One Hot CHRISTMAS

One Hot CHRISTMAS

VICKI LEWIS THOMPSON
KATHERINE GARBERA
KIMBERLY VAN METER
LIZ TALLEY

Published in Great Britain 2015
by Mills & Boon, an imprint of Harlequin (UK) Limited,
Eton House, 18-24 Paradise Road, Richmond, Surrey, TW9 1SR

ONE HOT CHRISTMAS © 2015 Harlequin Books S.A.

A Last Chance Christmas © 2014 Vicki Lewis Thompson
Under the Mistletoe © 2014 Katherine Garbera
Ignited © 2015 Kimberly Sheetz
Where There's Smoke © 2015 Amy R. Talley

Ignited by Kimberly Sheetz and *Where There's Smoke* by Amy R. Talley have been published digitally under the anthology title *A WRONG BED CHRISTMAS* (Mills & Boon® Blaze®, November 2015)

ISBN: 978-0-263-91785-7

024-1115

Harlequin (UK) Limited's policy is to use papers that are natural, renewable and recyclable products and made from wood grown in sustainable forests. The logging and manufacturing processes conform to the legal environmental regulations of the country of origin.

Printed and bound by
CPI Group (UK) Ltd, Croydon, CR0 4YY

A Last Chance Christmas

VICKI LEWIS THOMPSON

A passion for travel has taken *New York Times* bestseller **Vicki Lewis Thompson** to Europe, Australia and New Zealand. She's visited most of North America and has her eye on South America's rainforests. Africa, India and China beckon. But her first love is her home state of Arizona with its deserts, mountains, sunsets and—last but not least—cowboys! The wide open spaces and heroes on horseback influence everything she writes. Connect with her at www.VickiLewisThompson.com, facebook.com/vicki lewisthompson and twitter.com/vickilthompson.

To the Lone Ranger, my first crush.
A white horse, a deep voice and a mask.
What more could a girl want?

Prologue

Christmas Night, 1990
From the diary of Eleanor Chance

MY BROTHER SETH called tonight from Arizona, and we spent a good amount of time bragging about our grandchildren. Seth and Joyce ended up with four kids—three sons and a daughter—while Archie and I only had Jonathan. So it's not surprising that Seth has ten grandchildren to my three.

Not that I'm comparing or complaining. In fact, ten grandchildren on Christmas Day had worn Seth to a frazzle, even though he'd never admit it. I can only imagine.

We had enough ruckus with Jack, Nicky and Gabe trying out their new games. And don't get me started on the subject of NERF footballs. Yes, they're soft and supposedly can be played with in the house, but they inspire all manner of tackling and running and throwing. Archie bought them each one without consulting me.

Seth got a kick out of the NERF football drama.

Then he had to tell me about his three-year-old grand-daughter, Molly, who spent the entire day dressed as a princess, complete with tiara. About the only thing I envy Seth is that he has granddaughters as well as grandsons. Molly sounds like a pip, smart and funny. According to Seth, she has her two older brothers buffaloed.

Maybe next spring Archie and I can fly down to spend time with the Gallagher clan. We haven't visited in quite a while. Seth and Joyce came up to Jackson Hole two years ago, but I haven't seen my three nephews and my niece since they were kids. Now they have kids of their own.

According to Seth, everyone's doing great except his daughter Heather. She married a hard-drinking rodeo man, which means they travel a lot. Seth doesn't think they're very happy. They have one son, Cade, who's the same age as little Molly. Seth is worried about what will happen to that tyke as he's tossed from pillar to post.

Makes me thankful that my grandkids are all right here where I can see them every day. I cherish that most of the time. All right, I cherish it all the time, even when they're playing NERF football in the living room. I didn't need that vase anyway.

_1_

Present Day

AFTER BATTLING ICY roads all the way from Sheridan, Ben Radcliffe was cold and tired by the time he reached Jackson Hole and the Last Chance Ranch. But adrenaline rather than fatigue made him clumsy as he untied the ropes holding a blanket over the saddle he was delivering to Jack Chance.

Jack, the guy who'd commissioned it for his mother Sarah's seventieth birthday, watched the unveiling. The two men stood in a far corner of the ranch's unheated tractor barn in order to maintain secrecy. They'd left their sheepskin jackets on and their breath fogged the air.

This gift would be revealed at a big party the following night, so to keep the secret Ben was masquerading as a prospective horse buyer. It was a flimsy story because buyers seldom arrived in the dead of winter. But the combination of Christmas next week and a major birthday tomorrow had kept Sarah from questioning Ben's arrival.

The entire Chance family, including a few people who weren't technically related to Sarah, had helped pay for this elaborate saddle. Jack's initial reaction was crucial. Ben hoped to God he'd made something worthy of the occasion.

The last knot came loose. Ben's heart rate spiked as he removed the rope and pulled the padding away.

Jack's breath hissed out. "Wow."

"Good?" Ben dared to breathe again.

"Incredible." Jack moved closer and traced the intricate pattern on the leather.

That tooling had taken Ben countless hours, but he thought it showed well against the walnut shade of the leather. Even in the dim light, the saddle seemed to glow. Silver accents he'd polished until his fingers ached were embellished with small bits of hand-picked turquoise from his best supplier. He'd put his heart and soul into this project.

Jack stepped back with a wide smile of approval. "She'll love it."

"That's what I'm hoping." Ben's anxiety gave way to elation. The biggest commission of his life and he'd nailed it—at least, in Jack's opinion, and that counted for a whole lot.

"I have no doubt she will. It *looks* like her—the deep color of the leather, the classy accents, the tooling—she'll go crazy over this. Everyone will." With a smile, Jack turned and held out his hand. "You were the right choice for the job. Thank you."

"You're welcome." Ben shook hands with Jack and returned his smile. "I'll admit I haven't truly relaxed since you came to my shop in October. I wanted to get this right."

"You've obviously worked like a galley slave. I'm not a saddle maker, but I can appreciate the hours that must have gone into this."

"A few."

"Oh, before I forget." Jack took a check out of his wallet. "Here's the balance we owe on it. Now that I've seen the saddle, I'm not convinced you charged enough. That's amazing workmanship."

"It's enough." Ben pocketed the check without looking at it, but knowing it was there and that his bank account was healthy felt really nice. "I love what I do and I feel lucky that it pays the bills, too."

"I predict that soon it'll do more than pay the bills. You have a bright future. Once my brothers get a gander at this, I guarantee they'll both be trying to figure out if a new saddle is in their budgets. I know I'm thinking like that."

Ben laughed. "I'd be happy to cut a deal for repeat customers or multiple orders."

"Oh, yeah. Dangle temptation in my face. Thanks a lot." Jack grinned. "Come on, let's cover this up and get the hell into the house where it's warm. We have a heated shed for your truck, too."

"Sounds good." Ben replaced the blanket and together they moved the saddle stand to the far corner of the tractor barn, farther out of sight.

They passed by a sleigh, which had to be the one Jack had mentioned back in October. Jack had been worried that the carpenter wouldn't finish it before the holidays, but there it was, a one-horse open sleigh worthy of "Jingle Bells." Cute.

Ben gestured to it. "I see your guy came through for you."

"Yeah, thank God. And we've already gone dashing through the snow more times than I can count. Everybody loves it. Hell, so do I. The runners are designed for maneuverability. It can turn on a dime."

Ben laughed as he imagined Jack tearing around the countryside with his new toy. "I'll bet."

"You'll have to take it for a spin while you're here," Jack said as they walked toward the front again. "Oh, and I hope you don't mind the white lie that you're here to look at one of our Paints."

"I don't mind, but speaking of that, which horses did you supposedly show me?"

Jack paused before opening the door. "Let's see. How about Calamity Sam? He's a fine-looking gray-and-white stallion, five years old, could be used as a saddle horse and as a stud."

A gray-and-white Paint. The artistic appeal of a horse with a patterned coat fired his imagination. He'd never made a black saddle, but that might look good with the gray and white. "Any others?"

"You could say I tried to sell you Ink Spot, but you liked Calamity Sam better. Then tell everybody that you have to think about it before you make a final decision."

"And why didn't I bring a horse trailer?"

Jack adjusted the fit of his black Stetson. "That's easy. You saw no point in transporting a horse in this God-awful weather, but you were in the mood to go looking. If you decide on Calamity Sam, you'll pick him up in the spring."

"You'd hold him for me that long?"

Jack's brow creased. "We're making this up to fool my mother. It's not real."

"Yeah, I know, but supposing I actually wanted to look at your horses?"

"Ah." Jack's puzzled expression cleared. "Do you?"

"I might."

"Well, then." Jack stroked his chin and his dark eyes took on a speculative gleam. "In that case, maybe we could work out a little trade, one of our horses for some of your saddle-making skills."

"It's a thought." In the back of his mind, Ben was already designing a black saddle with silver accents. "Right now I don't have a place to keep a horse, but that could change."

"Especially if you take a liking to Calamity Sam."

Ben smiled. "Exactly." The idea of posing as a horse buyer on this trip had sparked his interest in actually buying one. He made saddles for everyone else but didn't have one for himself because he didn't own a horse. Stable horses were okay, but he craved a horse of his own with a custom saddle on its back.

"You're staying for a couple of nights, aren't you?"

"Just overnight. This is your holiday, and I don't want to—"

"Hey, you just brought the coolest gift my mother has ever had, so you can stay as long as you want. We have plenty of room."

"Well, if you're sure."

"Absolutely. The only person staying upstairs is Molly, which leaves three empty bedrooms. Cassidy, our housekeeper, is off visiting family, so you might have to fend for yourself. My brothers and I have our own places, now."

"Who's Molly?"

"My cousin from Arizona. She's here to do genealogy research on the family, but she'll go back to Prescott before Christmas. Don't worry. There's plenty of space if you want to stay on and scope out the horse situation. Unless you have to get back."

"I don't have any plans that can't be changed. So thanks for the hospitality. I might take you up on it." Much depended on whether he felt like an interloper once he met the rest of the family. As usual, he had no holiday gatherings back in Sheridan.

He'd never been part of a big family Christmas, and he was curious about whether it would be the way he imagined. But he was a stranger, so he wouldn't really fit in. On second thought, he shouldn't stay. The horse deal, though, was worth considering.

"You should stay at least three nights," Jack said. "I might not have time to show you the horses tomorrow because we'll be getting organized for Mom's party, but the next day I could."

"How about giving me a preview right now?"

"Now? Aren't you ready for a warm fire and a cold beer?"

"Yeah, but how long would it take to wander through the barn?"

Jack gazed at him. "You're right, and I'd be a damned poor salesman if I didn't take you over there right now, especially if you're considering swapping horseflesh for saddles. My brothers would kill me if I screwed that up." Jack opened the door and ushered Ben out into the cold late afternoon.

Darkness approached, and the two-story log ranch house looked mighty inviting with smoke drifting from the chimney and golden light shining in most of the windows. But the barn looked inviting, too, with its old-fashioned hip-roofed design and antique lamps mounted on either side of the big double doors. Each door had a large wreath on it, decorated with a big red bow.

"Well, look at that," Jack said. "My brother Gabe's over at the barn. That's his truck there. I wonder what he's up to."

"Is he the one who rides in cutting-horse competitions?" After Jack's visit to his shop, Ben had done some research on the Last Chance Ranch. He'd heard of the place, of course, but he'd wanted more in-depth information to guide him in his saddle design.

"He is, and I'm sure he'd love a new saddle. But I warn you he's picky as hell."

"I'd enjoy the challenge." Ben looked forward to meeting the other family members, and if any of them wanted saddles, so much the better. He navigated a narrow path that had been cleared between the tractor barn and the horse barn. Knee-high drifts formed a barrier on either side.

He was used to Sheridan, where snowplows kept the streets passable except during the worst storms. Out here, the Chance family had to use their own resources to deal with weather issues. In the barn where the saddle was hidden, he'd even seen a tractor with a plow attached.

Jack opened the barn door and they were greeted with warmth, light and the satisfying aroma of hay and horses. Ben decided that he wanted a barn. He'd need some kind of shelter if he planned to buy a horse. Some folks left horses outside through the winter, but he'd rather have a barn.

He could build a tack room for his saddle and other

equipment. If he had more than one horse, he'd make a saddle for each of them. Saddles on horses were like boots on a cowboy. If they didn't fit, no amount of padding or stretching would make them feel right. He winced whenever he saw a horse with an ill-fitting saddle. Had to feel damned uncomfortable.

A cowboy with a sandy-colored mustache walked down the wood-floored aisle toward them. "Hey, Jack."

"Hey, Gabe. I'd like you to meet Ben Radcliffe. He just brought Mom one hell of a saddle. You should go see it."

Gabe smiled. "Why do you suppose I'm here?" Then he shook Ben's hand. "Good to meet you, Radcliffe. Thanks for making the trip."

"Glad I could."

Jack unbuttoned his coat. "You snuck over here to get a look at the saddle?"

"I didn't sneak. I drove."

"Yeah, well, you'd better have given your kids a good excuse for doing that, especially Sarah Bianca. If she gets wind that there's a secret present for her grandma hidden somewhere on the ranch, we'll hear about it all day long. Mom will get suspicious and the surprise will be ruined for sure."

"I told them I wanted to check on Persnickety. He's been favoring his right front leg."

Jack frowned. "He has?"

"Well, he *was*. Sort of. But guess what? Now he's all better. Is the saddle in the tractor barn?"

"I thought that was the best place. Go all the way to the back in the right-hand corner. There's a blanket covering it. Take a flashlight."

Gabe pulled his phone out of his jacket pocket. "Get

with the program, bro. Nobody carries a flashlight anymore. We have an app for that."

"I'm sure you do. I'll keep using my Coleman lantern, which will still be functioning when your teeny battery is DOA."

Gabe laughed and picked up a battery-operated lantern sitting on a shelf. "I just say these things to get your goat, big brother. Works every time."

"Bite me."

"Nah, I've outgrown that. Say, have you done your homework for Molly yet?"

Jack groaned. "Hell, no. Have you?"

"Some of it. The form she gave us is longer than a dead snake. I got bored and quit." Gabe looked over at Ben. "Our cousin from Arizona. She's a history professor by day but a genealogist by night." He turned to Jack. "Which reminds me. Have you told her about the saddle? Morgan wanted me to ask if Molly's in on the secret."

"I haven't told her. I had to get to know her first and find out if she could be trusted to keep quiet. Now I know she's trustworthy, but there hasn't been a good time to say anything when Mom wasn't around."

"Yeah, and that'd be one more person who could slip up accidentally. Morgan seems to think we should tell her, but I say if it's gone this long, might as well not take the risk." He glanced at Ben. "That means as far as Molly's concerned, you're a prospective horse buyer."

"Got it."

"You might not see much of her, anyway," Jack said. "She spends a lot of time on the computer with her genealogy program. Once she has the family tree all completed, she's going to put it into some kind of book for all of us."

"Sounds nice." It also sounded like something done out of love for family. Ben doubted his family would ever create something similar.

Jack sighed. "I suppose it will be, but all the paperwork is a pain in the ass. I tried to get Josie to do it for me. She filled in her part, but she flatly refused to fill in mine."

"Yeah, Morgan wouldn't do mine, either." Gabe glanced over Jack's shoulder as the barn door opened. "Well, if it isn't Nicky. Whatcha doing here, Nick, old boy?"

"Oh, just happened to have a little spare time." Nick walked toward them.

Jack shoved back his hat. "I don't suppose you're here to check out the saddle or anything like that."

"Maybe." Nick smiled and shook hands with Ben. "You must be Radcliffe. I had a look at your website. Impressive work."

"Thanks." Ben's eye for detail took in the similarities among the brothers—same height and build, same mannerisms. But there were marked differences, too.

Jack's dark hair and eyes suggested he had some Native American blood, while Nick and Gabe showed no evidence of that. Gabe was the fairer of the two. He'd probably been a towhead once. Nick's green eyes made him look as if he belonged in Ireland. Interesting.

"Ben outdid himself on the saddle for Mom," Jack said. "But I hope she doesn't happen to glance out the window when you two yahoos head down to the tractor barn together."

"What about Ben's truck?" Gabe smoothed his mustache. "It's parked right in front of the tractor barn, but he's supposed to be here to see horses, not tractors."

"You can't see the front of that barn from the house." Jack crossed his arms. "But she could see you leave here and walk in that direction."

Nick looked over at Gabe. "Did you say the tractor hitched to the snowplow has a bad starter?"

"No, I didn't—oh, wait." Gabe smiled. "Come to think of it, you're right. You and I need to go check on that. They're predicting a blizzard in a couple of days and we don't want to be caught without a snowplow."

"Just what I was thinking." Nick turned up the collar of his sheepskin jacket.

Gabe did the same and pulled on leather gloves. "Hey, did you do your homework for Molly?"

"I did. Scanned it and emailed it to her this morning."

"Loser."

Nick laughed. "I take it you haven't?"

"Jack hasn't, either." Gabe looked to Jack for backup.

"Haven't found the time," Jack said.

"Yeah, right." Nick sent them both a knowing grin. "Just do it, okay? She's very into this, even if you two aren't."

Gabe blew out a breath. "Yeah, I know she is. Morgan thinks it's endearing. She also thinks Molly should be told about the saddle. You haven't said anything, have you?"

"Nope. If she knows, she didn't get it from me."

"She doesn't know," Jack said. "And she might want to contribute if we told her about it, but we've dealt with the money situation already. Gabe and I think we should just keep it a secret since we're this close and she wasn't part of it from the beginning."

"Fine with me." Nick glanced at his two brothers. "But you really should fill out those forms for her. It's not so much to ask."

"You're right." Jack grimaced. "Otherwise, she'll bug me until I do."

"Yep, guaranteed she will," Gabe said. "I like her okay, but she sure can be a bossy little thing."

Ben listened to the conversation with amusement. Jack had said he'd be sharing the second floor with Molly, who sounded like a determined woman. This trip was becoming more interesting by the minute.

2

SOMEONE WAS PLAYING "Silent Night" on the harmonica. Nostalgia washed over Molly Gallagher and she paused, fingers resting on the computer keyboard. Her Grandpa Seth had played the harmonica, and the gentle sound, especially at Christmastime, always made her think of him.

Harmonicas and cowboys seemed to go together, and her grandpa had been an old-fashioned cowpoke who'd grown up right here in Jackson Hole. He'd even lived in this house for a little while with his sister, Nelsie, and his brother-in-law, Archie. If Molly believed in ghosts, she might think Grandpa Seth had taken up residence down the hall from her bedroom.

"Silent Night" was followed by "O Little Town of Bethlehem." Talk about atmosphere. Snow drifted down outside her window and the scent of pine filled her room. Yesterday she'd helped Aunt Sarah arrange fresh boughs all over the house. With her bedroom door open, she could hear the logs crackling in the giant fireplace downstairs.

Feeling all warm and cozy, Molly went back to entering data in her Excel file. The harmonica player was likely the guy Jack had mentioned was staying down the hall. His name was Ben something-or-other. He'd come to look at the ranch's registered Paints and would be around for a couple of nights. Molly had offered to help out by making his bed and putting clean towels in his bathroom.

Being alone upstairs with four empty bedrooms had been a little spooky. She was glad to share the space with someone, especially if he chose to serenade her every so often with Christmas carols on the harmonica. Hard to believe she'd be leaving in four days. The time had flown by.

Although she'd love to stay and meet everyone who'd be coming in to spend Christmas Eve and Christmas Day, that would mean she'd miss the big Gallagher family celebration in Prescott. So far, she had a perfect record—twenty-eight consecutive holidays spent at the Double Down Ranch. Her parents ran it now that her grandparents were gone, and it was her favorite place in the world.

"O Little Town of Bethlehem" came to a close with a long, drawn-out note embellished by some vibrato. Ben was pretty good on that thing. Then he switched away from carols to play the theme from *Beauty and the Beast*. She'd loved that movie from the first time she'd seen it as a little girl. Belle was the perfect heroine—pretty, brave and well-read.

Plus she was a brunette, and Molly had been thrilled about that, too. The scholarly Belle had been her role model for years. She'd never heard the theme played on a harmonica before, but it worked. It worked so well that she left her chair and moved into the hall so she could hear it better.

What a lovely sound. He really was talented. She moved a few steps closer and then a few steps more. He played with heart, and she could almost imagine him as the Beast longing for his Beauty to show up. That was plain silly, of course. The way her luck went, he'd be old as the hills, or middle-aged and balding.

His bedroom door was open. As the music continued, she edged closer. Now that her curiosity was aroused, she wanted to find out what the man who created such a heavenly sound looked like. But she decided to wait until he'd finished the song. She liked it way too much to interrupt him, and if she suddenly appeared, he'd probably stop playing.

The last note trailed away, and she walked up to the doorway, prepared with a little speech. "That was…" She forgot what she'd intended to say. Ben something-or-other was drop-dead gorgeous.

Why hadn't she brushed her hair before walking down here? Why hadn't she checked to see if she had anything in her teeth? Why hadn't she taken *two measly seconds* to glance in a mirror and find out if her glasses were smudged?

Thinking of that, she whipped them off and cleared her throat. "I'm Molly Gallagher. I live down the hall." *What?* "I mean, I'm *sleeping* down the hall. That is, my room's…that way." She actually pointed. Good God, now she was giving the beautiful man directions.

His eyes were the color of dark chocolate, and they crinkled at the corners when he smiled. "Good to know."

Heat flooded her face. "I didn't mean that as a…

well, never mind. I don't know why I said it. Mostly I wanted to tell you how much I like your harmonica. Your harmonica *playing*, that is."

"Thanks. I didn't know anybody was up here. You were quiet as a mouse."

"Just nibbling away on my computer." Her laugh sounded much too breathless, but he had *such* broad shoulders, and his dark hair curled gently around his ears in a very sexy way. She liked his chin, too, with its little cleft, and she adored his mouth. A harmonica player would be good with his mouth and his tongue. She'd never thought of that before.

"I promise not to play in the middle of the night."

"I wouldn't care." And didn't that sound like she'd become his adoring fangirl? She licked her dry lips. "Actually, I grew up hearing harmonica music. My grandpa would sometimes play me a lullaby before I went to sleep."

"That's very sweet."

"It was more of a bribe. I always put up a fight about going to bed." She had no idea where these idiotic remarks were coming from, but she couldn't seem to make them stop.

She'd prepared herself for some old geezer, probably because she associated harmonicas with her grandfather. Instead she'd found this amazing man, who couldn't be much older than she was. He sat on the edge of a king-sized bed she'd personally made up earlier today. Her filter must be working a little bit, because at least she hadn't blurted out that piece of information.

"I'll bet you did put up a fight about bedtime."

Amusement flashed in his brown eyes. "I'll bet you were one feisty little girl."

"Jack would probably tell you I still am. I think he and Gabe are a little irritated with me."

"Why is that?"

"Oh, there's something I asked them to do and they're both procrastinating. I'm leaving in four days so I gave them each a little nudge. I don't think they appreciated it."

He seemed to be working hard not to laugh.

"Did Jack mention that to you?"

"Just in passing."

"It's only two pages of information for my genealogy research. You'd think I'd asked him to write a book."

"Some people hate filling out forms."

She sighed. "I know. Everybody's not detail oriented like I am. I should probably just sit down with each of them and do it interview style. I'll text them and suggest that. I mean, if Jack's complaining to you, a virtual stranger, I guess he *really* doesn't want to do it."

"He didn't complain all that much. Don't quote me on this, but I think he plans to finish it soon."

"Then I'll wait and see. He might be insulted if I offered to write it down for him, as if he's not capable."

"I've only spent a little time with the guy, but I think you're right."

Discussing this matter with Ben had been a good ice-breaker. He felt like a potential friend now. She was still ogling him a little, but she'd recovered from her first stunned reaction. "Sarah told me you were here to look at horses."

"That's right." Something flickered in his gaze the

way it did when someone wasn't telling the whole truth and nothing but the truth.

She caught it because she'd thought all along that driving around looking at horses in this weather was strange. She couldn't shake the suspicion that he was here for some other reason, but she couldn't imagine what that would be. "Did you see any you might be interested in?"

"I did, as a matter of fact. I really like the looks of Calamity Sam."

"Oh, yeah. Me, too. He's one beautiful stallion. Pricey, though, since he gets pretty good stud fees."

"I know. Jack said maybe we could work something out."

So maybe he really was interested in buying one of the Last Chance horses. He might hope to get a better price by coming when business was slow. But asking any more questions would make her seem nosy—which she was, of course. She'd been nosy all her life.

But sometimes she caught herself doing it and backed off. This was one of those times. "Well, I've bothered you long enough. I should get back to my work. If you need anything like more towels or extra pillows, the linen closet is right down there." She gestured to a door on the far side of the hallway. "The housekeeper's on vacation so we're on our own up here."

"Jack told me. I'm pretty good at looking out for myself."

"Great. That's great. Anyway, thanks for the harmonica concert. Please play any time you feel like it. Brings back fond memories for me."

"I'll remember that. Actually, I was about to head

downstairs. Sarah and Pete invited me to have a drink with them before dinner."

"Oh! Is it happy hour already?" Whenever she became involved in a genealogy project, she lost track of time.

"Almost six."

"Then I'll turn off my computer. Last night Sarah had to come upstairs to get me or I would have worked through the whole evening. I'd have hated that because I love hanging out with her and Pete. I'll see you down there, then." She turned to leave.

"I can wait until you shut off your computer."

Thank God she wasn't facing him, because she wouldn't have wanted him to see her reaction to that comment. For sure, her eyes and mouth had popped wide open exactly the way a cartoon character would look when startled. "Um, sure, that would be great. I'll just be a sec. Meet you at the top of the stairs." And she skedaddled out of there.

As she hurried down the hall, she calculated how much repair work she could get away with. Changing clothes was out, so she was stuck with the blah jeans and her old green turtleneck. If she had time to pop in her contacts, Ben might notice that the sweater nearly matched her eyes, but she didn't so he wouldn't.

The best she could hope for was a quick brush through her hair, a fast polish of her lenses and a glance in the bathroom mirror to make sure she didn't have food in her teeth. Refreshing her makeup would take too long, and besides, he'd already seen her like this. If she showed up with lipstick and blusher, that might telegraph her interest in him.

But, truly, she might as well forget about having

any interest in him. It didn't matter how yummy he looked, or how much she loved his harmonica music, or how talented his mouth might be as a result of playing said harmonica. She was leaving in four days and didn't expect to be back in Wyoming any time soon.

She should forget about Ben, whose last name she still didn't know. It wasn't like she was thirsting for male companionship. For example, there was Dennis, the new guy in the history department. He was cute in a nerdy kind of way, and he'd seemed quite fascinated by her when they'd talked during the faculty Christmas party. He'd promised to call after the holidays.

So, there. She had a potential boyfriend and a potential relationship waiting to be cultivated back home. No need to get starry-eyed over some horse-buying, harmonica-playing cowboy who had his feet firmly planted in Wyoming.

Then she walked out of her room and saw those booted feet braced slightly apart as Ben waited for her at the top of the stairs. Oh, Lordy. She'd never looked at a man and instantly fallen into lust. Well, except for unattainable movie stars.

But it was happening this very minute. He'd been impressive sitting on the bed. Standing upright in all his six-foot-plus glory, he made her forget her own name, let alone the name of that guy in the history department.

Then he smiled at her and her knees actually weakened. She'd thought that was a stupid cliché, but apparently not. When she went back for second semester, she'd get one of her friends in the biology department to explain how a brilliant smile from a handsome man could adversely affect a woman's tendons, ligaments, joints and kneecaps.

She hoped she didn't wobble like a Weeble as she joined him at the top landing. "Thanks for waiting for me."

"No problem. By the way, I never introduced myself. I'm Ben Radcliffe."

"I know. I mean, I knew about the Ben part but I'd forgotten your last name." If she'd known he was a walking female fantasy, she would have paid more attention when Sarah mentioned it.

"Okay, now that we have that out of the way, we can—whoops. Hold still for a minute." He leaned toward her.

Her heart leaped into high gear as he reached a hand toward her hair. She'd been told it was her best feature because it was so many rich shades of brown. Maybe he couldn't resist running his fingers through it. That would be a good start.

Then, after he'd buried his fingers in her hair, he could lean even closer and kiss her. Maybe she should take off her glasses to make that maneuver easier, but he'd told her to hold still. She'd have to move a little, though, because he was almost a foot taller than she was. She'd have to stand on tiptoe for a proper kiss.

As his fingers made contact, she closed her eyes and tried to breathe normally. That sure wasn't working. Finally she gulped in some air so she wouldn't pass out and tumble down the curved staircase.

"There you go."

She opened her eyes to discover a piece of dental floss dangling in front of her face.

"It was in your hair."

"Oh." Her cheeks hot, she grabbed the floss and rubbed it between her palms until it was a tiny ball. Then she shoved it in the pocket of her jeans. "Thanks. That's what I get for rushing." She couldn't make herself look at him.

"You have great hair."

That brought her head up. She gazed into his warm brown eyes and said the first thing that popped into her head. "So do you."

"Thank you." The crinkles reappeared at the corners of his eyes because he was smiling again. "I got teased about it as a kid. I guess I looked too girly."

Not anymore. "What do kids know?"

"Not just kids. My dad, too."

"Oh." That made her heart hurt. "Guess you proved him wrong, huh?"

He shrugged. "Doesn't matter if I did or not. We're not that close, anyway."

"Well, that's…" She stopped herself before saying it was too bad. She knew nothing about him, really, or about his family. For him, distance from his father might be a good thing. "That's the way it happens sometimes." She'd honor his obvious wish to make light of what, for her, would be a devastating situation. She couldn't imagine not being close to either of her parents.

"Yep, sure does. Ready?"

"You tell me. I was prepared to walk downstairs wearing dental floss. Do I pass inspection?"

"Now that you mention it, I don't know if you do or not. Back up and do a slow turn for me."

She followed his instructions, although she didn't kid herself that he had ulterior motives for the request.

There wasn't much to see because she'd always been slender, not curvy. If she'd been taller, instead of only five-four, she could have been a runway model.

But not really. The idea had been an obsession of hers as a preteen, when her egghead status had made her feel uncool. A career as a high-fashion model would have soothed her ego. But she'd abandoned that plan when she'd realized, first, she'd never grow tall enough, and second, she'd only be modeling to improve her social standing, which was a dumb reason to get into any line of work.

So, instead, she'd embraced her brainy side, especially her passion for details, specifically historical details. Teaching history during the day and studying genealogy in her spare time made her incredibly happy. In her chosen profession, being an egghead was a good thing.

She finished her circle and glanced up at him. "Okay?"

"Perfect."

Of course he didn't mean that literally, but she couldn't help the squiggle of happiness that danced through her. When a man who looked like Ben declared that she was perfect, she'd take it with a grain of salt, but she'd take it. "Then let's go down."

"Now I'm not sure if I pass inspection or not."

"Don't worry." She smiled at him. "You're perfect, too." That was the main problem with him, in fact. If she were to design her ideal man, he would look exactly like Ben. She just hoped he wouldn't turn out to be the guy who would haunt her dreams once she left Wyoming.

3

BEN WASN'T SURE what to do about his instant attraction to the impish woman descending the staircase beside him. He tended to go for tall and curvy. Molly was short and on the skinny side. He'd never finished college, which didn't matter for his saddle making, but he'd steered away from dating scholars because he wasn't sure how to talk to them. Molly was a college professor.

And yet she didn't act much like one, or the way he thought a college professor would behave. He didn't have a lot of experience to go on, but he'd had no trouble talking to her. He liked talking to her, in fact. She was so full of energy, so *happy*. He imagined that he could see her glowing, and not just when she blushed because she'd put her foot in her mouth.

That was part of why she charmed him. Apparently he flustered her, which made him want to fluster her more just to see the pink bloom on her cheeks. But that didn't explain the visceral tug he'd felt when she'd walked down the hall toward him, or the surge of desire he'd felt when she made a slow turn, allowing him to view her from all sides.

She hadn't done it in a suggestive way, as if trying to showcase her body. Yet he'd had the almost irresistible urge to get his hands on her. He still had that urge. He had no trouble imagining what she'd feel like beneath him, a small but explosive bundle of heat. He had a hunch she'd drive him crazy.

Maybe he was drawn to her because of the advance billing. He'd been curious to meet the woman who had no problem pestering all three Chance men for what she wanted. After watching his mother's mouse-like behavior for years, he admired any female who stood up for herself. He might never marry, but if he did, it would be to someone who refused to be intimidated by anyone, especially him.

"So, where are you from, Ben?"

Her question brought him back to reality. He'd already pictured them in bed together and she didn't even know where he lived. "Sheridan."

"Really? That's fabulous! Maybe you can help me track down two of my relatives, an aunt and a cousin."

"Maybe. I've lived there for seven years."

"I hope so. It's not a huge place. My aunt's married name was Heather Marlowe. At least, that's what it was last time we heard from her, although that was a long time ago. She was in Sheridan then."

"Doesn't ring a bell."

"My cousin's name is Cade. His dad was a bull rider, Rance Marlowe, although he'd be too old to do that now. From what I've heard, he wasn't a very nice guy. Aunt Heather might have divorced him, but nobody knows because she stopped writing or calling."

"Sorry, but I don't think I've met anybody named Marlowe."

Molly sighed. "It was worth a shot. I've investigated online but I got nowhere. Rance followed the rodeo circuit and was never in one place for long. My aunt trailed after him and brought little Cade along, too. Well, he's not so little anymore. He'd be the same age as I am, twenty-eight."

He considering pointing out that she was still little, even at twenty-eight, but he figured she'd probably had her fill of short-person jokes. "So they might have had some tough times financially along the way?"

She paused at the foot of the stairs and turned to him. "I wouldn't be surprised. Why?"

"They might have made use of social services there. I know a retired social worker. Maybe she'd remember something, or could ask around."

"That's a great idea. I didn't think of that, but it gives me another avenue. Thanks!"

"She lives not too far from Sheridan at a place called Thunder Mountain Ranch. I—" He caught himself right before he screwed up. He'd been about to announce that he'd made a couple of saddles for Rosie and Herb, but his profession wasn't supposed to be common knowledge yet. "The Padgetts are good people. He's a retired equine vet. For years they also took in foster boys, but they don't do that anymore. Anyway, Rosie knows a lot of people in town. She might have information."

The tension eased from her eyes and she smiled. "I'd run out of ideas, so I'm thrilled to have a new lead. My family always wondered what became of Cade, especially my grandpa."

"The harmonica player."

"Yes. Losing touch with Aunt Heather and Cade made him sad. And of course Heather's my dad's sister. I think he's resigned to the idea that she doesn't want to hang around with the Gallagher family anymore, but he's told me that he wonders where she is. When I started working on this family tree project, tracking them down was one of my goals, especially because my dad still thinks about them."

"Then I wish you luck with it. Now that I know what names to listen for, I'll pay more attention once I get back home. Maybe I'll stumble across somebody who's heard of them."

"Excellent! I'll give you my phone number in case you find anything. You'll be my man in Sheridan."

He couldn't help grinning. "Okay."

Her cheeks turned that wonderful shade of pink again. "That didn't come out quite right."

"It came out fine as far as I'm concerned."

Her blush deepened. "Um, well…I didn't mean to imply that I considered you *my*…" Then she groaned. "I'm going to stop now before I make this worse than it already is. Sarah's going to wonder what the heck we're standing here yakking about. Let's go get us some drinks."

"Works for me." Still smiling, he walked beside her into the living room. She was not a flirt by any stretch, and yet she was clearly interested in him. Earlier he'd wondered what to do about his attraction to her. He might not have to do a damned thing except wait and let nature take its course.

The ranch's beautiful setting wouldn't hurt, either. The living room looked like a scene out of a Christmas card, with pine boughs and ribbons everywhere, plus candles on the mantel. Flames danced in the big stone fireplace, and a ten-foot Scotch pine in the corner glittered with lights, ornaments and garlands.

Sarah and Pete both got up from their leather armchairs. Through Ben's cursory internet research, he'd discovered that Sarah's first husband, Jonathan, had died several years ago and she'd since married Pete Beckett. Pete was tall, like Sarah, and lanky, with gray hair and gentle blue eyes. He was a philanthropist who'd dreamed up the Last Chance's summer program for disadvantaged kids. He had the relaxed air of someone who'd found his place in the world. Ben wondered if that time would ever come for him.

Sarah put down her wineglass. "I thought I heard you two out in the hall."

As Sarah made the introductions, Ben stepped forward and shook hands with Pete, who'd been one of the biggest contributors to the saddle fund. "It's a pleasure."

Obviously Pete wasn't about to give anything away at the zero hour. "I admire your can-do spirit." He raised his glass in Ben's direction. "I'm not sure I'd drive all the way from Sheridan to look at horses in this weather."

"I'm used to the weather and I had some free time. Jack promised I wouldn't be in the way." Ben had been prepared to like the guy, and Pete's casual friendliness didn't disappoint him.

"Heck, no," Pete said. "Always room for one more at a party. Right, Sarah?"

"Absolutely. The more the merrier. It isn't every day a girl turns seventy."

Pete gasped and placed a hand over his heart. "You're that old?"

"Stuff a sock in it, Peter." Sarah laughed. "I'm still younger than you. Now, please get Ben something to drink while I pour Molly a glass of wine. I already know that's what she wants."

"Yes, I sure do. That's a terrific red wine. I'm stocking up on some when I get home."

Pete turned to Ben. "What can I get for you?"

"Jack and I each had a bottle of dark beer this afternoon. Can't remember the brand. I wouldn't mind another one of those if you have it."

Pete set his glass on a coaster. "Let's mosey down to the kitchen and find out if there's a cold one in the fridge. If Jack likes it, we probably have a supply." Once they were in the hallway and out of earshot, Pete lowered his voice. "I had a chance to talk to Jack and he raved about the saddle."

"Good. I'm glad he's happy."

"I want to see it, but I haven't come up with a good excuse to go out to the tractor barn without making Sarah suspicious."

"Nick and Gabe have looked at it, and they seem satisfied."

"Damn. My curiosity is killing me. I wish everybody who chipped in could be here tomorrow for the big reveal, but several couldn't come for both her birthday *and* Christmas. So they asked her when she'd rather have them arrive, and she picked Christmas."

"So, who won't be coming tomorrow?"

"Jack's two half-brothers, Wyatt and Rafe Locke and their wives will wait and come for Christmas. I'm pretty sure their mother Diana also will be here then.

She's Jack's mother, too, of course, but it's hard for me to think of her that way."

"Hang on. Sarah isn't Jack's biological mother?"

"No. She adopted him after she married Jonathan. I don't blame Jack for procrastinating on that family tree project of Molly's. His part is complicated. His biological mother, Diana, divorced his dad when Jack was a toddler. She left Jack here, ran off to San Francisco and married this guy Locke. They had twin boys, Rafe and Wyatt."

"That must have been tough on Jack."

"Yeah. Having his mom leave was bad enough, but he didn't know she'd had two more kids until Wyatt showed up here one day, a couple of years ago." Pete led Ben through the large dining room and into the kitchen, Mary Lou Sims's domain.

Ben had met her earlier when he and Jack had come into the kitchen looking for beer.

Mary Lou closed a door on the double oven and turned, her fly-away gray hair curling in the moist heat. "Hi, guys. Let me guess. Ben wants another beer like the one he had before."

"That's right," Pete said. "We got any more?"

"You know we do." Mary Lou crossed to the commercial-sized refrigerator. "Jack sees to it." She took out a bottle. "Want a glass, Ben?"

"No, thanks. The bottle's fine."

Mary Lou twisted off the cap and smiled as she handed the bottle to him. "I've been hearing great things about that saddle. Everybody says it's gorgeous."

Pete rolled his eyes. "And everybody needs to quit talking about it. Sure as the world, Sarah's going to overhear one of those conversations and figure out what's up."

"Aw, we're all being careful." Mary Lou waved a dismissive hand. "We have less than twenty-four hours until the unveiling. It'll be fine."

"I hope you're right. How soon before dinner's ready?"

"Give me another thirty minutes or so."

"Will do. Thanks, Mary Lou." Pete put an arm around her for a quick hug. "You're the best."

She laughed. "Yes, I am, and don't ever forget it."

"I wouldn't dare. Sarah would kick me out. Come on, Ben. Let's go join the women."

Ben had been sorting through what Pete had told him about Jack and his biological mother. "Is Diana Native American?"

"Half-Shoshone, half-Caucasian, which is where Jack gets his coloring."

Ben nodded. "I wondered about that. So, Jack has two half-brothers on his mother's side, Wyatt and Rafe, and two on his dad's side, Nick and Gabe. That's wild. How does Sarah feel about Diana coming around?"

Pete smiled. "I think the first time was awkward, but she's…amazing. She's forgiven Diana, even though the woman left her kid and never looked back."

"Wow."

"That's not all. Diana also kept his existence and her former marriage a secret from her new family for years. But when Sarah realized how miserable Diana was about it all, she accepted her as part of the family. I don't know if Sarah's forgiven Nick's mother, though."

"You mean Sarah isn't Nick's mother, either?"

"Nope. After Diana left Jonathan, he went sort of

crazy and had an affair with a free spirit who was just passing through. She kept her pregnancy to herself and had Nick without notifying Jonathan. When Nick was six months old, his mother died in a sky-diving accident. Baby Nick arrived in a cab with a lawyer, and Sarah took the little guy in and raised him as her own. But she doesn't have kind words for Nick's mother."

"I'll bet not. Sounds like one flakey lady."

"One who paid the price for it." As they neared the end of the hallway, Pete lowered his voice again. "Regarding the saddle, I figure we'll just leave it on display in the living room until Christmas. I doubt the weather will be good enough for her to try it out, anyway, and everyone can see it when they walk in."

"Sounds good. Oh, and don't be surprised if I end up buying a horse. I asked Jack to show me some prospects this afternoon."

Pete laughed. "You did? That's terrific. Everything's working out great, isn't it?"

"Looks like it." They entered the living room and he noticed Sarah sitting alone, sipping her wine and gazing into the crackling fire. "Where's Molly?" He hadn't realized how much he'd anticipated seeing her until she wasn't there.

"She told me your suggestion about her cousin Cade, and I thought she should call right now. After dinner might be too late, and tomorrow it'll be a zoo around here. She could get sidetracked and forget. So she went to look up the place online to see if she could get the number."

"That's great." Ben hadn't expected Molly to act on his suggestion this fast. He had the number saved in his phone, but no doubt she'd found it online by now.

Which meant she was already calling. If she mentioned that she'd heard about them from him, they could easily tell her that he'd made a couple of saddles for them. That, in itself, wouldn't be bad unless she came down and asked about his saddle-making business in front of Sarah.

If Sarah learned what he did for a living, she'd probably put it all together. His only hope was that if Molly got the information from the Padgetts, she'd figure out the secret and keep it to herself.

Pete sat in the chair next to Sarah's. That left one empty chair and the sofa. Ben noticed Molly's wine glass on the coffee table in front of the sofa, so he sat there, too, hoping to be next to her. Close proximity would give him more options if he had to suddenly keep her from saying something incriminating.

"What's this about Molly's cousin?" Pete picked up his drink.

Sarah combed her silvery hair back with one hand. "She wants to pick up his trail in Sheridan, which was the last address they had for him and his mother. It's a happy coincidence that Ben is from there. You're sure you don't know anybody named Marlowe, Ben?"

"I'm still thinking, and I'll keep my ears open once I get back, but the name doesn't sound familiar."

"I haven't paid much attention to rodeo stars over the years," Sarah said. "So I wouldn't recognize the name Rance Marlowe even if he had been well-known."

Pete shook his head. "Me, either. Did Molly ask the boys?"

Ben got a kick out of Pete's reference to three grown men as *boys*, but the Chance brothers would probably always be *the boys* to Sarah and Pete.

"I'm sure she asked them." Sarah chuckled. "That girl is like a quiz-show host when it comes to questions. She has a million of them. And she loves to dig into what she calls *archives*. I let her look through Jonathan's old trunk full of papers and souvenirs, which she adored, and then I let her read my mother-in-law's diaries covering all the years she and Archie lived here. You'd have thought I'd offered Molly a sack of gold."

"She's fun to have around," Pete said. "I'm going to miss her when she leaves on Monday. But getting back home for Christmas is important to her. She's really big on family."

"I gathered that," Ben said.

"Well, so am I." Sarah took another sip of her wine. "I'll admit when I married Jonathan I didn't realize how important the whole concept of family would become to me. I'm an only child, so my original family consisted of three people. Now I find myself surrounded with an entire clan and it's wonderful."

"And I'm lucky enough to be part of that clan," Pete said. "I'm so thankful that Sarah agreed to let me into the club."

Ben felt as if he'd stumbled into a foreign land where he could barely speak the language. He'd heard people talk about the importance of family, but he'd never understood it on a gut level. His experience growing up had taught him the destructive nature of family ties.

Sarah glanced over at him. "Speaking of that, do you have any siblings, Ben?"

"An older brother in Colorado." He never knew what to say when such questions came up, or how to answer them so the questions would stop. But in this case, with all the talk about bonding, he might have a way out. "We're not close."

Sympathy flashed in Sarah's blue eyes. "I'm sorry."

Ben shrugged and used Molly's earlier response, one he'd thought was brilliant at the time. He'd keep it in mind for any future conversations regarding his family. "That's the way it happens sometimes."

"I know it does, but…" Sarah hesitated. "I hope being in the middle of this crazy group doesn't bother you."

"Not at all." This much he could say with conviction. "I like it."

4

MOLLY KEYED IN the number for Thunder Mountain Ranch with some misgivings. Despite what she'd told Ben, she was conflicted about what she might uncover with this phone call. If Rosie Padgett had no knowledge of Heather or Cade, then Molly was back where she started.

But if the woman had heard of them, that meant they'd contacted social services and very likely had struggled to make a life for themselves. Molly didn't remember her Aunt Heather much at all, but her dad sure did. Heather was his sister, after all, and the news might not be very good.

A woman answered the phone. "Thunder Mountain Ranch."

Well, she'd come this far. Molly took a deep breath. "Hi. I'm Molly Gallagher, and I'm looking for information on my cousin, Cade Marlowe, or his mother, Heather. A friend suggested I call and see if you knew anything about them."

"Cade Marlowe?"

"Yes. His father's a bull rider named Rance, but I'm

sure he's retired from that by now. The last letter my family got from Heather was postmarked in Sheridan, but that was years ago. I'm trying to find out if any-body remembers them or has a forwarding address."

"I'm sorry, but I don't know anybody named Cade Marlowe."

"Oh." In spite of her desire for information, she was relieved.

"But if you want to leave your number, I could ask around. Someone might have heard something."

"Thank you. You must be Mrs. Padgett. The friend who suggested I call is Ben Radcliffe."

"Oh, Ben!" The woman's voice warmed. "Yes, I'm Rosie Padgett. Ben's such a great guy, and when it comes to making saddles, he's a real artist."

"Um, yes, he certainly is." *Ben was a saddle maker?*

As she gave her number to Rosie Padgett and said her goodbyes, she kept thinking about Ben's profes-sion. His odd timing for coming to look at horses coin-cided with Sarah's birthday—a significant one, at that. She'd wondered all along why Jack would agree to host a potential customer during his mother's big celebra-tion. Jack didn't strike her as the kind of man who put business ahead of family gatherings.

Ben could have come after Christmas, or he could have waited until the weather warmed. Yet here he was, staying in the bosom of the family and attending Sarah's birthday party. But if he'd designed a custom saddle for Sarah, then his sudden appearance the day before her birthday made perfect sense. And of course he'd be invited to stay so he could see her reaction to it.

After booting up her computer, Molly searched for Ben's saddle-making operation. Once she found the site and scrolled through the photos of his work, she was almost positive this was why he was here. And it was supposed to be a surprise.

Well, cool. She'd always loved uncovering secrets. Knowing that Ben was an artisan on a secret mission made him more intriguing than ever. She wasn't the least bit artistic, but she admired those who were.

She knew Ben was good with his mouth because he played a damned fine harmonica. If he'd landed a commission from the Chance family to create a saddle for their beloved matriarch, then he must be good with his hands, too. Add in his fine physique, and it amounted to the sort of man very few women could resist.

She wondered where the saddle was hidden. Probably not in the house where Sarah might accidentally find it. He wouldn't have left it in his truck where it would be difficult for her cousins to see it. The barn wasn't a good spot, either, because Sarah might go down there. She loved taking bits of carrot to Bertha Mae, her favorite horse.

"Molly?" Sarah's voice traveled up the stairs. "Are you having any luck? Dinner's ready."

"I'll be right down!" She shut off her computer.

Then, because she could, she brushed her hair again and put a touch of blusher on her cheeks and the merest hint of gloss on her lips. She'd lived with two brothers, so she knew that most men didn't notice subtle makeup. They just thought a woman looked good and assumed it was her own healthy color coming through.

When she reached the bottom of the stairs, Sarah was there holding a wine glass. "I thought you'd want to take the rest of your wine in to dinner."

"Great! Thank you." She followed Sarah over to the hallway where Pete and Ben waited for them.

"What happened with the Padgetts?" Ben asked. "Did you talk to them?"

"I talked to Rosie Padgett. Very nice lady. She didn't know anybody named Cade Marlowe, but she took my name and number in case she can find out anything through her contacts with social services." She couldn't spend much time looking at Ben because she was liable to start smiling. She knew his secret, and it might show.

"Well, that's something, anyway." Ben sounded wary. He might be worried she'd spill the beans. "You never can tell. She might turn up some information that would help you."

Molly wished she could reassure him that she wouldn't reveal the secret. "She might, although I realized when I made the call that I had mixed feelings. What if she finds out something bad happened to my aunt or my cousin, or both of them? I've always assumed I'd find them and orchestrate a touching reunion with the rest of the family."

"That's because you're an optimist," Pete said. "Don't ever apologize for that. It's an admirable trait."

"Yes, but given the fact that we've heard nothing from either of them in years, what are the odds that they're both okay?" She saw the hesitation in each of their expressions. "See, maybe I don't want to keep searching. Maybe I don't want to know the truth."

Sarah put an arm around her shoulders. "You could call that lady back in the next few days and tell her you've changed your mind. It's nearly Christmas. I doubt she'll start investigating until the New Year."

"Thanks. I might do that. Hey, aren't we supposed

to head to the dining room? As I recall, Mary Lou doesn't take kindly to people who are late for dinner."

"She doesn't," Pete said. "And she told me to give her thirty minutes or so. It's been forty. I think we'd better move it." He started off with Sarah at his side.

Ben followed, but Molly put a restraining hand on his arm. When he turned to her, she mouthed the words *I know.*

His eyes widened.

"I won't say anything," she murmured before starting down the hall.

"Thanks." Ben matched her stride and kept his voice low. "I was worried."

"Don't be."

He let out a breath. "I'm so glad you have a brain."

That made her laugh. "Me, too."

They continued down the hall to the small family dining room adjacent to the larger one used when the hands gathered for lunch every day. Molly loved that meal, too, because the atmosphere was completely different. The main dining room had four round tables that each seated eight, and many days they were all filled.

The Chance brothers attended whenever possible, sometimes with their wives. Gabe's wife, Morgan, often brought all three of their kids when she came, and Jack's wife, Josie, would bring little Archie so he could play with his cousins. Nick's vet practice sometimes kept him away, but his wife, Dominique, liked to be there if she wasn't in the middle of mounting one of her photography shows. When their adopted son Lester wasn't in school, he came to lunch, too. Add in the ranch hands, and the room became a noisy free-for-all.

Tonight, though, the room was in shadows and light

beckoned from the more intimate family dining room through a set of double doors. A rustic metal chandelier hung over a linen-covered table set with china, crystal and silverware. Molly felt the family connection here, because gracious living had been a part of her heritage, too.

She'd researched her great-grandfather and great-grandmother Gallagher, parents of her Grandpa Seth and her Great Aunt Nelsie. The Gallaghers, it turned out, had traveled from Baltimore and had brought with them the customs of a genteel society. So when she sat at this table at the Last Chance Ranch and unfolded her cloth napkin, she thought about how the tradition of elegant dining had been passed down through three generations.

Hers was the fourth, and she already used cloth napkins in her small rental home. She was collecting silver and china. After she had her own family, she'd pull out all the stops.

Sarah and Pete sat across the table from Molly and Ben. While Mary Lou served the dinner, Ben asked questions about the breeding program at the Last Chance. He mentioned his interest in Calamity Sam and suggested he might begin a breeding program of his own in Sheridan. If Molly hadn't known his actual mission had been to bring Sarah's birthday gift, she'd swear he'd come for the reason he'd given.

Pete and Sarah discussed the horses with great enthusiasm. Molly was out of her depth when it came to horse breeding, so she spent a lot of time listening and watching. Mostly she paid attention to the interaction between Ben and Pete as they kept up the fiction that Ben was here as a buyer.

They were both playing their cards very close to the vest. Once or twice she caught a look that passed between them, but if Sarah noticed anything, she didn't say so. Smart lady.

Sarah must have questioned Ben's presence here the night before her birthday celebration. She might suspect he had brought some big surprise with him. But, if so, she'd probably decided not to ask any questions and risk spoiling whatever surprise her husband and sons had cooked up for her.

Now Molly was part of the charade, too, and she loved that. When Ben glanced over at her and gave her a wink, her toes curled. Nothing like a shared secret to bring two people closer together.

She enjoyed their current proximity, in fact. Having him seated within touching distance was quite arousing. His aftershave tantalized her and she found herself listening for the pattern of his breathing and imagining she could feel his body heat.

But she had to find out if the attraction between them was mutual. That meant spending some time alone with him. A bolder woman might walk right down to his bedroom tonight, but that wasn't her style. She had something more subtle in mind.

They all lingered over dessert as the conversation turned to the party, which would begin at four the following day. Mary Lou came out with more coffee and stayed long enough to confirm tomorrow's itinerary.

Sarah glanced at her. "I'll be up by seven to help you bake cookies. Morgan and Josie will be over around ten with the kids."

"Got it." Mary Lou gathered up the dessert plates. "I'm off to bed so I'll be rested up for that crew."

Sarah grinned. "It'll be fun."

"It's always fun, but it's also exhausting. 'Night, all."

Molly had been so focused on Ben that she'd forgotten tomorrow morning Sarah and Mary Lou were going to let the grandkids decorate Christmas cookies. After Mary Lou left, she turned to Sarah. "Will I be in the way if I come down to help?"

"Absolutely not! I was hoping you would. The more adults to help manage the frosting and sprinkles, the better."

"Then I'll set my alarm and be down by seven, too."

"Great." Sarah picked up her coffee cup. "Those kids always look forward to it, and then they'll get to show off their work at the party." She looked over at Ben. "I'm afraid it'll be a little wild around here tomorrow. You might want to grab a book and hide out in the barn."

"Actually, I'd like to help. I'm no good at decorating cookies, but if you need furniture rearranged, I can do that."

"Then you're hired." Sarah smiled at him. "We have to move all the furniture against the walls to create space for dancing. With all the people coming, it'll be crowded out there."

"We'll manage," Pete said. "It wouldn't be a Chance party if we didn't dance."

"But we might have to do it in shifts." Sarah laughed. "Molly, you could make up an Excel sheet and assign us all time slots."

"I could, but I think Jack would tear it up. He's not the type to be assigned a time slot."

Pete smiled. "No, he's not. We'll work it out. So we bump into each other. So what? We're family."

"I don't have to dance," Ben said. "I'm a guest, not family."

"Nonsense." Sarah frowned at him. "As our guest you most certainly should dance. But I guess I should ask if you even like to."

"I do."

"Then you'd better join in," Pete said. "Jack is big on getting everybody out on the floor for at least a few numbers. He's currently teaching all the kids. I guess you could say he's the Last Chance's dance master. If I hadn't been able to two-step, I'm not sure he would have let me marry Sarah."

"And we'll have live music, Ben. A couple of our ranch hands play guitar." Sarah brightened as if inspiration had just hit. "Did I hear you playing a harmonica earlier tonight?"

"Yes, ma'am."

"I'll bet Trey and Watkins would love to have you add your harmonica to the mix, if you're willing."

"Uh, well…sure." Ben looked pleased. "I'd like that. Sounds like fun."

Sarah clasped her hands together. "I do love parties!" Then she beamed at Molly. "I'm so glad you could be here for this one. I wish we could magically transport your whole family up here, too."

"Me, too, but then you'd have to knock out a couple of walls."

"True. Your family's even bigger than ours. I'm losing track of who's who in the Gallagher clan. I remember you and your brothers very well, but I can't tell you the names of their wives and kids without looking it up."

"I know, and I'll be better about sending emails and

pictures from now on. I'm the one the family has put in charge of doing that. What a shocker."

Sarah took another drink of her coffee. "I don't know that we have anybody in that role. We should, though. Now that we can connect online, we should all be better informed about each other."

"We can work on that, but I hope you and Pete are serious about flying down next spring. My folks would love it."

"Oh, we are," Pete said. "I haven't been to Arizona in years. I'm stoked about going."

Sarah took a deep breath and pushed back her chair. "And I'm ready for bed. We have a big day tomorrow. The rest of you can stay here as long as you like, but I'm thinking Mary Lou has the right idea. Time to turn in."

"Yeah, it is for me, too." Pete stood. "But you kids are welcome to hang out here for awhile. Mary Lou won't mind if you help yourself to more coffee and dessert if you clean up after yourselves."

"I'll just finish what I have in my cup," Ben said. "It's great stuff. Then I'll be off to bed, too. It's been a long day."

"I'm sure, driving on those icy roads." Pete tucked an arm around Sarah's waist. "See you both in the morning."

Sarah said good-night, too, and then Molly had her wish, to spend some time alone with Ben. Once Pete and Sarah were out of earshot, she spoke, but kept her voice down. "Rosie Padgett said you were an artist with saddles, and then I knew what you were really here for."

Ben turned sideways in his chair and gazed at her.

"That was nice of her to say, but I sure as hell didn't think it through when I suggested you should call them. I guess it never occurred to me that you'd call now, before the birthday party."

She mirrored his position so she could look at him as they talked. "I probably wouldn't have if Sarah hadn't encouraged me. As you could probably tell, I wasn't sure I wanted to hear what Rosie Padgett had to say."

"I know, and I didn't think about the fact that if your cousin had ended up at Thunder Mountain, then your aunt…well, I can't see that being a good thing where she was concerned."

"No. But he wasn't there, so that leaves the mystery unsolved. I wonder if I should leave it alone and imagine they're doing well but have no interest in reconnecting with their family."

"That could be the truth. You might not have been aware of problems between your aunt and your grandparents, but that doesn't mean there weren't any."

She thought about that for a moment and finally shook her head. "I get what you're saying, and I suppose anything's possible, but Grandpa Seth and Grandma Joyce were kind, gentle people. According to my dad, Aunt Heather was a happy person until she hooked up with Rance Marlowe. Then she got pregnant with Cade and…well, there's never been a divorce in my family."

"Wow, that's unusual."

"I know, and most people who hear that assume it's because problems were swept under the rug. I think it's because they were brought out in the open and dealt with. Heather was the big exception. When she had problems with Rance, she cut off communication and hid their troubles from everybody."

"And you're worried about how that turned out."

"Yes. I thought we'd all be better off knowing the truth, but now I'm not so sure."

Ben sighed. "Well, I don't have any advice. My knowledge of family dynamics is sadly lacking."

"Why?"

He met her gaze and smiled. "I should have known you'd ask that. Which means I shouldn't have made the remark in the first place. Sorry. I'd rather not get into it right now."

Although his tone was friendly and he was doing his best to be polite, she felt a brick wall go up. She couldn't blame him. They'd met a few hours ago. Just because she'd blabbed some of her family information didn't mean that he'd want to do the same. "That's fine. Let's switch topics."

He polished off the last of his coffee. "To what?"

"The saddle you brought here. Where is it?"

He laughed. "You know, I've only been around you for a little while, but somehow I knew you'd ask that question. Now that you know about the saddle, its whereabouts is driving you nuts, isn't it?"

"Yes."

"I guess I can trust you."

"You can. I wouldn't ruin this surprise for anything."

"It's in the far back corner of the tractor barn under a blanket."

"Who's seen it?"

"Jack, Gabe and Nick. That's it."

She gave him her most winsome smile, the one even her brothers had never been able to resist. "Please take me out there. I want to see it, too."

5

BEN SHOULD HAVE seen this coming. Molly was the most inquisitive woman he'd ever run across, and now that she'd learned about the secret present for Sarah, of course she'd want to see it. She'd want to be one of the privileged few who knew what was coming when the saddle was presented tomorrow evening.

And the fact of the matter was, he wanted to show it to her. He was proud of that saddle and after all three Chance brothers had given it a thumbs-up, he felt pretty confident that Molly would like it, too. Still, he needed to think of the logistics.

He considered what they'd have to go through. "It's damned cold out there. I'm sure the temperature's dropped considerably since I was out, and it was freezing, then."

"I know. We'll bundle up and go fast."

"It's snowing."

"Not very hard. A few flakes. The shoveled paths should still be fine if we go right away. Please?"

That smile of hers was something. It made her eyes light up and put a cute little dimple in her left cheek.

He felt like kissing her, but her glasses would be in the way so he didn't act on the impulse. Besides, she'd asked him to take her out to see his saddle, not kiss her.

"Come on, Ben. It'll be fun." She pushed back her chair and picked up her coffee cup and saucer. "We'll just put these in the dishwasher, pull on our duds, and be off."

He stood and collected his dishes. "I'll bet you got your brothers in all kinds of trouble when you were a kid."

"Yes, but they never regretted it. I had great ideas. Even if we were punished…well, mostly they were punished because they got blamed…they still had fun."

Ben laughed. "I'd love to hear their side of that someday."

"You should! You totally should come to Prescott for a visit. It's a cute little town. You'd like it."

"We'll see." Whoops. He wasn't sure how it had happened, but suddenly she was inviting him to Prescott so he could meet her brothers.

He wondered how they'd react to a guy who had no intention of starting a family, ever. That wouldn't work for Miss Molly. Her brothers would probably escort him right out the door. If they thought for one minute he'd misled their baby sister, he might be run out of town on a rail.

But that was a moot point, because he wouldn't be going to Prescott. If he had any sense, he wouldn't have told her where the saddle was, but she had a way of making him say things he shouldn't. Now he had to take her there, because if he didn't, she'd go by herself. He wasn't about to let her do that.

They climbed the stairs together and separated at

the top to go to their respective rooms and suit up. He wound a wool scarf around his neck before pulling on his sheepskin coat. He left it open so he wouldn't roast, made sure his fleece-lined leather gloves were in the pockets and settled his Stetson on his head.

What he needed was a lined hat with earflaps, but he hadn't brought one on this trip. He hadn't expected to be going outside in subzero weather. But then, he hadn't counted on a little bit of a thing winding him around her pinky finger, either. At the last minute, he pocketed his phone so he could use its flashlight feature. Jack might not think much of that convenience, but Ben used his all the time.

As he walked out of his room, Molly appeared wearing a puffy, bright-red jacket, a red knit hair band that covered her ears, a red knit cap and rubber boots. She looked adorable.

They met at the top of the stairs once again, and he realized she held mittens in her hand, not gloves. Who wore mittens anymore? She did, apparently.

She waved them at him. "A gift from one of my sisters-in-law," she said in a low voice. "She's just learning to knit. This is their first and maybe their only outing, but I wanted to tell her I used them in Wyoming and this trip to the tractor barn won't require me to do anything complicated with my fingers."

Her low-pitched comment, probably designed to keep from waking the household, shouldn't make him think of sex, but it did. He pictured the interesting things she could do with her fingers if they were free to roam over his naked body. Presently they were about as far from naked as they could get without being zipped into a hazmat suit.

Something was different about her, other than all the stuff she'd put on to guard against the cold, but at first he couldn't figure out what it was. Then he did. He kept his voice down, too. "Where are your glasses?"

"I popped in my contacts. My glasses would just fog up the minute I stepped outside and started breathing."

"So why don't you wear contacts all the time? Do they bother you?"

"Not really. I just…like my glasses. I know that sounds silly, but I started wearing them when I was a kid, and they're *me* in a way that contacts aren't. It's a cliché, but I feel smarter with them on. Now, see, you're smiling because you think that's ridiculous."

"No, I'm smiling because I like you."

"You do? How do you mean that, exactly?"

He laughed softly. "I keep forgetting that you have to analyze everything."

"That's true, but I just realized I'm getting very hot in this coat, so forget about that question for now. We can talk about it after we come back from the tractor barn and take off all these clothes."

"Depending on how much you plan to take off, we should definitely talk about it."

She blushed. "I didn't mean it like *that*."

"Too bad." Chuckling, he started down the stairs. She was the wrong woman for him. The absolute worst choice he could make. But when she stood there looking so cute and talking about taking off her clothes, he couldn't seem to remember that.

He paused in front of the door to button his coat and put on his gloves. Then he turned up his collar.

She pulled a knitted red scarf out of her pocket. "My sister-in-law knitted this before she tackled the mittens." Molly wrapped it around her neck and then around her nose and mouth so only her eyes showed.

When that was all he could see, he became aware of what a beautiful green they were, and how her long lashes framed them. She might love her glasses, and in a way he preferred that look on her, too. But without her glasses, he could more easily picture her stretched out in his bed, gazing up at him. He'd be wise not to dwell on that or he'd really overheat standing in the entryway.

Last, she put on her mittens, which were too big. "Don't fit very well." Her voice was muffled by the scarf as she moved her hands and the mittens turned into flippers.

He bit the inside of his cheek so he wouldn't laugh. Then, moving cautiously, he opened the front door.

She gasped as frigid air engulfed them.

"We don't have to go."

She shook her head and stepped out onto the porch.

He followed her out, closed the door and took the action any man in this situation would. He wrapped his arm around her shoulders and held her close as they navigated down the steps. Close was a relative term in this case. Holding on to her was like holding onto a blow-up Christmas yard decoration. He kept losing his grip because she was so squashy and slippery.

It might have been the coldest walk he'd ever taken in his life. Without any pavement or large buildings giving off heat, the air bit through his coat as if he'd walked out bare-chested. His nipples tightened in response to the icy temperature until they actually hurt.

But she'd been right about the snowfall. The flakes were lazy and slow. That could change at any time, though, so he planned to make this a very quick trip.

The shoveled path led to the horse barn, then branched off to the tractor barn. It was narrow, but by hugging her against him, he was able to steer them along it without either of them stepping into the crusted drifts on each side.

The horse barn was heated, as he'd discovered this afternoon. He considered making a stop there to warm up and decided she wouldn't go for that. She didn't strike him as a woman who took very many detours in life.

Besides, the sooner they got to the tractor barn and looked at the saddle, the sooner they could get back to the cozy ranch house. He thought he'd become used to Wyoming winters, but he'd never been outside in a landscape like this, where security lights and a pale moon reflected off untrampled snow. Beyond the soft glow coming from the house and the barn, the surroundings were completely dark.

No sound greeted him, either, not even the hoot of an owl. He knew this was wolf country, but they were silent, too. The frozen world was completely still, without even a breeze. For that he was grateful. They didn't need a wind-chill factor right now.

The tractor barn was secured by the same method as the horse barn—a wooden bar that slid across when a person wanted to open the double doors, and slid back when they wanted to keep them closed. Ben had to let go of Molly while he pushed the bar aside, and he could swear he heard her teeth chattering, even with the scarf covering her mouth.

He hoped, after braving the cold, she'd like his saddle and feel good about having seen it. Tramping out here tonight was a lot of trouble, particularly if the saddle turned out to be anticlimactic.

The tractor barn wasn't wired for electricity, which meant no heat and no lights. Once they were inside and he'd pulled the doors shut, the air was marginally warmer, but not by much. He reached into his pocket, but before he could turn on his flashlight app, she'd pulled off one mitten and activated hers.

She tugged her scarf down from her nose and mouth. "That was intense." Her words came out in little puffs of condensed vapor.

"And we have to do it all over again when we go back." More clouds fogged the air between them.

"I didn't say I didn't like it. Challenges are fun for me." Mist from their conversation hung between them.

"Me, too, actually." He'd felt a sense of kinship when she'd said that. Not everyone welcomed challenges in their life. He thought it was the only way a person could grow. "Shine your light along the floor so we don't trip over anything as we walk back there."

"Thank you for bringing me." She held the light steady as they walked to the back of the tractor barn.

In warm weather the place probably smelled of gas and oil, but freezing temperatures cancelled out most of the odor. Ben caught faint whiffs of the metallic scent of machinery, but it was subtle. Light from the phone allowed him to see the hulking forms of tractors. In the dark the barn *was* a little spooky.

He couldn't imagine sending her out here by herself, even if she would have been perfectly safe. Maybe her size made him feel protective, but he thought it was more than that. He loved her enthusiasm for new experiences, but having someone around as backup wasn't a bad idea. He'd never want to suggest she wasn't capable of anything she put her mind to, but if he could provide a safety net, that would be okay, too.

And what a ridiculous idea that was! He didn't expect to see her after she left the state on Monday. She had a lifetime of adventures ahead of her and he wouldn't be a part of any of them. So he could stop fantasizing about his role in her life, because he had none.

"To the right," he said as they neared the back of the barn. "Over in the corner. Lift the light a little. See that thing over there with the blanket covering it? That's the saddle. Hold the light steady."

She did as he asked and he noted that she was excellent at following directions when the situation required it. Stepping into the glow of her phone light, he grabbed two corners of the blanket and pulled. He considered making it even more dramatic by whipping it aside like a magician revealing his completed trick. But that would be showing off, and he wasn't into showing off.

"Oh, Ben."

The awe in her voice thrilled him. "Glad you like it." He turned toward her.

She was in shadow with her flashlight trained on the saddle. "I don't just *like* it. I *love* it." She moved forward and angled the light as she examined the saddle more closely. "Rosie Padgett was right. You're an artist."

"I don't know about that." Good thing he was in shadow, too, so she wouldn't see him blush. Later, when he was alone, he'd savor those words, but at the moment they made him uncomfortable.

"Then you underestimate yourself."

"I think of an artist as being somebody like Leonardo da Vinci, not Ben Radcliffe, saddlemaker."

"Then maybe your definition is a little too narrow." She traced the tooling on the saddle's fender. "Did you copy this design from somewhere? Is that why you don't feel like an artist?"

"No, I made it up."

"There you go. This is original art. It happens to be on a working saddle instead of on the wall of a museum, but personally, I like the idea of art in everyday life. Useful art. You took something that serves a function and made it beautiful. Like Grecian urns. They were made to be used, but that didn't keep the potters from decorating them with amazing pictures and turning them into works of art we study today."

"I guess."

"Listen to a history professor. If Sarah takes good care of it and passes it down, it could someday end up in a museum as an example of Western art."

"I think that's going a little far." Even though the barn was very cold, he was growing warmer by the minute. No one had ever said such things to him. He didn't believe a word of it, but that didn't mean he didn't like hearing it. "I've never studied art, really. I took an art class in high school because it was an easy A, but that doesn't mean—"

"Be quiet, Ben." She caressed the saddle one last time and turned back to him, the light moving with her. "Where are you? Oh, I see you." She walked over to him until she was standing inches away. "What was that you said when we were inside? That you liked me?"

"I said, that, yeah."

"And I asked you to elaborate. Would you care to do that now?" She kept the light trained on the floor.

That meant she was still mostly in shadow, and she was still bundled up like someone about to ski the Alps. But he sensed something in the air, a yearning that matched his own. "Instead of trying to explain it," he said, "maybe I should show you."

"Show me how?"

"Like this." Tossing his hat onto the saddle horn, he gathered her into his arms. She squeaked in surprise, but when he located her mouth, her squeak turned into a sigh. Oh, yeah. She wanted this as much as he did.

6

AT FIRST BEN'S lips were cold, but Molly's weren't. She'd had them covered with a scarf. Warming his lips took no time at all. After the first shock of discovering he was going to kiss her, she threw herself into the experience with abandon.

Rising to her toes, she wound her arms around his neck and gave it all she had. So did he, and oh, my goodness. A harmonica player knew what it was all about. She'd never kissed one before, but she hoped to be doing a lot more of this with Ben.

Although she'd never thought of a kiss as being creative, this one was. He caressed her lips so well and so thoroughly that she forgot the cold and the late hour. She forgot they were standing in a cavernous tractor barn surrounded by heavy equipment.

She even forgot that she wasn't in the habit of kissing men she'd known for mere hours. Come to think of it, she'd never done that. But everything about this kiss, from his coffee-and-dessert-flavored taste to his talented tongue, felt perfect.

As far as she was concerned, the kiss could go on

forever. Well, maybe not. The longer they kissed, the heavier they breathed. His hot mouth was making her light-headed in more ways than one.

That was her excuse for dropping her phone on the concrete floor. It hit with a sickening crack, but in her current aroused state, she didn't really care.

Ben pulled back, though, and gulped for air. "I think that was your phone."

"I think so, too." She dragged in a couple of quick breaths. "Kiss me some more."

With a soft groan, he lowered his head and settled his mouth over hers. This time he took the kiss deeper and invested it with a meaning she understood quite well. Intellectually she was shocked, but physically she was completely on board. The stroke of his tongue delivered a message, one she received with a rush of moisture that dampened her panties.

This time when he eased away from her, she was trembling. Like a swimmer breaking the surface, she gasped. Then she clutched his head and urged him back down. She wanted him to kiss her until the voice of caution stopped yelling at her that it was too soon to feel like this about him. "More."

He resisted, but he was panting and obviously as hot as she was. "This is crazy. I think we broke your phone. The light's out."

"We don't need light."

"That's not the point."

"Yes, it is. Come back here and do what you were doing some more. I really like it."

His chuckle was a little strained. "Me, too." Apparently he had both a strong will and a strong neck, because he held himself away from her. "But I can do a better job of it in a warm house, plus then we can check out your phone."

"I don't care about the damned phone." She sighed. "Which is a measure of how you affect me if I'm unconcerned about my techie toy."

"I'm flattered."

"I hope you're also turned on."

"That, too." He sounded amused.

"You realize the minute we step out into that Arctic air we'll lose momentum." And she'd begin to question the wisdom of sleeping with him. She just knew it.

His gloved hand brushed her cheek. "Speak for yourself. The way I'm feeling right now, I could make love to you on an ice floe."

She shivered, and it had nothing to do with the cold and everything to do with picturing them naked and going for it on any available flat surface. Oh, boy. She was actually considering having sex with a guy she'd just met.

As the power of his kisses faded a little, her conscience resumed its tedious lecture about her wanton behavior. She tried not to listen, but it was no use. "Maybe we should lose momentum." She said it with regret, but her conscience applauded. "How long have we known each other?"

He was silent for a moment. "Yeah, you're right. For the record, I don't ordinarily move this fast."

"I *never* move this fast. I go through the normal steps—coffee date, lunch date, dinner date." More smug applause from her conscience.

"So we skipped a couple of steps."

"It's not just the steps." Her conscience was in full control, now. "It's the time between the steps, when you talk on the phone with someone, when you have moments to contemplate them when they're not around, when you begin to miss them if you don't see them for a couple of days."

He took a shaky breath. "I know you're right, but we don't have that kind of time. You'll be gone in a few days."

She noticed he still hadn't let go of her. She could wiggle out of his arms, but she didn't want to do that. "You make a valid point." *Take that, conscience!* "I've never met anyone special when I was on vacation. My dating steps work great in Prescott, but this isn't quite that situation."

"Same here. I've never been bowled over by somebody who's about to leave town. Guess I don't know how to handle—"

"Bowled over? Really?" Her conscience was speechless at that.

"Yeah." There was a smile in his voice. "Really. That little pirouette you did for me after I took the dental floss out of your hair knocked me out."

"Wow. No one's ever told me I bowled them over." And if she needed justification for ignoring her dating steps, this might do the trick.

"Surprised the hell out of me, too. You're not my type at all."

"Oh? In what way?"

"Uh…the women I date are usually more…full-figured."

With an internal sigh, she decided this cozy embrace was over and pushed against his broad chest. "Then maybe you're hot for me because, even though I'm not your type, I'm handy and you're in the mood."

"Hey, hey, I didn't mean it like that." His arms tightened around her.

"Let me go, Ben. I get the picture. Chances are you'd be disappointed once our clothes are off, which they won't be, because I'd sooner strip in front of a grizzly than you."

"Let me say my piece, okay? Then if you want to stay away from me for the rest of your visit, I won't bother you."

Curiosity had always been both a blessing and a curse in her life. "Go ahead."

"You're right about what I've always considered my type of woman." He rubbed the small of her back while he talked.

"Centerfold worthy." She tried not to be affected by his touch. Logically she shouldn't feel it much through her bulky coat, but when it came to Ben, she was extra sensitive. "I'm not built to those specs."

"You don't have to be. You have something more important."

"Here it comes. You even said it already. You like that I have brains, but trust me, women don't want to be adored just for their brains, even if they think they do. They want to be worshipped for their bodies, even skinny ladies like me."

His voice grew husky. "You have no idea how much I want to do that, Molly."

"Because you've been through a long dry spell?"

"No, I haven't. I broke up with somebody a couple of months ago."

"For some guys, two months is a long time. You could be one of those guys."

"I could, but I'm not. It wasn't a very intense relationship, anyway." He kept rubbing her back with slow, sure strokes. "But you—you would be intense. I thought so before I kissed you, and now I know it for sure. You're so full of energy. That's very sexy."

"It is?" She was feeling a little better about being in his arms. A *lot* better, actually.

"Oh, yeah. You glow, Molly, and I'm so drawn to that. I want…" He swallowed. "I want to touch you all over and see if you'll glow even brighter. I bet you will." His voice roughened. "I want to see the excitement in your eyes when you're about to come. I want to see you go up in flames."

She gulped. And quivered. And decided that maybe her dating steps weren't all they were cracked up to be.

"That's all I have to say. If you want me to let you go and keep my distance while I'm here, I understand. We just met. I'm not a sexual opportunist, but you don't know me well enough to be convinced of that."

"Yes, I do." Her words were barely more than a whisper.

"You do?"

She cleared her throat. "Yes." She was smiling, but he wouldn't be able to see that. "A sexual opportunist wouldn't have announced I'm not his type."

He blew out a breath. "That was so lame of me. I'm sorry."

"Except you told me the truth."

"It was the truth until I met you. And besides that, you were insulted. I didn't mean to insult you." His sensual back rub continued. "Your body excites me in a way I can't describe very well."

"You're welcome to keep trying."

He chuckled. "Okay, let me see if I can come up

with a way to say it that makes sense. It's like you're sneaky sexy. A stealth vixen."

"A stealth vixen. I like that." She also liked the way he'd brought her closer until she was pressed tight against his warm body. Even with the layers between them, she knew for a fact he wasn't making this up. He really did want her.

"It's taken me awhile to evolve, but I think I'm finally learning to appreciate subtlety." He paused in midstroke. "How am I doing? Is any of this making sense?"

"Sort of."

"Where are we on your dating chart?"

"Is this your way of asking if I'll go to bed with you when we get back to the house?"

"I wish." He hugged her a little bit closer. "Much as I would love that, all we can do is fool around a little. No grand finale tonight, I'm afraid. I wasn't expecting this and I'm completely unprepared."

She had a genius IQ, but it didn't take a genius to figure out what he was talking about. She debated telling him what she knew and finally decided that keeping the information to herself might not be right. He should have all the facts, too.

Besides, she liked the idea of rocking him back on his heels. "Actually, that's not a problem."

His sharp intake of breath was gratifying. "Why not?"

"There's a box in your bathroom."

"You're kidding."

"I would never kid about a thing like that, Ben. That would be cruel."

"And you just happen to know this?"

"I had a headache yesterday and I forgot to bring aspirin. There wasn't any in my bathroom, so I looked in yours."

"I see."

Honesty made her amend that statement. "Actually, I found the aspirin right away, but once I was in there, I wondered what else was tucked in the drawers, so I checked everything out."

"God almighty, you're like a little cat, poking your nose in everywhere. And I love it." He hesitated. "But I'm still trying to get a bead on where we stand. Are we at yes, no or maybe?"

"We're at maybe. I still think we need to slow down a little. Don't you?"

"Truthfully? No. We're two consenting adults and what happens upstairs stays upstairs. We've both proven we can keep a secret, and we only have four nights before you leave. By denying ourselves tonight, we've taken a potentially great experience off the table."

"What if it doesn't go well?"

"Then I'll leave first thing Saturday morning. You'll only have to put up with me another twenty-four hours and I'll be gone." His voice dropped to a sexy murmur. "But it'll go well."

Her heart beat faster. "You're sure about that?"

"Yes." And he kissed her again.

The second his mouth covered hers, he proved that he knew what he was talking about. A man who could kiss like this, who could use his tongue with such devastating effect, a man who knew exactly the right angle for maximum pleasure—that man would bring the same originality and expertise to lovemaking. She'd be a fool to miss out on even one night of sharing his bed.

When he released her, he didn't let go right away, which was a good thing because she might have collapsed onto the cement floor. She was just that unsteady. Mentally, though, she was extremely focused on returning to the house. So much so that she forgot both the uncovered saddle and her dropped phone. "Let's go."

Laughter rippled in his voice. "First I have to cover the saddle."

"Oh. Right."

He turned on his flashlight app and aimed it at the floor. "And there's your phone."

"Thanks." She leaned down and picked it up. The screen was cracked, but the phone itself might be operational. She activated it. "Everything looks fine. I just need a new screen."

"Good." He took his hat off the saddle horn and put it on. "Would you please hold the light for me?"

"Sure." She tucked away her phone and took his. "It really is beautiful. Now I wish I'd had a chance to contribute to the fund, but my trip up here was kind of a last-minute decision. I'm sure Jack had it handled long before I arrived."

"He did." Ben arranged the blanket so the saddle was completely concealed. "He took up a collection back in October and gave me half my fee then." He turned back to her. "You mean you almost didn't make it here?"

"Almost. Christmas is special at Mom and Dad's house, and I usually spend the first part of my Christmas break helping cook and decorate. Plus the weather's dicey this time of year. Originally I planned to wait until summer."

"Then we wouldn't have met."

"Probably not."

"What made you change your mind and come before Christmas?"

"Aunt Sarah's birthday party tomorrow, for one thing, but then she told me about this set of diaries that her mother-in-law, Nelsie Chance, had kept for years. I was very eager to read them, which I have, and they're wonderful. I even found mention of me in there. But I could have put that off until next summer, too. I just had this hunch that I should come up here now, for some reason."

"Hmm." He adjusted the fit of his Stetson. "Listen, do you think…" Then he shook his head. "Never mind. I don't believe in that stuff."

"What stuff?"

"Fate, kismet, that kind of thing."

She didn't say anything because she *did* believe in it and was beginning to wonder if her hunch had been about him. But she wasn't ready to announce that thought. She might never admit it to him. So much depended on how the next few days went for them. Or the next few hours.

But apparently he was over there interpreting her silence. "You believe in it, don't you?"

"A little."

"Well, I don't."

That made her smile. He was the one who'd brought it up in the first place, but she wouldn't point that out to him. The instant attraction between them excited him, but it probably made him nervous, too.

Not surprising. It made *her* nervous. Going to bed with him tonight was so far out of her comfort zone it was in the next zip code. But that didn't mean she'd decided not to. She was still thinking.

7

As they hurried from the tractor barn back to the house, Ben still wasn't clear on whether Molly wanted to have sex with him or not. She hadn't specifically said she would, but her kiss certainly tasted like yes.

Yet he should probably give her a little more information before they took that step. Her dreams had to include a family of her own, but all he could share would be this brief time with her. Then he'd bow out of her life.

She didn't realize that, and he should be straight with her before anything happened between them. Someday she'd settle down with a man who wanted a family, but in the meantime, here they were, crazy for each other. If she was willing to share her warmth for a long weekend, he'd take it.

On the porch they quietly brushed off the snow that clung to their jackets. The porch stretched the length of the house, and according to Jack, rockers lined it during the summer. If Ben came back this summer for Calamity Sam, he'd make a point to enjoy some time in a rocker and take in the view of the Tetons.

Molly wouldn't be here, though. A tug at his heart told him that he'd miss her cheerful presence. He'd have to get over that, because she was most definitely not for him, not for the long haul, anyway.

But now, as he carefully opened the door hung with a giant pine wreath, he thought maybe she could be his for a little while. While they wordlessly removed their boots and set them on a mat by the front door, he thought about what he wanted to say to her. He didn't relish giving a full explanation, but he had to tell her this wasn't a lead-in to something more.

That was assuming she would consider sharing his bed. As they climbed the stairs to the second floor, he unbuttoned his coat. Then he grabbed her by the hand before she could start back to her room. "Molly."

She turned toward him, her eyes bright and her skin flushed.

"You know I want you."

"Yes." She swallowed. "And I—"

"There's something you need to know about me." He took a deep breath. "Saying this might seem weird, except…you're so into family, and I'm…not."

Her expression grew thoughtful. "Okay."

"I never plan to have kids. I'm not even sure if I'll ever get married." He wondered if she'd laugh and say the topic was premature. Or maybe she'd ask him why he felt that way.

Instead, her gaze softened. "Thank you for telling me."

"Seemed like the right thing." And he'd probably ruined his chances, but at least he'd be able to live with himself. "I guess that's that, then." But he didn't let go of her hand, just in case he hadn't blown it with her.

A smile touched the corners of her mouth. "Giving up?"

His heart kicked into high gear. "I thought maybe, under the circumstances, you'd rather—"

"You thought wrong."

"Thank God." Watching the glow of anticipation return to her eyes made his body hum.

"But first I should probably…" She gestured toward her bedroom.

"You don't need anything. Come with me." He wasn't about to lose momentum now. He tugged her down the hallway. "First stop, the bathroom."

She started laughing.

"Hey, you know where they are. I could waste precious time looking for them."

"You're incorrigible."

He'd never been with a woman whose vocabulary included *incorrigible*. He liked it more than he would have believed. He hadn't realized that smart women turned him on. Maybe before this episode ended, he'd make love to her while she wore the glasses she loved so much.

She located the box of condoms and lobbed them in his direction. "Don't say I never did anything for you."

He caught them in one hand. "I'd never say that, not in a million years." Taking her by the hand again, he led her into the bedroom and nudged the door closed with one foot.

Reluctant to break the magical connection between them, he tossed the box of condoms on the nearest nightstand. Coordination came in handy sometimes. Then he sent his hat sailing toward the bedpost and was gratified when he scored a ringer.

"Impressive."

"That's nothing." Pulling her into his arms, he plucked off her knit cap. Her hair was another glorious thing about her, and he combed his fingers through it, marveling at the many shades of color caught in the lamplight. "Cowboys are known for their agility. I can have you naked in ten seconds flat."

Her green eyes flashed. "Only if I cooperate."

"Please cooperate." He unwound the red scarf and dropped it to the floor. "I'm a desperate man."

"In that case..." She unzipped her parka and shrugged out of it. "I wouldn't want to be responsible for causing undue stress."

"Now I'm a grateful man." He got a firm grip on the hem of her sweater and tugged it over her head. He'd expected a utilitarian bra underneath. Instead she wore a lacy black number that made him catch his breath.

She stepped back with a coy smile. "When a girl doesn't have much to show off, she goes for the prettiest underwear she can find. Allow me." She reached behind her back.

The action thrust her pert breasts forward, and his mouth went dry. Then she unfastened the clasp and slowly drew the wisp of black lace away from the sweetest breasts he'd ever seen. He reached out.

"Not yet." She backed away another step. "You're falling behind."

He'd been so eager to get her out of her clothes that he'd lost track of the fact he still wore everything but his hat. He tossed the scarf aside and took off his sheepskin jacket.

"Give it here."

"You want my jacket?"

"I've always wondered what sheepskin would feel like on my bare skin." She draped his jacket over her shoulders and wrapped it around her. "Nice." Turning her cheek, she rubbed it against the soft collar. "Smells like you."

Transfixed by the sight of her stroking her cheek with his jacket lining, he stood motionless in the middle of the room.

"You're still behind, cowboy."

And so he was. He unfastened the cuffs of his Western shirt and the snaps down the front popped in rapid succession as he wrenched it open. In no time he'd dropped it to the floor. "Better?"

Her gaze moved from his face to his chest and the heat in those green eyes told him all he needed to know. This would be quite an evening. He'd closed the door, but now he wondered if he should stuff a towel under it to further soundproof the room.

At least Sarah and Pete slept downstairs at the opposite end of the house. He hoped that created enough distance to muffle what could become a noisy interlude.

"Now you're the one who's behind." His voice sounded rusty. "You're wearing my jacket."

"I like it."

His first impulse was to tell her she could have it, but that would be stupid for many reasons, most of them centering on the impermanence of this arrangement. "I'm glad. Now drop it."

She allowed the jacket to slide from her shoulders onto the floor. It was one of the most seductive maneuvers he'd ever seen. Once it was gone, she shoved her hands in the back pockets of her jeans, thrust her breasts forward and lifted her chin. "Now what?"

He lost it. With a groan of pure lust, he eliminated the distance between them and cupped her breasts in both hands. Then he leaned down and kissed her hard. She kissed him right back, rising on her toes and gripping his shoulders for balance.

Her breasts felt perfect in his hands and her throaty moans told him how much she loved having him touch her there. He stroked her silken skin and his cock thickened. Beneath his palms, her nipples hardened in arousal. He pinched them lightly and she moaned again, louder this time.

Wrenching her mouth from his and struggling for breath, she gazed up at him. Her words came out in a rush. "Take me to bed, now. Please."

He didn't have to be asked twice. Sliding his hands under her firm bottom, he lifted her up. She was light as a sunbeam and twice as warm. When she wrapped her legs around his waist, he felt the heat coming from her core, and the crotch of her jeans was damp. Hallelujah.

Carrying her to the bed, he set her on the edge of the mattress so he could pull off her jeans and panties. She was so finely made, so delicate. As he caressed each new treasure he uncovered, he also found out just how hot and wet she was, how breathless with desire.

He dropped to his knees, eager to give pleasure to a woman who was so ready for it.

"Not now." She cradled his head in both hands, her fingers gripping him tight, her gaze intense. "I ache, Ben. I've never ached like this. I need you inside me."

So he stood and backed away as she stretched out on the comforter. He hadn't bothered to pull it down.

There was no need. The room was warm and about to get a whole lot warmer.

She turned her head to watch as he stripped off the rest of his clothes and freed his aching cock. Her eyes widened. "Oh, my."

For the first time, he worried that he'd be too much for her. If he hurt her, even a little bit, he'd never forgive himself. His voice tight with lust, he sought to reassure her. "I'll take it slow."

She swallowed. "Okay."

His blood pounded in his ears. "Don't worry. You'll be in charge."

"Oh." Her rapid breathing made her breasts tremble invitingly. "That's good." A tiny smile touched her kiss-reddened lips and a gleam lit her green eyes.

"I guess you like that idea. Big surprise." His hands shook as he rolled on a condom. He didn't need it for birth control, but he didn't care to get into that discussion.

He didn't care to get into *any* discussion. She craved relief and by God, so did he. Neither of them needed conversation. He'd never wanted a woman so much, which meant he had to watch himself or he'd take her with all the force of that wanting. She might be a tough little thing with a will of iron, but she was no match for him if he allowed his passion free rein.

He paused before putting a knee on the bed and took a shaky breath. "Scoot over," he said softly. "So I can lie on my back. That's how we'll do this."

She followed his directions and propped her chin on her fist to watch him as he settled down beside her. "So I'm in charge?"

"Completely."

She looked him up and down, and her gaze lingered on his cock, which projected upward with the rigidity of a sundial. "Oh, boy."

That's when he realized he was in for it. He hadn't intended for this to be a test of his control, but now it likely would be. The other part of wanting her so much was that he felt as if he could come any minute. That would be bad on many levels.

She wasted no time scrambling to her knees and straddling his thighs. Then she sat there, her bare bottom warm against his skin as she contemplated him, her cheeks flushed. "I need you so much, but you are *huge.*"

He resisted the urge to grab her and lift her into position. With the entrance to nirvana so very close, yet so very far, his brain was on tilt. "You don't have to take it all." But how he hoped she could.

"I want to." She wrapped her fingers around his latex-covered cock.

He shuddered. "Then…just try." *Dear God, please try, before I go out of my effing mind.*

Slowly she rose on her knees and leaned over to flatten her hands on his chest. Her hair tumbled over her shoulders in waves of abandon. "Hold still."

"Right." His breathing roughened and he fisted his hands at his sides.

"Here goes nothing." She closed her eyes in concentration while she shifted her hips. Eventually, after what seemed like forever, she pressed the blunt tip of his cock right where it needed to be for the next stage.

He swore under his breath as her slick heat taunted him almost beyond endurance.

"Mmm." She looked into his eyes. "Ready?"

"Hell, yeah."

She eased down a little and sucked in air.

"Too much?"

"Oh, no." She moaned softly and took him slightly deeper. "This is…amazing. I thought it might be, and now…now…"

He didn't dare speak. He was too busy going through his multiplication tables and naming the U.S. presidents while he fought off his climax. She picked up another inch of real estate and he started counting backward from a hundred by threes.

Although he'd been worried that he'd be too big for her, he hadn't contemplated the flipside of that. He hadn't considered that her tight sheath would intensify the friction for him, too. He was thinking about it now as she continued her slow downward journey and he forgot how to breathe.

She also wasn't quiet about her plan to take all he had to give. She heralded each bit of progress with heartfelt moans and blissful sighs, which made it even tougher for him to stay in control. Then her core muscles clenched.

He drew in a sharp breath and glared at her. "Don't."

"I can't…help it." Her eyes were dark with excitement. "Nothing has ever felt…" She gasped as she settled further down. "Like this."

He lifted his head to gauge her progress. That was a mistake. The visual of his cock almost completely buried except for a mere inch sent a spasm through him. He groaned and fought against coming.

"I'm going for it." Taking a ragged breath, she moved the rest of the way and erupted, her climax rolling over his cock as her wild cries filled the room.

That wiped out his last ounce of control and he arched upward, claiming whatever fraction remained with a deep bellow of satisfaction as he came. *Yes, oh, yes!* Her tight channel clenched as he withdrew and thrust again. Pleasure pulsed through him in a dizzying spiral that left him gulping for air.

He couldn't say how long the moment lasted. He lost all track of time as he lay immersed in the incredible sensation of coming inside Molly Gallagher. When she slid down to rest her cheek on his damp chest, he finally allowed himself to hold her.

Until then he'd been true to his promise that she was in charge, but now he felt safe wrapping her in his arms. She relaxed against him, and her weight was no more than that of a pillow. The top of her head only reached his chin and her waist wasn't much bigger than his thigh. Yet she'd taken his cock deep into her body and treated it to the best time of its life.

"I loved that," she murmured.

"Me, too."

"Next time you can be in charge."

He smiled and combed her tousled hair with his fingers. "So you want to do this again?"

She laughed softly. "I do. And now that I know we fit, I'll let you direct the action."

Normally he required some recovery time. Apparently not with this woman. All she had to do was say she wanted more, and his body was willing to give her what she wanted.

8

WHILE BEN LEFT the room to dispose of the condom, Molly got under the covers and snuggled down to savor the most satisfying orgasm of her life. And she'd had it with an honorable man who'd admitted he was the wrong guy for her. She wanted to know why he'd decided against having a family, but something told her the reasons were extremely private.

Funny, but even though they'd just had great sex, she didn't feel as if she knew him well enough to pry into his personal business. He'd given her the truth, and she admired him for doing that much. They only had a short time together, and that might not be long enough for him to let down his guard. She wouldn't push, either.

Instead, she'd be grateful for this amazing experience, although she didn't know whether Ben was good in bed or not. Maybe with a package like his, he didn't have to try very hard to make a woman extremely happy.

He did, however, have to be gentle if the lady in question was built the way she was. She'd been intimidated when he'd first unveiled that bad boy, but intrigued and curious. Besides that, his kisses had aroused her to the point of no return, and although he'd offered oral sex to begin with, she'd wanted the full-body experience. She just hadn't realized how full he'd make her feel.

They hadn't moved much. They hadn't needed to. But she'd like to find out how a little movement would work out for them. She'd put his restraint to the ultimate test, and he'd controlled himself admirably. After that go-round, she didn't have to worry that he'd forget himself and take her too hard or too fast.

His consideration and tenderness said a great deal about him. He'd stockpiled some trust while holding himself motionless as she slowly discovered whether she could accommodate him. Putting him in charge didn't scare her a bit.

It aroused the hell out of her, though. He was by far the most exciting man she'd ever had sex with. When he walked back in the room, closing the door behind him, she sat up. "Could you just stand there for a minute and let me look at you?"

He grinned. "So I'm not in charge, after all?"

"You are, but once you climb into this bed, I won't get the same view as I have now."

"All right." He stayed where he was.

She took her time surveying his powerful chest sprinkled with dark hair before moving lower to his abs.

He shifted his weight. "You know what? Fair is fair. Throw back the covers so I can look at you."

She did, although she couldn't believe her body would affect him the way his affected her. The soft sheen of lamplight on his broad shoulders made her moist and achy. And when she gazed upon the equipment that could relieve that ache…

Hello. Maybe her body held the power to arouse him, after all. As his dark eyes focused on her, his penis, looking as impressive as it had the first time, rose from its base of dark curls.

"See what you do to me?" His voice was a soft caress.

She nodded. Her body quivered as he walked over to the bed and brought all that wonderfulness with him.

"It's not nearly as easy for me to see what I do to you." He sat on the edge of the bed and cupped one of her breasts in his hand. "Your nipples tell me a little something." He brushed his thumb over the one that was most accessible.

She moaned and arched into the caress.

"That tells me you like me to touch you." His thumb flicked her nipple in a lazy rhythm.

"Yes." Her blood heated.

"Now your skin is flushed, which tells me you're becoming excited." His glance roamed over her. "But in order to find out exactly how much you want me, I have to investigate further." Leaning forward, he nibbled on her mouth. "Spread your legs for me, Molly. Let me explore."

Heart pounding, she opened her thighs. He continued to give her teasing little kisses and nips as he slid his hand down over her stomach, tunneled through her curls and found what he was looking for.

"Ah, Molly." He probed her with knowing fingers. "Now I know how much you want me." He stroked deep.

Without warning, her body tightened around his fingers. She gasped at the sudden onslaught of an impending orgasm.

His soft chuckle tickled her mouth. "You're ready now, aren't you, sweet lady?" He pumped his fingers back and forth. "You're going to come for me in a minute or two, aren't you?"

She had no words for him, only whimpers as he increased the pace, curving his fingers and thrusting with devastating skill. The rhythmic, liquid sound of his moving fingers made the caress even more erotic. She lifted her hips, wanting deeper, wanting more.

"That's my girl. Take what you want. Ask for it." He slipped his arm behind her hips, supporting her as he worked his magic.

She'd wondered if he was really good in bed. He was giving her the answer. Maybe she should be embarrassed by how easily he'd seduced her with his words and his touch. But she didn't have time to be embarrassed.

She didn't have time for anything but this…letting go…coming apart…coming…crying out his name— over and over and over as he coaxed a shattering response from her willing body.

At last, panting and quivering, she sank back to the mattress and looked up at him, dazed by her own abandon.

He smiled. "I knew you'd be like this." Slowly he withdrew his hand and trailed his moist fingers up her body.

The brush of his fingers over her hot skin ignited the fire again. It burned low, but it still burned. She swallowed. "Like how?"

"Eager. Responsive. Sensual. Easily aroused. I shouldn't take advantage of that. I should let you rest, but…" He reached for the box of condoms. "Once more, Molly. Then we'll sleep."

She doubted that once more would be enough, at least for her. He was a powerful aphrodisiac. The memory of his thick penis filling her brought back the familiar ache deep in her core.

"You have such an expressive face." He tore open the packet. "You don't agree with my plan, do you?"

She shrugged. "Why set limits?"

"Because I think you need to get used to me." He rolled on the condom.

"So you say."

"I'm not taking any chances." He moved over her. "Our nights together should be nothing but pleasure. No pain." Grabbing a pillow from the other side of the bed, he lifted her easily and tucked it under her hips. "That's better. Now, bend your knees."

If he hadn't already loved her so thoroughly, she might have been shocked at the way he pushed her knees back and opened her to his gaze. But then he nudged her with his penis, and as he pushed slowly inside, she understood. He'd positioned her so that she could take him in this way, too.

And, oh, it was heaven. When he stopped halfway, she moaned in protest. "More."

"Give me a second or two." He clenched his jaw and lowered his head. "You tempt me to come like no one ever has."

"I do?" She liked that.

"You fit me like a glove." His chest heaved. "A

smooth, velvet glove that's been warmed by the fire. The deeper I go, the better it gets."

His description turned her on even more, making her voice husky. "For me, too."

"I thought maybe the second time would be…less intense." He shuddered and gazed at her with eyes filled with lust. "I think it's more, not less."

"You can come." She felt her own response building fast. "You don't have to hold back for my sake."

He gave her a crooked smile. "It's not for your sake. It's for mine." He took another ragged breath. "Okay. Moving on." He eased forward slowly and paused again. "You all right?"

"Never better." She tingled all over, and deep inside, her womb tightened in response to the glide of his penis. "Keep going."

"I don't want to hurt you."

"You won't. You fit, remember?"

"Oh, I remember, Molly. I remember *this*." He groaned and pushed home.

She sucked in a breath. So did he, and it was glorious. He wouldn't have to do another thing, and she could reach orgasm just because he was locked tight against all the places that needed contact. All she had to do was squeeze a little bit…

"Molly." Her name was an urgent warning. "Ah, hell, I have to move or go crazy. Hang on."

She clutched his shoulders because they were within reach. No sooner had she grabbed hold of him than he groaned and began to thrust, slowly at first, then more rapidly.

"Tell me…" He panted as he increased the pace yet

again, lifting her off the bed with each forward motion of his hips. "Tell me if it hurts. I'll stop."

"No!" She was on the wildest ride of her life and loving it. "Don't stop!" If she was sore later, she didn't care.

The headboard thumped against the wall in an ever-faster rhythm until he plunged into her with a cry that was half groan, half growl. His last surge tipped her over the edge, and as he pulsed within her, she came with a long, wailing cry of release, pleasure and total surrender.

All movement stopped as the room filled with the sound of their tortured breathing.

"Oh, Molly." He gulped in air. "I'm so sorry."

"Don't you dare be sorry!"

He leaned his forehead against hers. "But I lost control. I swore I wouldn't do that."

She struggled to breathe. "Because I made you, right?"

"Yes. No! I should be able to—"

"I'm too powerful."

Slowly he lifted his head and gazed down at her. Then a slow smile turned into a low chuckle. "Yeah. You are small but mighty. I'm a helpless servant who worships at your feet."

"Or sometimes a little higher."

"Whenever I can get away with it." He searched her expression. "Are you really okay?"

"Yes."

"Would you tell me if you weren't?"

"Of course. That was incredible. I've never had sex like that."

"Me, either." He leaned down and kissed her gently. "Thank you. I'll be right back. Don't go away."

"I have no intention of going away. Not after a performance like that."

"We're sleeping after this, just so you know." Easing away from her, he left the bed. But as he started out of the room, he paused and swore. It wasn't an angry response, just an irritated one.

She couldn't imagine what had made him react like that. "Is something wrong?" She sat up.

"Not really. No worries." He left the room quickly.

She thought about the incident until he came back. Only one thing explained his behavior, and if she was right about what had happened, she needed to know about it.

When he returned, she was ready for him. "Ben, did the condom break?"

His expression gave her the answer.

"That's what I thought." Her mind sorted through the options. She'd never been in this position before, but she'd figure it out. "I think we need to—"

"We don't need to do anything."

"That's not exactly true. We just met, so pregnancy wouldn't be a good thing under the circumstances. I—"

"You won't get pregnant."

She didn't appreciate his cavalier attitude. "You don't know that. My family is extremely fertile. They get pregnant like that." She snapped her fingers.

"I've had a vasectomy."

She had her mouth open to offer more arguments for treating this as a serious situation, but she closed it and stared at him. "I guess you *really* don't want kids."

"No."

She waited to see if he'd elaborate. He didn't, which told her she'd guessed right. This was a sensitive topic. "I guess you wore the condom for health reasons."

"No. My last girlfriend was a nurse. She wouldn't go to bed with any guy unless he had a clean bill of health. Once she found out about my vasectomy, she was thrilled that we didn't have to use anything."

"Oh." The thought of him having sex with another woman didn't sit well with her, but that wasn't the issue here. "Were you worried about me?"

"Of course not. I'm sure you're squeaky clean."

She was, but that wasn't the issue, either. "So why didn't you suggest we go without?" He'd been willing to have this frank discussion with another woman, after all.

"Partly because we'd just met, and it's one of those lame things guys try to get away with."

"You thought I wouldn't believe you."

"Right."

"Why did your last girlfriend believe you?"

He sighed and walked over to sit on the side of the bed. Then he took her hand in his. He laced his fingers through hers but didn't look at her. "Because I told her why I'd gotten a vasectomy."

"Then please tell me."

"I think it's a little harder to tell you."

That hurt. "Do I come across as judgmental? If so, I don't mean to."

He looked into her eyes. "You come across as someone who's known nothing but loving kindness all her life. I hate the idea of bringing ugliness into that world. Maddie wasn't like that. She was…I guess you could say she was jaded. Oddly enough, that was why I broke up with her. She was too cynical and that began to bother me."

"Oh, Ben." Heart breaking for him, she cupped his cheek and searched his gaze. "What in God's name has happened to you?"

"Let's just say I didn't have your upbringing, and I'm afraid I might repeat that pattern. I can't risk it."

She thought he probably was wrong about himself, but he might not believe her if she said so. She could also sense that he didn't want to talk about his past and how it had shaped him.

"Ah, Molly." He lifted their clasped hands and kissed her fingertips. "You feel so absolutely right, but I wonder if I'm being selfish. I can't offer you any of the things you want."

"That's not entirely true."

"Sex doesn't count."

"Who says?"

"I do." He touched her cheek. "You'll find someone who'll give you great sex and lots of babies."

She squeezed his hand. "Fine. I'll keep an eye out for that person. But in the meantime, could I please have more great sex with you? Because I really like how you do it."

9

BEN DIDN'T KNOW a guy in the world who could refuse a request like that. Besides, after two climaxes, he had the staying power to make long, slow love to Molly. She seemed to like that as much as she'd liked the wall-banging kind.

Turned out, so did he. A whole hell of a lot, in fact. Afterward, he gathered her close and they drifted off to sleep in each other's arms.

He woke up before she did, experiencing an emotion that didn't come often to him. At first he had trouble naming it, but finally he settled on the description that seemed to fit. He was contented.

The reason was easy to figure out. He'd enjoyed amazing sex with a woman he liked well enough to sleep with in the literal sense. He hardly ever woke up with a woman. Usually he went to their place and left that same night. Staying for breakfast gave the wrong impression, as if he might be considering a more permanent arrangement.

But he and Molly had put everything on the table, or enough that she understood why he wasn't the one for her. He didn't have to dredge up the past and talk about his crummy family or his fears about turning into his dad.

Instead, they could enjoy each other and part ways as friends. If he didn't want to think about the leaving right now, so what? Philosophers said that the trick to happiness was staying in the moment, so he'd do that. And in this moment, he was extremely happy. He couldn't remember being happier, in fact.

He could faintly smell cookies baking and the muted sound of people talking on the floor below. It must be after seven if the cookies were already in the oven. He still cradled Molly against the curve of his body, his arm tucked around her waist. She'd wanted to be part of the cookie situation, but setting an alarm had been the last thing on his mind and probably on hers.

No surprise that they'd overslept. They'd worn each other out, in a good way. He'd love to stay like this a little longer, but she might not thank him for it.

He murmured her name.

She stirred in his arms and yawned.

So cute, that little yawn. Funny how his feelings for her were more tender than lustful this morning. "If you still want to bake cookies, you need to get up."

"Cookies!" She scrambled to a sitting position and stared at him in dismay. "I forgot the cookies!"

"Sorry. Me, too."

"It's okay. Not your fault, but I have to boogie." She left the bed, gathered up her clothes, and began tugging them on. "Thank you for a wonderful night."

He propped himself up on his elbow. "You're welcome. Doing anything special tonight after the party?"

"I hope so."

"Would it happen to involve coming back here?"

She laughed. "Yes, unless you'd rather come to my room where we'd probably end up falling off the double bed."

"No, thanks. I'll meet you back here in about…" He glanced over at the small clock on the nightstand. "About eighteen hours, give or take."

"That's a long time."

"I know. Want to schedule a rendezvous in the middle of the day?"

After pulling her sweater over her head, she looked at him. "I'd love to, but I don't think we dare. The house will be full of people today. I'll be pretty busy, and besides, somebody might come up here. I wouldn't want them to hear us, or worse yet, walk in on us."

"Which brings up another important point. How do you want to play this?"

She was quiet for a little too long. "I don't know."

He couldn't blame her for being hesitant to reveal what was going on between them. She was a part of this family and her behavior would come under some scrutiny as a result. Even though she was an adult capable of making her own decisions, Sarah might feel a certain responsibility for her.

"We'll keep it to ourselves," he said, letting her off the hook.

"Thank you." Relief showed in her expression. "It's not that I'm ashamed of what we've done. It's just—"

"Never mind. I get it. You don't want your relatives to know you hopped into bed with a virtual stranger on his first night here."

"When you put it that way, it sounds pretty wild, doesn't it?"

He smiled. "It *was* pretty wild."

"Yeah." Her voice was filled with wonder, as if she couldn't quite believe what had happened in this room. "This is not like me, at all."

He sat up. "Regrets?" He said it lightly, but her answer meant more to him than he wanted to admit.

She met his gaze. "No. Last night was amazing. I didn't know sex could feel like that, or that I could respond the way I did. I'll never forget what we've shared."

"That sounds like a kiss-off speech." His chest felt tight. "Are you reconsidering meeting me after the party?"

"Oh, no, I want to."

He let out his breath.

"But last night I didn't give much thought to how our choice could be interpreted by the rest of the family. To be honest, I wasn't doing much thinking at all. I wanted you and that wiped out every other consideration."

"And now you're worried about what others might think."

"I am. Maybe that's cowardly and I should be stronger, but—"

"Hey, you don't have to explain." He was a little disappointed, but he did understand. Tossing back the covers, he searched the floor for his underwear. "I *am* a virtual stranger."

"Not anymore."

"Nobody else will find out." He located his briefs and pulled them on. "Not from me, anyway."

"Thank you, Ben."

"Just don't go ogling my butt or someone might notice."

"I promise not to ogle your butt, although I have to say, it's very ogle-worthy." She grabbed her boots and jacket. "So is the rest of you."

"Likewise." He stepped into his jeans.

"Don't be silly."

"I'm not being silly." After picking up his shirt, he glanced at her. "Your body drives me out of my mind."

"Come on. You don't have to say that."

"No, I don't, which is why I *am* saying it." He took a deep breath and let it out. His intense gaze locked with hers. "I look at you and think of how you rode my cock, your breasts bouncing, and how wet you are for me, always, and how tight, and how sliding inside you makes me want to come the minute we connect."

Her cheeks flushed.

"I won't be able to not think about that today, Molly."

She swallowed. "Me, either. So we'd better stay away from each other—at least, most of the time." With a little moan of frustration, she whirled toward the door. "I'm getting out of here while I still can."

"Check the hall and make sure the coast is clear."

"I will. Tonight I'll come over in my robe. That might help."

He chuckled. "It'll certainly make it easier to get started."

She glanced at the box of condoms on the night-stand. "Put that back, okay?"

"You bet."

Opening the door, she peered out. "Looks deserted." Then she turned and her gaze swept over him. "You're a beautiful man."

His throat tightened. "You're a beautiful woman."

She gave him a quick smile before running out into the hall.

He stepped to the door and watched until she disappeared into her room. Then he sighed. Although he wouldn't change a single thing that had happened, she was working her way under his skin. Eventually he'd have to face the truth—a long weekend with her wouldn't be nearly enough. But he wouldn't worry about that today. Today he would practice ignoring her. That would be challenge enough without thinking about a future that didn't have Molly in it.

10

MOLLY HAD NEVER thought of herself as much of an actress, but she hoped she gave a convincing performance as she moved through the day of party preparations. Ben made good on his offer to help, which meant he was tantalizingly close by most of the time. He moved furniture with ease and his height came in handy for attaching decorations to the exposed ceiling beams.

Not for the first time, she turned and found herself staring at his impressive package, which was currently at eye level while he stood on a ladder to hang a cluster of balloons and a Happy Birthday banner.

She hoped nobody had caught her sudden intake of breath or the blush she'd felt rising to her cheeks. Or maybe they'd think she was a modest little thing who wasn't used to getting up close and personal with a man endowed like Ben. Little did they know she knew all about what he kept tucked away inside his jeans.

The bustle of preparations helped to cover any slip-ups on her part. Holiday traditions at the Last Chance felt familiar to Molly, which wasn't surprising considering that her Grandpa Seth had been Nelsie's brother.

The Christmas carols blasting from the sound system in the living room were by the same artists Molly's family loved.

She was thrilled to arrange the nativity scene on the mantle. Her parents had an identical set that was also a little chipped, yet beloved. Nelsie had bought both sets more than seventy years ago and had given one to her brother and his wife.

Tasks like this temporarily distracted her from thinking about Ben. Each time she finished a chore, she'd turn around, and there he'd be, doing something helpful and manly. He was the most tempting man she'd ever met.

He treated her with casual courtesy, as if he barely noticed her. She had the perverse urge to pinch his butt and remind him that she was standing behind him as he showed off his perfect ass to every female in the vicinity.

That urge was so unfair. She was the one who'd been reluctant to let anyone know that they'd established an extremely intimate connection on a very brief acquaintance. He was only acting the way she'd asked him to.

Possessiveness on her part was not only unattractive but uncalled-for. They'd struck a deal—a fun romp for however long he was here followed by a cheerful parting of the ways. Under those circumstances, she had no claim on him, and he had no claim on her.

The arrangement felt completely unreal to her, though, because she'd never entered into one like it before. She'd never gone to bed with a man who hadn't been a potential mate. None of her three previous lovers had turned out to be her one and only, but she hadn't

known that until they'd spent some quality time together, including having sex.

What she'd shared with them hadn't come within a
mile of what she'd discovered with Ben, and now she
had a whole new concept of what made for a perfect
partner. She hoped that Ben wasn't one in a million.
If so, she was in for a long search.

Molly arrived early for lunch in the big dining room.
She sat down with Sarah and Pete, who were the only
two at their table so far. Ben moved on past, as if heading for a spot on the other side of the room.

But Pete called out to him, and he turned back.
"Come and sit with us," Pete said. "I had some more
thoughts on your potential breeding program. You
might be interested in one of our mares, as well."

Ben sat down next to Pete, across the table from
Molly. "Don't know if I can afford that, yet."

"Maybe we could work out a deal. Time payments,
or first look at the foal. There are all sorts of creative
ways to do it. Jack and I talked and we want to help in
any way we can."

Ben nodded. "That's good to know. Where is Jack,
anyway?"

"Josie had an emergency at the bar. A pipe broke,
so he's helping her handle it."

"I've heard of that bar." Ben picked up his sandwich.
"Supposed to be haunted, right?"

"Yes." Sarah laughed. "That's why Josie renamed it
the Spirits and Spurs. Some claim my late father-in-law
is one of the ghosts who makes an appearance from
time to time. He used to stop in for a beer whenever
Nelsie went into town to shop."

"Archie's supposed to be one of the ghosts?" This

was the first Molly had heard of it. "That needs to go into my notes. I have this feeling I'm missing all kinds of things that will just come out in casual conversation if I hang around long enough."

"That's true." Sarah sent her a fond glance. "You need to come back. You have summers off, right?"

"Sort of. I usually teach one session of summer school." She felt Ben's gaze on her. If she returned this summer, they could pick up where they left off. He'd be in Sheridan, which wasn't that far away, and in summer the drive would be easy. They wouldn't have to say goodbye forever.

"Then think about flying back up here," Pete said. "We've loved having you. You fit right in."

"Thank you. That sounds great." But she wasn't so sure it was a good idea. This time with Ben was short and sweet. When they parted, they'd make a clean break. If she came back, though, the relationship automatically became more complicated.

"Good." Pete seemed satisfied the issue was settled. He turned back to Ben. "You'll need to figure out where you're going to put these horses. Do you have some ideas about that?"

As the meal continued, Ben described his plans for buying a small spread on the outskirts of Sheridan, and Pete offered enthusiastic advice. The two of them seemed to have bonded. Nick and Gabe joined them, and soon the four men were deeply involved in a subject they all held dear.

Sarah glanced over at Molly and lowered her voice. "Are you okay?"

"I'm fine." She smiled to add emphasis to the statement.

Sarah leaned closer. "I hope you didn't have a disagreement with Ben."

"Heavens, no." Molly tried to control the heat in her cheeks but knew it was no use.

"You did, didn't you?" Sarah spoke in an undertone. "I thought you were getting along great last night, but you've avoided each other all morning. Was he rude to you?"

"No, Aunt Sarah. Everything's fine."

"Because I don't care if Pete likes him. If he's not nice to you, then he can take a long walk off a short—"

"Really, it's *fine*."

Sarah turned in her chair and skewered Molly with a look. "You're sure about that?"

Molly gulped. "Yes."

"All right." Sarah leaned even closer. "But since he's right down the hall from you, if there's any reason for concern, you let me know immediately. Is that clear?"

"Yes." But as she looked into Sarah's blue eyes, Molly didn't kid herself that she was fooling her aunt. Sarah knew that something was going on. She just didn't know for sure what it was.

But with the big party only three hours away, now was not the time to confess everything. No one had discovered the liaison with Ben yet.

Sarah nodded. "Good. Glad that's settled." She resumed her normal tone of voice. "I'm worried that we don't have enough wineglasses for tonight. We've lost more to breakage than I thought. I'm thinking of ditching the stemmed glasses completely and going with whiskey glasses for the wine. We have a ton of those. What do you think?"

"I think it's very European." Over Sarah's shoulder,

Molly caught Ben looking straight at her. One of the hands had come by to talk with Pete, temporarily interrupting the men's conversation.

Ben took the opportunity to wink at her. Then the ranch hand left and Ben returned to the topic of breeding horses. But that wink had undone her. He'd chosen the perfect moment to send her a covert message, a secret communication to remind her of their connection.

Molly had been looking forward to Sarah's party ever since she'd made plane reservations. She'd created a special photo album of all the Gallagher relatives, and each of them had written a birthday greeting next to their picture. Molly could hardly wait to present that to her aunt tonight, and now she was eager to see Sarah's reaction to the magnificent saddle.

And yet, her thoughts had already moved beyond the party to the moment when the guests had left and she could climb the stairs. She pictured slipping into her room and taking off her clothes. Unfortunately her bathrobe was fleece and had moose pictures on it, but that couldn't be helped.

"I just don't want the kids to think that the wine is their favorite cherry drink and guzzle it by mistake. I sometimes let them have the cherry drink in a whiskey glass, so help me keep an eye on them, okay?"

"I will." Molly did her best to concentrate on the conversation. "One sip and they'll spit it out. I've never known a kid who thought wine tasted good."

"Oh, I know one. Sarah Bianca took my glass when I wasn't looking the other night. When I asked if she'd tasted my wine, she assured me that she had, but it was okay because we had the same germs."

Molly laughed. "Sounds like her."

"So then I asked her opinion of the wine. She said it was yummy. I explained that it was for grownups, but I'm not convinced that she won't try it again."

"Then I'll keep close track of her." Sarah Bianca, SB for short, was Morgan and Gabe's oldest. During the cookie decorating session, the little redhead had informed Molly that she was not four, but four and a *half*, thank you very much. She thought her Grandma Sarah had hung the moon, and if her beloved grandmother loved red wine, so would SB.

Nick and Gabe said their goodbyes and left the table. Soon afterward, Pete and Ben pushed back their chairs and Pete glanced at his wife. "Unless you need me for something, Ben and I thought we'd head down to the barn and take another look at Calamity Sam, maybe turn him out so Ben can see him run."

"I think we're in pretty good shape." Sarah smiled at him. "I have a few more things to check on in the kitchen, but as far as I'm concerned, the work's done. We're ready for the party."

"Excellent." He leaned over and gave her a quick kiss on the cheek. "See you soon."

"Bye." Sarah gazed after the two men as they left the dining room. "You know, when Pete and Jack first told me a horse buyer was coming, I was so wrapped up in the preparations for the party and Christmas that I didn't think much about it." She turned back to Molly. "But don't you think his timing is a bit strange?"

"I guess it worked with his schedule." Molly hoped her expression gave nothing away.

Sarah gazed at her with a knowing smile. "That's BS."

"It is?"

"It is, and you know it. There's a secret connected to that guy. There has to be, and it has something to do with my birthday. I just hope it's not a horse. I love Bertha Mae and I don't need another one. But I don't think that's it. He didn't haul a horse trailer in here, just his pickup with a camper shell on the back."

Molly laid a hand on her arm. "My advice is to stop thinking about it."

"Oh, I intend to. But I had to test you and see if you were in on it, whatever it is. You definitely know what's going on. Maybe that's why you've been avoiding Ben all morning. You're afraid to talk to him for fear you'll give something away. Is that it? Did I guess?"

"I'll plead the Fifth."

Laughing, Sarah glanced out the window. "Sun's shining. If you want to take a walk, you could touch base with my husband and Ben and plot some more. I'll be in the kitchen with Mary Lou so I won't be able to hear a word you say."

"So you really aren't going to pry into this?"

"Nope. That would spoil the fun. I know better than to do that with this family. They do love their surprises."

"Then maybe I will walk down there." She thought it would be safe enough, even if temptation lurked in the form of Ben Radcliffe. He'd be with Pete, and ranch hands would likely be around, too. "I haven't spent much time at the barn. According to Nelsie's diary, she and Archie and my Grandpa Seth lived in it for a few months."

"Yes, they did. They were hardy, those two. I wish I could loan you her diaries to take home for your research, but I don't dare let them out of this house. The boys would kill me."

"I wouldn't dream of borrowing them, either. They're too precious. I feel lucky that I was able to read them, and I took copious notes and a few pictures of certain entries with my phone."

"The one where she mentioned you, I'll bet."

"Absolutely. I texted that one to my folks because I knew they'd get a kick out of it. I kind of remember her, but not very well. I was pretty young when she and Archie made their last trip to Arizona."

"That's too bad, because you would have loved her. I did." Sarah got a faraway look in her eyes. "When I first met her, she was younger than I am now. Hard to believe." She shook her head and scooted back her chair. "Enough of that. Go take your walk and don't let on that I suspect a thing."

"I won't."

"It doesn't matter if I do, anyway, since I have no idea what they could possibly be up to." She stood. "I have everything in the world a woman could want."

Molly stood, too. "Just remember that they love you and want you to know it."

"Oh, I do know it." She smiled. "They demonstrate how much they love me all the time and I return the favor. Life's too short to live any other way, don't you think?"

"Yes." Molly gave her a hug. "Thanks for letting me be a part of things for a few days, Aunt Sarah. I've thoroughly enjoyed it."

"You're more than welcome. Now, go put on your coat and get some fresh air. We might not get to keep this weather much longer. I heard there's a storm moving this way."

"See you in a few hours." Molly left the dining room and hurried upstairs. First she popped in her contacts. She probably wouldn't get to kiss Ben behind the barn, but she didn't know that for sure.

Then she put on her winter gear. She'd given the mittens their outing and was back to her leather gloves. She checked the weather app on her phone. Sarah was right about the approaching storm. With luck, the storm would blow through before Monday, when her plane left.

She had confidence it would. And Christmas Eve wasn't until Wednesday. Surely the storm, if it hit, would be over in time for her to spend the holiday with her family. She didn't intend to break a perfect record.

Dressed for winter, she bounded down the stairs and out through the front door. Someone had scraped the snow and ice from the porch, and the steps were clear, too. Sunlight glinted off the snow. She pulled on her gloves and shaded her eyes as she glanced toward the barn.

Ben and Pete stood by the fence watching Calamity Sam romp through the drifts in the pasture. The air was still cold enough that she could see her breath, but the sun helped warm her as she followed the path toward the barn.

A Paint horse running through snow proved to be a dramatic sight. As he frolicked, the white part of his coat blended into the background. If she squinted, she could almost see disembodied gray spots dancing in the air.

Mesmerizing though that was, Molly was more interested in studying Ben. She could get away with it because he had his back to her. The tilt of his Stetson, the sheepskin coat stretched across his broad shoulders and the booted foot he'd propped on the bottom rail of the fence all branded him as a cowboy, even though she'd never seen him ride. He made Western saddles and was thinking of buying one of the Last Chance horses. She figured he could ride.

She easily pictured him investing in a small ranch and adding a little horse breeding to his saddle-making operation. Like her, he was full of energy and ideas. He seemed to love life as much as she did. But she couldn't help thinking about his decision not to have children. If she and Ben were only destined for a brief affair, it shouldn't matter to her if he liked kids. She had no right to question his choices, either. Their relationship was based on sex, and she'd told him she was fine with that.

Except she wasn't. He'd already become more than a sex partner. His good nature and cheerful willingness to help out with the party preparations had impressed her. She was beginning to care about him and hated to think he was closing himself off from certain aspects of life out of fear.

His tenderness with her indicated he was a kind man, and she found it hard to believe that he'd mistreat a child. She also hadn't forgotten the emotion he'd put into his harmonica rendition of the theme from *Beauty and the Beast*.

Then there was his artistic side. He wouldn't have been able to create that magnificent saddle unless he had an empathetic, sensitive nature. His contradictions fascinated her. She wanted to know what made him

tick and why he nurtured some dreams while rejecting others.

He'd said that he'd come from an unhappy home and
didn't want to repeat the pattern. Tonight she'd watch
how he acted with Sarah's grandchildren. If he was
abrupt with them, she'd know that his concern was le-
gitimate and he was right not to want kids.

As she stood there contemplating this puzzle of a
man, he turned, along with Pete, and walked toward
her.

Pete called out a greeting. "Coming out to see Calamity Sam strut his stuff?"

"Sort of. Mostly I just craved a little fresh air."

As she drew closer, Pete lowered his voice. "Ben
said you know about the surprise."

"I do. The woman I called in Sheridan mentioned
that Ben made saddles, and I knew that had to be the
reason he was here."

Pete gazed at her. "Do you think Sarah has
guessed?"

"No."

"That's a relief. Ben and I mostly came out here to
discuss how to get the saddle into the house without
her noticing."

"Did you figure it out?" She had wondered about
the logistics.

"I think so. I'll keep Sarah busy in the bedroom
while...wait, that didn't come out right."

Molly grinned. "Whatever it takes, Uncle Pete."

He looked a little flustered. "What I meant to say
was that I'll distract her and keep her out of the living
room for the ten minutes it'll take for a couple of guys
to carry the stand and saddle into the house."

"We moved it to the front of the tractor barn first thing after we left the dining room," Ben said.

"And I finally got to see it," Pete said. "I was blown away. I've seen some gorgeous saddles, but this one... you made something very special, Ben."

He flushed. "Thanks."

"As long as Molly's out here, you should take her over to get a look."

Ben looked at her, his expression carefully neutral. "Would you like to do that?"

She smiled, enjoying the fact that they had their own special secret. "Of course!"

"You have never seen such a beautiful saddle in your life, Molly. Anyway, I need to get back. I forgot to check the supply of Scotch in the liquor cabinet. Usually I'm the only one who drinks that, but lately Alex has taken a liking to it."

Then he turned to Ben. "My apologies. I shouldn't throw out names like that. You'll need a scorecard to keep everyone straight tonight, but for the record, Alex Keller is Jack's brother-in-law. He and Jack's wife Josie are brother and sister."

"And Alex is married to Tyler, who is Morgan's sister," Molly added.

"Exactly." Pete nodded. "Stick close to Molly, Ben. She's been studying this stuff all week and she has it down cold."

"I'll be sure to do that." Ben's tone was carefully nonchalant.

"See you two later, then." Pete's long strides carried him back toward the house.

Ben glanced at her, laughter dancing in his brown eyes. "So, Molly, would you like to see that saddle?"

"Yes, Ben, I would love to."

"After you." He gestured toward the narrow path leading to the tractor barn.

As she walked ahead of him, she wondered what sort of scenario was going through his mind and if it was as X-rated as the one going through hers.

11

BEN DECIDED HE must be living right. From the minute he'd turned away from the fence to find Molly standing several yards behind him, he'd been trying to figure out how he could get her alone. Pete had handed him the perfect excuse.

But he wasn't going to mess things up by saying anything incriminating while they made their way to the tractor barn. Noise carried in the crisp air, and ranch hands were in the barn cleaning out stalls while some of the horses exercised in the pasture. The tractor barn was empty as far as he knew, though.

They couldn't be noisy in there, either. The place echoed like crazy and he figured that sound could possibly be heard in the horse barn. He didn't want anyone showing up to investigate.

Once they reached the tractor barn, he opened the door for her and she slipped inside. They couldn't stay long. Her red coat was a beacon that could be glimpsed for miles.

He followed her in and called out. "Anybody here?" The echo came back to him. No response, though. He turned back toward the door, but there was no locking mechanism on the inside.

"What are you doing?" She moved close, almost touching him.

He breathed in her scent and his body responded immediately. "I'm looking for something to wedge the doors shut."

She left his side to prowl around. "There's a small workbench over here with a few tools on it."

"Perfect." He located a couple of wrenches and jammed one under each of the double doors. "That's just in case."

The interior of the barn was dim, but her smile lit it up. "Anyone would think you had plans to do something secretive in here."

"Anyone would be right." Unbuttoning his coat as he walked, he closed the gap between them. "You put in your contacts. Anyone would think you were hoping something like this might happen."

She laughed breathlessly. "Anyone would be right."

"We can't stay long, so we have to make every second count. Unzip your coat."

She pulled off her gloves first and tucked them into her pockets. Then she glanced around as she unzipped the puffy coat. "I don't see much in the way of a welcoming spot."

He chuckled. "Except you." He grabbed her around the waist and lifted her to the back fender of the first tractor in the row.

"Ben!"

"Shh. This place is an echo chamber. No matter what happens, don't yell, okay?"

"That could be a challenge."

"You're up to it." He pulled off one of her boots. "Unzip your jeans." He did the same.

"You seem to have this all worked out."

"I do." He freed his cock, which was ready for action. "My brain's been focused on the problem ever since Pete suggested I bring you in here to look at the saddle."

"Apparently other parts of you are focused on it, too."

He glanced up and discovered she was ogling his equipment. "I've had this problem all day long. You just didn't know about it." He took off his coat.

"You've been aroused all day?"

"Yep. Every time I looked at you I wanted to drag you into a dark corner and have my way with you." Reaching around her, he spread his coat on the fender, lining side up. "That's how you affect me."

"That's very flattering."

"That's very tough on my package. Now hang on to my shoulders, wrap your legs around my waist, and lift your cute little tush." When she did, he slid the coat under it.

"I have a feeling you've done this maneuver before."

"Never in a very cold tractor barn."

"Then maybe you shouldn't have taken off your coat."

"I plan to be plenty warm in a minute, and you need it." He set her back down so he could pull off her jeans and panties and work one of her legs completely free.

Her breathing sped up as she positioned herself on his coat, wiggling her bare fanny against it. "Kinky."

"Sorry. You're not staying there. Hang on to me." His heart was pounding by the time he slid both hands under her bottom and lifted her off the fender. "Wrap your legs around me again."

Once she did that, he found her entrance with the tip of his cock and let gravity take care of the rest.

"Mmm." She closed her eyes.

"I know." He tightened his jaw against a groan of pleasure.

She opened her eyes and excitement gleamed there. "I feel so decadent."

"Good. That should make it all the better." He sucked in air as she squeezed his cock hard. "Easy."

"You said we had to do this fast."

"Yeah." His grin was tight. "But we should have a little bit of fun, first. I'll lift you up and then you push yourself back down. I have a firm grip on you. You won't fall."

"I know I won't. I trust you."

"But you *will* come."

She held his gaze. "I know that, too."

"You have to be quiet, though."

She nodded. "You're still wearing your hat."

"No good place to put it. You're still wearing yours, too." He smiled. "I kind of like having sex with a woman wearing a red knit hat. I've never done that before."

"And I kind of like having sex with a man wearing a Stetson. I've never done that before, either."

"Then here we go." He eased her upward and she used the leverage gained from his shoulders to push back down. Dear God. He kept thinking that sex with her couldn't be as good as he imagined, but then he'd bury himself in her again and realize that, yes, it was just that good.

They established a tempo, one that slowly picked up as if by mutual consent. He watched her eyes darken and her lips part. Neither of them groaned or whimpered.

Even their breathing, though it was rapid, seemed softer. Without words or moans filling the silence surrounding them, the rhythmic beat of his thrusting became the dominant sound. The quicker the beat, the more he throbbed with anticipation.

Sweat trickled down his spine as he pumped faster. "Soon," he murmured.

She gulped. "Yes." Her fingers dug into his shoulders. A tremor moved through her.

"Come for me." He squeezed her smooth bottom as he pushed her upward one last time.

She shoved down again and he gasped as heat and motion swirled over his cock.

He watched her climax reflected in her eyes. Dragging in a breath, he surged upward and claimed his own climax. Holding her steady as he pulsed deep inside her took all the strength he had. If she'd weighed an ounce more, he wouldn't have been able to do it. She was perfect...so perfect.

When he began to shake, she smiled gently. "You need to put me down."

He nodded, but he didn't want to let her go. Easing away from her felt wrong. He wanted to carry her to the back of the tractor barn and find somewhere they could lie down and rest. Then they'd do it all again.

Instead, he tucked his still-twitching cock back inside his briefs and zipped up. Then he pulled a bandana out of his pocket and handed it to her so she could clean up. She kept it.

He didn't know if she planned to wash it and return it or keep it as a souvenir. Either way worked for him. He helped her back into her jeans and slid her boot on.

Once she was standing, he retrieved his coat and brushed the dust from the part that had come in contact with the tractor fender. The lining carried the subtle odor of sex, and that was fine with him, too. He put the coat on and breathed deep.

Then he laid his hat on the newly dusted fender and gathered her into his arms for one long, lazy kiss. He didn't want to leave the tractor barn without paying attention to her wonderful mouth.

In a way, kissing her was more personal than having sex, although he couldn't explain why. All he knew was that kissing Molly felt like a special privilege she'd granted him and he loved it. She responded with her signature enthusiasm. Apparently she enjoyed kissing him, too. Good to know.

With great reluctance he finally pulled back. "We need to go."

"I'm sure we do." She gazed up at him, her expression dreamy. "Your saddle is beautiful, but I doubt anyone would believe I spent this much time admiring it."

"Let's hope no one was clocking us." He stepped back but kept hold of both her hands. "I have such an urge to throw you over my shoulder and carry you off to…I don't know. Somewhere with a soft surface."

"I have such an urge to let you do that."

"But this party is important for both of us. You flew here so you could help your aunt celebrate, and I'm pretty excited about how she'll react to that saddle."

"She'll love it, but we'd better get moving, cowboy."

"Yeah." Squeezing her hands, he released her and picked up his hat.

"I'll get the wrenches." She pulled them out from under each door and handed them to him.

He put them back exactly where they'd been. Then he walked over to the doors. Just his luck, Jack's red truck pulled up in front of the tractor barn. Ben swore softly under his breath and closed the door.

"What's wrong?"

"Jack just drove up."

"So what? You brought me to the barn for a quick look at the saddle. He doesn't know how long we've been in here."

"No, but…" He surveyed her from head to toe. "You look well-kissed and extremely satisfied."

"You just think that because you know what we've been doing."

"I think that because it's true. And your hat's on crooked."

She straightened it. "Better?"

"A little. You still look…ah, never mind." One truck door slammed followed by a second. "Sounds as if Jack's bringing someone with him."

Ben walked over to where the saddle was perched on its stand and whipped the blanket off right before the door opened. He turned with a smile of welcome as Jack came in with a woman who wore her blond hair in a long braid down her back. Probably Josie. "Hey, Jack! Heard you drive up. Pete said there was some trouble with the plumbing at Spirits and Spurs."

"There was, but it's handled. Josie, this is Ben Radcliffe. Ben, my wife, Josie." Jack's tone was casual, but his gaze wasn't as he glanced from Ben to Molly.

"Pleased to meet you, Josie." Ben focused on her and tried to ignore the fact that Jack was sizing up the situation.

"Same here, Ben." Josie looked over at Molly. "Guess you couldn't stand the suspense either, huh?"

"Nope." Molly smiled. "And it's a beauty."

Ben still thought she looked like the cat that ate the canary. Intuition told him Jack was picking up on it. Could be trouble ahead.

Josie was protected from the cold like everyone else, in a bulky parka and a blue knit cap much like Molly's red one. Fortunately she was there to see the saddle, and it seemed to absorb all her attention. "Oh, my." She moved toward it and caressed the leather. "I'm no expert on saddles, but I've never seen one this pretty. Love the turquoise and silver accents."

"It's designed to fit Bertha Mae perfectly," Jack said. "We haven't tested that, but—"

"It'll fit," Ben said. "If it doesn't, I'll rebuild the saddle."

Josie's blue eyes widened as she turned to stare at him. "You'd start over?"

"If I have to. I stand by my work."

"I'm sure that won't be necessary," Jack said. "We provided Bertha Mae's measurements along with Mom's measurements to make sure that the saddle would be perfect."

Josie chuckled. "Sarah's measurements? How'd you get those, if you don't mind my asking?"

"Pete." Jack looked smug. "I didn't tell you about his scheme?"

"No, I missed hearing that story. I'm sure I'd have remembered."

"Pete's a sneaky guy. He bought her a one-of-a-kind outfit in Jackson that he knew for sure was too big. When she had to have it altered, he got all the specs from the seamstress."

"Goodness." Josie shook her head. "FYI, if you ever decide to give me a beautiful saddle like this, just ask me for my measurements instead of going through all that rigmarole. I'll be happy to give them to you."

Jack tipped his hat back with his thumb. "No need. I know your measurements."

"You most certainly do not! I'd bet there's no husband on the planet who knows his wife's measurements exactly."

"Test me sometime." Jack grinned at her.

"I will, and you'll be way off. Anyway, I love this saddle, Ben."

"I'm glad."

"Sarah will, too," Josie continued. "Don't you think so, Molly?"

"I do. Ben's done a wonderful job."

"Thanks, Molly." He knew she would have said that no matter what, and she'd told him last night the work was good, but hearing her say it again warmed him. He had come to value her opinion quite a bit.

He was in the awkward position of wanting her to think well of him, yet knowing in his heart he didn't deserve her good opinion. She trusted him when he didn't even trust himself. For the short time they'd be together, he could keep his flaws hidden, though. That was the advantage of knowing she'd leave on Monday. He wouldn't think about the sunshine that would leave with her.

"I texted Pete before we left Spirits and Spurs," Jack

said. "He seems to think we can risk moving the saddle up to the side of the house so it won't take so long to bring in after the party starts. I told him Josie and I would do that, but since you're here, Ben, you and I can carry it."

"Sure." Now that the unveiling was less than two hours away, Ben's chest tightened with anxiety. Everyone had praised the saddle, but Sarah was the one who had to be pleased. He'd know the minute she saw it whether she was or not.

"I think you should text him again and make sure Sarah's otherwise occupied," Josie said. "After all this, we don't want her to glance out the window and see you and Ben carrying something from the tractor barn. I don't care if it is covered with a blanket. She'll know what it is."

"Yeah, I'd better do that." Jack nudged back his hat and pulled out his cell phone. "Never would have believed I'd depend on this silly thing the way I do. I carry it everywhere now. Phone calls are bad enough, but texting is unmanly."

Josie held out her hand. "Want me to text Pete and protect your manhood, cowboy?"

"No." Jack scowled and moved his thumbs over the keyboard. "I'm just sayin'."

"Personally, I love that you carry your phone everywhere." Josie stuck her hands in her pockets. "Then you can't perform your manly disappearing act when there's an unpleasant chore to be done."

"My point, exactly." Jack glanced up from the phone. "Go ahead and cover the saddle, Ben. I'm sure we'll be hauling it out of here in a couple of minutes."

His phone chimed and he read the text. "Yep. Mom's taking a shower, so we're good to go."

Ben settled the blanket back over the saddle. The next time it was pulled off, he wouldn't be the one doing it. Something he'd labored over every day for two months was about to leave his care. That always felt strange. He had a picture of it on his phone, but he might never touch it again. He always felt a little sad when he had to part with one of his creations, and he'd put more of himself into this one than any other.

Jack tucked his phone into his jacket pocket. "Ladies, if you'll hold the doors for us, the manly men will carry this precious cargo out of here and over to the house."

Ben got on the front and Jack took the back, which was the same way they'd carried the saddle and stand into the barn. So much had happened since then.

"I'll back down the path," Jack said. "I know it better than you do."

"Okay." Maneuvering carefully, he guided the saddle through the door and let Jack set the pace. Molly and Josie followed. Judging from the bits of conversation Ben caught, they were talking about Molly's genealogy project.

"What's between you and Molly?" Jack's quiet question was abrupt, but not unexpected.

Ben met his gaze. "We like each other."

"Thought so. And I just realized I know almost nothing about you." Jack's breath fogged the air between them. "Careless of me."

"What do you want to know?"

"Are you unattached?"

"Yes."

"Where's your family?"

"Colorado."

"Visit them much?"

"No."

Jack frowned as if not happy with that answer. "Why not?"

"We…don't see eye to eye."

"Does Molly know about that?"

Ben hesitated. "I've mentioned it."

"Did you give her the details?"

"No."

"Then I suggest you do that." Jack's dark gaze hardened. "I suggest it very strongly. It's important information for a woman like Molly."

"You're right." Ben's gut clenched. He'd told himself Molly was better off not knowing the gritty details of his past. But she was an open book, so the scales weren't balanced when it came to their relationship. And they had one. He could no longer pretend otherwise. She might be coming back to Wyoming this summer. What then?

Yeah, it was time to give her the whole story. She deserved to know that she was dealing with a man terrified of losing his temper, afraid of who he'd become.

"And Ben?"

"Yeah?"

"If you don't treat her like the extremely valuable person she is, you'll answer to me. And it won't be pretty."

"Understood."

"You're one hell of a saddlemaker and I love what you've made for my mother, but hurt one of my own, and you'll wish we'd never met."

"I won't hurt her. You have my word."

Jack's smile was colder than the breeze sweeping down from the snow-covered mountains. "Break your word, Radcliffe, and I'll have your ass."

12

MOLLY HEARD JACK and Ben talking about something, but they spoke in low tones, as if they didn't want her or Josie to hear them. A couple of times Jack glanced in her direction. She couldn't shake the feeling they were discussing her. If so, then Jack suspected something.

Josie might, too, but Molly hadn't spent as much time with her as she had with Jack. Josie might not feel comfortable asking about Ben. Jack, on the other hand, allowed nothing to stand in the way of protecting those in his care. Sarah had told her that the other day, and now she'd seen it in action. When Jack had stepped into the tractor barn and spied her there with Ben, his whole manner had changed.

Sure, he continued to joke with his wife, but underneath that banter something in his tone made her think he was mentally arming himself to confront a potential threat. She appreciated the impulse, but she didn't want Jack to protect her from Ben. He reminded her so much of her brothers, who'd been intimidating her boyfriends ever since she'd turned sixteen and had been allowed, with major restrictions, to date.

Extreme protectiveness, both from her brothers and her parents, had been one of her reasons for moving into town instead of continuing to live at the family ranch. She was the only girl, which meant she'd had to fight for her sexual freedom. If she hadn't moved out, she'd probably still be a virgin.

No doubt her brothers would disapprove of her relationship with Ben, but they weren't here. Unfortunately, Jack was filling their role to perfection. She'd have to politely ask him to butt out, but finding a private moment to do that might be tough.

Right after Jack and Ben hid the saddle under a large tarp at the far end of the house, Jack slung an arm around Josie's shoulders. "Come on, babe. We need to shower and change for this shindig." They both hurried back to Jack's big red truck and drove away.

The wind had picked up, so Molly helped Ben tuck the canvas tarp more securely under the stand so it wouldn't flap. Maybe she was being paranoid about Jack's conversation with Ben. She should ask Ben about it before accusing Jack of meddling in her business.

Ben beat her to the punch. "Molly, we need to talk." He straightened. "Maybe out here's as good a place as any."

"Was I just the topic of conversation between you and Jack?"

"Yes, and—"

"Is he trying to protect me from you?"

"In a way, but that's not the point."

"It is the point. I'll speak with him. I'll let him know that this was mostly my idea. I don't want him to get the wrong impression of you. After all, you're hoping to do more business with him. I don't want to interfere in any way with that."

"That's fine, but I still—"

"Hey, are you Radcliffe?" A middle-aged ranch hand with a handlebar mustache walked toward them, his boots crunching through the snow drifts.

"I am."

"I'm Watkins." The man shook hands with Ben. "Glad I caught you. Hey, Molly."

"Hey, Watkins." Aunt Sarah had filled her in on the stocky cowboy's background. Two years ago, after a long courtship, Watkins had won Mary Lou's hand in marriage. Watkins had a first name, but nobody remembered what it was. He was also one of the guitar players scheduled to perform for tonight's party.

"Is the saddle under there?" Watkins peered at the tarp.

"Yep," Ben said, "but we'd better not uncover it again. I think we've finally got the blanket tucked around it good and tight."

"That's okay. I can wait until the party. I'm not here about the saddle." He was a good ten inches shorter than Ben and had to push back his hat and lift his chin to make eye contact. "I heard you might be willing to play a little harmonica with Trey and me tonight."

"I'd like that, if I wouldn't be in the way."

"Hell, no, son. We're not that slick. We'd love to have you, and I thought you might want to come on out to the barn. Trey's already down there with some of our music and our guitars. If you'll go fetch your harmonica, we can have a private jam session before the party and see what tunes we have in common."

"You bet. I'll be there in five minutes."

"See you then." Watkins headed for the barn.

Ben gazed at Molly. "What I have to say shouldn't be rushed, and I'd better go. I said I'd play tonight, so I don't want to duck out of it."

"You shouldn't. It'll be fun."

"But we'll have to talk later."

"Are you thinking of changing the plan?"

His hesitation gave her the answer.

"Maybe I shouldn't come to your room tonight. Jack must have put pressure on you to leave me alone." And she'd deal with Jack, but she might not be able to sway him. She'd also discovered he was stubborn. "I don't want to jeopardize—"

"Please come to my room tonight. But before we… before we do anything, I have some things to say."

"You have a crazy wife tucked away in an asylum?"

"No." His smile was sad. "Nothing that dramatic. Ready to go in?"

"Sure." They walked around the house and up the porch steps without speaking.

Once they were inside, Ben turned to her. "See you tonight." Then he bounded up the stairs to get his harmonica.

She debated whether to go up to her room and start getting ready. Normally she wouldn't need an hour to primp, but tonight was special. She wanted to wash her hair and spend time on her makeup. An hour might not even be enough.

Ben was coming back down as she pulled off her hat and started up the stairs. She gave him a quick smile. "Have fun."

"Thanks." His return smile was polite and brief.

With a sigh, she continued to her room. Too bad

her situation with Ben had come to a head this soon, but the family would have discovered their relationship eventually, maybe even during the party tonight.

Jack's reaction wasn't all that unusual, now that she had time to think about it. She was his youngest cousin from Arizona, and he'd never had sisters. That could make him even worse than her brothers when it came to interfering in her social life.

His concern was sweet, and she didn't want to be rude since she was a guest at this ranch. Although he wasn't the only one in charge, he had plenty to say about what went on here. On the surface, it looked as if Ben had taken advantage of Jack's hospitality by showing an interest in her.

Without giving offense or revealing how far the relationship had progressed, she wanted to convince Jack it was a two-way street. Ben shouldn't be blamed for something that she'd encouraged every step of the way. As Ben had said, they were both consenting adults and what they did in the privacy of his room was nobody else's business.

She didn't intend for anyone to know that she'd spent the night in his bed and hoped to spend tonight there, too. The layout of the huge house made it unlikely that anyone knew. If she was careful not to be seen entering or leaving his room, that part of their secret would be safe.

But Jack had planted a seed of doubt in Ben's mind. Clearly he was wondering if he should back off. The thought made her stomach twist. They might only have this brief time together, but she'd counted on making use of all of it.

If she were honest with herself, she'd have to admit

that she hoped this affair wouldn't end when she left Wyoming on Monday. Every moment she spent with Ben made him more precious to her. She didn't want to give him up at all, much less have their time shortened by Jack's influence.

If Ben's mind had changed, she'd just have to change it back. Fortunately, she had a killer dress in her closet. She'd brought it even though it might be a bit much for a family gathering. Jeans weren't right. She'd packed a more casual dress in case that had seemed more appropriate, but she was going for the wow factor tonight.

Thinking about the dress lifted her spirits. If her jeans and sweater turned Ben on, then this outfit would send him up in flames. If he had any thoughts of backing out of their agreement, she wanted him to know exactly what he was rejecting.

An hour later, she descended the stairs carefully, her wrapped gift in one hand, gripping the railing with the other. She looked hot, if she did say so herself. But her hotness quotient would be eliminated if she tripped in her four-inch heels and stumbled on the curved staircase. She also might damage the album she'd so carefully created for Aunt Sarah.

Laughter and the hum of conversation told her most of the guests had arrived. Her beauty routine had taken longer than usual, so she was about fifteen minutes late. The results, in her humble opinion, were well worth it.

She'd picked the knit dress off the rack because the moss green exactly matched her eyes. Then she'd tried it on, thinking that the long sleeves, ankle-length skirt and high neck would make it a fairly conservative choice. Oh, no. The dress slithered over her body like a second skin, leaving nothing to the imagination.

That alone would have made it sexy as hell, but the skirt was slit up one side to several inches above her knee. She hadn't noticed that, either, when she'd decided to try it on. Looking at herself in the dressing-room mirror, she'd seen a different Molly Gallagher, a seductive woman capable of driving men out of their minds. This was the dress's first outing, and after her wild night and stolen afternoon session with Ben, she felt qualified to wear it.

She'd bought teardrop earrings with stones the same color as the dress. She wore no other jewelry. The dress spoke for itself. Her hair was piled on top of her head and she had left a few tendrils dangling in front of her ears.

"Molly?"

She was halfway down the stairs when Ben called her name. She turned and looked over her shoulder. "Hi," she said. "You look nice." That was an understatement. He wore a crisp white Western shirt with silver piping that made his shoulders seem wider than ever, and his black dress jeans were sinfully snug.

His black leather belt was intricately tooled, and she wondered if he'd made it. He wore no hat tonight, and his thick hair gleamed in the light from the hallway. The scent of shampoo and shaving lotion drifted down the staircase. She had an almost irresistible urge to climb back up and kiss his smooth jaw. But judging from the heat in his brown eyes, she didn't dare.

"You look..." He swallowed. "I don't even know how to describe how you look, Molly. That dress really…it fits you like…I've never seen a dress look as good on anybody as that one does on you."

"Thank you." It was exactly the response she'd hoped for. She'd never felt more beautiful or desirable in her life.

"Hang on a minute. I'll walk down with you." He started toward her.

"Got your harmonica?"

He patted his breast pocket. "Right here. Watkins and Trey are good. I'll have to bring my A game tonight."

"From what I heard before, you'll be fine." She smiled at him.

He paused and caught his breath. "Damn, Molly. You're so…damn."

"What?" She pretended not to know what he meant. But she knew, and exulted in a sexual power she'd never claimed before.

"That dress. It moves when you move. It slides right over your breasts and your sweet little bottom. I don't—hell, I know it's unworthy of me, but I don't want other men to see how great you look."

"Too late." Jack stood at the bottom of the stairs with Josie. "Put your eyes back in your damned head, Radcliffe." He held out his hand. "Come on, Cousin Molly. Let's go join the party. You look terrific, by the way."

"Thank you." She walked down the stairs, took his hand and allowed him to steady her for the last few steps.

"That dress is dynamite," Josie said.

"Yours isn't too shabby, either." Molly admired the ice-blue, long-sleeved sheath that Josie had accented with silver shoes and jewelry. Instead of her usual braid, she'd created an updo that showed off her slender neck. She was a knockout.

Jack gave Josie a possessive once-over. "Not shabby at all," he said softly. "I'm a lucky man."

He crooked both arms. "Ladies, make me the envy of every poor slob in the room."

"I'm honored, Jack." Molly looked into eyes that glowed with the pride of his Shoshone ancestors. She might as well make her stand now as later. She knew instinctively that he'd respect her for being direct. "But I'm going to wait for Ben."

Jack's glance flicked from Molly to Ben, who'd remained standing midway down the staircase. "All right." He held Ben's gaze. "Don't forget our conversation."

Ben's voice was steady. "I won't."

Jack and Josie walked into the living room and Molly took a shaky breath. Round One. She thought maybe she'd won it, but time would tell.

"Thank you." Ben descended the last few steps and stood before her. "But you didn't have to do that."

"Yes, I did." She looked into his eyes. "I'm capable of choosing my own…friends. Jack needs to understand that."

A smile teased the corners of his mouth. "I'm glad you consider me a friend."

"I do." She longed to touch him. But while they were within sight of the front door where anyone could come in and discover them, being affectionate might not be the best plan. "You may not realize it, but you've given me enormous confidence."

"You?" He looked surprised. "You were already confident. You didn't need me for that."

"Ah, but you're wrong." She lowered her voice. "When you asked me to pirouette for you at the top of the stairs twenty-four hours ago, I wasn't completely convinced of my sexual power. Thanks to you, now I am." She stretched out her arms. "Behold the result."

He laughed, his eyes sparkling. "So as I struggle to make it through this evening of torture, watching you move through the crowd in that incredible dress, I have only myself to blame?"

"Pretty much."

"In a twisted kind of way, that helps. Shall we go in?"

"Yes." She linked her arm through his. "I can hardly wait to hear you play."

"Then know this. Every note will be for you."

His words ran in a continuous loop in her mind as they walked into the crowded living room. They were the kind of words that could turn a girl's head. If Ben were a different sort of man, she'd think he'd used them as a seductive line.

But he didn't need to spout pretty words to get a woman into bed. He'd already accomplished that with her. She'd spent enough time with him, especially quality time in which emotional barriers had come down, to know that he didn't say anything he didn't mean.

He'd announced from the beginning that he was the wrong man for her, long-term. She still didn't know all the particulars, but he hadn't tried to fool her by implying that they could have more than a brief fling. He'd been honest about that from the beginning.

Jack might not completely trust him, but she did. She really should corner Jack and discuss his dealings with Ben. Jack hadn't turned in his genealogy homework yet, and that would give her a good excuse to talk with him.

For right now, though, she was a party girl on the arm of a handsome man as they walked into a kaleidoscope of color and movement. As Molly deposited her wrapped package on the gift table, Ben went to get them both drinks. Before he made it to the temporary bar set up along the far wall, Watkins grabbed him and pulled him into the corner where Trey was setting up their sound system.

Molly hadn't thought about the fact that Ben would be needed over there. She'd never attended a function with someone who was part of the evening's entertainment. Making her way over, she tapped him on the shoulder.

He turned. "Oh, sorry. I'll get our drinks in a second. First I need to—"

"Never mind. You have things to do. Can I bring you something?"

He grinned. "One of those dark beers would be outstanding."

"Got it." She wove through the crowd, greeting those she'd already met, like Pam Mulholland, Nick's aunt and one of Sarah's best friends. Last Christmas Pam had married Emmett Sterling, the tall, sixty-something ranch foreman standing between her and his daughter Emily. Emily was in line to be foreman after Emmett retired.

Emily's husband, Clay Whitaker, director of the stud program at the ranch, arrived loaded down with two bottles of beer and two glasses of wine. "Hey, Molly. Can I get you something from the bar?"

"Thanks, but I promised Ben I'd fetch his drink, so

I need to go there, anyway. By the way, who's the couple standing by the Christmas tree talking to Jack?"

"They're good friends of Jack's," Clay said. "Nash and Bethany own the ranch that borders this one."

"And Bethany writes self-help books," Pam added.

"Right! I remember Aunt Sarah mentioning that."

"Except for the ranch hands, they might be the only ones who aren't somehow part of the extended family," Pam said. "But apparently Nash and Jack were inseparable in high school, so I think Sarah thinks of him as another son."

Molly glanced around at the crowd gathered in the living room. "Such a happy group."

"I know." Pam smiled. "It's a real tribute to Sarah that everyone's so eager to help her celebrate her big birthday."

"Yes, it is. I'm so glad I made the trip. Anyway, I did promise Ben that drink, so I'd better get going. I'll catch you all later!"

But she got sidetracked briefly when she stopped to talk to Regan O'Connelli and his fiancée, Lily King. Regan shared a veterinarian practice with Nick, and he was also Morgan and Tyler's brother. Lily ran an equine rescue operation on the outskirts of Shoshone.

Eventually Molly reached the bar. It was so tempting to stop and talk to people. Tonight was a genealogist's dream. She was finally able to put faces to some of the names on her chart.

A guy with a buzz cut was tending bar. She'd never seen him before, so she held out her hand. "Hi, I'm Molly, a cousin from Arizona."

He smiled and shook her hand. "I'm Steve, a bartender from Spirits and Spurs. I'm absolutely no relation to anybody here, which Josie thought would be a good thing so I can concentrate on the job at hand. What can I get for you?"

She asked for a glass of the red wine Sarah had introduced her to and a bottle of dark beer. Then she returned to the makeshift bandstand and handed the bottle to Ben.

"Thanks." He glanced toward the hallway that led to Pete and Sarah's bedroom. "Pete just coaxed her back there on some pretext or other. I think this is it."

She noticed his breathing had changed and lines of tension bracketed his mouth. "Nervous?"

"Hell, yes. What if she doesn't like it?"

"She'll love it. Everyone else has."

"I know, but they're not the ones I made it for." He looked over at the front door. "They're bringing it in." His voice was strained.

She'd never dreamed that he'd be so worried about whether Sarah would like the saddle. So far, everyone had raved about it, but he was right that Sarah's reaction was the crucial one. If she gave the slightest indication that she didn't love it, Ben would be cut to the quick.

His anxiety became hers, and she longed to hold his hand, touch his arm, anything that would let him know she was there for him, but he wouldn't appreciate that. She might know he was feeling vulnerable, but he wouldn't want anyone else to figure it out. Outwardly he projected calm confidence in his ability to do his work.

She'd never thought about the pressure on an artist when a creation was unveiled. Ben's work was more than just a job, and she wondered how many of his customers understood that. Now that she'd seen this saddle, she longed to visit his shop and ask more questions about the process. That wouldn't happen if they ended things when this interlude was over.

Gabe and Nick carried the still-covered saddle into the middle of the room and moved back as conversation hummed all around them. Jack called down the hall to Pete before walking back to stand beside the saddle. Everyone's attention shifted to the arrival of the birthday girl.

Pete held Sarah's hand as he ushered her into the living room. She'd chosen to wear winter white, a stunning dress that showcased her cherished turquoise jewelry. Her cheeks were pink with excitement.

Molly held her breath along with everyone else in the room. She desperately wanted Sarah to love the saddle for Ben's sake.

Then little Sarah Bianca, her evergreen dress decorated with ruffles and a tiara balanced on her red curls, jumped up and down with cries of glee. "Do it, do it, Uncle Jack!" she shouted. "Show Grandma her surprise!"

"Yeah, yeah!" Archie, her blond, three-year-old cousin, started jumping, too. "Do it, Daddy!"

With a smile, Jack stepped forward. "Happy birthday, Mom. From all of us." He whipped off the blanket.

Sarah stared at the saddle in complete astonishment. Then she began to cry.

Ben sucked in a breath. "Is that good?"

"Oh, yeah." Molly's eyes filled as she watched tears of joy flow down Sarah's cheeks. "She loves it."

"But she's *crying.*"

Molly sniffed. "That's because she's happy, and

touched and overwhelmed by the generosity of every-one. The saddle's a hit, Ben. You did it."

"Thank God."

Sarah wiped her cheeks and accepted a handker-chief from Pete. She blew her nose and handed it back to him, which brought a laugh from the group and broke the tension. Everyone clapped and cheered as Sarah walked over to stroke the leather of the saddle and exclaim over the beauty of it.

Finally she looked up and searched the room until her gaze settled on Ben. "You made this, didn't you?"

"Yes, ma'am."

"It's magnificent."

"Thank you." His voice was husky.

"I knew you weren't here to buy a horse. But I never imagined…" She went back to stroking the leather with reverence. "I've never had a saddle like this. Bertha Mae will strut like a queen."

She lifted her head again and glanced around the room. "Thank you, all of you. It means more than I can say." Her voice caught, and she swallowed. "I can't imagine a better birthday gift than this, except to have you all here to share it with me."

More cheers followed. Then the grandchildren crowded around and asked to sit on the saddle. She lifted each one in turn, while camera phones clicked. Everyone laughed at the kids looking so proud sitting on their grandmother's birthday saddle.

Molly turned back to Ben. "Do you mind that the kids are sitting on it?"

"Why should I?" He watched with a smile.

"I don't know. It's a valuable saddle. Maybe you'd rather not see little kids bouncing on it."

"They can't hurt it. Obviously they're having fun, so why not?"

From the corner of her eye, she studied him. He didn't seem to be faking his enjoyment of the scene, which seemed odd for a man who'd decided not to have kids. The puzzle of Ben Radcliffe became more complicated than ever.

13

THE MUSIC STARTED after that, and Ben threw himself into the first set. He knew most of the tunes, and they were lively and easy to play. Because they didn't challenge him too much, he could watch Sarah with her grandchildren.

The saddle still sat in the middle of the room and dancers maneuvered around it. Sarah stood beside the saddle and rotated the kids on and off, giving each a turn, even Gabe's youngest, a months-old baby.

An older boy, who could be a teenager but looked younger because of his small size, climbed up and smiled at Nick. "What d'ya think, Dad?"

"I think you need to start saving your allowance, Lester," Nick said with a grin.

Such a simple exchange, and yet so filled with subtext. Lester had hinted he wanted a fancy saddle, and his father had good-naturedly told him he'd have to save for it. That's what a loving relationship between a father and son looked like. Ben had never experienced it.

He never would have dared to hint that he wanted

something. That would have been a sure way to get a lecture on his ungrateful behavior, or maybe even a beating. He'd learned early to keep his mouth shut and his head down.

The scene of Sarah with her family affected Ben in ways he hadn't anticipated. Unexpected yearning tightened his throat and at times made him screw up a note. He doubted anyone noticed, but it bothered him.

Then he'd catch a glimpse of Molly laughing with some of the women, or dancing with one of her Chance cousins, and he'd miss another note. Her joyful smile stirred longings he'd kept buried for years.

He didn't like feeling this way. He'd carefully avoided strong emotions for most of his life because he'd seen the dark side. When gripped by powerful emotions, people became unpredictable. The line between love and hate was thin and easily breached.

When he'd taken on this commission, he hadn't planned on having it throw him off kilter. He'd known that spending a couple of days at the Last Chance Ranch would be intellectually interesting, a scientific trip to observe a normal family. He'd planned to hold himself emotionally distant.

Molly had blown that plan all to hell on his first night here. He wanted her in a way he'd never wanted another woman, despite knowing he couldn't make her happy. She'd gotten under his skin. No, he'd *allowed* her to get under his skin. For some reason, he'd let down his guard and she'd stormed the castle.

That was bad enough, and he dreaded the conversation they would have tonight after the party. He was pretty sure she was fantasizing that they had a future, after all. She couldn't help it, optimist that she was, and he glimpsed dreams of forever shining in her green eyes. He'd have to destroy those dreams and watch the sunshine disappear.

Adding to that disaster, he was currently surrounded by the intense love that permeated the Chance family. He'd tried to maintain his position as an outsider, but Sarah had brought him right into the center of the celebration with her gratitude. With her tears. Her reaction had annihilated his defenses. He'd seen his mother cry in despair, but he'd never seen any woman cry with joy. His world had shifted.

He wanted this, all of it, but he didn't trust himself to create it. He could build a saddle, but he didn't know how to build a life. Not this kind of life where people hugged each other, watched out for each other, defended each other from any threat.

As Jack had. Ben didn't blame him one damn bit. Jack was right to worry about Ben getting too close to Molly. And he was too close to her. If he cared this much, then she probably cared more. Her heart was in shape for loving. His wasn't.

The set ended, and Sarah glanced up. Her gaze steady, she excused herself from a conversation with Josie and walked toward him. He braced himself.

"I don't know how to thank you." She placed a warm hand on his arm as she looked into his eyes. "It's obvious to me that you put all kinds of love into that saddle."

He hadn't known what to expect when she'd come over, but certainly not that. Damn it, his throat was tightening up again. He cleared it. "I enjoyed making it."

"I know you did. Jack said you made it in only two months. You must have burned the midnight oil."

"It was a pleasure." He kept thinking of how she'd cried when she'd first seen it. "I...I hoped it would be what you wanted."

"It's as if you knew what would suit me. I suppose Jack helped give you an idea of who I am, but you must have used your instincts, too."

"Maybe so." He didn't trust himself to say more without emotion roughening his voice.

"It's been wonderful having you as a guest, Ben. You're like a long-lost member of the family. I hope that's all right for me to say. From things you've said, I gather you're not...close...to your family."

He swallowed

"I just want you to know that you're welcome here anytime." She squeezed his arm. "Anytime at all." Then she gave him a little pat and walked away as if sensing that he wasn't in command of himself.

Tucking his harmonica into his shirt pocket, he walked out of the room and took the stairs two at a time before he did something embarrassing like break down. He had the urge to pack his things and leave, but the wind had begun to howl outside. The storm would hit any minute. He was a fool, but not that much of one.

So, instead, he sat on the edge of the bed, his head in his hands, while he struggled to breathe. In one precious moment, with a few words of praise, Sarah had warmed his heart in a way his own mother never had. His father had forbidden any gentleness for fear his boys would become sissies. His mother had never argued with that.

"Ben?"

He glanced up. Molly stood in the doorway. He

should have known she'd see him leave and follow him up here. That was Molly. Caring, compassionate, loving.

"What's wrong?"

He looked into those green eyes filled with concern. "Everything."

"How can that be?" She walked over and knelt at his feet as she placed her hands on his knees. "Aunt Sarah loves the saddle. I saw her come over and tell you again how much she loves it. I couldn't figure out why that made you take off like you did."

He cupped her sweet face in both hands. "That's because you come from a loving family where gestures like Sarah's happen all the time. But I...I can't handle it."

"Why?"

"I was raised with fear instead of love. My dad's anger was a terrifying thing to me and my older brother. He didn't hit us a lot, but the threat of it was always there. I don't know that he ever hit my mother, but he criticized her constantly. Still does. She has zero self-confidence."

"Oh, Ben." Moisture gathered in her eyes. "I was afraid that's what you'd hinted at before. I'm so sorry."

"Please don't cry." He heard the frantic note in his voice and hated it.

She blinked and her jaw firmed beneath his touch. "I won't. Tell me what you need."

"To be magically transported out of this house and back to a life I've learned how to handle."

"Sorry, that's beyond my powers."

He smiled as the tight band around his chest loosened. "And here I thought you could do anything."

"I'm awesome, but I can't teleport people. At least, not yet."

She was so good at this, he thought. So good at comforting people and putting them at ease. He'd even recovered enough to joke with her. "Sex is another good option, but we're not doing that, either."

"I'm afraid you're right. Sorry. Now is not the best time for wild monkey sex."

"Damn. Then I may just have to go back down there and act like everything is peachy." But thanks to her calming presence, he felt as if he could do that.

"Ben, I have to ask, although I think I know the answer. Is your family background why you don't want kids?"

"Yep, that's it." Saying it was easier than he'd thought it would be. "I hate the way my father ruled the household, and my brother swore he did, too, but he's exactly the same kind of father to his kids. And he intimidates his wife, who scrambles to please him."

"And you think you would turn out that way, too?"

He brushed his thumbs over her warm cheeks. "It's all I knew growing up, so I could easily slide right into that pattern. If I do marry someday, it would be with the understanding she should leave me the minute I start behaving like my father. But kids—they can't just leave."

"I know, but—"

"I'm not having kids, Molly. I won't risk repeating the cycle the way my brother has." He looked into her eyes. "Jack wanted me to make sure you understood all that. He said it was important information for a woman like you."

"A woman like me?" She bristled. "What's that supposed to mean?"

"Well…" He suspected he might get into trouble if he didn't choose his words carefully. "You come from a big, loving family, so logically, you probably want that for yourself."

"Yes, eventually! But *a woman like me* doesn't hand every guy I date a checklist to make sure he wants marriage and a big family, and the sooner the better!"

He shouldn't smile, but he couldn't help it. "You might want to tell Jack that. He probably thinks you do."

"Don't worry. I plan to have a talk with Cousin Jack."

"He's just afraid that you'll get hooked on me, and I'm not the right man for you."

"Jack's not in charge of my love life."

"I know."

"You told me right away that you weren't the right guy for me because you didn't want a family. Then I found out that you'd had a vasectomy. Now I have the whole story as to why. That doesn't mean I don't want to have sex with you anymore."

He searched her gaze. "Can you honestly say you've never thought that maybe, with time, we'd work something out between us?"

"Um…" Color darkened her cheeks.

"See?"

"Mostly after I saw the way you watched Sarah with her grandkids. I had wondered if you disliked children, but you don't."

"No. I like them a lot. That's why I can't take a chance on lousing up my own."

"You don't know that you would!"

"I don't know that I wouldn't. Listen, Molly, I made up my mind about this when I had the vasectomy."

"Sometimes those can be reversed."

"I don't want it reversed. I've read enough to know my dad has a borderline personality disorder. Maybe that's genetic. I didn't know my grandfather, but from the stories I've heard, he was the same way. Maybe that's just what he was taught, but maybe not."

"Then you could adopt."

He sighed. "I'd still be putting some innocent kid at risk. I can't take that chance."

"But—"

"Molly, the way you keep arguing the point, I have to wonder if you *are* thinking I'll change my mind about a relationship."

"That's bullshit." She scrambled to her feet and tee-tered as she regained her balance on her high heels. "And don't look so shocked. I know how to swear. I have brothers."

He closed his mouth, which had, in fact, dropped open when she let loose with that word. "Then you can probably outswear me. I only lived with one older brother."

She didn't smile. If anything, she looked angrier than ever. "As for your assumption about why I'm sug-gesting that you could find a way to have a family even with a vasectomy, has it occurred to you that I'm say-ing that for *your* sake?"

"My sake?"

"Yes, your sake. You should have seen the expres-sion on your face while Sarah played with the kids on that saddle. You were eating it up with a spoon. Just try and tell me that you wouldn't like to have cute little kids like that running around, and eventually grand-kids, and a family gathering like this one. Because I know you would!"

"So what?" He stood, too. He wished she couldn't read him so well, but it was partly his own damned fault. He'd been more open about his feelings since he'd met her and that needed to stop. "Doesn't matter what I want. My brother went into his marriage bound and determined not to be like Dad. Now he's exactly like him. When I mention that, and I have, he yells at me and says I don't know what I'm talking about."

"That doesn't have to be you! Don't cut yourself off from life just because —"

"Stop it, Molly. They're starting up the music again. I need to get down there." He walked past her and out the door. It hurt like hell to be so abrupt with her. He'd probably hurt her, too.

But she didn't understand the terror he felt at the possibility he'd recreate his parents' lives, or his broth-er's. If she understood, she wouldn't keep arguing with him.

She might think she'd known what kind of man he was, but she hadn't, not really. Even when faced with the truth about him, she was trying to make bargains and change things so it would all come out roses and lollipops. Of course she was. That was Molly, a bun-dle of sunshine.

It was the quality that had drawn him to her. Appar-ently he'd thought he could use her light and warmth to ease the cold darkness in his soul. That had been so damned selfish of him.

When he walked back into the living room, he discovered the configuration had changed. The saddle had been moved next to the Christmas tree, which opened the entire space for dancing. A woman Ben hadn't met was harmonizing with Trey on the Tim McGraw and Faith Hill number "I Need You." And only two people were out on the floor. Pete and Sarah danced looking into each other's eyes as if, in this moment, no one else existed.

Ben stood at the edge of the room, his heart once again lodged in his throat.

"Beautiful, isn't it?" Molly appeared next to him and gazed at the couple circling the floor.

"Yes."

Her fingers slipped through his.

God help him, he tightened his fingers and held on, needing her more than he needed to breathe. Jack could take him out and shoot him at dawn, a fate he no doubt deserved. But if Molly couldn't be turned away by all that he'd said to her, if she was willing to hold his hand and give him comfort for the short time they were together, he would take it.

The dance ended with Pete giving Sarah a soft kiss. Then he grinned and beckoned to everyone surrounding the dance floor. "Show's over. Get out here and we'll all play bumper cars again."

"Come on." Molly tugged him forward. "Dance with me. My extra four inches should make it way easier. I won't have to stare at your belt buckle."

That made him smile. Molly didn't stay down for long. She might have been arguing with him five minutes ago, but she wasn't going to let that spoil her mood. "It's a great offer, but I should get back to Trey and Watkins."

"They can manage without you for one more song. It's a slow one, so you'll have plenty of breath left over to play your harmonica. Come on. You know you want to. You've been giving me cow eyes all night."

"Cow eyes? I don't *think* so." But he let her pull him out into the crowd. Once she was in his arms and his palm felt the slide of that green knit material against the small of her back, he was very glad she'd talked him into it.

"Cow eyes." She looked up at him. "Like this." Her expression changed to one of complete adoration.

He lost it. Maybe it was the tension he'd been under, but he started laughing so hard he could barely dance. He twirled her around and bumped into Jack and Josie. "Sorry. Brakes just went out."

Jack gave him a long-suffering look, but a smile twitched the corners of his mouth. Maybe Jack wasn't quite such a hard-ass after all. Ben hoped not, because he'd rather be the guy's friend than his sworn enemy. And that was disregarding the possibility of doing more business with him. Ben plain liked him. Admired him, in fact.

Jack had it figured out. He and Josie seemed to be on equal footing in a loving relationship. Just then, Sarah danced by with her grandson Archie in her arms. He looked overjoyed to be there. Apparently the kid was bright and well-adjusted, which was no surprise given his environment.

Molly snuggled closer and laid her head against his shoulder. Whereupon Ben forgot all about Jack and the rest of the Chance clan. Resting his cheek on her hair, he forgot everyone in the room except the woman in his arms.

If he had Molly in his life, maybe he could learn how to create what Jack had. For one shining moment he allowed himself to imagine what that could be like. But it would be a gamble, and a huge one at that. He'd be gambling with her life as well as his own.

He cared about her more than he'd cared about any woman he'd been with, maybe more than any person he knew. His shiny picture collapsed into a heap of dust. He simply couldn't ask her to take that risk. They'd have this interlude, and he'd make the most of it if she was willing. But then he'd get out of her life. It was for her own good.

14

MOLLY KNEW THERE was an excellent chance Ben would break her heart, especially after their dance. She'd admitted to herself that this was no longer a fling, and not just for her. He was way more invested than he'd ever confess.

But his psychological wounds ran deep. They had to, in order for him to undergo surgery so he wouldn't father any children. Not many men would take such a step, but ironically, it showed how much he cared about those children he would never have. He was protecting them before they even existed. What a selfless act.

He wouldn't see it that way, of course. And she wouldn't point it out to him, either. Instead, she'd drop the subject completely and savor whatever time they had together. If she hoped for a miracle, some epiphany that would allow him to see he would never be like his father or his brother, then that only made her human.

During the next break in the music, Sarah sat in one of the easy chairs pushed back against the wall and opened the rest of her presents, including Molly's album. Her face lit up as she turned the pages carefully, reading the birthday wishes written beside each picture.

Molly was thrilled with Sarah's reaction, but not surprised. Sarah was easy to predict. Ben, on the other hand, was not.

To her amazement, he stood beside her in the crowd gathered around Sarah and rested his hand on her shoulder. He no longer seemed worried about Jack's dire warnings, and when Sarah exclaimed over the album, he gave Molly's shoulder a quick, affectionate squeeze.

Once during the opening of the presents, she caught Jack giving Ben an assessing glance. But his expression wasn't nearly as fierce as it had been when he'd confronted Ben at the foot of the stairs. Maybe Jack had noticed the exchange between his mother and Ben, and had decided to give the newcomer the benefit of the doubt.

Food was served buffet style. Molly found a footstool to sit on, and Ben crouched next to her to share the meal.

"Jack seems to have mellowed," she said quietly.

"Yeah, I noticed that, too." He glanced at her. "Wouldn't have mattered if he had or not. You seem to be willing to take me as I am, so unless Jack orders me out of the house, I thought I'd stick around."

Warmth flooded through her. "Good."

"'Course, I might not have a whole lot of choice. The storm's kicking up pretty good out there. Sarah and Pete could have some unexpected overnight guests."

"I hadn't thought of that." She held his gaze. "If it's too dangerous for everyone to head home…"

"I'll be giving up my room and moving somewhere

else. I could sleep on the floor down here, if necessary, but I can't justify keeping a king-sized bed all to myself."

"I suppose not." She took note of the snow hitting the living room windows with more force.

"We'll roll with whatever happens. But I figure I'll stay on until Monday, in any case, and drive you to the airport. It's on my way and everyone will be involved in Christmas stuff so it makes sense for me to do it."

She smiled. "I'd like that. Thank you."

"Consider it settled, then. And if we lose tonight, we'll just have to make up for it tomorrow night."

"Make up for what?" Sarah Bianca showed up, her green eyes focused on Ben.

"Sleep," Molly said immediately.

"I know." The little girl regarded them with a smug expression. "I get to stay up really, really *late*. Mommy says we might even sleep over. We do that sometimes when it snows hard." She took a sip from her glass.

"That'll be fun," Molly said. "Whatcha got there?"

"My cherry drink."

Molly remembered her promise to keep an eye on SB's choice of beverage. "Can I taste it?"

"Sure." Sarah Bianca held it out.

Molly took a quick sip and confirmed that it wasn't wine. "Delicious." She handed the glass back.

"Grandma already tasted it. Then Uncle Jack wanted to taste it, too! Everybody wants to taste my drink all of a sudden." She looked at Ben. "Do you want to?"

"Thank you, but no. I have my beer."

"I don't like that beer. I tried Uncle Jack's once and it was yucky. But I like Grandma's wine. She says I can't have it until I'm waaaaay older, like *you*." She pointed a finger at Molly.

Ben's lips twitched as if fighting the urge to laugh. "She's right. Your Grandma's a smart lady."

"I know." She studied him with the solemn intensity of a four-year-old. "Did you really make that saddle?"

"Yes, I did."

"How?"

"Well, I start with a frame that's made of wood, and the frame has to fit the horse, in this case, Bertha Mae."

"Wood?" Her smooth forehead creased in a frown. "I didn't see any wood."

"That's because it's covered with leather. Stretching the leather over the wood is tricky. I never know if it'll work out the way I hope."

SB took a sip from her glass with the sophistication of a debutante. "Sometimes that happens to me when I make things."

Ben smiled. "It happens to me *all* the time. But I just keep working at it until I get it right."

"Me, too." She paused to take another drink. "Someday I'll make a saddle."

"Excellent." Ben nodded. "It's a challenge, but it's worth it."

"And I'll make it pretty, like you did. With stuff on it. And maybe even *ribbons*."

"That would be very interesting. I'd like to see that."

Molly's heart melted. He was a natural with kids. If only he'd give himself credit.

"When I make my saddle, I'll show you it. Well, I have to go. My mommy said I shouldn't stay over here too long."

"Oh?" Ben lifted his eyebrows. "Why not?"

"Because. She said you might want to be alone with *Molly*." She giggled and walked away.

Ben chuckled. "She's quite a kid."

"You were very good with her."

He gave her a long look. "It's easy when they're being cute. Anyone would do the same."

"Not necessarily." She knew she was on thin ice with this topic, but she desperately wanted him to see all the things he was doing right. "They might brush off her question about how they made the saddle. They might belittle her announcement that she was going to make one of her own someday. You didn't."

He gazed at her silently before taking a deep breath. "So I was nice to Sarah Bianca, the granddaughter of my hostess. I was taught to be polite. It proves nothing."

What a stubborn, damaged man. She longed to take him by the ears and force him to see reason, but she'd only drive him away. No one wanted to spend time with a person who was trying to fix him. "Guess not."

His expression gentled. "I know you mean well, Molly. Your belief in the goodness of others is one of the things that I'm drawn to."

She was drawn to the goodness in *him*, but if she said that he'd hear it as another attempt to influence his thinking.

"I'm sure I frustrate the hell out of you." He smiled. "I must seem like a man from a foreign country who doesn't quite understand your language. It's a wonder we get along as well as we do."

She didn't think it was a mystery. They were more alike than different, but he wasn't willing to see that. Maybe he never would. He certainly never would if she pestered him about it.

"But we do get along." She looked into his eyes. "Especially in one particular area."

His breath caught. Then he lowered his voice. "Then we still have a date after this party is over?"

"Assuming everyone goes home and you're not too tired."

"You're kidding, right?"

"Not really. Your mouth has gotten quite a work-out on that harmonica. You might want to rest it."

"That's how much you know." He grinned. "Playing the harmonica just warms up my mouth for…other things." He waggled his eyebrows.

She sucked in a breath as her blood heated.

"Careful," he murmured. "You look like you're ready to jump my bones, and there are children everywhere." With a wink, he got to his feet.

She sighed as he walked away. He was everything she'd ever dreamed of in a man—sexy, funny, intelligent and more empathetic than he knew. He had so much to offer for the long haul. Yet he thought he was only good for a short trip.

He wanted more. He wanted it with an intensity that had caused him to run for cover earlier tonight. He'd been desperate to conceal his emotional reaction and his vulnerability.

Sarah had sensed it, though. And Molly understood it better than he thought she did. She'd discovered tonight how fiercely he clung to his belief about himself. That wouldn't change overnight.

If he could spend a couple of weeks surrounded by this loving family, his rigid stance might shift. Maybe he would come back for visits, and over time, he might realize that living without the joy that he witnessed here was unacceptable. She clung to that hope for his sake.

She, however, would stick to her resolve not to discuss this again. That wouldn't be easy. But unless she wanted him to avoid her completely, she'd have to keep her opinions to herself for the next two days.

Yet she couldn't dismiss his behavior with Sarah Bianca, even if he was ready to. He'd treated the little girl with respect and hadn't tried to put her in her place when she boasted about things she might never do. Molly remembered being that age. Her parents had backed her on all her dreams and schemes.

She wondered if he understood that his kindness and generosity of spirit were unlikely to disappear if he became a husband and a father. No, he probably didn't understand that, and she had to keep herself from pointing it out.

Still, she was convinced that they'd been destined to meet. Whether their meeting was to end up in a brief interlude or something more was a big question mark. So much depended on the next two days.

As Watkins, Trey and Ben prepared for their next set, Mary Lou came down the hallway from the kitchen carrying a three-tiered chocolate birthday cake. It was topped with candles arranged in a circle, although certainly not seventy of them.

The guest sang along as the musicians played "Happy Birthday." Mary Lou set the cake on the bar and Sarah blew out the candles with one breath. A cheer went up. Then plates appeared and Sarah parceled out the cake, starting with the grandchildren.

Molly walked over to where Morgan stood jiggling her youngest, baby Matilda, on her hip. Morgan had tamed her curly red hair with a Celtic-patterned silver clip at her nape, and the fabric of her dress swirled around her in a shimmering cascade of blues and greens. She looked like a Celtic goddess. "Hey, Molly! Having a good time?"

"I'm having a great time. But I have to ask, was that just a random number of candles?"

"Oh, no. Seventy would have made a bonfire, so Sarah asked for a candle for each of us—her three boys and their spouses, her five grandchildren, and Pete. Twelve candles."

"What a great idea."

"I love it. I'm going to steal it for my birthday. I don't need thirty-plus candles on my cake, for God's sake. By the way, I made Gabe email you his genealogy form before he came to the party."

Molly laughed. "Thanks. I know he wasn't overjoyed at having to do it, but I think he'll be glad when he gets the final result. I'll have it bound, with room to add information about the next generation." She smiled at Matilda, who reached up and tried to grab one of her earrings. She dodged out of the way and let the baby catch her outstretched finger, instead.

"That's mind-boggling, you know? People tell me that once SB starts school next fall, time will fly. I can't imagine her in high school, let alone college. And after that, who knows? She could be anything, do anything."

"She told Ben she planned to make a saddle."

Morgan laughed. "I wouldn't put it past her. She was fascinated with that saddle and asked if she could go talk to him about it. I was watching. He seemed to treat her plans very seriously."

"He did. He was so good with her, but—"

"But?"

Molly shook her head. "It's not my place to say. I shouldn't have added that. He was good with her. End of story."

"I doubt it." Morgan's aquamarine eyes filled with understanding. "If you're noticing his behavior with kids, that's a sure sign you're getting invested."

"I am."

"But I'm guessing there are issues."

"Yes."

"There usually are." Morgan plucked a tissue out of a hidden pocket in her dress and dabbed some drool from Matilda's mouth. "But that doesn't mean you can't work them out. It's just too bad you have to leave on Monday."

"Yeah, the timing sucks, but I want to be home for Christmas."

"Of course you do, but you two could keep in touch. You get a spring break, right? Come back up then. Sheridan's not that far. I'll bet he'd drive over to see you."

"Maybe."

Morgan chuckled. "Oh, I'd count on it. I've seen the way he looks at you. And this place has a way of bringing couples together." Her attention shifted back to where the three musicians had been joined by her sister Tyler and Tyler's husband, Alex. "There's a classic example. My little sister was determined to travel the world, but then she met Josie's brother and now she seems perfectly happy in Wyoming working for the Shoshone Chamber of Commerce and doing gigs with Watkins and Trey."

"I really wish I didn't have to leave so soon." Molly

clapped her hand over her mouth. "I can't believe I said that. I've never missed a Christmas with my family. I'd be devastated and so would they."

Morgan's gaze was compassionate. "Well, then, I hope you make it home."

"Me, too." But she was more conflicted than she'd realized. For the first time in her life, she wanted to be in two places at once. And it all had to do with the man who was currently playing a haunting rendition of "Greensleeves" on his harmonica.

Although it was a Christmas song, it was also a love song, and she remembered Ben's promise that every note was for her. He played with an emotional depth that silenced the chatter in the room. Watkins and Trey muted their playing so that Ben's harmonica took center stage.

When the number ended, applause erupted and Molly clapped loudest of all. A man who played a song with that much heart was incapable of becoming a cruel dictator. Maybe someday she would be able tell him that.

After the applause died down, some of the guests took their leave. The crowd gradually thinned out until it included only the core group honored by those twelve candles plus Molly, Ben, Mary Lou and Watkins. Trey had left with his fiancée, Elle Masterson, but Watkins shared Mary Lou's apartment next to the kitchen, so he could continue to provide music without having to worry about the weather.

At last Jack asked for everybody's attention. "It's time we made a decision. If we all leave now, we can probably get home okay. But if we wait much longer, the ranch roads will be impassable."

"You know you can all stay," Sarah said. "Pete and I would love to have you. With Cassidy away on vacation, you'll have to make your own beds, but I know you're all capable of that."

"I wanna stay!" Sarah Bianca said. "I can make my bed!"

"Me, too!" Archie clutched Jack's hand. "Me, too, Daddy!"

"I'd like to stay." Lester stepped forward and put a hand on Archie's shoulder. "I like it when we all sleep over. It's cool."

"Yeah, man." Archie gazed up at Lester with adoration.

Lester blushed. "Sorry. I taught him that."

"You could have taught him a lot worse things, son." Nick glanced around at the group. "I'm for staying and finishing this birthday up right. Who's with me?"

"I am." Dominique stepped up beside him. A tall, elegant brunette, she was a professional photographer who'd been snapping pictures all night. "But when it's bedtime, I get the top bunk."

Nick laughed. "Nice try. We'll draw straws like we always do."

"Somebody can have my bed." Ben said. "I'll camp out in the living room."

"I'll accept your generosity, Ben." Jack looked extremely happy about the turn of events. "Josie and I will take your room. If I know Archie, he'll want to be in with Lester."

Archie grabbed Lester's hand. *"Yeah, man."*

"But you don't have to sleep on the floor, Ben," Sarah said. "Move into Cassidy's room across the hall. She won't mind."

"And our family will take the other bunk room," Morgan said. "See? It works out perfectly!"

"It does, doesn't it?" Jack smiled.

Molly could tell that Jack was glad that they'd all be together on this special night. But he also might be pleased about the bonus. Thanks to the weather, she and Ben had a dozen chaperones staying in the house.

15

Now that no one had to leave, the party became even more boisterous. Ben wouldn't have thought that was possible, but being snowbound seemed to bring out the goofiness in the Chance brothers. They didn't get drunk, but now that they didn't have to worry about driving, they sure got happy as they allowed themselves to imbibe more freely.

As the music continued, courtesy of Watkins and Ben, Jack organized a dance-off and appointed Molly to judge.

"Oh, no." She waved both hands in denial. "Not doing that, cousin, especially all by myself. I'll get in way too much trouble." Along with the other women, she'd taken off her heels and added them to the pile in the corner.

"I'll help her judge!" Sarah Bianca stepped up next to Molly.

"So will I." Lester joined SB.

Jack surveyed the trio. "Looks like we have us a panel of judges, just like *Dancing with the Stars*. Does that work better for you, Molly?"

Sarah Bianca gazed up at her. "Please?"

"Okay." Molly hugged the little girl. "If you and Lester are going to help me."

"We will." SB nodded solemnly. "Lester and me will be very good judges, right, Lester?"

"Good but tough," Lester said with a grin.

"But *tough*." SB's eyes gleamed. "Very tough."

"All righty! That's settled." Jack clapped his hands together. "And to make it interesting, we'll draw for partners. I'll put all our names in a hat."

Gabe choked on his beer. "*All* our names?"

"Yep." Jack had located a pad of paper and was tearing a sheet into strips.

"So I could end up with you?"

Jack smiled. "Yes, and you'd be lucky to have me."

Ben began to get a sense of just how crazy this family could be. He really was a stranger to this kind of nutty behavior, but as he watched the joking and laughter he realized it could only happen when people were accepted and loved for themselves.

Mary Lou came out of the kitchen to watch as names were drawn. She walked over to Watkins and Ben. "Bet you've never seen this kind of nonsense before, have you, Ben?"

"Can't say as I have." Pete drew first and got Nick as his partner. Ben chuckled as they went into the hallway to practice their moves. "But it's fun."

"I've been the cook at this ranch for thirty-three years, and I thank my lucky stars every day that Archie Chance decided to hire me. I love those boys as if they were my own."

Envy pricked Ben once again. Jack, Nick and Gabe had been blessed with not one, but two mother figures.

Then he remembered Sarah's earlier comment that he was welcome here anytime.

Maybe he couldn't make up for twenty-eight years in a few days, but if he came back often enough, he might begin to feel like part of this family. Sarah seemed to be very good at adopting people. He'd noticed during the party that she'd acted as if Trey was one of her boys. Emmett's son-in-law, Clay, also seemed to be like a son to her. In fact, he could count a bunch of guys he'd put in that category—Josie's brother, Alex. Jack's friend, Nash. And Morgan and Tyler's brother, Regan.

He'd have the perfect excuse to keep coming back if he bought Calamity Sam and got serious about starting a small breeding program. He'd use this family as a role model, and maybe, with continued exposure, he'd gain enough confidence to ask a woman to share his life. Sadly, it might take months or even years, and by then Molly would have found her perfect family man.

That was as it should be. She had no business waiting around for him to get his act together. Besides, it might never happen. He'd had a few beers himself, so he could be building castles in the air.

Pete and Nick took the floor as the first couple in the dancing competition, and Ben quickly forgot his problems. Both of them were determined to lead, and it looked more like a wrestling match than dancing. Watkins had it easier because he could laugh all he wanted to, but Ben struggled to keep a straight face so he could play the harmonica.

"No swearing!" Dominique called out, grinning broadly. "Remember the kids!" Then she raised her camera.

"Don't you dare!" Nick scowled at her and kept trying to steer Pete around the floor. In the process he stepped hard on his partner's toe.

"Sh—ugar!" Pete gritted his teeth and limped through the final bars of the tune.

Meanwhile Molly had been busy making notes as she watched the performance. When the dance was over, she consulted with her panel and they each held up a number. Lester gave them an eight, but SB and Molly each held up a five.

Cheers, groans and raucous comments followed. Josie and Gabe were up next and did much better, getting a seven and two eights. Then Morgan partnered with Dominique, and Ben was impressed with how smoothly they danced. The judges gave them all nines.

That left Jack and Sarah. From the moment they took the floor, Ben knew it was no contest. Obviously mother and son had been dancing together for years, probably at every family event since Jack was a kid.

It was beautiful to watch them dance, but Ben was even more captivated by the expressions of love on the faces surrounding the dance floor. Obviously no one objected to losing to this pair. They'd probably expected it as soon as Jack and Sarah had turned out to be partners. Everyone cheered and hollered when the judging panel gave them three tens.

As the commotion died down, Nick held up his phone. "I just checked the weather, folks. It's not looking so good through the weekend."

Like old-time gunslingers, every man in the room except Ben pulled out his phone. After some muttered comments, Jack was the first to speak. "Good thing we all like each other. We may be here for a while."

THE BLIZZARD RAGED through Sunday night, and Ben had never been through forty-eight hours quite like it. He couldn't so much as kiss Molly. No corner of the house was safe and he was frustrated as hell.

On the other hand, he was given an education in the inner workings of a large, happy family that spanned three generations. Sure, there were disagreements now and then, and sometimes the kids got on everyone's nerves. But inevitably someone would crack a joke to diffuse any tension, or dispense a hug, or suggest a new board game.

Sarah was the linchpin of the operation. She made sure that clothes were washed and a schedule was kept. The littlest ones took their naps as if they were at home, and after the free-for-all buffet of Friday night, the menu shifted to plenty of healthy food and only occasional sweets. Sarah also hauled out colored construction paper to make chains and tissue paper for snowflakes. The adults created some impressive popcorn-and-cranberry garlands.

Fortunately the electricity stayed on all weekend. The ranch hands in the bunkhouse had enough food to last them for a couple of days, and they were close enough to the barn that they could keep the horses fed. Blizzard conditions weren't uncommon and the hands knew what to do.

Ben also noticed that although everyone felt free to joke about most anything, there was never an edge to their teasing. Family members respected each other and were never mean. At first, Ben had wondered if they were putting on a good face for him, and maybe for Molly. But as the weekend continued, he realized that was impossible. Nobody could fake it for that long.

He would have preferred more alone time with Molly, but if he couldn't have that, at least he was getting a crash course in healthy family dynamics. He couldn't tell for sure how Molly was handling the situation because they literally had no private time to talk. She'd mentioned to the entire group that she was worried about getting out on Monday, but other than that, she'd thrown herself into the activities with her typical sunny optimism.

Sometime during the night on Sunday, the snow stopped, and the weak morning sunlight revealed a world covered in generous dollops of whipped cream. Ben hadn't been able to see anything through the frost-covered window in the small room he'd appropriated that normally belonged to Cassidy, the housekeeper, so he'd dressed quickly and headed downstairs to look out the windows protected by the porch roof. He found nearly everyone else down there, too, peering at the snowfall and discussing the options.

Molly was among them, wearing a fleece, moose-print bathrobe on it. The robe made him smile, but it filled him with regret, too. She'd promised to wear it when she headed to his room on Friday, back when another three nights of great sex had seemed possible. Now it seemed unlikely that he'd ever get to watch her take it off.

Jack was there, unshaven and obviously intent on a plan. "According to what I'm finding online, the snowplows are out and the airport is hoping to be operational today. If we can get the road cleared from the house to the highway in time, then Molly can make her flight."

Ben nodded and avoided Molly's gaze. "Sounds good. Do you need help with the plowing?" He didn't want her to go, but this was what she wanted. He'd do what he could to make it happen.

"We'll handle it. You and Molly get yourselves packed, have some breakfast, and be ready to head out."

"I'm outta here." Molly hurried up the curved staircase.

Ben forced himself not to gaze after her like some adoring puppy. Instead, he kept his focus on Jack.

"I'll clear as much as I can," Jack said, "but I may end up plowing in front of you for the last little bit."

"Got it." Ben glanced around at everyone gathered by the window. "What about the rest of you? You must want to get home, too."

"We do," Nick said, "but Molly is the priority. That's the road that needs to be plowed first. We'll worry about the ranch roads once she's on her way."

"Okay."

"Oh, and not to alarm you unnecessarily," Nick added, "but there's another storm headed this way. Molly will probably get out okay, but if the road to Sheridan looks dicey, just come on back here instead of risking the drive."

"Thanks." Ben was touched. "I will. I'll go get my stuff together."

Less than twenty minutes later he sat in the kitchen eating the eggs, bacon and biscuits that Mary Lou had prepared in large quantity. Morgan, Josie and Dominique were there making sure their kids had some breakfast before the start of what promised to be a rigorous day.

Ben glanced at Morgan, who was directly opposite

him with her three kids. "So, you'll all go back home today, I guess."

"We will." Morgan sat with Matilda in her lap while her two-year-old son, Aaron, perched on a booster seat on one side. Sarah Bianca was kneeling in a regular chair on the other side. "I hope you can make it home okay, though. Promise you'll turn around and come right back if there are any issues with the road to Sheridan."

SB gazed at him across the table, her expression grave. "You don't live here?"

"No, I live in Sheridan."

"I've never been there. Do you live with your mommy and daddy?"

"No. I live by myself."

"All by yourself?" She looked dismayed. "Do you even have a Christmas tree?"

He was tempted to lie because he could imagine how the truth would shock her. Finally he compromised. "Not yet."

She cocked her head and stared at him as if digesting that information. "You'd better come back here for Christmas."

"Well, thank you, but I plan to spend Christmas in Sheridan."

"Why?"

A very good question for which he had no answer. "It's where I live."

"But you're all by *yourself.*"

Morgan put a hand on her daughter's shoulder. "SB, some people enjoy that."

Her little face puckered up in thought. "Do you?"

He was saved from answering by Molly's arrival.

Molly was one of SB's favorites, and the little girl quickly abandoned him. Nobody could ask as many awkward questions as a four-year-old. She'd zeroed in on the very subjects that had been troubling him all weekend. After spending nearly four days at the Last Chance Ranch surrounded by happy people, he would be damned lonely in the small apartment attached to his saddle shop.

He took one last gulp of coffee before excusing himself to go fetch his truck while Molly ate her breakfast. The trip to Jackson would be bittersweet. At last he'd be alone with her, but he'd be busy navigating the road and driving her to catch a flight that would take her far away from him.

His truck didn't want to start, but eventually he coaxed the engine to life. After letting it warm up, he backed it out of the shed and drove along the plowed lane Jack had created that led to the circular driveway in front of the house. He left the motor running and the heat blasting as he headed back into the house.

Although he'd promised himself he'd return, and often, leaving created a hollow feeling in his chest. Or maybe it was the thought that he would soon have to say goodbye to Molly. He hadn't allowed himself to think much about that, but the knowledge hovered in the back of his mind, ready to take center stage when he dropped her off at the airport.

Molly's suitcase and carry-on sat by the front door. She'd put on her red coat and she was busy hugging everyone within reach and thanking them for their hospitality. She had a catch in her voice.

But when she noticed Ben standing there, she gave him a bright smile. "Ready?"

"When you are."

She turned back to the little group that had gathered to tell her goodbye. "I'll email, and I'll see about coming during spring break. If that doesn't work out, then I'll definitely be back in the summer."

"Make sure you do that." Sarah gathered her close for one more hug. "But regardless, Pete and I will see you in Arizona."

"Great." She took a shaky breath. "I'd better get out of here before I start bawling." She picked up her carry-on.

Ben took that as his cue. He stepped forward and held out his hand to Sarah. "Thank you for your hospitality. It's been an incredible experience."

She glanced at his outstretched hand, bypassed it and gave him a fierce hug. He hugged her back and was worried for a moment that he might lose his cool. But he cleared the huskiness from his throat and promised to visit soon.

Then he smiled at everyone, grabbed Molly's suitcase and beat it out the door. Their warmth toward him felt great, but he didn't trust himself not to go all sappy and mushy as a result. Molly could get away with it, but he was a guy, and one who'd only just met them all.

He didn't feel that way, though, as he helped Molly into the truck. When he got behind the wheel, he glanced over at the house and saw them all massed in the open doorway, waving. His eyes misted.

Beeping the horn, he pulled out. "They'll freeze their asses off doing that."

"They don't care."

"I know. That's what makes them all so wonderful."

"They are, aren't they?" Molly's voice was a little

shaky as she turned to look at the receding view of the house. "I wish I hadn't taken so long to come up here."

"So you're coming back over your spring break?" He shouldn't ask, but he couldn't seem to help it.

"I might." She faced forward.

Now what was he going to say? That he wanted to see her if she flew up here again? Of course he did, but he was still the wrong guy for her, so he had no business continuing the relationship.

"From your silence I gather you won't be driving over here to see me." Her voice was tight and she stared out the windshield instead of looking at him.

"You know I want to."

"Then why not do it?" She glanced over at him. "What's the harm?"

"Damn it, next you're going to suggest we can be friends."

"You'd be wrong there, cowboy. We can be friends if you want, but mostly I crave your body."

He risked a quick look at her and she had a saucy little smile on her face. He couldn't help laughing. "I see how it is."

"I should hope so. We'd planned on another three nights of hot sex. That didn't happen."

"You noticed." He grinned.

"I certainly did. So if I come back up here on my spring break, do you think you could work those three nights into your busy schedule?"

"Yes." God, but he didn't want her to leave. She was everything he'd ever wanted and more. "I think that can be arranged."

16

MOLLY HAD TWO objectives for this trip to the airport with Ben—to put them both at ease, and to establish that this wasn't a permanent goodbye. She was proud of herself. She'd accomplished both goals in the first two minutes.

Now they could talk easily for the rest of the trip. They caught up with Jack and followed the tractor as it slowly carved a path to the highway. At the end of the road Ben honked the horn in farewell and they were on their way to Jackson.

"Are you definitely coming back for spring break?"

She turned toward him. "Are you definitely driving over from Sheridan if I do?"

"Yes."

"Then I'll be here for spring break."

"Good."

She cherished the enthusiasm in his voice. This wasn't the end, after all. She didn't need promises of forever. It was too soon for that, but at least she'd been given a reprieve from the awful prospect of never seeing him again.

"I'll probably visit the ranch before then, though."

He drove below the speed limit. The road had been plowed, but patches of ice remained. "I'll be making saddles for all three of the guys in exchange for Calamity Sam."

"That's terrific." Thank God she hadn't somehow screwed up his business opportunity at the Last Chance. "They're getting a great deal."

"So am I. Calamity Sam will bring in stud fees that should eventually allow me to buy a mare. Morgan gave me the name of a real estate agent she knows in Sheridan, and as soon as I get home, I'll start looking at horse property. If I can find a place that has a studio I can use for my saddle business, I can give up the shop I'm renting in town."

"I'm excited for you, Ben. Sounds like fun." It also sounded like permanence. He'd already established a business there. Once he bought property and horses, he'd be there to stay.

All weekend she'd watched him interact with the Chance clan and she'd detected a subtle shift in his attitude. He no longer tried to protect himself from the emotional pull of that family. He might think his business deal with the Chance brothers was the link between him and the ranch, but she thought it was more likely an excuse to spend time there.

She predicted that by summer he'd be making regular trips between Sheridan and Jackson Hole, and the visits wouldn't always be about horses and saddles. He was going to let the Chance family adopt him.

Moisture gathered in her eyes, and she quickly blinked it away. They were happy tears, she told herself. This was the best thing that could happen to Ben.

But it meant the end of a dream she'd barely ad-

mitted to having. Now that it was dead, she realized
how much she'd wanted it. What a foolish fantasy, too.
There'd never been a real possibility that he'd someday
bond with her immediate family and move to Arizona.

As much as she longed to see him at spring break,
maybe it was a dumb move on her part. She should have
thought it through before making that suggestion. Early
this morning her plan had seemed brilliant, a way to
stay connected as, over the next few months, Ben gradually changed his mind about having his own family.

But she hadn't put all the pieces together. The dis-
cussions he'd had with the Chance brothers about saddles and horse breeding hadn't included her. Although
she'd known he was considering buying property, she
hadn't grasped what that meant. By coming back over
spring break, she'd only get more hooked on someone
who'd put down roots hundreds of miles away.

On the other hand, knowing their parting at the
airport wasn't a permanent goodbye would make that
moment easier for both of them. But if she was only
postponing their inevitable split, was that fair to either
of them? Her head began to hurt.

"You're awfully quiet over there."

"Just thinking."

"About what?"

She could admit that she'd been reconsidering
whether they should see each other again, after all.
But why make the rest of the drive a miserable one for
him? "It's not important."

"If it's not important, then you'd tell me, which
means it is important and you don't want to tell me."

She liked knowing that he was a smart guy, but in
this case, she wished he'd been a little slower on the up-

take. Maybe she could talk around the subject. "Leaving you today is going to be hard."

"I know, which is why I'm glad we have the spring break plan. In fact, if you can give me the exact dates, that would make it more real. I can put it on my calendar so I can look forward to it."

So much for that strategy. "I was just thinking that if leaving you today will be tough, then leaving you in the spring will be even tougher."

"Maybe not. You said you could come back in the summer."

She swallowed. She'd done this to herself. If she was willing to come back in the spring and enjoy some good times, then why not repeat it? If she was mostly in it for the sex as she'd implied, then periodic visits to Wyoming made perfect sense.

But although she'd tried to convince herself that great sex was the drawing card, it wasn't anymore. At first it might have been, but she wasn't positive of that, either. She was the optimist who believed everything would turn out all right in the end.

So, naturally, she'd believed a miracle would come along so they could solve their issues. Even his statement about not wanting children hadn't stopped her. Vasectomies could sometimes be reversed, or there was always adoption.

Now he might marry and adopt kids. He seemed to be moving in that direction. But she had a vision of how her life would unfold—her parents as loving grandparents, her brothers and sisters-in-law as cherished aunts and uncles, and their children as cousins and playmates. In Arizona. Within thirty minutes of each other.

"I may be all wet," Ben said, "but I can't shake the feeling that you're reconsidering that spring break plan."

She took a deep breath. "I am, and I'm sorry." She clenched her hands in her lap. "I didn't think it through."

"I wondered about that," he said softly. "It did seem a little too good to be true." He sounded sad, but resigned.

Her heart ached for him. "I *hate* the thought of never seeing you again."

"Likewise."

From the corner of her eye she could see his jaw clench, and she hated that, too. "But I'm...really beginning to care for you."

"I'm not surprised." His voice was tight. "You care for everybody."

"Not the way I care for you."

"Well..." He cleared his throat. "We both know you shouldn't fall for me. So if that means saying goodbye today, that's what we'll do."

She didn't respond to that for fear she'd start crying. And here she'd been so proud of herself because she'd supposedly found a way to make the drive relaxed and fun. It sure wasn't fun now.

After an eternity of silence except for the crunch of the tires on icy patches of road, Ben flipped the turn signal to go into the airport's parking lot.

"You can just drop me off."

"I'm going in with you. I want to make sure you get on the flight okay."

She couldn't very well argue. He was driving. "All right. Thank you."

He insisted on taking charge of both her suitcase and her carry-on, so she was left with only her shoulder bag as they battled a stiff wind on the way into the terminal. The place wasn't very crowded. Several flights had been canceled.

She glanced at the flight information monitor to double-check her flight. Then she blinked and looked again.

"It's canceled," Ben said.

"It wasn't when I checked my phone ten minutes ago!" She heard the desperation in her voice, but she had to get out of here. Part of it was her eagerness to be home for Christmas, but most of it had to do with the man standing by her side. Being with him had become too painful to bear.

Leaving him with the suitcases, she went to the counter, but the woman only confirmed what was on the monitor.

Molly fought panic. "But it's not snowing."

"No, but it will soon. And the winds are treacherous right now. All planes have been grounded until further notice."

Molly groaned. This couldn't be happening.

"I'm sorry." The woman's smile was sympathetic but firm. "We hope to resume service in the morning, so your best bet is to stay close, either in the airport or at one of the hotels nearby."

"Thank you." Taking a deep breath, Molly turned and walked back to where Ben waited with the luggage. "I'll just stay here. Something might open up."

He searched her face, his dark gaze troubled. "How soon?"

She shrugged and did her best to look unconcerned

about it. "Not sure, exactly, but I'll be fine. You'd better take off. Everybody was worried about the road between here and Sheridan, so I don't want you to get stuck."

He blew out a breath and nudged back his Stetson. "Look, Molly, I'm not leaving you here when there's only some vague promise of a flight eventually. Did they say if it would be today?"

"It won't be today, but that's no problem. I can—"

"Damn it, Molly. Did you seriously plan to spend the night here by yourself?"

"Why not?"

He shook his head. "I don't even know where to start. Sure, I know you could do it if you had no other option, but you have another option. Come on." He picked up her suitcase and started toward the door.

"Where are you going?" For one wild moment she wondered if he planned to drive her all the way to Arizona.

"To a hotel."

"Okay." That made more sense. She might have taken a cab to a hotel if he'd left anyway. "You can just drop me at whichever one we come to first."

If he replied she didn't catch it. She was too busy staying upright as they went back to his truck. Maybe the airport authorities knew what they were doing when they'd grounded the planes because of the wind.

He helped her back into the truck and stowed her luggage. She called a couple of nearby hotels to find out which had vacancies. In short order she was able to direct Ben to a medium-priced place that had several rooms available.

As he pulled the truck under the portico at the entrance, she unbuckled her seatbelt and turned to him. "Thank you, Ben. I'm not going to make this a long, drawn-out speech, but I will always cherish what—"

"Good God, woman."

"What?"

"I'm not dropping you off here, either! What do you take me for?"

She gulped. "So, what were your plans?"

"To stay with you until you get a flight out of here, of course, like any decent human being would do. I suppose we could book two separate rooms, but all things considered, that seems like a waste of an opportunity." His gaze was steady.

"Oh." Her heartbeat tripled, at least.

He reached out and brushed a knuckle over her cold cheek. "What do you say, Molly? It seems Fate has thrown us together again. Shall we have one last fling before we call it quits?"

Her chest and throat were so tight it was a wonder she could talk at all. "Okay."

He smiled. "That's my girl."

She thought about those words as they registered and rode the elevator to their third-floor room. *My girl.* It had sounded so sweet, so natural. He'd only meant it as a casual endearment, not a statement of fact, but how she wanted to be his girl. If only the price weren't so damned high.

But she didn't have to think about that, now. Once again, the parameters had been set. They'd enjoy each other for whatever time they had and go their separate ways.

As Ben swiped the keycard, his hand trembled slightly. That was the only outward sign that he wasn't calm and composed about spending the night with her. For her part, after a weekend of wanting and not having, Molly felt like a hand grenade with the pin pulled out.

He stood back and gestured her inside. She walked into an ordinary hotel room with a built-in desk, matching bedspread and drapes, and one easy chair in the corner. There was nothing remarkable about the place.

Then Ben came in and put down her suitcase. When he closed the door and flipped the security latch, she turned to him. In that instant, the room ceased to be ordinary. Her heart pounding, she held his gaze as she unzipped her red parka.

Ben stepped toward her, his dark eyes filled with heat. A shudder moved through his large frame.

She couldn't say who groaned or who moved first, but suddenly they were in each other's arms and tearing at each other's clothes and kicking off their boots. In mere seconds she was down to her underwear, and her glasses were gone…somewhere. She had no idea if she'd taken them off or he had.

And she didn't care, because his talented mouth was covering her with kisses as he stripped off her bra. Her panties ripped as he pulled them down and she didn't care about that, either. When he picked her up, she wound her legs around his waist and pushed her bare breasts against his soft mat of chest hair. Then she bit his shoulder.

His low laugh was the sexiest sound she'd ever heard. "Want this, do you?"

"Desperately."

"That makes two of us." He laid her on the bedspread and followed her down, his rigid cock nudging her damp folds. His first powerful thrust lifted her off the bed.

This time she laughed. "Yes!"

"Yes." The word was almost a growl. Then he began to move, each stroke delving deep into her quivering body.

How she loved the way he claimed her! And there was no other word for it. She surrendered to the delicious sensation of being taken by a man who'd been pushed to the limits of his control.

His heavy breathing blended with her gasps of pleasure as he drove home again and again. His eyes burned with a fierce urgency that sent fire through her veins. She held his gaze as the first tremor rocked her body.

The flame in his eyes leaped and he pumped faster. He coaxed her up, up, until she lost herself in the glory of an orgasm that whirled her like a carnival ride and brought breathless cries to her lips.

He didn't pause, and his command tore through the mists of her climax. *"Again."* He bore down, the rapid friction of his thick cock sending her back to the top of the roller coaster and over into a second screaming descent.

This time he hurtled down with her, bellowing in satisfaction as he pushed deep, his big body shuddering in the grip of his release. Braced on his arms, he gazed down at her as he gulped for air. Gradually his intense expression relaxed into a bemused smile. "You bit me."

She took a shaky breath and smoothed her hand over the red spot on his shoulder. "I know. That's so unlike me."

His glance slid over her and heat smoldered in his eyes. "I don't think so. I think it's exactly like you."

"It isn't! I've never bitten a man in my life!"

"Until me." He sounded pleased with that.

"Unusual circumstances. We had one night of great sex, and one crazy moment in the tractor barn, and then we couldn't do anything because the house was full of people. Naturally I was a little frustrated by that."

His smile was more than a little smug. "I noticed."

"So were you, smarty pants."

"Oh, I won't deny it. This weekend was pure torture. By the time we walked into this room, I was a ticking time bomb. However, I'm not the one who bit." He chuckled. "You are."

"You aren't going to let me forget that, are you?"

"Nope. Because the thing is, under that college professor persona you have going on, you're a wild woman, Molly Gallagher. And until the weather clears, I'm going to prove it to you."

17

BEN HAD BEEN given a few more precious hours with Molly, and he planned to make the most of them. When she flew out of here, he would never see her again. He'd known from the beginning he was wrong for her, and now she'd apparently accepted that, too.

But he wouldn't have to face their final goodbye until tomorrow. At this very moment he had a naked Molly lying beneath him, gazing up with those amazing green eyes. He was already getting hard again.

He could stay right where he was and start all over, which would be fine, but he had an unfulfilled fantasy to satisfy. "Let's find your glasses." He eased away from her and climbed out of bed.

"That's very sweet." She sat up. "But if we broke them during that episode, that's okay. I have a spare pair at home and I can wear my contacts in the meantime."

"I hope *I* didn't break them." He surveyed the carpet as he searched for them. "But thanks for being willing to share the blame."

"They're my glasses, so I should have taken them off if I was worried about them."

A rush of emotion took him by surprise. Pausing in his search, he gazed at her. "Thank you."

"For what?"

"For not blaming me."

Her breath caught. "Oh, Ben." She started to leave the bed.

"Stay there. I can see better than you and you might step on them."

"All right." Her voice was warm with compassion.

The man he used to be would have rejected that compassion. Instead he allowed it to flow over him as it gently soothed a pain he'd never let anyone else see. Dear God, he was going to miss her.

He found her glasses, intact, lying on the carpet. "Got 'em."

"Thanks. Just put them on the nightstand." She smiled and gestured toward his erect cock. "You're blurry, but I can still see that I won't be needing them anytime soon."

"That's where you're wrong." He walked to the side of the bed and handed them to her. "I want you to wear them."

"While we have sex?"

"Yep."

She laughed. "Why, for heaven's sake?"

"Because I love the way you look in them, and it'll be kind of kinky fun to do it while you're wearing glasses and nothing else. But that's not all of it."

She put them on and glanced up at him. "What's the rest?"

"You said you feel more like yourself when you

wear them. I want to make love to you when you're one hundred percent Molly."

She held his gaze. "That's the most romantic thing anyone's ever said to me."

"Really?"

"Yeah."

He soaked up the way she was looking at him, because it made him feel about ten feet tall, and he wanted to remember that warm expression for a long, long time. "Well, good, then." His pulse beating with anticipation, he climbed into bed with her and knelt between her thighs.

"I should warn you they might get in the way of kissing."

"Much as I love kissing you, I have something else in mind." Leaning back, he lifted her legs and propped her heels against his chest.

"My goodness."

"Ever tried it this way?"

"Not while wearing my glasses." Her gaze swept over him and she smiled. "They definitely improve the view."

"For me, too." He took a moment to be thankful for the canceled flight. Otherwise he would never have made love to Molly this way. "I'll take it slow."

"Okay." Her breathing had picked up speed and her skin was the sweetest shade of pink.

His cock throbbed. "Tell me if it doesn't feel good." Cupping her bottom, he lifted her up and watched her reaction as he pushed a little way into her. "All right?"

She groaned softly. "Very right."

Holding her gaze to make sure she didn't flinch, he sank up to the hilt. "Still okay?"

"Yes."

He eased back and rocked forward again. "How about that?"

"Uh-huh."

It was certainly working for him. His fingers flexed as he massaged that firm little bottom of hers while he stroked in and out. Her breasts quivered each time he pushed home and she seemed to grow wetter with each thrust. And those glasses knocked him out. She really was pure Molly with them on, and he was the guy who was about to give her a climax.

She clutched the sheets and gasped. "Ben...I'm...ready to..."

"I know." He felt her first spasm. "Me, too." His climax hovered as if waiting for her. He marveled at how quickly they excited each other, how easy it was to give pleasure and receive it.

He pumped faster. She came, her cries filling the small hotel room. He followed right after. His groans drowned out hers as his climax roared through him.

Shuddering from the impact, he still managed to lower her to the mattress without falling forward and crushing her. Then he eased away from her quivering body without knocking off her glasses. At last, he flopped onto his back and lay there gulping for air. Molly at full power was a force to be reckoned with.

She drew in a shaky breath. "We might have peaked with that one."

Rolling to his side, he propped his head on his hand and gazed at her. "Think so?"

"It was pretty spectacular." She turned her head to look at him. "Or I should say *you* were pretty spectacular. I just went along for the ride."

"You did your part." He brushed his knuckles over her breasts and noticed with satisfaction that her nipples tightened. "Feeling you come is quite a rush for me."

"Feeling you come is amazing." Her gaze was soft and open as if she'd let down all her barriers. "I had no idea making love could feel like that."

She could have said *having sex* and he liked that she hadn't. He liked lying here talking with her about intimate details that only lovers shared. He'd never felt as emotionally connected to someone as he did at this moment.

But the day wasn't even half over yet, and he had more fantasies to fulfill. "Hold still." He gently removed her glasses. "You won't be needing these for a while."

She smiled. "Because we'll be kissing?"

"Showering." Brushing his lips quickly over hers, he left the bed and put her glasses on the nightstand.

"Good plan. You go first since you're already up."

"I have a better idea." He scooped her out of bed and she gave a little shriek. "Ever had shower sex?" He started toward the bathroom.

"That depends on your definition."

He laughed. "Good answer."

"I wouldn't be as likely to have shower sex with a guy wearing a condom, now would I?"

"That's why you're about to have shower sex with a guy who doesn't need one."

"Sounds exciting. I'll bet you're a pro by now."

He lowered her feet to the floor, gathered her close and tilted her chin up so he could look into her eyes.

"I'm not a pro. I've never suggested this to anyone before, but with you I want…everything."

Her eyes widened in obvious shock.

"Hey, I didn't mean it like that." Too late he realized that she might have interpreted that comment as a prelude to a proposal. "I was talking about sex. Don't panic."

"I wasn't panicking. I just wasn't sure what you meant."

"I know. Sorry." Then he kissed her, more to distract them both from a dicey topic than to arouse her. But kissing Molly always got him hot, and soon he had his tongue in her mouth and his hands all over her supple body.

It wasn't until he'd backed her against the bathroom counter and started to lift her up on it that he remembered where they were and why. Shower sex. He set her down with a smile of apology. "Got carried away."

Her eyes were heavy-lidded with desire. "I didn't mind."

"We really are going to get in that shower."

She glanced at his jutting cock. "Better hurry."

"Um, yeah." He had the shower running in no time. He settled the bathmat on the floor and glanced over his shoulder.

She stood there smiling at him.

He held out his hand. "Ready?"

"You know it, cowboy." Sashaying toward him, she put her hand in his.

He helped her into the combination tub and shower and stepped in after her. With her back to him, she stood under the spray and combed her wet hair back from her face. Water cascaded over her curves and made her skin glisten.

A primitive urge that he didn't question took hold of him. Wrapping his arms around her, he drew her close, her back against his heaving chest. Her slippery body drove him wild as he fondled her breasts and slid his hand between her thighs.

She moaned as he thrust his fingers deep. So hot. He made her come in mere seconds, and her cries echoed in the small room. His balls tightened and his cock strained as his body demanded release.

Soon. Easing his fingers free, he turned her to face him. "Wrap your arms around my neck and hold on tight."

She was breathing fast. "Like…in the tractor barn?"

"Exactly like that." Under the shower's liquid caress, he braced his feet apart and lifted her the same way he had in the barn. She wrapped her moisture-slicked legs around his hips as he lowered her onto his waiting cock. He almost came. It felt just that good.

"Ohh." Her low moan told him she completely agreed.

He held still for a couple of seconds while he fought the climax that threatened to overwhelm him. Then he lifted her up and she pushed back down with another throaty moan of delight.

Because they were both so slippery, he didn't dare move too fast, but he didn't have to. The combination of warm water sluicing over them and the gentle slide of his cock was more than enough to send her over the edge, and the minute she clenched around him, he was done for. He came hard with a triumphant cry wrenched from deep in his chest.

Gasping, he held on to her and willed himself to stay steady as he set her gently back on her feet. He didn't let go, because if she was as blindsided by her orgasm as he was by his, she might lose her balance. Or he might. He wasn't absolutely clear on whether he was keeping her from falling or vice versa.

The shower continued to pelt them. When she gazed up at him, her eyelashes were beaded with water. "Shower sex is better than tractor barn sex," she murmured.

He grinned. "Riskier, though."

"No, it's not. You wouldn't let me fall."

Her trust humbled him. "I wouldn't mean to, but—"

"You wouldn't, Ben." Her expression was completely sincere. "Even if I started to go down, you'd block my fall with your body. That's why I was determined *not* to fall. I didn't want you getting hurt trying to protect me."

He bracketed her face with both hands. "And that's the most romantic thing anyone's ever said to me."

She frowned. "You think that's romantic?"

"You just said I'd do anything to keep you safe. No one's…" His stupid emotions were making his throat close up. "No one's ever said that before."

Warmth filled her gaze. "Then I'm glad someone finally did. Now what do you say we get out of the shower before we turn into prunes?"

"Good idea." But he thought about her comment as they dried each other off, as they started fooling around and as they went back to bed to fool around some more. She trusted him. That was huge.

As the day continued, he ordered room service whenever they got hungry because he didn't want to share even one minute of Molly with the outside world. He refused to think about the pain he'd feel the next morning when her plane lifted off.

Except it didn't. The second blizzard arrived before dawn, and when Molly called the airport, she learned that the planes were still grounded. If she was disappointed about that, she didn't show it. Her phone call to her folks in Arizona sounded positive.

Listening to her talk to them, he could tell how much she wanted to get home for Christmas. The snow continued to pile up, though, and he wondered if she'd make it back, after all. But he hid his doubts. Maybe the planes would fly the following morning, December twenty-fourth. Maybe not. She was running out of time.

Now that they'd taken the edge off their sexual hunger, neither of them felt the need to have sex constantly. They watched a movie on TV and then played Candy Crush Saga on her laptop. Whoever scored highest was allowed to choose their next sexual position.

Late in the afternoon, during another game of Candy Crush, played while they sat naked on the bed, she adjusted her glasses and gazed at him. "You're pretty good at being snowbound."

He smiled. "It's easy when I'm snowbound with you." The image of Molly sitting there playing a computer game wearing nothing but her glasses would stay with him a long time.

"Maybe for the first few hours it was, when it was a novelty and we were wild for each other, but you've been stuck with me since yesterday. You've had to use my razor and my deodorant. You've faced the same boring room service choices for every meal. You haven't complained once."

"Neither have you."

"Yeah, like I would. I'm in this fix because I insisted on traveling in December. I have only me to blame, but you've volunteered to keep me company and you've done an admirable job under trying circumstances."

That struck him as funny. He'd been allowed to stay in this cozy hotel room and spend time playing games, watching movies and having amazing sex with Molly Gallagher. The more he thought of her description of that as *trying circumstances,* the broader his grin. Finally he fell back against the pillows, unable to hold back the laughter.

"What's so funny?"

He turned his head to look at her. "You."

"Why?"

"Do you really think this has been a hardship for me?"

"Well, most people would—"

"It's been a privilege, Molly. There's nowhere I'd rather be than right here, keeping you company. The trying circumstances will come later."

Understanding shone in her green eyes and her expression grew tender. She took off her glasses and pushed aside the computer. "We're not there, yet." And she eased her warm body over his and began doing things that made him forget all about what would happen later, when she left Wyoming. And him.

18

BY THE NEXT MORNING, the snow had stopped, and Ben was feeling selfish enough to wish it hadn't. Molly propped herself up against the headboard with pillows, put on her glasses, and called the airport for an update. The news was inconclusive.

She might be able to fly out and she might not, depending on how quickly the snowplows cleared the runways and how dangerous the wind-shear factor was estimated to be. She was advised to come to the terminal and wait it out like everyone else.

"Then that's what we'll do." Ben was willing to spend the day in the terminal if it meant she might eventually be able to fly home.

"But it's Christmas tomorrow. Drop me off there, Ben, and drive back to Sheridan. I insist."

"You can insist all you want, but I'm not going to leave you at the terminal when there's a possibility you'll end up spending Christmas Eve there. And Christmas Day, for that matter."

She pushed her glasses up the bridge of her nose. "Much as I hate to admit it, that could happen."

"It certainly could, and after all this, I won't have you spending Christmas alone in an airport terminal. I can't substitute for your family, but at least you won't be with a bunch of strangers."

She regarded him silently for a minute or two. "Even if I get a flight out, I'll have to make the drive from Phoenix to Prescott, and they've had snow up in the mountains. I'll probably arrive late, after most of the stuff is over. I'll miss the big dinner and the Christmas carols and the kids hanging up their stockings."

The thought of her driving alone into the mountains on Christmas Eve in bad weather chilled his blood, but it wasn't his decision.

"And that's assuming I get a flight out."

He waited for her to sort through this on her own.

"I want to be home for Christmas, but looking at all the facts, I might not make it." She sighed and glanced at him. "If my chances of going home are slim to none, I know what my second choice is. Would you be willing to drive us back to the Last Chance today?"

"Of course, but don't you want to go over to the airport and see if—"

"If we intend to land on the Chance family's doorstep the day of Christmas Eve, they deserve the courtesy of knowing it well in advance. I'll call Sarah and ask if it's okay." She scrolled through her contacts.

"Molly, wait. If we arrive together, and they know I've been with you since Monday, they'll make assumptions. Are you sure that's what you want?"

She lifted her chin. "I'm proud to know you, Ben. They can make assumptions all they want. It won't bother me." Then she hesitated. "Would it bother you? I don't want to come between you and them, either."

"No." He'd already considered whether this would affect his dealings with Jack and had decided that giving Molly a decent Christmas was more important to him. "I'm honored that you've chosen to spend this time with me." He gestured toward her phone. "Make your call."

She did, and of course Sarah told them to come back immediately. In less than an hour they'd checked out of the hotel and were driving back toward the Last Chance. If he'd worried about intruding on Sarah's birthday celebration, that was nothing compared to crashing a Last Chance Christmas. But for Molly he'd risk anything.

Listening to her talk to her folks on the phone was heartbreaking, though. She'd called them as soon as he'd pulled away from the hotel, and the catch in her voice told him how much she'd miss being with them. That was another good reason why she was wrong for him. She'd naturally want to live in Arizona surrounded by her family.

He, on the other hand, had a growing business in Sheridan, and for the first time in his life, a place that felt like home—the Last Chance Ranch. If his business continued to grow, he might rent a storefront in Jackson and hire somebody to run it.

He could even take on an apprentice saddlemaker and teach someone else the skills he'd learned from his mentor. He smiled at the thought that someday Sarah Bianca might go into business with him. Probably not. Kids changed their minds all the time as they grew up, but it was fun to think about.

Molly gazed at the freshly ploughed highway stretching in front of them. Very few vehicles navigated the road. Her pitiful little sigh tore at his heart. "I'm sorry it didn't work out."

"Me, too."

She gave him a quick smile and returned her attention to the road.

When she didn't say anything more, he wondered if she was battling tears. He probably ought to let her work through that by herself.

"My mother said something that surprised me."

"Oh?"

"She thinks this might be a good thing. She doesn't want me to feel tied to the tradition of always being there for Christmas. She pointed out that my brothers have missed a few times."

He proceeded with caution because this sounded like a loaded topic. "What do you think?"

"I don't know. I've always assumed she'd be crushed if I didn't make it home for the holidays. Of course she'll miss me. She said that. But knowing it won't ruin Christmas for her is…liberating, in a way."

"Your mom sounds great."

Molly smiled. "She is great. You would love—well, anyway. Yes, my mom's terrific."

She'd been about to say he'd love her mother. He probably would, but that was beside the point. He would never meet her.

Perversely, now he wanted to. People said you could tell what a woman would be like in twenty-five years by looking at her mother. Despite having no future with Molly, he couldn't help fantasizing about what one would be like.

"I'll bet Jack's out plowing the ranch road so we can

get through." Molly chuckled. "I could be wrong, but I think he likes doing that."

"I can guarantee he does. Most little boys never outgrow their obsession with tractors."

"So I guess you'll be getting one of those, too."

Ben hadn't thought of that. "Guess I will. If I have horse property, I'll need a tractor for raking the corral. And I'll need a blade attachment so I can get in and out in winter."

"You'll also need a name for the place."

"I suppose so. Got any ideas?"

"Oh, tons!" She rummaged in her purse. "This will be fun. Let's make a list."

He smiled at her burst of enthusiasm. God, how he loved…her. *He loved her.* The thought hit him with stunning force. His pulse raced and he lost track of what she was saying. "Hold on to that thought. Let me get past this icy stretch." If he pretended that the road had suddenly become more of a challenge, she might not notice his distracted behavior.

Taking a deep breath, he refocused on the conversation. "Okay, run those past me one more time."

She rattled off several potential ranch names, some decent and some hysterically funny. They debated the merits of those names and came up with more. The subject occupied them for the rest of the drive, but all the while, in the back of his mind, lurked his newfound knowledge. He was in love with Molly Gallagher. And she would never know.

BEN PULLED INTO the circular drive in front of the ranch house behind two vehicles he didn't recognize.

"Oh, I just remembered!" Molly practically bounced

on the seat. "Jack's half brothers, Wyatt and Rafe Locke are supposed to arrive today with their wives. I'll bet that's who's here. Yay! I've been in touch with them for my project, and now we'll meet face-to-face!"

"Then you're okay with not making it home?"

She glanced at him. "I feel like a traitor for saying this, but I'm pretty excited about being here for Christmas now that it's a done deal, especially if I get to meet more family members." She unbuckled her seatbelt and reached for the door handle.

"Molly, hang on a second." He wouldn't bare his soul to her, never that, but he could take advantage of the last few moments of their time alone. "Once we go in there, we won't have any privacy."

She turned to him, her expression contrite. "That's true. Sorry. I didn't mean to rush out of here."

"You're eager to meet them all. I understand."

"But we really will be in a goldfish bowl for the next couple of days. I've considered braving it out and announcing that we'll share a room. I've been debating that ever since we agreed to come back, but I don't think it would be appropriate."

"No, it wouldn't. Before we go in, though, I want to wish you Merry Christmas." He gave her a wry smile. "Minus the gift."

"No apologies necessary. I don't have one for you, either." She touched his face. "But ever since I met you, you've been teaching me what a sexy woman I can be. That's quite a gift, when you think about it. You're precious to me, Ben."

"As you are to me." Nudging his hat back with his thumb, he slid her glasses off and laid them carefully on the dash. Then he cupped her face in both hands. "Merry Christmas, Molly."

"Merry Christmas, Ben."

He took her mouth gently, reverently. It wouldn't be the last time his lips touched hers. He planned to drive her back to the airport after Christmas, but that kiss would be all about goodbye. This one was all about gratitude…and love.

Her response was filled with such unspeakable tenderness that his breath caught. Slowly, reluctantly, he lifted his head and looked into her eyes.

They were filled with wonder, as if she'd just had a revelation.

Hope blazed within him. Maybe, just maybe…

The massive front door flew open and people he didn't recognize poured out chattering and laughing. They clattered down the steps toward the truck with an older woman in the lead, a brunette who had Jack's coloring.

Ben put his money on that being Diana, the runaway wife and mother, which meant the rest of the posse could be her sons and their wives. "Your welcoming party is here."

Molly put on her glasses just as the woman leading the pack rapped on her window. With a start of surprise, Molly looked out. Then she opened the door, letting in a cold blast of air. "Hi."

"Hi! I'm Diana, and these are your long-lost cousins, or step-cousins, or whatever the terminology is, Wyatt and Rafe. Oh, and their dearly beloveds, Olivia and Meg. Come on in! After all those emails, we're dying to meet you!"

Molly turned back to Ben. "Listen, I hate to—"

"Go ahead." He gave her a smile. "I'll bring the luggage."

Belatedly Diana glanced at Ben and seemed to remember her manners. "Sorry, how rude of me! And now I've forgotten your name."

"Ben."

"Kids, this is Ben, the guy who made that amazing saddle."

A chorus of greetings and compliments went up from the group. Then Molly climbed out, and their attention shifted to her. That gave Ben the leisure to study everybody.

One of the guys was the spitting image of Jack, only a few years younger, so he had to be Rafe, who managed investment portfolios. Ben should probably talk to him before the holiday was over, considering all his plans for expansion.

The sandy-haired stepbrother must be Wyatt, who owned an adventure trekking operation. Ben observed body language to figure out the pairings, and he found the matchups fascinating. The pulled-together woman, Olivia, was with Wyatt, while Meg, the wholesome one with the freckles, was Rafe's bride.

He waited until they'd all gone inside before unloading the luggage. After setting his duffle bag and Molly's suitcase on the porch steps, he drove his truck down to the barn and parked. Much scraping and shoveling must have gone on this morning, because the entire area was clear of snow. Huge mounds of the stuff had been dumped to the side of the buildings, though. Sled tracks and snowball forts told him that the kids had enjoyed themselves today.

As he walked back to the house, he thought about

the look in Molly's eyes after their kiss. If he didn't know better, he'd swear she'd just figured out that she loved him. If so, then what?

He was still a serious gamble for her. She obviously thought he had no reason to be concerned about his potential as a husband and father. But he was afraid that some little thing could flip a switch, and he'd become his dad.

He stepped through the front door into a world of joyful chaos. Christmas carols were on the sound system and Sarah's grandchildren raced through the living room in delirious glee. Christmas Eve was only hours away. Anticipation hummed in the evergreen-scented air.

His saddle—no, *Sarah's* saddle, was still in its place of honor beside the Christmas tree. Leaving the suitcases in the entryway for now, he meandered over to take another look at the project that had brought him to this place. To Molly.

Damn, but he was proud of it. He ran his hand over the seat and remembered how he'd struggled to fit the leather just right. The stirrups hung straight and true, and the tooling was…wait a minute. He crouched down and peered at the intricate work.

Dear God. Somebody, some *kid*, had scribbled on the leather with a neon green felt pen. His work, his labor of months, had been defiled, and recently. He could smell the acrid scent of fresh marker. Gut churning, he stood and scanned the room.

Archie, Jack's tow-headed three-year-old, met his gaze. He held a neon green pen in his chubby fist.

Anger seethed as Ben glared at the child. *"Archie."*

Archie stared back, his gaze stricken. "I made it... pretty."

All conversation in the room stopped. Jack put down his beer and looked from Ben to his son. "Archie, what did you do?"

"I...I colored it." His lower lip quivered.

Jack's expression was thunderous. *"You marked on Grandma's saddle?"*

"I wanted to make it nice, Daddy!" the little boy wailed.

Jack started toward him, fire in his eyes. "That is not acceptable, young man! You are in big—"

"Jack." In that moment, Ben remembered being that age and screwing up. Archie was so small. So vulnerable. Instinctively Ben knew that Jack wouldn't harm the kid, but anger was not appropriate here. Understanding was. Ben moved between father and son. "It's okay. It can be fixed."

"Archie needs to understand that he can't do this kind of thing."

Ben looked down at the little boy. "I think you already know that, don't you, sport?"

Archie nodded vigorously.

"So, tell you what. You and I will get some alcohol and we'll clean this off, okay?"

Archie nodded again, his eyes wide.

Sarah approached. "I'll help." She crouched down next to her grandson. "I know you were only trying to decorate it."

His voice was a faint whisper. "I was, Grandma."

Sarah glanced up at Ben. "Thank you for understanding. He's learning."

"Yeah, I know." Ben's throat felt tight. And he knew

something else. He'd been tested just now, and he'd passed with flying colors. He was *not* like his father.

Someone touched his arm and he turned to see Molly standing there, that same look of wonder in her eyes.

"Could I—" She cleared her throat. "Could I talk to you for a moment?"

"Sure."

Taking his hand, she led him out of the room and down the hallway into the large dining room, which was empty. Light spilled in from the busy kitchen, but the room was still mostly in shadow.

Molly took his other hand and faced him. "I love you."

His world tilted.

"You put your heart and soul into that saddle, and Archie messed with it. If you were ever going to become a bully like your father, you would have done it then."

"I know." And suddenly it was all so easy. "I'll move to Arizona. I'm sure there are people there who need custom saddles. As for Calamity Sam, I'll—"

"You'll buy him and stay right here in Wyoming."

"No." He shook his head. "I can't ask you to leave your family."

"You're not asking me to. I'm offering. My folks have a great ranch that they'll pass on to my brothers. Sure, they'd give me a share, but when you and I started tossing around names for your ranch, I realized that I want to be part of something that I've helped build, something that hasn't existed before. I want us to be like Archie and Nelsie, creating a life from the ground up."

Joy threatened to turn his brain to mush, but he

forced himself to ask the necessary questions. "What about your job?"

She shrugged. "You have a college in Sheridan. I'll apply to teach there, or get licensed for public school. I don't see that as a problem." She hesitated. "But I've done most of the talking. Maybe I'm jumping to conclusions. Maybe you don't—"

"Of course I love you." His heart thudded wildly. "I'm crazy about you."

Even in the darkness, her smile was dazzling.

"Excellent." She lifted her mouth to his. "You and I are going to make history."

As he kissed her, he had no doubt of that. Molly Gallagher, source of all things wonderful, would see to it.

Epilogue

CADE GALLAGHER HAD called home every Christmas Eve since he'd left Thunder Mountain Ranch, but he felt an unexplained urgency this year. Maybe it had to do with being several hundred miles away in Colorado and sitting in an empty bunkhouse. All the other hands had gone into town, but he'd chosen to stay here and make this special call. He missed Rosie and Herb Padgett, the people he'd come to call Mom and Dad.

He also missed Lexi, but that was nothing new. Missing her was a constant nagging ache that hadn't gone away even after five years. She was the reason he hadn't felt comfortable going back to Sheridan in all this time. Because her parents were good friends with the Padgetts, she'd spent plenty of time at Thunder Mountain Ranch. Still did, judging from stray remarks during phone conversations with Rosie.

He called the ranch's land line. Cade liked picturing Rosie answering in the kitchen while stirring her famous vegetable stew—a Christmas Eve tradition at Thunder Mountain. When all the boys had lived there, she'd made a huge vat of it. Now that it was just her and Herb, she probably made a smaller batch.

"Cade!" She always sounded as if his call was the best thing that had happened to her all day. "I just talked to Finn a minute ago!"

"Yeah? How's he doing?" Cade didn't know how many of the boys called home this time of year, but he, Finn and Damon were faithful about it. They'd been the first three to come to the ranch and their loyalty ran deep.

Homeless preteens within months of each other in age, they'd been desperate to establish an identity. They'd heard about a Native American blood-brother ceremony and had enacted it with typical adolescent drama. They'd named themselves the Thunder Mountain Brotherhood. They still kept in touch, but not as much as they should. Cade often got his news about Finn and Damon from Rosie.

"His microbrewery is keeping him busy, that's for sure. Seattle is a great town for it, apparently. But his divorce became final last month."

"Sorry to hear that. I'll give him a call. How about Damon? Have you heard from him yet?"

"Not yet, but I'm sure I will. He never misses. But you know him, probably out on the town with some woman he met last week. None of them last long, though."

"Nope." Unlike Cade and Finn, Damon had never fallen hard for anyone. Cade didn't ask about Lexi. That would make Rosie think he was still interested. He was, but it was complicated. "So, you and Dad are doing okay?"

"Couldn't be better. Retirement suits us both. Listen,

before I forget, someone called a few days ago. She's working on her family's genealogy chart and asked if I knew a Cade Marlowe. Of course I said I didn't."

A shiver ran down his spine. "If she's from the Marlowe side, I want nothing to do with her."

"Her name is Molly Gallagher, so she could be related to your mother, but don't worry. I didn't give her any information. She thinks she hit a dead end."

"Just as well. I have all the family I need."

"And I love you, too." There was a definite smile in her voice. "But I took her number in case you decide to call and find out if you're related in some way. For what it's worth, she seemed like a nice person."

"I'll think about it." He searched the empty bunkhouse for a piece of scratch paper and finally pulled an envelope out of the trash. "What's her number?" As Rosie read it off, he scribbled it down.

He had no intention of calling now. He doubted that he'd ever call. If his mother hadn't seen fit to contact her family, then why should he? But maybe he'd change his mind in the future, so he tucked the envelope in the cubby where he kept his stuff.

"Lexi's doing fine." Rosie tossed it out exactly as someone might throw a bread chunk to a bird.

He approached cautiously and took a nibble. "Good. What's she up to these days?"

"Teaches riding. She's talented in that area. She was dating some guy but they broke up."

And damned if that didn't make his Christmas Eve a little bit brighter.

"Should I tell her you said hello?"

"Better not."

Rosie sighed. "Cade, I wish you'd come home, just

for a weekend, and talk to her. I can't help thinking that both of you are pining away and are too bull-headed to admit it."

"I'll think about that, too. Merry Christmas, Mom."

"Merry Christmas, Cade. I love you."

"Love you, too. Give my love to Dad." He sat on his bunk long after he'd hung up. He wondered what Lexi was doing.

At least he didn't have to worry about her being with somebody else tonight. When Lexi broke up with somebody, she took her time about dating again. From what he'd heard, she'd waited a year after their split.

He'd waited a hell of a lot longer than that. Finally he'd eased back into the game, but he hadn't found anyone like Lexi. He had a bad feeling he never would.

* * * * *

Under the Mistletoe

KATHERINE GARBERA

Katherine Garbera is a *USA TODAY* bestselling author of more than fifty books and has always believed in happy endings. She lives in England with her husband, children and their pampered pet, Godiva. Visit Katherine on the web at www.katherinegarbera.com, or catch up with her on Facebook and Twitter.

Family and tradition define every moment of my Christmas holidays, so this book is dedicated to Charlotte and David Smith, who raised me to love the season and to never forget the reason for it. Also to my grandmothers, who are no longer with us, but who I miss more keenly at Christmas: Rose Wilkinson and Priscilla Tromblay.

_1_

PENNY DEVLIN HAD decided that she was giving herself an early Christmas present this year. A vacation from her life. Actually, making herself not read another email her former boss and ex-lover sent her was the best gift she could ever really give herself.

He'd made a mockery of her dreams of a white knight and cost her a job she loved. Rat bastard.

But really, who would keep working for a man like him?

Not her. Mentally she gave herself a pat on the back. She'd made the tough but right choice to leave her position as an event planner at Papillion Clothiers, and this place was her reward.

A ski chalet to herself for fifteen days at the luxurious Lars Usten Lodge in Park City, Utah. Her phone pinged again. She groaned as another text appeared on her screen from Butch—or actually from the label she'd assigned him.

JerkButtFace: Stop being a baby. I need to talk to you.

Penny: All my files are in my former office. You don't need me.

JerkButtFace: Not about work.

Penny: All we had was work.

JerkButtFace: Stop acting like I did something wrong. This is the 21st century.

Penny: Jerk is the same now as it's always been.

JerkButtFace: Name calling? You must still care.

As if. He was so frustrating. She *didn't* care, and was coming to realize she hadn't ever really loved him. That was the worst part.

Her phone pinged again.

That's it!

She flung open the front door of her very lovely, secluded alpine cabin, stopped to admire the gently falling snow and then chucked her cell phone out the front door.

"Hey!"

She glanced up just in time to see a man batting away her cell phone before it fell to the ground. She'd almost hit him in the face.

And what a face. A strong, square jaw with just the right hint of stubble, firm masculine lips curled in a sort of sneer, and bright, Chris Pine–blue eyes. He wore a heavy shearling jacket and a pair of faded blue jeans that clung to his thick, muscular thighs. His boots were covered in snow, and as she let her gaze travel back up his body, she forgot why she'd been so fuming mad just a second earlier.

"Sorry. I'm so sorry! I just couldn't take my phone one more second." She knew that sounded totally lame, but it was the only thing she could think of other than: *Yowza! Hot guy alert!*

He chuckled. The sound was deep and rich and echoed in the silent snow-covered land around them. It was cold, and the air seeped through the fabric of her chic lounge sweater, but she wasn't tempted at all to go back inside.

Full disclosure? This guy was the perfect distraction. He held a leather suitcase in one hand and a brochure from the Lodge in the other, so she assumed he had to be a guest. She glanced at his left hand to see if he was single, but he wore leather gloves. Plus some married men didn't wear their rings all the time. "I've been tempted to ditch my phone more than once," he said with a smile. "What seems to be the problem?"

"Problem?"

"I'm assuming part of the technology isn't working," he said.

He sounded logical and normal. All the things she just didn't feel right now. And he was cute. Really, really cute. So if she played her cards right, perhaps she'd be able to salvage this and flirt with him. She wanted to. Needed to reclaim a part of herself she'd lost when she'd learned the horrible truth from Butch. No denying it.

"Um…it wasn't picking up the Wi-Fi," Penny stammered, making up the very first thing that came to mind.

He bent over to pick up her phone. Seeing him holding her pink, jewel-studded case in his manly hands made her feel funny. But when he glanced over at her with those piercing blue eyes of his again, she still couldn't help but stare back. This time she noticed he had sun lines around his face. He spent a good deal of time outdoors, she figured.

"Mind if I give it a try?" he asked.

"Sure," she said. He was a really good-looking man with his thick brown hair styled to one side so just a swoop of it fell over his forehead. No way could his hair be as soft as it looked, but she wanted to touch it and find out.

He glanced at her screen and then back at her.

"It seems to be working. You've got a text from… JerkButtFace. Apparently, he's desperate to explain."

She groaned. When he said it, the name sounded… well, still funny to her.

Of course, even though Butch was married and his wife was pregnant with their child—something he'd failed to mention when they first met or at any point during their six months together—he still expected her to be his girlfriend. Something that she definitely didn't want to hear him try to justify again.

And he'd still managed to wriggle his way between Penny and the first attractive man she'd met in months. *Ugh.*

"I know. He's like a broken record."

"I take it you've heard enough?" the man asked wryly.

"You've got that right. But watch out, I seem to be a moron magnet," she said, moving out of her doorway to approach the man. Her UGG boots protected her against the snowy path as she did so.

He smiled at her and shook his head as he handed her phone to her. She put it in the pocket of her long lounge sweater.

"Will Spalding," he said, holding out his hand.

"Penelope Devlin." She took his hand to shake it. She worked in the business world and probably shook hands at least three times a day with potential clients, so she was used to weak ones and even clammy ones.

But his hand was smooth and dry as he enfolded her fingers in his, and the grip was firm, but sort of gentle, too. He looked to be in his early thirties, close to her own age. She stared at their joined hands for a moment as a tingle spread up her arm. She pulled hers back and then looked up at him again.

"You are a very interesting woman," he murmured.

She was not sure how to take that. "Not really. I get very boring once you get to know me."

"I highly doubt that," he said. Her phone beeped from her pocket and he raised one eyebrow.

"I'm sorry I almost hit you with the phone. I was aiming for the snowbank."

"Why don't you just put it on silent mode?" he asked.

"That would have been logical, but I'm afraid I was pushed beyond that," she admitted, hoping he didn't think she was crazy, but already suspecting that her first impression hadn't gone very well. "I know it's a sickness, really, but I'm waiting for an important work call."

She'd applied for another job with a big, high-end New York retail chain. And they were making the decision this week on who would get the position of senior event planner. If she got the job, she'd be in charge of the company's parties for the various fashion weeks around the world.

"See, to me…that part is logical. I can't ever really detach from work, either," he said, giving her a half grin that made him even sexier. "That makes you even more intriguing…"

"And mysterious? I've always wanted to be mysterious," she declared.

She liked the image he had of her. She could be that woman. Right now, she could be any woman she wanted to be. She was free of everything. A man who'd been way too secretive, a job that had been demanding and had that awful perk of working for Butch...

But that was behind her now. Will thought she was intriguing instead of old reliable Penny. That would be very exciting and different.

She'd be able to enjoy her holiday the way she'd planned. She thought of the framed print that she'd propped up in the kitchenette of her cabin.

No Regrets. Just Good Times, Love, Peace and Lots of Chocolate.

Will Spalding seemed the perfect man for that if he was single and interested, and she acknowledged there was a 50/50 chance he wasn't even single. Well, he *looked* interested. God, what if he was another loser? Granted, a very sexy-looking one, but still...

He didn't look like a loser, though. Not with that firm square jaw and serious expression on his face. He looked like someone who lived life on his own terms.

"I'll leave you to the snowbank. I look forward to seeing you again," he said.

He continued walking down the path and all she could do was watch him go. He had a seriously nice ass.

She didn't realize she was staring until he turned to the cabin next to hers and then put his key in the lock and looked back at her. She shook her head and waved and then dashed back into her own cabin.

He was cute and she felt incredibly attracted to him,

and for thirty seconds she just stood there letting all those feelings wash over her. She even felt a bit like her old self again.

Wild. Free. And ready for adventure.

WILL HAD BEEN on his own since he was fourteen. He didn't say that to gain sympathy, as he was a trust-fund baby used to having whatever he wanted—as long as it was something that could be purchased. And for the better part of the year being alone suited him just fine.

But Christmas was his Achilles' heel. He hated not sharing it with someone else. Christmas brought with it lonely memories that he had learned a long time ago would overwhelm him if he didn't ensure he was distracted.

Being a man of action, he'd developed a very simple way of dealing with it: affairs that lasted two weeks. That was the optimal amount of time. Plenty of days for fun and not enough time to form a real bond with another person. One week left him wanting more, and after two weeks the novelty was gone. No strings, no hurt feelings afterward, just two weeks of pure, frivolous pleasure for him and the lady of his choice.

He'd learned that the hard way during his brief marriage when he was younger, and had decided to limit himself to just two weeks.

Will put his leather suitcase in the corner and thought of Ms. Penelope Devlin next door. On the surface she seemed like his favorite kind of distraction.

She was cute and funny and a bit charming in her awkwardness. He'd been very good at keeping his affairs light and making sure the women he got involved with wanted exactly what he did from the affair—fun and temporary companionship.

Penny was definitely intriguing. Maybe she was looking for something to take her mind off her problems. Plus that one innocent little touch of their hands had shaken him to his core.

It had been a while since he'd felt the zing of lust at first sight. And he wasn't sure he was ready to write it off simply because she might be more than what he'd been expecting to find. Ah, hell, who was he kidding? He wanted her. And unless she shut him down, he was going to go after her. No bones about it.

Which made her dangerous, because he was simply looking for a casual affair, not a woman who could touch him all the way to his soul.

Shoving those troubling notions aside, he unpacked, checked his email and then realized that he totally sucked at relaxing when he glanced up and realized the sun had already set.

Where had the time gone?

He could eat dinner in his bungalow…but he'd be alone with just his thoughts, so he put on his shearling coat and snow boots and left his cabin. He stood in the doorway and looked at the night sky, so big and bright on this clear, cold evening. In the distance he saw the twinkling of lights down in the valley where the town was.

His breath puffed out in front of him as he locked the door and went down the path leading back to the main lodge. He glanced at Penelope's door as he passed it. Someone had hung a Christmas wreath on it and strung some lights around the door frame. It looked homey and festive and not at all like his dark doorway.

"It's beginning to look at lot like Christmas," he muttered aloud.

It was just the little nudge he needed to start thinking more about Penelope. Maybe she was just what *he* needed this Christmas.

The path to the Lodge was lit with gas-style electric lamps with holly wrapped around the posts. A light snow was still falling and he promised himself that tomorrow he'd take advantage of the ski slopes. But that left a solid twelve hours to fill and even though he had international business interests, he didn't want to spend the entire time working.

He climbed the steps that lead to the lobby past the lounge area that was dotted with fire pits and large padded chairs. There were families roasting marshmallows and couples snuggling under heavy blankets, and he just kept walking into the building away from all that…togetherness.

A blast of yuletide music hit him as he entered the lobby. "Last Christmas"…it had been his mom's favorite song. Funny that he could still remember details like that, but not her face without the help of a picture.

He paused for a moment to listen to the song and let those faraway memories wash over him. There were times when he wished for things that couldn't be. He shook himself and walked straight to the bar and ordered a seltzer water with a twist of lime. Though what he really wanted was a double shot of whiskey neat. Being a recovering alcoholic was a constant struggle.

But he'd never been good with self-control, especially when he felt like this. Truth was, he'd been unable to describe this feeling to any of his therapists, and there had been a lot of them during his teenage years. He just

knew when he felt this way, he could destroy things—
including himself—and not give a crap.

But the last time he'd done that, it had taken a lot of
time and money to clean up the mess, and he still had
some scars from that incident that hadn't fully healed.

"Gin and tonic?" Penelope asked as she slid onto the
seat next to his at the bar. She'd changed out of those leggings and the long sweater into a micro-miniskirt that
ended at the top of her thighs, and her furry boots had
been replaced with a leather pair that hugged her calves.
She looked chic and fashionable.

And drop-dead gorgeous.

She wasn't tall but sort of average sized and curvy.
Her blond hair was pulled back around her face but left
to hang free. It was stick-straight and looked like sunshine to him. She'd put on some kind of lip gloss that
made her mouth seem full and kissable.

Kissable? Really? Was he going to be the kind of
sap who—

He knew he shouldn't stare at her legs and forced his
gaze to her face. But the image of those long, shapely
calves lingered in his mind. He wanted to reach down
and put his hand on her leg but that was too bold. Even
in this mood.

Her eyes were a welcoming shade of blue. Different
from his own, darker and more exotic.

"Just tonic, unfortunately," he said. He waved the bartender over and ordered a gin and tonic for her.

"Did you get your phone sorted out?" he asked after
a long moment.

"Yes. I figured out how to block him for now," Penelope said, chewing her lush bottom lip. "So are you
married or engaged?"

He shook his head. "No. You?"

"Would I have someone labeled JBF if I was?" she asked.

He laughed, because he suspected she wanted him to, and he'd also noticed that people talked more when they felt at ease. Plus, he'd been told one too many times that his face could be intimidating when he wasn't smiling.

"I guess not."

She took a sip of her gin and tonic and leaned in toward him.

"Feeling really adventurous?" he asked, because despite the fact that his gut was saying it was a mistake to get to know this woman better, he wanted to. He wanted to know if her hair was as silky as it looked and if her skin was as soft. He wanted to know if she'd be as fun in bed as she was out of it.

She arched one eyebrow at him and gave him a wink. "What'd you have in mind?"

"Something daring and dangerous—dinner with a total stranger."

She tipped her head to the side. "That *is* really risky."

"Why do you say that?"

"Well, you never know what I might do or say if you stick around."

"Like I said, you're a very interesting woman, Penelope Devlin."

She nodded coyly. "Yes, I've decided I am. And I will have dinner with you."

"Good. Now, how adventurous are you? Will you have a private meal with me in my cabin, or is it the hotel restaurant for us?"

"I'm not stupid," she said. "We have just met so I'll take the hotel."

He smiled. "Perfectly understandable. Would a picnic dinner by one of the fire pits work for your comfort level?"

"Yes," she said, taking out her phone.

"What are you doing?"

"Texting my friend, who is the general manager of this lodge, to get the scoop on you," she said.

He reached over and put his hand on top of hers. "I'll give you the full rundown while we are eating. You did say you were ready for an adventure…"

She nodded again but it seemed more for herself than for him. "I guess you're taking just as big a risk. After all, you know I'm armed and dangerous."

She held up her cell phone and he chuckled.

"Yes, you are," he said. She fascinated him; there was no denying it. The more he got to know her the more he wanted to be around her. There was something about her smile and her body… Hell, there was no denying he wanted *her*. This was Christmas, after all, so why shouldn't he make it the best one possible?

2

WILL LEFT HER to go and make plans for their dinner, and asked her to be on the back patio in thirty minutes. She stood alone in the bar with her gin and tonic, thinking about life. She was excellent in a business situation. Give her an event for groups from fifty to a thousand to plan and she was in her element, but put her one-on-one with a guy—a smoking-hot guy—and she froze.

"You look like you are contemplating something serious," Elizabeth Anders said as she slid onto the bar stool that Will had just vacated.

"I am," she said.

"Why?" Her best friend had a more relaxed aura now that she was engaged to their college chum Bradley. The two of them had been friends forever, and over Thanksgiving had finally given into the steaming sexual tension that the rest of the world had always seen between them. Now they were madly in love and planning their life together.

She hitched in a breath. "Well, you know how I'm supposed to be giving myself Christmas this year?"

"You know I do," Elizabeth said, signaling the bartender and ordering herself a Drambuie.

"You're off the clock?"

"I am. Bradley and I are going for a moonlight snowshoeing walk as soon as he gets here."

"That's nice. I'm so happy for you." And she was. Truly. But she was also jealous. She wanted that kind of romance in her life.

Usually she was too busy with work to think about that kind of thing, but Will was making all those fantasies she'd tucked away for someday seem like a possibility.

"I got the idea from that photo you'd posted on Pinterest of the couple walking in the snow."

"No fair stealing my romantic fantasies." Penny pouted.

"I thought one of us should take advantage of it. Plus you are better at romance than I am." Elizabeth's blue-green eyes sparkled. "Bradley loved the idea." She smiled at her friend and then reached over and hugged her. Normally Elizabeth was all business so she struggled to make small talk and be social outside the corporate world but lately she'd been trying to change.

"I met a guy this afternoon," she said, picking up where she'd left off.

"You did? That's great! Where did you meet him? Why isn't he here?"

"I kind of tossed my phone out of the cabin and almost hit him in the head."

"Nice. I guess that's why he's not here," Elizabeth said with a grin.

"You'd think, but no. He said I'm *interesting*. We're

having dinner in thirty minutes. A picnic on the patio by one of the fire rings."

"You are? Who is he?"

"Will Spalding. He's staying in the cabin next to mine. Do you know anything else about him?"

Elizabeth withdrew for a second but Penny didn't mind. She knew her friend was using her razor-sharp mind to search for details about Will. "Last Christmas he stayed at the Caribbean resort that Lars owns. He always books in for two weeks at the holidays, and he's due to check out on New Year's Eve." She grinned at her friend. "I can pull up some info about him if you want? I know he asked for a Christmas tree to be delivered on the twenty-first and that's about it."

"That's okay. He's going to give me the scoop when we have dinner," Penny said.

Elizabeth gave her an incredulous look. "Yeah, sure he is. He's probably going to tell you whatever he thinks you want to hear."

"I'm pretty sure my bullshit meter is more than ready to weed out his lies," Penny said. "He's my holiday fantasy. And unless he is a complete troll at dinner, I think I've found my distraction."

"Really?"

"Uh-huh."

"Then why did you look so serious before?" Elizabeth prodded.

"It sucks having a best friend who calls you on the BS."

Elizabeth laughed. "Yes, it does. So what's up?"

"I like him, Lizzie. He's funny and charming, and I think he could be a lot of fun. But given what just hap-

pened with Butch, I'm afraid to just let myself relax and
enjoy it, you know?"

"I do know. But I also know that you aren't going to
let him slip away. If you want him for Christmas, then
make him yours," she said.

"My own Christmas hottie?"

"Definitely."

"Should I be jealous?" Bradley asked, coming up behind Elizabeth.

"No," Elizabeth said. "You're my hottie."

"And you're mine," he said, bending to give his fiancée a kiss.

"And that's my cue to go," Penny said, downing the
rest of her drink. She was happy for them and everything, but she might have misjudged coming here with
them so happy and in love. It made her wistful. Made
her wish she had some kind of radar that would help her
steer clear of losers. "Have fun on your walk."

"We will," Bradley said with a wink. "Where are you
heading off to?"

"Dinner with a tall, dark stranger…" Penny replied.

"Go, Penny!" Elizabeth said, holding her hand up for
a high five.

She gave her one, walking out of the bar. She wanted
to believe that this was simply dinner and nothing more.
Will Spalding didn't have to be anything other than who
he was. She needed fun and uncomplicated. A Christmas gift to herself before she had to make some serious
decisions about her future.

WILL HAD NO problems ordering the dinner he wanted for
himself and Penny. The concierge was more than happy

to secure a fire pit for them away from the families roasting marshmallows and singing carols.

Christmas lingered in his mind like a festering wound. Probably because it was the one time of the year that it really hit home that his family was gone and he was alone. He tended to wallow in it, starting around Thanksgiving. One year before he'd finally gotten sober, he'd spent the entire month of December drunk.

"Is that all, Mr. Spalding?"

"I'd like to do something after we eat. Any suggestions?"

"We have a horse-drawn sleigh that I can reserve for you. Our guide will take you on a path out toward the ski lifts. It's scenic and on a clear night like tonight it should be beautiful."

"Sounds perfect," Will murmured. "Is the gift shop still open?"

"Yes, sir, until nine."

"Thank you," he said, turning to walk away. He went to the exclusive, high-end women's boutique that was tucked off the main lobby. He found a Scottish-wool scarf that had the colors of Penny's eyes and had it wrapped up, and asked the sales girl to send it to the concierge with instructions to have it in the sleigh later.

These kind of romantic gestures he'd learned early on. Women appreciated them and he found that a happier woman made for a more enjoyable evening. And money had never been an obstacle for him. He knew the gift was small, but he also had realized pretty early on that it was the small things that mattered most in life.

And he wanted Penny. Wanted two weeks alone with the pretty blonde. He headed back to the bar and noticed her high-fiving her friends.

Maybe he was kidding himself by thinking she would agree to a two-week Christmas romance. Despite her throwing her phone earlier, she seemed like someone who was a bit healthier in relationships than he was.

He doubted she'd need anything from him. After all, it wouldn't be the first time he'd misjudged someone. But this time he hoped he was wrong. Because, more than anything, he wanted her to need him so he could focus on making her Christmas special and ignore the gnawing emptiness that he still felt deep inside. She pushed off the stool and turned to walk toward him. He watched the way she moved. Her hips swaying with each step she took. Her breasts bouncing the slightest bit. The effortless grace that was arresting to behold. He realized he was staring but didn't care. Penny smiled when she noticed him watching her, and for the first time since he'd started thinking about Christmas, he felt lighter. He didn't care if nothing else came of this evening than dinner in a pretty woman's company. For tonight that was enough.

He didn't have to think of the past or the bruises he always pretended weren't there. He could just enjoy this evening with a sweet, uncomplicated woman. Someone who could make him forget the truth of who he was.

"Ready?" she asked, coming up to him.

"I am. Are you going to be warm enough?"

"I think so. If not, you can keep me warm," she said with a wink.

"I can?"

"Unless you don't want to, but then that's the whole point of inviting me to dinner, right?"

"Indeed. Let's go." He nodded toward the bar. "Were those your friends?"

"Yes. They just got together so they are still kind of too cutesy each time they see each other."

"Too cutesy? I don't know what that means," he said.

"Kissy and huggy. Wow, now that I said it out loud, I really do sound jealous."

"I'll hug and kiss you if it makes you feel better," he drawled. "I believe in giving a lady what she wants."

"You're quite the white knight."

"What can I say? It's fun to make another person happy," he replied.

She slipped her hand into his. "Dinner is a good place to start."

He led the way to the semisecluded area where his name was on a chalkboard under the word *RESERVED*. They had a thick, camel-colored blanket on the padded bench and the fire was roaring. There were thick potted pine trees placed around the area with brightly colored Christmas lights on them.

Will gestured to the bench and she walked over and sat down on it. Joining her on the comfy seat, he draped the blanket over both of their laps. He saw one of the waitstaff standing discreetly out of the way and signaled the man to bring their meal.

As the food and a table were arranged in front of them, he stretched his arm behind her on the bench and leaned in. The clean floral scent of her perfume surrounded him. He closed his eyes, reminded of a spring day in the mountains near his home in California.

"I didn't ask if you had any dietary needs," he said.

"None," she admitted. "Healthy as a horse."

She shook her head and covered her mouth with one hand. "Maybe this would be more romantic if I didn't talk."

"Not at all. I like hearing you talk. So you think this is romantic?"

She gave him a sardonic look. "As if you didn't know. Yes, any woman worth her salt would think this was romantic."

"What's the problem then?" he asked, because there was definitely something more going on here.

"Just me being me. When I'm in a setting like this, I want to be perfect and all the ways that I'm not seem to make me stumble. I'm sorry… I want to be the glamorous sort of girl who'd fit right in here, but I'm going to say dumb things."

"No, you're not," he said softly.

"Trust me—I am."

"Honey, you're going to say things that are going to show me who you really are." Turning toward her, he stared into her captivating blue eyes. "Besides, I'm not interested in someone who is pretending to be perfect."

PENNY ENJOYED THE dinner that Will had ordered. It was just a smorgasbord of meats and cheese and artisanal breads from the Park City Bakery. But what made the dinner so lovely was Will. He was funny and urbane. Obviously well-traveled and cultured.

Being with him made her realize how lacking Butch had been in those departments. He put her at ease. Made her feel like it was okay to be herself. And for the first time since she'd learned Butch was married, she felt a spark of hope.

"You look very determined," Will said as he finished off the last of a cheese straw.

"Do I? I was hoping to look intriguing," she said with a self-deprecating laugh.

"It's hard when you keep laughing. Femme fatales don't laugh," he said.

"They don't? I've met a few spies and they do laugh," she said.

"Do they? How do you know they were spies? Maybe they were just pretending," he said.

"I wouldn't be surprised if they were. My mom is a lobbyist so I've met all kinds of people in DC. Speaking of which…what do you do? You haven't said."

"Sorry to say, I'm not a spy. In fact, I'm in commodities, so not even a really exciting job."

"I don't know that that means. Are you a trader?"

"More of a speculative investor. Commodities are things so I invest in things, not in people or ideas."

"Interesting," she said, still having no idea what he did.

He laughed. "I spend a lot of time on the internet doing research and reading company profiles before deciding if I should invest in them and their products."

"Is it profitable?"

"Usually," he said. "What do you do?"

"I'm sort of between jobs at the moment. I was the senior event planner for Papillion Clothiers," she said.

"Interesting," he said with a half grin.

She arched a brow. "Don't tell me you don't know what that is."

"I've heard of Papillion and I know what an event planner does, but I'm struggling to put the two together."

"Mostly I plan events around the various fashion weeks for our high-end clients," she said.

He glanced at her curiously. "Do you like it?"

"I love it. Clothes and parties, what more could a girl ask for?"

"Truly? Is that all it takes to make you happy?" he asked quietly.

Suddenly, she didn't feel like being light and pretending everything was perfect, but she knew she had to keep up the charade. No matter that he made her feel like it was okay to be herself. The past had taught her it wasn't. "Most days. Especially at work. It's a world I enjoy and I like getting paid for it."

"But in your personal life?"

"I like clothes and parties in that, too, but that's not all I need to be happy," she told him.

"What is?"

"I think defining happiness isn't a first-date subject," she said evasively.

"Is that so?" He leaned in closer and the scent of his spicy aftershave surrounded her. "As far as I'm concerned, there's not a better time."

"Why?"

"Because we don't know each other well enough to put up barriers. Right now there is just potential and we can be as honest with each other as we want to be."

"Okay, then. What makes *you* happy?" she asked. "If you want to do this, then you can go first."

"Touché," he said.

"It's harder than you thought it would be, isn't it?"

"Not at all. I'm just not all that into happiness. I'm more a contentment sort of guy," he replied.

"Really? Why is that?"

Will shrugged his broad shoulders and gave her an inscrutable look. "Happiness is a chimera. Something shimmering in the distance that most of us keep striving toward but never really reach. But contentment is easier. I mean, right now I've had a nice dinner with a very beautiful woman in front of a roaring fire. Nothing could be simpler than that."

Penny thought about what he'd said. There was more truth to it than she wanted there to be. He'd been honest and now she had to be, too. She owed it to the man who saw happiness dancing just out of his reach to stop pretending to be something she wasn't. Ultimately, she knew that she couldn't make another person happy. She never had been able to do it and doubted that in this moment with this man it would be any different. Contentment was all he was aiming for and she suspected she could manage at least that, but a part of her wanted more.

"I don't know if I buy into that. I've been truly happy at times, usually with my friends when I can let my guard down and be myself," she admitted.

"Are you being yourself now?" he asked softly.

"I am. Coming off a bad relationship makes it so clear to me that I can't stomach lies," she said.

Then wished she hadn't.

"I can't, either," he admitted. "Which is why I have a proposition for you."

She looked at him, trying to read the expression in his blue eyes, but in the flickering light of the fire that wasn't easy.

"I'm listening."

He rubbed his chin and gave her a rueful grin. "Don't take this the wrong way."

"Um…if you keep hedging, I'm not going to have much of a choice."

"I have a theory that has served me well most of my adult life about relationships and it's that the maximum time for them is two weeks."

"Two weeks?" Great. Sounded like he was another

guy who wasn't for her. But at least he was being honest. "Go on."

"Before I do, there is something I want to make sure of first."

He put his arm around her shoulder. Drew her closer to him, and she let him. Given that this might be their one and only date, she wanted to go for it.

Their eyes met and held, and she couldn't look away from his intense blue eyes and the expression in them. Whatever he meant by two weeks she wanted to know more. His breath brushed over her lips as he exhaled and he lowered his head slowly, giving her a chance to retreat, but she didn't want to back away.

She wanted his kiss. But she needed some answers first.

3

PENNY PUT HER hand on his jaw and felt the stubble of his five o'clock shadow. She liked the way it abraded her fingertips and she sighed.

"Sex. That's what you're proposing, isn't it?" she asked, withdrawing her hand from him and getting to her feet.

Penny shivered a little bit from the cold but stood her ground. She'd never been wishy-washy in her life. Even with her bad relationships, she'd gone into them with her eyes open.

"No. I'm talking about the fact that we both know we're going home in two weeks. It would be silly to pretend we didn't."

"Go on, I'm listening," she said as her teeth chattered.

She got back under the blanket and he tucked it around her. He smiled at her—it was tentative and roguishly charming, and she had to smile back. "The next two weeks, leading up to Christmas and then New Year's Eve, we spend together. We do all the things that couples do and we enjoy it."

She nodded, trying to be analytical about it, to treat

Will as if he were a businessman pitching an idea to her. "What's the catch?"

"That we both know it ends on New Year's Eve. That this is just temporary. To pretend this could be anything else is a lie."

She thought about it. She'd had her fill of lies that were told to her by men. "So you're proposing a vacation fling?"

"No, a Christmas affair…a sort of gift to each other," he said. "Unless you're not interested in me."

"I almost kissed you," she reminded him.

"The almost is the part that I'm concerned about," he said, frowning slightly.

"You kind of said you had a proposition for me. I needed to see what you meant before I took this any further." She hitched in a breath. "But for the sake of argument, why not try to make this into something real? Don't you believe in love at first sight?" she asked. "I know not everyone does, but some people do."

He rubbed the back of his neck and reached for his drink, taking a couple of swallows before looking her in the eyes. She knew stalling when she saw it.

"No lies," she said. "That's my rule if we even consider doing this. I don't care if it will hurt my feelings or if it's too raw for you. I will not tolerate any falsehoods."

"I think there is a story there," he said wryly.

"You haven't convinced me you should hear it yet," she retorted. "But it involves Jerk Butt Face."

He laughed. "I am not good at relationships. Courtship and romance I can do—no problem—but the heavy-duty lifetime-together crap, not so much."

She arched her eyebrow at him. "Might have something to do with the fact that you call it crap."

"Might be. But experience has taught me two weeks is my maximum," he said.

She wanted to know more about that but didn't push. He offered her something temporary. "You're proposing that we just both go into this with our eyes open. Have a great time and keep it light?"

It seemed almost too good to be true, but she was tempted. She needed something to make her remember all the things she loved about her life. And all the things she liked about being with a man.

Before Butch had come along and made her feel nothing but bitter resentment… "Yes," he said. "That's precisely what I'm looking for. But I'll understand if this isn't for you. Not everyone is good at compartmentalizing."

"I take it you are?" she asked.

"I am. But as you said, we don't know each other well enough to go into all that."

"The nice thing about what you're offering is that we don't have to. I don't have to try to make you into the man of my dreams."

"No, but I wouldn't mind being the man of your *fantasies*." His voice dropped a seductive notch. "I find that when women and men are too focused on making 'it' work, they lose out on experiencing all the things they truly want."

Boy, was that the truth. She hadn't been too pushy with Butch because he was her boss, but also because he had seemed like a nice normal guy. She'd called that wrong.

"Can I have some time to think about it?" she asked, biting her lip.

"You can, but we only have two weeks," he reminded her. "So don't take too long."

That was true. But— No, no buts, she thought. Thinking and weighing the pros and cons had netted her a holiday by herself. The gift she'd really wanted was a sexy man to share it with. Will was offering her that very thing.

It was only her fear that was keeping her from leaping into it. She didn't want to make another mistake. Who did?

"I have arranged for a little surprise for you," he said, breaking into her thoughts. "Why don't you think it over and meet me in the lobby under the mistletoe in thirty minutes if you're interested."

"What kind of surprise?" she asked, but she already realized that she liked his surprises.

"An outdoor one, so you might want to get changed," he said.

"What if I don't show up?" Penny asked. She tried to imagine him standing there waiting for her. No guy she'd dated in the past would have done that, would have left themselves so obviously open to being stood up. "Won't you feel silly standing there?"

"Not at all. I'll feel like a man who missed out on knowing a very special woman. I hope you'll take the chance and let me make this a Christmas we can both remember."

Penny wasn't too sure about Will or letting herself know him any better. Two weeks sounded fun in theory, but the truth was that she wasn't always supersmart when it came to love. She fell for all those losers and the sweet promises they made—but seldom kept—because inside she desperately wanted to be loved.

She knew it. Her therapist had confirmed it. And let's face it, all those bad boyfriends over the years had just reinforced it.

But Will was different. He wasn't making her any promises. All he'd said was, *Let's be each other's Christmas present. Meet under the mistletoe to accept.* And now she stood in the corner of the Lodge's big reception area, waiting to see if he was going to show up.

She'd taken her time with her hair and makeup, wore a pair of slim-fitting black pants and a cream-colored silk top that showed off her curves. She looked her best. But now she just had to believe in herself. That was part of why she kept falling for those guys who couldn't give her what she needed.

But believing in herself in a relationship was always a slippery slope.

"Hello, gorgeous," Will said, coming up behind her.

She flushed and turned toward him. A few snowflakes still clung to his thick brown hair, and his bangs fell forward, brushing his face. His blue eyes were bright, but she noticed that he was watching her carefully.

He wore dark jeans and an olive green sweater that accentuated his muscular physique and broad shoulders. A few snowflakes still clung to his thick brown hair and his bangs fell forward, brushing his face.

"Hello." She reached up on the premise of brushing the snow away but really just wanted to touch his hair.

"Are you waiting for me? Or hiding?"

"Neither," she said. "Just giving myself a swift mental kick in the attitude."

"Why is that?" he asked.

"I'm not sure about you yet, Will. I don't have a good track record with men—something we've discussed. And I have to be honest here, you are almost too good to be true."

"A sort of Christmas miracle?"

She had to laugh at the way he said it. He had enough confidence for both of them.

"I haven't decided yet. You could be a mean old Jack Frost just blowing chilly air and leaving ice in your path."

He gave her an enigmatic look as he peered down at her. "I have no way to prove I'm not. But we both know the girl who threw her phone in the snowbank wants to take a chance on me. So I'm going to go stand under that mistletoe and wait."

He walked away, his stride long and confident, those jeans still hugging his butt. Trans-Siberian Orchestra's "Christmas Canon" played in the background and Penny stood there, hesitating for a second before she realized that she wanted Will. Wanted him enough that she was going to go for it.

He'd said two weeks was the optimum time to just enjoy each other, and she was going to just have to take him at his word. Besides, Will seemed like the perfect sort of Christmas surprise that she couldn't *wait* to unwrap.

She walked slowly toward him, the music dipping and swelling, the scent of the large pine Christmas tree in the lobby filling the air. Her courage and her hope were building with each step.

She stopped right in front of him and he gave her a cocky grin. "Knew you couldn't resist me."

"Maybe I just felt bad for you standing all alone under the mistletoe," she said, leaning in to kiss him.

His mouth was soft and firm as his lips moved under hers. With their breaths mingling together, sheer physical need inundated her senses. She felt the tip of his tongue brush against her lips, then gently part them. Shivers ran down her spine until she forgot everything except this man. Will.

He put his hands on her waist to draw her closer, but she broke the kiss and stepped back. Just because she'd decided to take a chance on him didn't mean she was going to lose her head. She was going to keep her attraction to him under control.

"What was that?"

"A kiss," she said.

"A pity kiss? I expected more from you," he said.

"You're going to have to show me a little more of the man who thinks two weeks is enough time to get to know someone."

"Fair enough. I have a surprise for you," he said, sliding his hands up her back and pulling her into his arms for a more thorough kiss. He took his time with it and she was struck with how good he tasted. It wasn't just the fresh taste of his mouthwash; it was more than that. Something that seemed to stem entirely from Will.

He angled his head to the side and thrust his tongue deeper. She lifted her hands and framed his face with them. Spread her fingers over his five-o'clock shadow and then drew back.

"Where's this surprise?" she asked, even though she wanted to pull him into a nice private corner and have her way with him. Keep kissing him until they were both so turned on that they could forget about everything except each other.

"Outside. Did you bring a coat?"

"I did," she said.

She'd left it at the coat check and they walked over to get both of their coats. Then he led her out the door, which led to the ski slopes and outdoor area with fire pits and trails. A chill wind blew a light snow around them as they walked. Her neck was cold and she wished she'd brought a hat with her, but she'd forsaken it for vanity's sake—so her hair would look good.

Warm sounded better than nice hair at this moment, however. She turned her collar up around the back of her neck and shoved her hands deeper into her pockets.

"Damn, it's cold. We'll be warm in a few minutes," Will said. "Wait right here."

She watched as he strode away in the lightly falling snow. She almost felt the first tingles of that same worry that had bothered her in the lobby but she pushed it to the back of her mind. She'd made her decision. She had two weeks of just being with Will before she had to deal with the fallout from it.

THE SLEIGH WAS big and looked like it had come from a scene from one of the Currier and Ives lithographs that had hung in her grandparents' hallway when she'd been little. The driver introduced himself to them and as Will talked to him, Penny moved to the front of the sleigh to get a closer look at the horses.

She'd grown up back East in a fairly suburban area, but her best friend growing up had been raised on a horse ranch and Penny had always loved the animals.

"Ready?" Will asked.

She nodded, even though she felt a little nervous. Hell, after the way her last relationship had broken down who would blame her…but she'd made her decision and it was time to enjoy it.

"This is for you," he said.

"I didn't get you anything," she responded, taking the long square box that was wrapped in plain brown paper and tied with a simple red bow.

"You can owe me," he said with a wink.

"Have you done this a hundred times before?"

"It's a little unflattering you think I'm old enough to have experienced a hundred Christmases," he said flippantly.

"You know what I meant." Penny held the package with one hand and just watched him, wondering if he'd been serious about not lying. She was sorely tempted to embark on a red-hot affair with this handsome stranger, but if he was going to hedge and evade questions, she'd call the whole thing off.

"I do. And to answer your question—no, this isn't my normal MO. But I have had two-week affairs before. As I mentioned earlier, I pretty much don't do long-term."

She nodded. "Should I open this gift now?"

"Yes. The driver has gone to get the hot cocoa I ordered."

Penny turned the box over in her hands. Her first present from Will. She untied the red ribbon and took a moment to slip it in her pocket. It was that soft fabric kind. Then she carefully undid the wrapping paper.

"I've never seen anyone take as long to open a present."

She laughed. "Sorry about that. I like to savor things."

He reached over, pulling off his glove, and touched the side of her face. His hand was warm against her skin. "Me, too."

She leaned over and kissed him, just a quick brushing of lips before removing the rest of the paper. He took it from her and wadded it up in his hand and tossed the ball of wrapping into the nearby trash bin. "Open it."

She took the lid off the box and pushed the tissue paper aside to reveal a pretty, thick wool scarf. The colors were soft and muted, almost like the sky just after dawn. The wool was so soft that she couldn't stop touching it. It was an exquisite gift. "Thank you."

He nodded then reached into the box and took out the scarf. He stepped closer to her and wrapped it around her neck, tying it carefully before pulling her hair from the back where it had gotten trapped by the fabric.

"I really like it," she said.

He cupped her face and tipped her head up so that their eyes met. Even in the darkness his were still brilliantly blue. "I really like you."

He kissed her then, slowly, as if they had all the time in the world. Passion built inside her as his mouth moved over hers. His tongue was gentle but firm as he thrust it into her mouth and she dropped the box to the ground to reach for him. Putting her arms around his broad shoulders, pulling him close to her, she reveled in his power and strength. His chest was solid against hers even through the layers of their winter coats. And the snow that fell lightly around them was a counterpoint to the heat they generated.

He wrenched his lips from hers and then dropped a series of soft kisses on her face before he stepped back and bent to retrieve the box she'd dropped. He walked over to toss it in the trashcan. As he slowly headed back toward her, she watched the way he moved, with that confident stride and the languid grace of a man sure of himself and his woman. *His woman.* She had pretty much agreed to be that. Penny rubbed her lips, which still tingled from his kiss. She was electrified from his touch. Couldn't wait for him to kiss her again and to see how this evening turned out. What kind of lover would he be?

"Why are you watching me?"

"I like the way you move," she said, getting more excited by the prospect of this Christmas romance. There was no pressure to be what he wanted so they could make things work out. There was nothing for her to do except enjoy her time with him. Something about him just made her feel warm inside. When he was just a few feet away, she leaped toward him and saw a look of surprise before he opened his arms to catch her.

She laughed as he hugged her close and spun her around. She threw her head back as the snowflakes fell on her face and she released all the past hurts and emotional baggage that she normally carried with her. For this Christmas, she was ready to let go and enjoy it.

He slowly lowered her down the length of his body and she kissed him with all the fierce desire building up inside of her. She couldn't believe that it had only been this morning when she'd met him.

Savoring the moment, the feel of his lips ravaging hers, she marveled at how someone's world could change that quickly. How a chance encounter could completely make her open her eyes to a world she had never realized existed until now.

"I guess you like the scarf," he said wryly as he put her on her feet.

"I do. But I like you more. I think this is going to be the best Christmas I've had in a long time."

"Me, too," he murmured.

The attendant returned and the driver climbed into the front of the carriage while she and Will were seated in the back. The blankets they had for their legs were thick and woven in a traditional red, green and gold plaid. They were handed a thermos and two insulated mugs for their drinks, which were stowed in a small basket on the floor.

"Ready?" the driver asked.

They nodded and the sleigh took off, pulling them through the snow with only the sounds of their breathing, the bells on the horses' necks and the whistle of the blades over the snow to accompany them.

4

WILL WRAPPED HIS arm around Penny as the sleigh traveled over the path in the moonlight. The snow had stopped falling and the trees on either side of them were all aglow with white lights that made the snow twinkle as they moved past it. The high back of the sleigh kept them protected from the wind.

He hadn't expected his present to generate the reaction it had from her. She was cute and sexy and all signs pointed to her being everything he wanted in a lover. But he'd felt something else when she'd thanked him for the scarf.

A stirring of unfamiliar emotion that had been so intense he'd had to force it back down inside himself. He wanted Penny, he reiterated to himself. He was going to enjoy Christmas with a woman instead of by himself, but that was it.

"Do you know how to pick out any of the stars?" Penny asked, jarring him out of his thoughts. "I've always really liked looking up at them, but I'm afraid I can't ever pick any of the constellations out."

He tipped his head back, gazing up at the sky. "I know the basic ones. Like right there is the Little Dipper."

He pointed to it.

She looked up. "Do you see the star the wise men followed?"

"I can't really, but I bet we could find a bright star that would work."

"Or we could each find a star that is leading us," she said. "My mom used to do that whenever we couldn't find an answer. Or if we didn't have a tradition, she'd say let's make up something we both like."

He liked the sound of her mom. He'd come to terms with the fact that he'd never have that kind of family. His parents' death in a car crash had left him set for life financially, but there were times when he was reminded of the stuff he'd missed out on. Penny made him want to have that. She was spontaneous, he realized. The phone throwing, the jumping into his arms...

Did she always leap like that?

"Have you ever followed something like a star?" he asked curiously. It seemed like something she'd do. "Just took off believing it would lead you to something special?"

"No... Well, that's not true. One time I followed a dog I spotted after school. Every day after that, for a straight week, it waited for me outside of my classroom. I thought it was a stray and that maybe I could keep him."

She turned to face him, her pretty gaze serious, and she licked her pink lips. His eyes tracked the movement and his blood flowed thicker in his veins. "What happened next?"

"When I approached the dog it sort of took off, not running but just heading somewhere. I had saved half of my sandwich at lunch so I could sort of bribe the dog. It was a cute little poodle and in my head I'd named it Fifi."

"Sounds like you had a plan," he said.

"And a big imagination. It's part of the reason I'm good at creating events," she said. "So I followed Fifi and she turned down my street. I was eight at the time so please don't think this is too lame."

"I'd never think you were lame," he said, enjoying the way she told the story. Seeing how her eyes sparkled and hearing that note of excitement and joy in her voice was truly infectious.

"Okay, I was so excited. Fifi trotted past my house, but instead of stopping at my place, she ran straight past it. I followed her round the corner and saw her disappear through a redbrick house with a doggy door."

"I'm sorry you didn't get your dog," he said.

She laughed good-naturedly. "I was so disappointed, but it wasn't meant to be. I did have a fun adventure following the dog, though. And my mom got us a cute miniature dachshund when I told her the story." He thought about Penny's story. He'd never been that aware of his environment, sure he'd followed things on the internet, but in the real world he tended to just keep his head down and move forward. He couldn't remember ever being different even as a child.

"That's sweet."

"Thanks," she said. "She was good about making sure I had what I wanted. Not that I was spoiled or anything."

His lips twitched with humor. "Sure you weren't."

"It's hard to not be a little spoiled when you're the only child," she admitted with a cheeky grin.

"What about you? Spoiled? Siblings?" she asked.

"Only child, as well."

She arched her eyebrow at him. "We both are used to getting our way, then. That could make things interesting."

"I wasn't spoiled," he said. He left it at that. He didn't want to talk about his parents' deaths or being raised by distant relatives. It created an image that he wasn't comfortable sharing with her. They were temporary playmates, nothing more.

"Did you ever follow anything home?"

"No. I'm usually very focused on getting what I want. Instead of following dogs or stars, I'd use my computer and do a load of research before starting out."

She rolled her eyes. "Sounds kind of boring."

"Perhaps, but I don't waste time and I get my end result every single time. I try to eliminate all the variables so I don't have to deal with surprises."

"But surprises are the best part of life," she said.

"That hasn't been my experience."

Shaking her head at him, she countered, "That's not true."

He gave her a look from under his eyelashes.

She punched him playfully in the shoulder. "You're wrong. Today I bet you weren't expecting an iPhone to come flying through the air at you."

She had him there. She knew it, too—he saw it on her face. "That's true."

"Also you didn't expect that I'd be so intriguing," she said.

Right again. He definitely hadn't expected Penny, and he was learning that even though he'd thought he'd managed all the variables with this Christmas liaison, perhaps he had forgotten something very important. The Penny factor.

SHE WAS HAVING FUN—despite the fact that after the past few months, the stress of quitting her job and hoping for a new one, she still hadn't gotten the call she'd been hoping for today. But given that the East Coast was two hours ahead of them, she doubted they would be calling before tomorrow.

Her real life was still a mess but tonight that didn't seem to matter as much. Will had wrapped his arm around her shoulder and tucked her against his side. He had gone quiet after she'd told him about Fifi but maybe he was thinking…who knew what. The bells of the horses rang across the empty fields as they continued their ride, and she felt the hope and joy of the season all around her.

Suddenly, she found herself humming the beginning of "Jingle Bells" under her breath. The song was stuck in her head now. Ugh. She couldn't start singing. Wouldn't let herself do that.

But there it was.

"Dashing through the snow," Will said, under his breath, too.

She tipped her head back and started laughing. "Is that song also in your head?"

"It's impossible for it not to be. We are in the middle of a freakin' Norman Rockwell Christmas scene."

"I would have said Currier and Ives."

He shook his head. "You like to argue, don't you?"

She thought about that for a long minute. She did have to always make sure she had her own opinion. "I never thought of it that way. I just want to make sure I'm standing on my own, not following someone else."

"Me, too. And this is definitely Norman Rockwell. You'll never convince me otherwise."

"Are you sure?"

"How could you possibly? I've made my mind up and I never change it," he said.

"Never? Are you sure about that?"

He nodded. "I can promise you I will never change my mind. Once a decision has been made I stick to it."

"Duly noted," she said. It was something that she might see as a red flag if they were going to date long-term, but for two weeks…what did that matter? "Jingle bells, jingle bells…"

He squeezed her close, putting his finger under her chin, and when he tipped her head back, she looked up at the strong line of his jaw. There was a tiny birthmark under his chin. Something she wouldn't have noticed if they hadn't been sitting so close. She reached up and touched it.

"Beauty mark," she said.

"Beauty?"

"That's what my mom always calls them. She has one that looks like a strawberry along her neck, and she says it's a mark of inner beauty." Penny missed her mom but she was in the Caribbean with her new husband celebrating the holidays. Exhaling softly, she stroked his neck. It was strong and had the tiniest bit of beard stubble on it. His light brown hair brushed the side of his face and she pushed it out of the way.

"No one has ever suggested there was anything beautiful about me," he said gruffly.

She looked into those incredible blue eyes of his and wondered about this man. She had a bunch of questions about his past. What had shaped him into the person he was today? Why would anyone be satisfied with two-week relationships?

But she kept those questions to herself. "You have to know you are a very beautiful man."

"Rugged maybe. And I get charming a lot…but beauty? Nah." She understood where he was coming from. But there was something about his confidence and the way he pushed her to take him on his terms that contributed to what she saw when she looked at him.

Or at least what she saw now, on this magical snow ride. "Well, we can agree to disagree."

"Which we've already established you like to do," he said, winking at her.

She pretended to elbow him in the gut. Playing around to control her emotions so she didn't let things turn too serious. "Keep it up and I'll show you what a fierce competitor I can be."

"Are you one?"

She shrugged. "I sometimes say it doesn't really matter to me if I win, but it does. I hate losing. Not that I want to beat anyone else—I just like being right."

She laughed and so did he.

"Me, too." He rubbed his chin on the top of her head and held her lightly in his arms.

"What are you thinking?" she whispered.

Their sleigh ride was getting close to its end and the snow started to fall a little more heavily. They huddled together but the snow was cold as it fell on them. Will maneuvered around and pulled the blanket up over their backs and then their heads. She looked at him and realized how safe he'd made her feel tonight.

Not just physically safe, but emotionally. He'd listened to her and didn't judge her. Just let her be who she was. Probably because they weren't trying to impress each other. Though, frankly, he'd more than done that with dinner, the gift and this sleigh ride. She had relaxed her guard.

He kissed the tip of her nose as they returned to the Lodge. "Thank you for making this a very special night."

She shook her head in bewilderment. "How have I done that?"

"By sharing your stories and that sparkle that I think might just be you."

"I *sparkle*?" she asked with a giggle. "Did you really just say that?"

He freed them both from the blanket and stood up, holding his hand out to her. She took it and he helped her to her feet and then out of the sleigh.

She stood to one side as he thanked the driver and tipped him and then turned back to her. The snow still fell over him, making him look even more strikingly handsome, and for a moment she wondered if she might have made a huge mistake. This arrangement was just supposed to be about having fun, but she saw signs that Will might be the kind of man she wanted in her life for a lot longer than one Christmas.

Two days later, Will walked through the quaint Park City streets looking for some new ski gear. He and Penny had said good-night at her front door after their sleigh ride and he'd walked away without a kiss. But the ride hadn't gone exactly to plan. He had meant it as a prelude to seduction but the truth was he liked her. She stirred things deep inside him that he liked to pretend he never felt and didn't care about.

But that was a lie.

He'd always been one of those men who knew where he was going. When he'd gotten out of rehab, he'd made choices that had pointed him toward his future. He eliminated all the things that were enablers for him.

First order of business: he'd stopped partying 24/7 and started working. A part of him found it surprising that he had the golden touch when it came to making money. But he had found his niche and that was enough for him. However, two nights ago, he'd felt like that had begun to change. He hadn't slept well since then and he wondered if he would again.

And it was all *her* fault.

As Will continued his stroll through the town, he paused at the corner where a mural of the Wasatch Mountain Range was on the side of Fresh Sno's retail store. It was really well done.

"Nice picture, eh?"

He glanced over his shoulder to see Penny standing there. She had a Fresh Sno bag in one hand. Her blond hair was hanging around her shoulders under a pink knit hat. Her coat was a deep turquoise wool and she had it buttoned to the top with the scarf he'd given her wrapped around her neck.

"Yes, it is. Are you following me?" he asked with a grin. For the first time in a long time, he was struggling to keep his flirtations light. He knew that was a danger sign. It might be better for both of them if he just walked away now. They hadn't even slept together. No harm, no foul.

"Following you? No, not at all. I decided I need a little retail therapy and my friend Bradley owns this place. He's the guy half of my cutesy friend couple. I stopped by to get some new ski gear. Want to join me on the slopes?"

Just like that, she made it seem normal that he hadn't

talked to her in one entire day. They had only a limited number of days to spend together and he'd wasted one.

"Sorry about not being able to see you yesterday." He'd sent her a note via the hotel concierge desk that he'd had to work.

"It's fine. To be honest, this arrangement is harder for me than I thought it would be. But I understand about having work commitments so it's not a big deal." She spared him a look. "Of course, if we were a *real* couple, it might have bothered me. But that's clearly not the case…"

Work had been a convenient excuse, but he'd needed distance and now he regretted it. He'd never been a coward— *Ha!* his conscience jibed. Alcohol had been his crutch a long time ago and now seemed like Penny was.

"Any word from the people in New York on your new job?" he asked.

"Just that they were still weighing their options and would be getting back to me in the new year. So I have nothing else to do in the meantime." She flashed him a coy look. "And the way I see it, I have two options here. I can either distract myself by having fun with you, *or* I can just relive my interview over and over again, trying to come up with all the things I could have done better."

He was willing to bet she'd wowed them. Penny had that thing that made people notice her. Made her stand out.

"I don't want to be responsible for all that misery," he deadpanned. "So skiing? That's your idea for today?"

"Yes. I'm not an expert at it, and I'm certainly not very daring, but I do like to spend a few hours on the slopes. Want to join me?"

"I would enjoy that. But I could use some new ski gear, too," he said. "That's why I'm here at Fresh Sno. I've heard about the brand and directed several of my investment clients toward them, so I thought I'd check out their retail space."

"I'll leave you to your shopping, then. Want to meet me at the ski rental at the Lodge in two hours?" She was being more cautious with him today. But then in the light of day that wasn't too surprising. Night seemed to be the time for daring.

"Want to join me? Where else are you going?"

"That kitchen shop up the block. I need some sprinkles for cookies," she said.

"I think the ones at the Lodge's bakery come with sprinkles."

She flashed a grin. "They do, wise guy, but I'm making my own. I mean you have to bake cookies at Christmas. I think it's a law or something."

"I've never done it. I hope the cops don't find out," he said.

"You're kidding, right?"

He shook his head.

"That's sad, Will. *Really* sad. You've spent your whole life missing out on eating the batter and broken cookies."

He wrinkled his nose. "I'm not sure that's a bad thing."

She nodded. "Well, it is. I'm not baking cookies until Saturday. Want to come to my place and help me?"

"Okay," he said. "I'll do that. Which kitchen store are you going to?"

She pointed to the big chain kitchen store down the block. The streets were draped with festive garland. "If you meet me there after you get your ski gear, you can pick out a couple of cookie cutters, too."

He nodded. "Sounds like a plan."

She smiled at him. "Later then."

He stood where he was, watching her walk away and wondering when he'd lost control of this affair. He had a feeling that it had started the moment her cell phone had come flying out of nowhere. As soon as he'd seen that pink jewel-covered case, and those long legs, he should have run in the opposite direction.

She was different than what he was used to. He didn't know if that would have any impact on him, but he hoped not. He didn't want his world to change.

Change. It was the one thing he feared the most. But he was coming to realize that there was a certain thrill in facing his fears, and he certainly wasn't ready to throw in the towel where Penny was concerned.

5

THE KITCHEN STORE was jam-packed with high-end appliances and prepackaged baking mixes. But what Penny was interested in wasn't the baking section. Why hadn't Will ever baked Christmas cookies? She didn't mean as a man, but as a kid. Even her co-workers all had stories, men and women alike, of being in the kitchen at the holidays. Even if they didn't bake them, most men stood in the kitchen, pretended to decorate and ate them fresh out of the oven.

It was one of those things she and her mom had made a tradition of when Penny was about ten. Prior to that, they'd bought cookies from a small mom-and-pop place that was a few blocks from their house. But the bakery had closed since the couple wanted to retire and move to Florida, so her mother had suggested they make their own. Penny had a chuckle at the way they'd both been very unskilled at first, but over the years, they had gotten a lot better. Still smiling to herself, she browsed the baking section. Her chalet had a small kitchen with a tiny oven so she took a few moments to get all the necessities.

"Is an elf going to be cooking with you?" Will said

as he joined her like they'd agreed. He reached into her basket to remove the small spatula she'd just tossed in her bag.

"No, silly. That's a cookie spatula—it enables you to get the cookies from the tray without scrunching them up."

He furrowed his dark brow. "Interesting. What kind of cookies are you making?"

"We are making a basic sugar-cookie dough and then rolling it out, cutting it into cookies, baking them and then frosting them."

"Sounds like a lot of work," he said with a grimace. "I think I might have to wait for the *eating them* part. Maybe just supervise you working…"

"Are you good at supervising?"

"If I'm honest?"

Penny nodded but was only half listening to his answer. She bit her lower lip as she looked at him, with his thick brown hair falling loosely around his face and scarf tied nonchalantly around his neck. Part of her wished she'd just invited him back to her chalet two nights ago. Got rid of the desire that made it impossible for her to do anything but watch his lips move and wonder how they'd feel on her skin.

She wanted him. She'd dreamed of him in her bed last night. And she knew that today, unless he really screwed up, somehow she was going to have him there. Two days were gone of her fourteen with him. She didn't want to waste another second like she had yesterday by giving him space to work. She was in as much control of this affair as he was.

"What?" she asked, upon realizing he'd stopped talking and was staring at her.

"I said I'm not good at supervising but I can tell you are. Are you okay?"

She tipped her head to the side. "I'm…fine. I was just, uh, looking at your hair and wondering how it would feel between my fingers. I really didn't get to touch it when we were on our sleigh ride because I had my gloves on."

His eyes darkened and he stepped closer to her in the busy shop. No one was paying them the least bit of attention, as they were all busy getting their own purchases made. He stood pressed against her front, the cookie-cutter baskets to her back, and he put his hands lightly on her waist, bringing his face so close to her that each exhalation of his breath brushed over her mouth.

His breath was minty again, his aftershave outdoorsy, and she breathed it all in. Breathed *him* in. Closed her eyes and tried to make a sense memory that she could carry with her forever. But then she forced her eyes open. Not forever. Just for Christmas.

"Touch it now," he said.

She lifted her hand and tangled her fingers in the thick, rich strands of his dark hair. It was cool from him being outdoors without a hat on and a few snowflakes that hadn't melted were caught in it. She pulled her fingers downward, letting the strands spread out and then fall back against his head.

He had his eyes half-closed and watched her carefully. She felt her pulse racing and her blood seemed to be pumping a lot faster. She wanted him.

Penny licked her lips, which felt dry, and noticed he tracked the movement with his half-hooded gaze. She felt his hands in her hair, slowly winding a lock around his finger before letting it go. They he cupped the back of her head, spread his fingers out and angled her head before he brought his mouth down on hers.

The kiss was quick and hot. Full of passion and promise, determination and desire. He wanted her, too.

He pulled back and her lips were tingling and every nerve in her body awakened. Suddenly skiing and baking cookies didn't seem like anything she had to do today. She wanted to find a private place and rip his clothes off. Explore the rest of his body and then take him and make him hers.

Someone bumped into them and Penny looked down into the face of a five-year-old girl with a gap-toothed grin.

"I'm looking for a princess cookie cutter," she said. "Can you help me?"

Will laughed and stepped back, crouching next to the little girl to start searching in the baskets with her. And Penny took several breaths to try to feel normal again, but as she picked through the cookie cutters, she had a sinking feeling that she wasn't going to find her way back to normal that easily.

She found a tiara and finally a princess cutter. "Here you go."

"Thank you," the little girl said, racing away.

Will had two in his hands when he stood up.

"What do you have there?"

"A rolling pin-shaped cookie cutter, because I never want to forget standing in this store with you," he said with a devilish gleam in his eye, "and a sleigh."

She took his cutters and added them to her basket. The cashier was friendly as they approached, smiling warmly at them.

"You are the cutest couple," she gushed.

Penny realized she didn't know how to respond, but Will threw his arm over her shoulder. "Yes, we are."

THEY TOOK TWO runs down the slopes before calling it a day. For Will, if he'd been on his own, he would have kept skiing, but honestly even the most interesting ski slopes couldn't compare to the excitement he felt with Penny.

He'd been turned on since the cookware shop, and their ride back to the Lodge and then up the mountain on the ski lift hadn't changed that. The bulk of their afternoon had been touching, sort of kissing and a lot of teasing.

He thought that Penny knew she was keeping him in a state of semiarousal with those teasing touches, and it really didn't bother him too much since he had plans to end all the teasing tonight.

"Want to warm up by the fire pit?" he asked after they'd turned their skis back in to the rental stand.

"I'd love to. Grab our spot and I'll get us a couple of hot drinks," she said.

"That's nice, but I'm the white knight, remember? Why don't you sit down and I'll get the drinks?"

She gave him a sweet smile. "That's very old-fashioned. But I like it."

"Cocoa?"

"Sounds great," she said.

He watched as Penny took a seat and went to the bar to order their drinks. She glanced up and caught him watching so he pulled out his phone to check his email instead. He needed to keep his priorities straight. There wasn't anything urgent on his phone, and he shoved it into his pocket trying to pretend that he didn't feel tense again.

"Hello," the bartender said. "What can I get you to drink?"

"Cocoa please. Two of them."

"Enjoying a getaway with the girlfriend?" the bartender asked as he made the drinks.

"Um…yes, I am." But Penny wasn't his girlfriend. Not the way the bartender meant it.

Normally when he went away for Christmas it wasn't this Christmassy. He went to the Caribbean and stayed at all-inclusive resorts and just hung out on the beach or in his beachfront room with his lover.

There were no holiday-themed dates in the Caribbean. So different from this year. The very essence of what he was doing with Penny was holiday-themed.

A part of him was okay with that because each year needed to be different. Snow instead of sand this year. He had no desire to be like Bill Murray in the movie *Groundhog Day*, reliving his life over and over again.

He hoped he'd learned and moved on.

But as he watched her walking toward him, he realized he was skating on a very fine edge. He had to be careful to remember that no matter how much this seemed like a "real" holiday, it was still a two-week dalliance. And that was it.

That was all it could be. She was smiling as she sauntered toward him, and he had that feeling that he was on the cusp of something that could change him. Maybe he should just walk away now. Because if he were completely honest with himself, he'd have to admit that sex might not be enough with her. That even an afternoon of skiing left him wanting to do a lot more with her.

He handed her a mug of frothy hot cocoa before sitting down next to her.

"Do you like whipped cream?" she asked.

"I do," he said. Then realized that even if he didn't, he might be tempted to drink it just to see her keep on smiling. There was something about her smile that got to him.

"You are a really good skier," she remarked.

"Thank you. When I was young, when my parents were still alive, we used to ski every winter. I grew up on the slopes."

"You can tell. So your parents are dead?" she asked, then made a face. "I know that sounds dumb and wasn't a very tactful way of saying it. I'm sorry about your mom and dad."

"It's okay," he said. "They died when I was ten. I was already signed up for boarding school and summer camps so my relatives who inherited my care weren't burdened by me."

"*Burdened* by you?" she asked incredulously. "That's not a very nice way of saying that. Didn't they want you?"

How had he gotten on this topic? He was usually more careful with how he talked about his past. "All I meant is they had busy lives and I was already established in mine."

She wrinkled her nose at him. "I'm not sure if I should hug you because of that, but you seem okay with it. Was there any fallout to growing up that way?"

He definitely wasn't going to get into all that. "One perk is that I get to spend my holidays in the company of lovely women like you."

She pursed her lips. "That's…flippant. But I guess that's all that we really have between us."

He shook his head. "It isn't. Already you feel different to me, but we both know we are going back to our real worlds on January 1."

The reminder wasn't just for Penny; it was also for himself. He'd tried relationships in the past, and if he was being honest, they simply didn't work for him. He'd shut down all of his emotions when his parents died. He'd been left alone and hadn't really understood how to cope. There were no relatives clamoring to take him in and he'd been sent back to school and camp. Not having a "home" after his parents died had left something broken inside of him. He knew that.

"Don't worry. I'm not looking for serious," she promised him. "Just fun. Christmas fun! With a man who could ski me under the table, but stuck to the moderate runs. Thank you for doing that."

"Why would I want to ski by myself when I could share it with you?" he said huskily.

She smiled at him. "I will say this—whoever taught you to talk to women did a very good job."

"How so?"

"You seem to always know the right thing to say," she said.

He winked. "I like to think it's part of my charm."

"It might be," she said.

They sipped their cocoa and talked about current events, but he noticed she'd stopped the teasing touches and worried that she might have changed her mind about a no-strings-attached affair.

IT WAS REASSURING to hear Will's comments. Really, it was. That's what Penny told herself as she stood in the living area of her chalet and painted her toenails before she went to see Will later that evening.

He wasn't going to change the rules halfway through this. He'd said two weeks, he meant two weeks. That was what she'd wanted to hear. What she'd needed to hear. He said he wouldn't lie to her and he hadn't.

Except now she sort of wished he had. She sort of needed him to at least pretend—what? That he'd changed his mind? Well, she wasn't going to change hers. She wasn't ready for a serious relationship. Not now.

She had to sort out her real life and figure out her next steps—she had no time for a man. Even one who made her remember all the reasons why she wanted a lover in her life.

The day had turned unexpectedly for her when she'd seen Will in town. She'd enjoyed flirting with him all afternoon, and touching him had been pure bliss. God, she wanted him. She knew that the sex probably wouldn't be as good as she was anticipating. Nothing against Will… it was simply that in the past, when she'd had this much buildup, the guy came after three thrusts and she was left lying there wondering what the heck had happened.

But another part of her was convinced he might be the best lover she'd ever have. So far he was an ace at shattering all of her illusions. Every time she thought she had him figured out, he did something else to force her to look at him again.

For instance, this afternoon when he'd talked about losing his parents so nonchalantly, it had been like a knife in her heart. No child should think of themselves that way—of "not being a burden" to the adults in their life. But Will did. He hadn't said it to gain her sympathy or anything like that, just stated a fact that would warp a lesser man.

To be fair, there was something maybe a little damaged about only wanting a two-week relationship, but he seemed to be okay with it.

Now she just had to be okay with it, too.

She finished painting her nails and leaned back on the couch, putting her feet on the coffee table. With a heavy sigh, she stared up at the ceiling. What was wrong with her? She owed it to Will to keep her emotions in check.

Her mind was still going a million miles a minute when her phone rang. She glanced at the screen to see Elizabeth's name on the caller ID.

She contemplated not answering it, but Elizabeth was her best friend. The one she could talk to about anything. "Hey," she said before she changed her mind and chickened out.

"Hey, you. I'm calling to see if you'd like to have dinner with me tonight. Bradley is heading to Europe for a few days on business."

"I can't tonight," she said. "Maybe tomorrow?"

"Okay, sounds good. What are you doing tonight?" Elizabeth asked. "It's none of my business but I'm nosey."

Penny laughed. "Remember that hottie I almost hit with my phone? I might see him later."

"Sounds like fun," Elizabeth said.

"I'm sure it will be," Penny replied. She just had to remember that it was the holidays. She could be free and do what she wanted to do. There were no rules that said every guy she dated had to have the potential to be the one. Hell, half the time she never thought beyond the next date, but because she and Will had set a time frame, all she could hear was the clock ticking down the days until he was gone.

"Are you okay?" Elizabeth asked.

"Yes, I'm fine. Will is a lot of fun. We went skiing

this afternoon and I'm sure he has some over-the-top romantic thing planned for tonight."

It was just like Will to do that. She didn't know much about him, if she was being honest, but she had realized that romance was something he was good at. And she supposed if a man asked a woman to have a short-term affair it was in his best interest to make it the best two weeks of her romantic life.

"Like what? I'm not very good at romantic gestures. Maybe I can steal a few ideas and blow Bradley's socks off."

"He took me on a sleigh ride on our first date. It was sweet and sexy."

"Have you slept with him?"

"Elizabeth!"

Her friend didn't say anything for a few minutes. "Did you?"

"Not yet. I want to. But he's so good at being all the things I want in a man, and you know my past with lovers hasn't been great…so I'm sort of afraid to. I don't want it to ruin that perfect image I have of him."

"Fair enough, but if he's as good at romance and all the other stuff as you say, I'm willing to bet he won't let you down in bed."

That was what she was afraid of. If he were a disappointing lover it would be a lot easier to accept that this would end.

"I've got to go, hon," Elizabeth said a moment later. "Bradley is calling me on the other line. But I want to hear all about this hot date tomorrow."

"Of course," Penny said, hoping she'd have something

good to tell her friend. She knew she just had to get her head around this Christmas present she was giving herself. But it was a lot harder than she'd anticipated.

6

WILL HAD PLANNED the evening carefully. He was tired
of waiting and suspected Penny was, too. Tonight that
would end.

He'd take her to his bed, make love to her, and she'd
go back to being like every other woman he'd ever met.
Although he was happy with his plan, it had to go off
without a hitch. Which meant that the ambiance had
to be ultraromantic. To that end, he'd ordered dinner
from the Lodge's Cajun-inspired restaurant, and had the
food warming in the little kitchenette. He had a blanket spread out on the floor, and had even asked the staff
at the Lodge to decorate the mantle with garland and
brightly colored Christmas lights. Glancing around the
room, he smiled to himself. It had taken some finesse,
but finally everything was the exact way he wanted it
to be. After smoothing his hands over the blanket one
last time to make sure it was soft enough for Penny, he
checked the timers on the oven and the bottle of red
wine he had opened, then got his coat on and left to go
and collect his date.

He adjusted the wreath on the front of his door and

flicked on the switch to the lights, which framed his entryway. Now the exterior of his place looked just as festive as the inside, and as he stepped out into the lightly falling snow, he let the wind and the snowflakes carry away his apprehension about pursuing a relationship with Penny.

Somehow he'd managed to mess himself up when it came to this woman by letting her grow too big in his imagination. Once they had sex, however, and this settled down to something similar to his normal dating routine, everything would be fine.

He arrived at her chalet and knocked on her door.

"Coming."

He waited, looking distractedly at the tiny Santas that were dotted around the wreath on her front door.

"Hello," she said as she opened it.

A wave of warm air surrounded him and he caught his breath as Penny stood there in a form-fitting black velvet dress that ended at her midthigh. She had her blond hair curled and then piled high on her head with a tendril on either side framing her face.

Her blue eyes sparkled and her lipstick was shiny, drawing his eyes to her mouth. He leaned in for a kiss before he could think better of it. She pulled back.

"No mistletoe."

"I didn't think I needed mistletoe to kiss you," he murmured.

"That depends," she said coyly.

"On?"

"If you will give me time to fix my lipstick before we leave," she replied, with a tinkling laugh that made his gut clench and his cock harden. He wanted her. He realized he'd been carefully playing a game with himself and not with her. He had been trying so hard to make her blend into the pack of women he'd had in his life when she clearly stood out.

"You won't need to. We are having dinner at my place," he said.

She reached for a long cream-colored wool coat and handed it to him. "So I guess we're done with playing the slow game?"

"I am," he said, looking her in the eye. "Aren't you?"

She nodded. "But to be honest, I'm kind of nervous. I keep making myself more and more anxious by try-ing to make this—"

"Don't overthink it, sweetheart. It's just you and me. There are no right or wrong actions here. Just whatever feels right to us." He smiled down at her. "And if we just enjoy dinner by my fireplace and you want to go home alone, then that is what will happen."

She smiled back. "Thank you."

"You're welcome," he said, taking her coat and hold-ing it up for her to put on.

Despite his outward bravado, Will realized her nerves mirrored his own. There was something different about her…and maybe it was just that he was experiencing a white Christmas, or the fact that it had been two years since he'd had a holiday affair, but something made Penny seem special.

The Penny factor.

He kept forgetting that. As soon as she had her coat on, she closed and locked her door and looked over at him. She licked her lips and tipped her head to the side as she watched him.

He let his gaze drift down over her from the top of her head to those ridiculously sexy high-heeled stilettos she wore on her feet. She was pure temptation and he didn't have to deny himself. It was a heady feeling. Made him feel like he was on a wild binge and on the edge of doing something crazy. Much the same as he had back in the days when he used to drink too much.

He lifted her off her feet and swung her up in his arms. She clutched his shoulders and asked breathlessly, "What are you doing?"

"You're wearing heels. Not ideal for walking on a snowy path," he said, walking carefully down the steps toward said path.

"No one has ever carried me before. I mean my mom probably did when I was little, but I can't remember anyone carrying me."

"I'm glad," he replied. He wondered where her father was. She never mentioned the man, but that was *real life*. Not this special, magical Christmas they had promised to spend together.

"I like it," she said giddily. "I might let you carry me again."

He planned to carry her to his bed later tonight, but for right now he was content to set her on her feet at the front door of his chalet. He unlocked it and held the door open for her.

Will took her coat and hung it on the peg near the door, and then pulled her into his arms for the kiss that she'd denied him earlier. She came up on her tiptoes, meeting him halfway, and put her hands firmly on his shoulders. Her lips parted under his as he thrust his tongue deep into her mouth.

She moaned and leaned forward, brushing her breasts against his chest. He slipped his hands down to her waist, lifted her off her feet again, and spun so that he was leaning against the wall and could hold her nestled against him.

Penny's hands slid up his shoulders to his neck. Her fingers stroked his neck and his erection grew with each touch. She sucked his lower lip between her teeth and bit down carefully, then pulled back.

"Dinner first," she said.

Nodding, he set her down and away from him. He gestured for her to go into the living room as he went to the kitchen area. "Would you like a glass of wine?"

"Yes, please," she said.

He poured her one and then poured himself a highball glass of Perrier. "To new beginnings."

She lifted her glass to his and took a sip. "You don't drink?"

"No, I don't."

She perched on one of the stools that were set by the breakfast bar, putting her wineglass on the counter. "Why not?"

"I used to drink too much. Found I was losing control and decided I didn't like it. So I stopped."

She narrowed her eyes at him. "Why is it that everything that happens to you fits into some neat explanation?"

"How do you mean?" he asked, setting his glass next to hers on the counter and taking out the tray of cheese, bread and olives he'd prepared for an appetizer.

"Just that you seem to bottle everything up in a neat little jar after you deal with it."

He led the way to the living room and heard her following. "Can you sit in that skirt?"

She nodded. "But I'm not going to unless you give me some answers."

"I promise you I will," he said, offering her his hand as he set the tray on the blanket. She walked over, carefully sitting down, and a moment later he joined her.

He didn't like to talk about his problems. Drinking, lack of parents, the fact that he sometimes had to deal with some unexplained anger. He'd managed all of these things by carefully putting them in compartments and locking them away.

"I'm waiting," she said carefully. "I've known a few friends who have had addiction problems, and not one of them could have an open bottle of wine in their home and not drink it."

He leaned back against the sofa and took a moment to figure out the best way to answer her. The truth of course had to be an element of his answer, but *his* version of it. He didn't want her to see him too clearly.

"Tonight there is little chance that I will be in the state of mind where I'd be tempted to drink. I knew I was having you over, and with you, I'm focused entirely on the night to come."

She took a sip of her wine and then set her glass down. "So if you were alone you wouldn't have wine here?"

"No, I wouldn't. I know what my triggers are and a date with a pretty women isn't one of them," he said, reaching for a piece of baguette and spreading some of the soft herbed cheese on it. He held it out to her.

She took it but didn't seem interested in eating. "This is difficult. I know we said this is just temporary, but I want to know you. It's odd because already there are things about myself that I've shared with you that normally I wouldn't."

"Like what?" He wanted to know so he could understand her better. Figure out what it was that made her tick…what made her different.

"The story about following Fifi. Kissing in the cooking store. Okay…that wasn't something I said, but something I did. I'm not a PDA kind of girl. This feels too big."

"It's not any bigger than you and I. And just for the record, Penny, I don't kiss women in public. The way I am with you is special." He scrubbed a hand across his face. "Most of the time I don't like to talk about myself. There is something about dredging up my past that makes… Well, I don't like to go there."

"Then why have you?" she prodded gently.

"Because you asked me for the truth. I said I would give it to you and I am a man of my word," he said.

"Okay. Well, I'm glad to hear that," she said. "I'm sorry about your addiction, and to be honest, I'm okay with not having wine. So from now on, why don't we just skip the alcohol?"

"It's not going to tempt me," he reiterated. "I've been sober for a long time."

"Oh, okay," she said. But he could tell that it wasn't.

"What is it? Why is this a hot button for you?"

She shrugged.

"The truth street goes two ways," he reminded her.

She chewed her lower lip and then looked away from him. "My dad was an addict. That's why he wasn't around when I was growing up and isn't a part of my life now. He just never could handle it."

Will leaned over, shifting so that they were eye to eye and she'd be able to read the truth in his gaze. "If I'd had people in my life who'd cared for me, I'd never have started drinking. And it's the fact that I don't want to lose anyone I love again that has kept me from committing to a long-term relationship."

She swallowed. "So two weeks is really all we're going to have?"

"Yes. I told you I'm a man of my word."

She nodded. "Okay, I believe you. Let's enjoy this dinner. I didn't mean to bring you down."

"You didn't. We needed to share these things. And to be honest, I was curious about your dad." He reached over and stroked her cheek. "Like you said, we aren't just lovers. I want us to be friends even after we part ways on New Year's Eve."

"I'd like that, too," she said softly. The timer went off in the kitchen and he got up to take care of the dinner. He turned it off and leaned back against the counter, unsure of how to move forward. Each thing he learned about Penny made it harder and harder to keep his promise to himself. To reassure himself that she was just like every other woman.

PENNY NEVER THOUGHT of her dad and she wasn't about to let thoughts of him ruin her night with Will. She put her wine to the side then stood up and walked around his little chalet. It was the mirror of hers and she noticed that he'd had some decorations for the holidays put up. Or maybe he'd put them up himself.

She wandered around the room as Will was in the kitchen area working. She felt odd. Not really herself. This truth thing wasn't as great as she'd thought it would be. And a part of her realized that was because not all lies that were told between couples were like the horrible one Butch had been living. Most of the time they were told to protect one other.

"Want to put some music on?" he asked.

"Yes," she said, picking up her wineglass and setting it on the counter next to the Bose speaker system. "Then I'll help you with dinner."

"No need. I've got it under control," he told her.

She took her iPhone and put it in the dock, then flipped through her playlists, looking for something that would be good for dinner. Lana Del Rey and "Summertime Sadness" didn't seem right. She settled on a playlist she used when she was working on planning events. A mix of adult contemporary songs mixed with some top-forty hits.

Then she leaned her elbows on the counter and watched as Will worked. She was back in that place where things were starting to get gray again. She wanted to fix that problem he had with shoving everything into his safely labeled jars. That wasn't healthy. Something she knew from personal experience.

"Why are you staring at me?"

"Just admiring your butt. I don't think I noticed how cute it was before," she said lightly. Enough truth had been shared for tonight. Time to remember she was young and this was a temporary affair.

He turned his back to her and looked over his shoulder with a wink. "Like the view?"

"Very much. What do you do to stay in shape? I can tell you like to ski and I did notice you have sun lines on your face."

"Pretty much anything I can. I love being outside. I work long hours on my computer, but I always take the weekends for myself. I compete or train for a lot of cycling road races. What about you?"

"Nothing that ambitious. I'm doing that run for breast

cancer with my friends in May so I've been training, but it's kind of hit-or-miss. I don't mind running once I get dressed and get outside, but convincing myself to get out of bed when the alarm goes off is hard."

"You lack motivation," he said.

"I do," she said with a grin. "So what's for dinner?"

"Cajun-inspired salmon and dirty rice."

"Sounds delicious," she said.

"I thought so," he replied with a wink. He carried their plates to the blanket and she brought the bread basket and the cutlery. As they dined it was easy to fall back into the rapport that had been between them from the beginning. She ate and listened to his tales from college Mardi Gras trips he'd taken when he'd been young and, as he put it, a little too wild.

"Spring Break was never my thing. And Mardi Gras sounds like it would be so packed and just too many people acting nuts for me."

"Like your crazy people in smaller doses?" he countered.

"Or not at all. I like crowds when I'm controlling an event so I at least have the illusion that I am in control. That I'm taking care of everything and staying one step ahead."

"That's part of my job at times. Analyzing risks and then mitigating them."

"Does it work?" she asked. "In business it's easier to predict, don't you think?"

He took her plate and carried it into the kitchen before he came back and sat closer to her. He pulled her into his arms so that she was nestled against his chest and they were both facing the roaring fire.

"I think business is sort of easier to predict. Markets

have trends and you can spot them. But sometimes I am wrong and then I have a huge loss."

She snuggled against him. "What do you do then?"

"Regroup, figure out what I read wrong and make sure I don't do it again," he said.

"Wow, you must be pretty good to never make the same mistake twice," she mused.

"Not really. I try not to but sometimes I'm tempted to go down a path just because it seems like it might be worth the risk," he said, tipping her head back and looking down into her eyes.

There was some emotion in his eyes that she couldn't read. She wanted to ask him another question but he leaned down and kissed her. Not like their previous ones, but this was sweet and leisurely. An awakening of the passion that had been simmering between them since the moment they'd met. She knew that all the talk of being hurt had been masking her very real fear that she'd made the wrong choice when she'd agreed to be with Will.

But his mouth on hers and his tongue slowly seducing her with those long, languid movements made her push those doubts aside. She knew there was no place she'd rather be on this cold December night than right here in Will's arms.

7

PENNY SHIFTED AROUND until she was kneeling next to Will, and then straddled his lap, something her short skirt accommodated very easily. She framed his face with her hands, relishing the feel of his strong jaw under her fingers.

"Thank you for a very nice dinner."

"I like the way you say thank you," he said in response.

She kissed him again. His lips were soft yet firm under hers. She pushed herself up on her knees so that he slanted his head back against the cushions of the couch. She felt his hands on her hips, sliding up and down the sides of her thighs and then cupping her butt and squeezing.

She tilted her head for deeper access to his mouth. Thrust her tongue in again and again. God, his taste was addicting, but she shoved that thought out of her mind.

She pulled her mouth from his and dropped soft kisses along the line of his jaw to his ear. She settled back down on his lap, felt the firm ridge of his erection between her legs and rocked against it. He was so long and thick between her legs.

She shivered a little as a pulse of desire went through her entire body. Her breasts felt fuller in the cups of her bra and her nipples started to harden.

He groaned and squeezed her butt as his hips jerked forward to rub against her. She sat back on her heels, felt the buckle on her ankle strap sting her foot, but she didn't want to stop touching Will long enough to remove them.

She had a plan to do a striptease for him when the time was right. She'd read a lot of articles over the years, trying to make her love life more exciting, and finally she had a guy who might be the right one to test it out on.

She slowly unbuttoned his shirt, pausing to kiss each bit of his chest that was revealed. He had a light covering of hair on his chest that tapered from his pectorals down to his belly button. She scooted back and untucked the tails of his shirt from his pants and then spread it open so she could look her fill at his taut chest.

He flexed his muscles as she looked at him. "Like what you see?"

"I do," she admitted. Penny ran her finger down the center of his body from his Adam's apple, following the line of his sternum. Then she leaned in, inhaling the scent of his aftershave combined with his own natural musk. She lowered her mouth and dropped nibbling kisses on his neck, then shifted to caress her way down his chest. A few exquisite moments later, she bit at the flat flesh around his belly button and then leaned back to see his reaction.

He had his arms spread on the cushions behind him and his head was tipped back again. She leaned up to take his mouth again in a slow, tantalizing kiss that left no doubt how much she wanted him.

She thrust her tongue deep and tangled it with his as she shifted on his lap, rocking her center over the ridge of his cock. Breathing hard, she scraped one fingernail over his chest, found his flat nipples and teased them, then let her touch roam lower.

Penny pulled her mouth from his and he ran his fingers through her hair, bringing her mouth back down to his. She shifted a little, let him dominate the kiss for a few moments, forgetting that she was seducing him, exploring him.

Making Will hers. Unwrapping him like he was the one Christmas present she'd been waiting a lifetime to find. She didn't want to think, just feel. Just make this as physical as it could be. She felt his hand on the back of her thigh and wished she hadn't worn sheer tights under her dress.

Pulling her mouth from his, she leaned forward to start kissing her way down his body again. This time she shifted even farther back so she could get to his flat stomach. She reached for his belt and slowly undid it.

Once she drew it through the loops, she tossed it aside. He shifted his hips forward, rubbing his cock against her hand. She curved her fingers around his length and tightened her grip as he shafted her hand.

She unfastened his pants, pushing her hand inside to fondle him through his boxers, stroking up and down while she shifted again so she could kiss him. But just briefly. She skimmed her tongue over his jaw before she leaned in to whisper in his ear. "Are you ready for me?"

She felt him shiver in response, and when his cock jerked under her hand, she claimed his lips once more.

"Hell, Penny, I'm more than ready for you," he bit out, his voice raw and husky as he drew his hand down the center of her back.

She felt like she was already on the edge of her climax and she wasn't ready for it yet. Wanted to draw this moment out for as long as she could.

"Good," she said, pushing herself off his lap and standing up. She spread her legs as she drew the skirt of her dress up toward her waist, stopping when it was at the top of her thighs.

"Want to see more?" she asked.

"Yes," he growled, coming up on his knees as she lifted her skirt higher.

She turned around to reach the zipper that ran down the back of her dress. Then she began to slowly lower it, but he was on his feet to help her.

His breath was hot as he kissed his way down her spine and unzipped the garment. She shrugged her shoulders and the fabric fell forward as she turned away from him and let the dress slip slowly down her body to the floor.

Penny stepped out of it and stood in front of him in just her demi-bra and a pair of sheer black hose. She still wore her stiletto heels and she could tell that Will liked the way she looked. He'd toed his own shoes off and pushed his pants down his legs, along with his boxers. She walked slowly forward, taking her time so that he watched each sway of her hips.

She put her finger in the middle of his chest and pushed him backward until he was sitting on the couch. A moment later, she turned her back to him and bent forward to unbuckle her shoes and slowly slip them off her feet.

He touched her, traced the line of her buttocks and the curve of each cheek. But he didn't stop there; he let his fingers drift down to the backs of her knees and then up between her thighs. She moaned as he rubbed his finger back and forth between her legs.

Penny stepped out of her shoes and pivoted to face him again. She stood there and saw him sprawled out in all his masculine glory, and so in the moment. Turned on by her. She'd never had a man watch her like Will was right now.

A wave of feminine power swept through her. She was responsible for this moment, for making him want her this badly, and it was a heady feeling. She shivered as she slowly removed her stockings, pushing them down her legs and stepping delicately out of them before moving to stand closer to him.

Will kept his hand between her legs, his fingers tracing over her lips, dipping lower to graze the opening of her feminine core. Then he wrapped his arm around her waist and pulled her forward. The feel of him kissing her stomach and pushing his tongue into her belly button was strangely erotic. He nibbled at the skin of her lower belly and then he moved lower. Parting her most intimate flesh with his fingers and flicking his tongue over the exposed bud.

He curled it around and around and then flicked his tongue against her until she spread her legs to offer him greater access to her body.

She moaned and her legs quivered then buckled as he continued to nibble at her clit. He held her up with his arm around her waist, his mouth on her. She braced one leg on the couch and threw her head back as sensation after sensation rippled through her.

She reached for his head, tunneled her fingers into this thick, dark hair and gasped as he drove her higher and higher.

Every nerve in her entire body was pulsing and reached for orgasm. And she put it off, afraid to come before he was inside of her. She wanted to feel that big cock of his stretching out and pushing her over the edge.

Penny pulled back but he tightened his grip on her, maneuvering his body on the couch so he could get better access to her center. He cupped her butt and held her still as he traced his tongue around the opening and then thrust it inside of her. She arched her back, rocking her hips against his mouth.

"Come for me," he said. "Let me see how you look when you come."

His voice was rough and raw and the last bits of her control shattered as he pushed one finger up inside of her. Curling it deep within her as he brought his mouth back to her clit and sucked on it. She felt everything in her tightening, saw stars as she rocked harder against his mouth…and then it happened.

Her orgasm washed over her in a huge wave that left her feeling weak and at the same time so alive. She fell forward against him, catching herself on the back of the couch and in his arms. He wrenched his mouth from her body but kept his finger pumping inside of her.

She felt his free hand rubbing up and down her spine. Felt him flick the fastening on her bra open, and then his mouth was on the curves of her breasts, kissing them as he pulled his hand from her body.

"Are you on the Pill?" he asked.

"Yes," she said. "I'm healthy, too."

"Me, too," he said. "I want inside of you."

"I want that, too," she said. But not yet. She wanted something that every other man had demanded as his due, but this time with Will, she needed to taste him. Wanted to feel that thick cock in her mouth. She shifted so she could stroke him and he stopped her.

"I'm about to come," he said. "I want to be inside of you."

She shuddered as she moved over him and felt the tip of his cock at her entrance. He put his hands on her waist and drew her forward and down on him. It was a slow penetration, each inch coming after the other.

She rocked her hips forward, trying to hurry him, but he gritted his teeth and shook his head. "I want this to last."

"Why?"

"It's our first time," he said, looking up at her with those bright blue eyes of his so intense she felt like he could see all the way to the center of her soul.

She tunneled her fingers through his hair and slowly took him all the way inside of her. Refusing to break eye contact as she rode him with intent.

In her romantic dreams, she and her lover always came at the same time. She knew it was hard to time something like that, but she wanted it. Anticipated that happening with Will. He was so big, filled her so deeply and completely.

He held her with one arm against the middle of her spine as he sucked one of her nipples into his mouth and continued to thrust deep inside of her.

She felt her orgasm coming again. Fingers of sensation spreading out from her center. She leaned forward. "I'm close."

"Not yet," he rasped. "Not yet. You can take more of me, can't you?"

She wasn't sure but then he turned them on the couch, shifted so he was over her, and drove harder and deeper inside of her. And she finally came. Her orgasm rushed over her in waves, and she felt his hips moving faster as he reached for his own release.

He whispered hot, dark, sexy words in her ear as he spilled himself inside of her. The heat of him filling her as he continued to thrust two more times.

He slumped forward, resting his head on her breasts, and she kept her legs wrapped around his waist and stroked his back with her hand.

He felt big and solid. She tightened her arms and legs around him, brushed a kiss against his shoulder and thought, *Mine*.

He was hers. And for now that was more than enough. He'd exceeded her expectations when it came to sex.

"You okay?" he asked huskily, and as he pushed up on his elbows and looked down at her with a soft smile on his face, her heart beat a little faster.

He looked happy and relaxed. His smile was intimate and sweet and it made her crave something that she'd never really thought she wanted before.

And she wanted to hold him to her. Vow that she'd protect the man who smiled that sweetly.

"Yes. Are you?"

"Definitely. Woman, you just about blew every one of my preconceptions of you."

"Did I?" she purred.

"Yes."

She smiled. "Good. I don't like being predictable."

"No chance of that," he said. He rolled them to their

sides, keeping himself inside of her and holding her to him like he didn't want to let go, either.

Their new position put her with her head on his chest right over his heart. She heard the slow and steady beating of it, felt the heat from the fireplace on her back and the slight tickling of his chest hair against her cheek.

She'd never have thought to find this kind of satisfaction with a man. He stroked his hand over the back of her head and down her spine and neither of them said anything for a long time.

But then he shifted on the couch and picked up a blanket off the chair, draping it over her.

He lifted her in his arms and carried her blanket and all to the stairs that lead to the loft bedroom. He set her down on the bed and then opened the curtains so that the stars and moon shone into their room.

"When I was little, I used to think the moon followed me everywhere I went," he said. "You know, we talked about following things… I thought I was so special that the moon always wanted to watch me."

"I like that," she said softly.

"Me, too." He crawled into the bed beside her, wrapped his arms around her and kissed the top of her head. "I've never told anyone else that. Just you, Penny."

Snuggling against him, she realized she had a million questions. She wanted to know what he was feeling and if he usually spent the night with his lovers. When she turned to face him, he was watching her carefully, as if he knew what she was about to ask. She opened her mouth, but he brought his down on hers, kissing her and rebuilding the passion between them. He made love to her again, moving over top of her, and this time they came together. Afterward, she was so exhausted she drifted off to sleep before he pulled out of her body.

She dreamed of flying across the sky in a sleigh with Will and that the world was theirs. That she could have anything she wanted if she had the courage to stop trying to control all the elements and just reached for it.

Then a strong breeze blew, rattling around them, and the sleigh twisted and she fell out. Will reached for her but missed, and she had the feeling that because she was just his temporary lover he simply adjusted his course and kept on moving.

She fell through the night sky, expecting to crash, but fell softly. Nonetheless, she jerked awake with a start.

Will snored softly next to her and she sat there, looking over at him, desperately trying to steady her racing heart. And she realized that as much as she wanted to be cool about this and pretend that she could do temporary tonight, the dream had confirmed that it was going to be harder for her than she'd anticipated.

But she wasn't about to let worry and fear keep her from having the best Christmas of her adult life.

8

THE NEXT MORNING he woke to the smell of coffee, and a naked woman pressed to his side. Penny smiled at him through her thick mane of blond hair, which was falling around her shoulders. The sunlight was streaming in through the windows behind them and he caught his breath as she gave him a tentative smile.

"Morning," she said.

"Morning," he replied, taking the cup of coffee from her. He took a careful sip and then sat up and shifted around so he could lean against the headboard.

"I'm not sure what to do now," she admitted. "I've been up for a while thinking."

"What to do about what?" he asked.

"You," she admitted. "Mornings after aren't my forte."

"Why not?" He was intrigued, as always, by each new thing she revealed to him.

"I'm just awkward…and this conversation would be a perfect example of that. It's just hard to know what to do. I don't want to assume we'll do something together and worry that even just asking puts undue pressure on you."

He shook his head as she talked. That was a lot to

dwell on before he even had his first cup of coffee. "Actually, I do want to do something with you today. I picked up a trail map in Fresh Sno yesterday that showed some paths for snowshoeing. And the gal behind the counter said if you go early enough, the snow is pristine and undisturbed. You interested?"

She nodded. "That sounds really nice. What time do you want to go?"

She seemed anxious, like she wanted to leave, and he understood that she might want some time alone to process what had happened last night. God knew he was forcing himself to keep it light and act like nothing had changed, like two weeks was still suitable for him, but deep down inside something had shifted.

She'd seduced him with her body and her soul and he wanted to figure out how he'd let that happen.

He was the one who'd proposed a temporary fling and he was a bit surprised to find his defenses not as strong as he'd hoped. Penny was different. He already knew that. But he'd been confident that he'd be able to conquer that. After all, his own will was strong and he just didn't form emotional attachments the way that others seemed to.

But now he wasn't so sure.

"This morning. What if we both shower and change and meet at the front of the Lodge in an hour or so?"

"That sounds great," she said, jumping out of bed. He was struck again at the beauty of her body.

She was all creamy skin and long limbs. She smiled over at him as she grabbed his bathrobe from a hook by the bathroom door. "I'm borrowing this."

"Okay," he said. "Want to borrow some boots, too?"

"Ah, I see how it is—give you what you want and

now I have to walk back to my chalet instead of being carried."

He got out of bed and scooped her up in his arms. "I haven't come close to getting everything I want from you."

She gave him a serious look from beneath her eyelashes. "What more do you want?"

There it was. The real fear that had her waking him up with coffee and talking a mile a minute before she escaped his chalet.

He didn't know how to answer it. How to give her the response she wanted. To be fair, he didn't have a clue what to say to smooth this over...and that wasn't like him.

He was known for his charm. Known for his romantic gestures. Neither of those would work. Not for her and not this morning.

"Christmas," he said. "A sexy Ms. Claus to spend the holiday with so that when I look back on this year, I'll have no regrets."

She squirmed and he put her down. Then she arched one eyebrow at him. "Sexy Ms. Claus I can do. So you said an hour? I might need a little longer."

"No problem. We have all day and we're on vacation," he said, reminding himself that this was meant to be light and easygoing. But he wasn't sure that suited him any longer.

It didn't take Sherlock Holmes to figure out that he'd disappointed her with his answers, but the fact was, he was simply doing what they'd agreed to.

"Have you changed your mind about this?" he asked suddenly. "I'll understand if you have. My intent was to make sure we both got what we wanted."

Locking eyes with him, she wrapped her arms around her waist. The sleeves of his robe fell over her hands in the process, and she looked small enveloped in it. She kept watching him, searching his face for some sign, and he had no idea what she was looking for.

She said nothing but continued to stare at him. The silence was growing between them.

He tried to look solemn and thoughtful, but imagined he might look odd. So he sighed. "I don't know what you want."

"I don't know, either. I do want to spend more time with you," she said, then lifted her hand to run it through her hair. He watched as the silky strands fell around her shoulders and she tossed her head.

He closed the gap between them, reached for her, but she stepped away and he realized that she was walking a fine line between wanting to be what he needed and needing be what she wanted. It was something he'd seen before but usually at the end of his time with a woman.

"What part was it?" he asked thickly. "What was it that crossed the line?"

She shrugged and looked down at her feet. He noticed the pretty red toenails for the first time. "I don't know. I think it's something inside of me—I should have left last night."

He nodded. "I want to be sure you know that this can't go beyond these two weeks."

She didn't say anything else but walked downstairs and collected her clothing. He watched from the loft as she put on those sexy heels of hers and walked out the door. And in his gut he knew he'd lost something, but he wasn't sure what.

A SHOWER PUT everything into perspective for Penny, plus she had sent a text to Elizabeth and was going to catch up with her friend at the ski lodge while she was having breakfast with Lindsey Collins, the ski pro at the Lodge.

She needed something else to do. To see someone else so she'd stop feeling like Will was her Mr. Perfect. Lesson one: Mr. Perfect wouldn't say, *Let's be lovers for two weeks only.*

Except despite what he'd said, this morning when she'd woke cuddled up next to him, cradled close to his body, it had felt like something more than temporary.

"Good morning," Penny said as she approached.

"Morning. Penny, this is Lindsey. Lindsey, Penny," Elizabeth said.

"Hiya," Lindsey said. "Nice to meet you officially. I think we chatted about that yummy fondue at Elizabeth's promotion party."

"You, as well. Thanks for letting me invite myself to breakfast."

"No problem. We both used to sit at tables by ourselves and one morning we decided to share and chat. And now we're friends," Lindsey said with a smile.

Penny sat down and ordered coffee and oatmeal. She knew it wasn't sexy but she'd always loved it for breakfast and it was healthy.

"You're a guest here?" Lindsey asked in a friendly way. The woman had Nordic good looks and was taller than Penny. She still had the look of an athlete. Penny had watched with the rest of the US as Lindsey took her super-G warm-up run in Sochi and careened off the path into a barricade, sustaining a career-ending injury.

"Yes, but Elizabeth and I were roommates in college," Penny said with a smile. Girl talk. Yes, this is just what she needed. Even at home she didn't have any close friends to talk to since she'd left her job.

"And we've been best friends ever since," Elizabeth said with a wink. She looked so happy and relaxed these days. It wasn't that she needed a promotion or a man to be content, but Penny could tell that having those two things had really helped Elizabeth find her center. "She planned my fab celebration party for my promotion."

"That was a great party," Lindsey said. "I enjoyed it a lot. So thank you for planning it."

"You're welcome. That's sort of what I do for a living," Penny said, taking a sip of coffee and trying to settle into her normal-girls'-brunch mind-set. She could do this. This was what she needed.

"Sort of?" Lindsey asked.

"Yes. I'm between jobs. Do you like being the ski pro?" Penny asked. *Better to keep the spotlight off of me,* she thought. She didn't need to dwell on the fact that her career was as much in limbo as her personal life.

"I do. It's not as rigorous as training was. But I get to ski every day and my knee can handle what I do so it's the best of both worlds." Lindsey cleared her throat, looking slightly uncomfortable. "How are you settling into your new position, Elizabeth?"

Penny noticed how fast the other woman had switched gears, and couldn't help wondering if Lindsey, like herself, wasn't as happy as she was pretending to be.

"It's great. Lars has finally started recovering from his health scare and is relaxing a lot more, giving me a freer hand in management. But I still need his advice. A bigger problem for me is Bradley."

"In what way?" Lindsey asked.

Frowning, Penny added, "Is there trouble in paradise?" She hoped her friends weren't having relationship problems.

"Not at all. But he's pressing me for a wedding date now that we're engaged. I think he wants to get married on New Year's Eve, but I'm not so sure I can plan something that quickly."

Penny thought about it for a moment. It was the kind of project she could use to distract herself from her mono-focus on Will. "I could do it for you. But I need to know what you want. I'm guessing you'd want the ceremony to be small and intimate?"

"Yes, definitely. I think Bradley would be happy with just us and two witnesses."

Penny pulled a notebook out of her bag and started to jot down some notes. "Do you have a venue yet?"

Elizabeth shook her head.

"That's too bad. That could be a challenge for us, especially around the holidays." She chewed thoughtfully on the end of her pen. "But first things first…are you going to take time off or just work and then get married?"

Elizabeth laughed. "Bradley would kill me if I didn't take time off. Do you think you can do this?"

Penny nodded. "I can. Let me know if you want me to."

"I have to check with Lars and the board. But if we do it on New Year's Eve, I think it might be okay. January is actually a pretty slow month for us at the Lodge. Everyone goes back to work after the holidays. Do you think finding a location will be hard?"

"Yes," Penny said, "but not impossible. I've got a little over ten days to plan this. The hardest thing will be to get you a dress."

"I can help with that," Lindsey said.

Penny looked at the former Olympic skier, as did Elizabeth.

"My cousin is a wedding-dress designer in LA. I will call and ask her if she has some dresses in your size."

"Thank you," Elizabeth said. "Ladies, do you really think we can do this?"

"It won't be perfect," Penny cautioned. "I can't work miracles, but I think we can get you a really lovely wedding."

"I think so, too. Bella—that's my cousin—she's always up for a challenge."

Penny was up for one, as well. Something that reaffirmed there was more to life and romance than hot sex and temporary lovers. She needed this. Needed to pour all those emotions that Will stirred to life in her into something constructive so she didn't dwell too heavily on what was missing in their relationship.

Affair! she reminded herself. Just a Christmas affair.

PENNY MADE TWO calls before she went to meet Will. The first was to a florist she'd frequently worked with on events back in Maryland to get a recommendation on someone local who could do the flowers for Elizabeth's wedding. The easiest place for Bradley and Elizabeth to have their ceremony was probably here at the Lodge. Given that Elizabeth was the GM, she should be able to find a room or location they could use.

Penny rubbed her hands together and felt that charge of energy she got from planning parties. She loved doing it. She'd forgotten how much over the past few months while she'd been dealing with Butch and quitting her job. He'd tainted something that was a part of her and so personal.

She seemed to have beaten Will to their meeting point; she checked the time on her iPhone and realized that she was about four minutes early. Then she realized she had a call from a number labeled "private number." One without a name. Was it New York?

"Hello?"

"Penny, it's Butch."

"Why are you calling me?"

"Because you won't answer my texts and we need to figure something out. I think if you would just stop being so stubborn…"

"No, Butch. There isn't any way that this will work."

Will walked up as she was talking.

"Please, just listen. I think we had a good thing—"

"We didn't. I've got to go. Don't call me again," she said, hanging up before he could say anything else.

Will didn't say anything, just stood there next to her, and she felt the differences between the two men so clearly. Butch had seemed like he was a solid kind of guy. The type of man who she had a lot in common with, but despite their working together that had been so untrue. And Will, who was so his opposite, had offered her a better relationship.

He'd done it with honesty and no false promises. She realized that he had given her more than Butch ever had. Her former boss had made her believe she might marry him someday when he had already committed himself to another woman. Something that Will would never do.

"You okay?" he asked quietly.

"Yes, much better. I think I was hungry this morning. Must be all that physical activity last night," Penny said, forcing a smile. She was going to enjoy this time with him.

Will Spalding was the man she'd picked to do that with, so no more doubts or wishing for more. Relationships ended all the time and usually long after they had turned to bitterness. This way she'd always have just the good stuff with Will.

"I think I finally get what you meant by two weeks being the best part of the relationship," she remarked.

"You do?"

"Yes. No time for real life to take something special and make it mundane," she said.

He gave her an odd look and she wondered if she were trying too hard to make him think she accepted everything the way it was.

"I can't imagine life with you ever being mundane," he told her.

"Don't do that. Let's not talk about the future, okay? I'm having a really hard time keeping myself from falling for you, Will."

His jaw tightened and he nodded. "You're different for me, as well."

She felt a spark of hope that maybe things would last between them. But then she knew that was false hope. She didn't even know where he really lived or how they would make anything work. And for now, she needed this to be about the two of them and the holiday season. Nothing else.

"So…snowshoeing," she said. "I've never been before, but I read an article in a magazine about it in my room."

"I did, too. That's where I got the idea and thought it might be a bit of fun. Plus with all the snow it seems like staying indoors, while fun for certain things, would be a waste."

"I agree," she said. She needed to keep moving, keep

busy so she didn't have any time to think. "Do you have a vehicle?"

"I rented one from the front desk. A big all-terrain one," he said. "And I had a lunch packed for us. Ready to go and explore?"

She nodded. He led the way to a big Ford Explorer that looked way too big for two people, but given the trail that Will had marked on his map, they might need the all-wheel-drive SUV to get them to the start of it.

"What kind of car do you drive at home?" she asked after she'd climbed up into the passenger seat and he was seated behind the wheel.

"Lamborghini. It was my dream car growing up."

"So you finally made enough to get one?"

"Sort of. I've got my eye on a Tesla electric sports car next. But I'm waiting to make sure they have the bugs worked out of it before I buy one." He shrugged his broad shoulders. "The Lambo is a status thing and I like driving fast. I spend a lot of time online with my investor group and they are all from the Middle East. Those boys have roads where driving over 150 is no big deal. Makes me jealous."

"Why would you want to drive that fast?" she asked, fully admitting to herself that she liked driving under the speed limit when she did take her car somewhere. But most times she was a mass-transit traveler.

"The thrill of it. Makes me feel like I'm alive when I'm going that fast and controlling my car. I'm not dangerous and I'd never want to hurt anyone, but seeing the world flying past my windows always makes me feel like I'm not missing anything."

9

IT WAS COLD and quiet as they walked through the thick pine forest. He huddled deeper into his coat and looked over at Penny to make sure she was warm enough. She had her head tipped back to stare up at the trees.

The wind shifted and the trees swayed, a large clump of snow falling with a dull thud from the branches. It was nature at its most tranquil. He took his phone out and snapped a picture of Penny with her head back and the thick snow blanketing the ground around her. The only signs of disturbance were the tracks they'd left where they'd been walking earlier.

He wasn't any closer to finding answers about her today. He knew that she was struggling to find her place in the dynamic that had changed between them since they'd become lovers. He was, too.

But they were both ignoring that and acting like they were just in Utah to enjoy themselves this holiday break.

The scent of the pines in the woods made it feel like Christmas to him. Brought him back to the house he'd grown up in. The home he'd had before his parents had died. He'd forgotten about that big pine tree that had been in the foyer of the house and how his mother had asked the housekeeper to put pine boughs in each of the rooms.

He missed his mom.

Will didn't think of her often…but today, when he was standing in the quiet woods with Penny, he wished she were still here so he could talk to her. He had a hunch she'd like Penny. Who wouldn't?

She was beautiful and funny but also very caring. He'd seen the signs more than once.

"Sorry about that. Were you waiting for me?" she asked as she caught up with him. She'd been sort of lagging behind him and he'd let her have her space.

"I was. I wanted to take a selfie," he said, wriggling his eyebrows.

She smiled at him. "I'd like that. It's so lovely out here. I never realized what I was missing living in the city but I like all this rural space around me."

"Me, too," he said. "I live on the outskirts of town on fifteen acres of land so I have it right in my backyard." He wrapped an arm around her shoulders and pulled her up against him, and then stretched his arm with the phone out.

He lifted his arm and Penny moved around, tipping her head from one side to the other.

"What are you doing?" he asked.

"Trying for the right pose. I want to make sure I don't look funny," she said with a grin.

He smiled back and pulled her close, pushing the shutter button as he leaned down to kiss her. She was surprised. He felt it in the way her cold lips parted, but then she sighed as her tongue rubbed against his. She wrapped her arms around his waist as he deepened the kiss and forgot about selfies and preserving this moment. He needed to live in it.

He felt that rush of excitement in the pit of his stomach. A feeling he normally only got when he was making a risky hedge-fund investment or driving his car too fast down an empty highway. And now it was coming from Penny.

He lifted his head and her lips were damp from his kisses, her eyes wide and slightly dazed. He had to get himself under control. Forcing a smile to his lips, he said, "Sorry…couldn't resist."

"Do you hear me complaining? Ready for the photo?"

"Yes," he said and snapped one of the two of them.

"Let's see it," she said.

He showed her the photo and noticed her radiant smile in it.

"Will you send it to me?" Penny murmured.

"I will, what's your email?" he asked. "Weird that we haven't exchanged that info yet. Or friended each other on Facebook."

"I know. But you have a big advantage over all my Facebook friends since we are actually doing stuff together."

He laughed. "True."

She rattled off her email address and he sent the photo to her. "I always loved the smell of pine trees," she told him. "In the winter my mom would buy those Christmas-scented candles and put them all over our house. She tried apple-pie scent but it made us too hungry."

They moved quietly through the trees, following the trail that he'd marked on the app on his smartphone. "My mom used to make the best apple pie."

"Did she?"

"Yes. She didn't do the two-crust thing but instead put some kind of crumble on top of it. It was so good," he said with a smile. "I remember one year, I must have been about six, that my dad and I snuck in and ate the crumble off the pie while my mom was at her bridge club." He chuckled fondly, realizing he hadn't thought of that in years.

Something about Penny brought his old memories up. Reminded him of the power of having a family and how much he'd enjoyed it. He didn't feel that aching loneliness he'd felt in the past when he'd thought of his mom and dad.

"That's funny. Did you get in trouble?"

Will shook his head. "My dad and I left a present for her next to the pie."

"What was it?"

"A bracelet my dad had picked out at the jewelry store and a charm he'd had made from a drawing I'd done of the three of us. Looking back on it as an adult, my dad knew the exact right thing to get her. She loved it."

"Sounds like your parents had a really good marriage," Penny said.

"They did. It was perfect. In a way, again as an adult, I think they would have been miserable if one of them had lived while the other died. They were so connected to each other."

"How did they die?" she asked, slipping her gloved hand into his.

"Car accident," Will said. An over-the-road eighteen-wheeler that a trucker had been driving for too long had swerved. The driver lost control of his vehicle, careening into their path and changing Will's life forever.

"I'm sorry," she said. "But I'm glad you have those happy memories with your parents. Memories are important, aren't they?"

More and more he was coming to realize that.

PENNY ENJOYED THE afternoon with Will. They spotted some fallen pinecones and she picked two of them up to take back to her chalet.

"What are you going to do with those?"

"Just keep them as a little reminder of this outing. I really enjoyed it." She glanced over at him. "I saw a poster in town the other day that said there is a nativity performance on Saturday afternoon. You interested in going?"

"It's not really my kind of thing," he admitted.

"Fair enough," she said, trying not to feel too disappointed. It was a family thing, wasn't it? Watching little kids reenact the night that Jesus was born. Not something that a bachelor who wasn't interested in commitment would attend.

"I have one other event to invite you to and if you don't want to go it's okay. But my friends Elizabeth and Bradley—the cutesy kissing couple, remember them?"

"I do," he said, opening the back of the truck and getting out a thermos. "Would you like some hot tea?"

"Yes, please," she said, taking the insulated mug he handed to her. "They are getting married on New Year's Eve. I'm actually helping to plan it and I wondered if you wanted to make that our last date."

He watched her carefully. "I'd like that."

She imagined he would. It would be a public ceremony and then party, and he could walk out the door at midnight without a backward glance. Or maybe she would. But that was a long ways away. She didn't have to think too much on that right now.

"What's the one thing you have to do for it to feel like Christmas?" he asked suddenly.

She thought about it. Christmas was tied to a bunch of different things that she had to do in order to get into the spirit of the season. "Watch *A Charlie Brown Christmas* some years. Others, it's singing 'Santa, Baby.' And sometimes it's kissing a guy under the mistletoe."

She didn't want to share too much more of herself with him. Spending the afternoon together, hearing about him and his dad eating that pie his mom had baked, it had touched her. Made him even more real than he'd been last night after they'd had sex that first time and she'd seen that tender look on his face. That look that she wanted to see again, but had to be so careful she didn't interpret as anything other than lust.

"I would love to hear you sing 'Santa, Baby,'" he said with a grin.

"I haven't done it since college. My sorority used to put on a show each year to raise money for our charity. And we'd all dress in those cute little Ms. Santa red velvet dresses and sing it." She met his eyes. "I haven't heard that song yet this season."

"I haven't, either. But then I'm not into a lot of the sentimental stuff that is associated with the season."

She wondered if that was because his parents had died when he was young. Parents built traditions for their families. She'd seen that with her mom. Everything that was important to Penny about Christmas either came from her friends or her mom. "So what makes it Christmas for you?"

Will tugged her into his arms and dropped a kiss on

the end of her nose. "This year, you do, Penny. Without you this would be just one more vacation getaway. But you are making it seem very festive."

"Does that mean a different woman each year is how you know it's Christmas?" she asked. No sense lying to herself if that was how he felt. She needed to keep her vision clear and not blurred by sugarplum fairies or snowshoe walks through pine-tree forests.

"Not like you mean it. It's just for me the holiday always starts when I find someone I can share it with."

"So a different girl every year," she reiterated.

A muscle ticked in his jaw as he gazed down at her. "It's not as black-and-white as you make it sound. I have two choices when it comes to Christmas. I can work myself into oblivion and try to miss the fact that most everyone else is celebrating being together. Or I can find a woman who is also a little lost and make the most of that time together until the world sorts itself out and we can both move on."

She took a deep breath. She understood for the first time how much he needed this affair that they were having and how much she sort of needed him, too.

WILL DROVE INTO Park City instead of back to the Lodge and noticed that Penny didn't say anything. He wanted to show her that she was special to him, not like all the others. And as he pulled to a stop in front of the Christmas-tree lot and she turned to him, he thought she was beginning to see that.

"I thought you were getting a tree delivered," she said.

"I am. But I guess I could have two trees," he told her. "I think anyone who likes *A Charlie Brown Christmas* must like going to the Christmas-tree lot."

She nodded. "It's one of my favorite things to do. I actually haven't ordered a tree, so unless you really want two of them, we could pick one out for my chalet."

"Sounds perfect," he said.

He put his gloves and scarf on before coming around to open the door for Penny. She smiled as she hopped down from the truck and then reached for him and gave him a big bear hug. "Thank you."

"It's no big deal," he said gruffly.

She shook her head and held his hand in hers. "It is to me. Thank you."

She closed her door and he hit the automatic locks as they walked to the tree lot. There weren't too many people here at this time of day: middle of the afternoon on Thursday a week before Christmas. Most folks were at work trying to cram in as much as they could before they took off for the holidays.

The two of them wandered through the lot looking at all the trees. "I love this one." She pointed to a Douglas fir that was full, round and way too tall for their little chalets.

"Might be a bit on the big side."

"You think?" she asked, laughing at him and at herself. "Just saying I like it. Most of these trees are pretty big. Let's try over there."

He followed a few steps behind her, listening to her humming along with the canned Christmas music that played from the overhead speakers. She stopped in front of a tree that was probably only five feet tall and a little sparse. It looked desperately in need of water. Lots of water.

"That's a fire hazard," he said.

She nodded. "It is. Reminds me of that pitiful tree that Charlie Brown picked out."

"So that's the one?" he asked, folding his arms across his chest. He doubted that her little dry tree could make it all the way to Christmas day. But who was he to argue with Penny when she was smiling?

"Not sure yet, but it's a definite maybe."

She had shaken the blues or whatever had been dogging her when they'd been in the forest earlier. He wished he could do the same as easily. But talking about his parents was bringing back all sorts of memories—good and bad—and he missed them keenly.

She continued moving through the trees but Will had stopped following her. "White Christmas" was playing over the loudspeaker and the scent of the pine trees brought him back to dancing in the living room with his mom while his dad sang along. It was a happy memory. So then why did his eyes burn and his heart feel heavy?

He wasn't sure how to snap himself out of this. He wondered if he should end this right now with Penny and get on a plane and go to Jamaica. Get his head out of Christmas altogether.

"Hey," Penny said, coming back around the corner and walking over to him. "You okay?"

He couldn't speak. He had promised not to lie and right now there was no way he was going to tell her the truth. He hadn't realized how much of his past he'd shoved away until little bits of it started coming out. Little bits that didn't mean much by themselves, but combined together were shaking him to his core. He had to get out of here.

Had to get away.

He turned and started walking toward the front of

the lot but Penny stopped him with her hand on his arm. "You can't outrun things in your head."

He looked down at her and saw in her eyes that she understood exactly where he was coming from.

"Let's pay for this little tree," she said, "and then we can go back to the Lodge and relax in my Jacuzzi tub and pretend that we both are okay."

"Aren't we?" he asked tersely.

"Let's face it, honey, you and I are both running from something. We don't have to talk about it but we know it. And together maybe I can provide you with a safe place to stop this afternoon. You've done that for me more than once."

She was wise, his Penny, he thought. He walked back to the SUV, carrying her tree, and the lot attendant helped him strap it to the roof before they left. When they got in the car, she put her hand on his thigh and talked to him about things that had nothing to do with Christmas, or family, and it helped.

He couldn't shake it completely, but she was slowly easing that tightness in his chest and that loneliness that was dancing just at the edges. The aching loneliness that promised him that temporary affairs couldn't fill the empty parts of his soul.

She arranged for her tree to be placed in a stand and delivered to her chalet later that evening, after it was watered and trimmed. Then she took his hand, leading him up the path to her place.

Penny didn't say anything, just walked up the stairs to the bathroom with the large garden tub. She turned on the heating and got out some candles from her overnight bag and then turned back to him.

"Ready to relax?"

10

PENNY DIDN'T KNOW what had happened at the tree lot but she knew that Will needed a distraction. She ran the water in the large tub and realized he stood behind her, just watching her.

"Would you go downstairs and get the travel speaker from my bag? It's on the end table by my books," she asked.

"Sure," he said, leaving the bathroom. She opened the box of bath amenities that Elizabeth had left for her the first day. There was a lavender-scented bath bomb as well as some bubble bath and those flower petals that dissolved into the water. She found two new fluffy towels and put them on the heated towel rack and then went to retrieve Will's bathrobe from her bedroom. She saw him on the stairs as she came back to the bathroom.

"Thank you."

"For?"

"Not asking questions. Just giving me space," he said.

What else could she do? She wanted to understand this man who was coming to mean more and more to her with each day they spent together, but a part of her knew that she would never fully understand him. That they both had to keep a few secrets from each other in order to survive Christmas with their hearts intact. She could do that. And she promised herself she could help Will do that, as well.

"No problem. It was cold outside today, wasn't it?" she asked.

"Indeed it was. Not too cold though, was it?" he asked.

They were both playing the polite game. She knew that it might bother her later, but not now. "Nope, it was perfect since I knew I had this big tub to come back here to."

"You seem prepared for it," he said wryly.

"It was the amenity that drew me to this chalet. I wanted that big garden tub from the moment I saw it," she said. "I live in a condo and my bathroom isn't the biggest. This year I might have it redone."

"I have a pretty decent-size bathroom with a big shower and that rain-type showerhead." He sighed. "It's heaven. You should think about putting one of those in."

She started to feel normal again. Started regaining her equilibrium and hoped that Will was, as well. She found the matches she'd been searching for and hung his robe on the hook by the door right next to hers.

His was thick and dark blue; hers was thick, also, but a pretty, deep red color. He followed her into the bathroom and she heard him disrobing behind her while she lit the candles and then fiddled with the light switches until just the light over the tub was on.

It was late afternoon but the sky was cloudy and they were forecasting more snow, so soon it would be falling again. She turned the taps off and spun around to find a totally naked Will standing by the sink waiting for her to finish.

"Your turn to get naked," he drawled.

She just smiled at him. She sat down on the bench under the heated towel rack and unlaced her boots, taking them off and setting them next to his. Hers were smaller than his, obviously, but also less worn. She took her socks off next and tossed them on the floor next to his, as well.

Will moved into the tub and sat down along the back, stretching his arms out on either side of his body. He tipped his head back as he sank lower into the water and she almost wished they had a different kind of bond. One where he would be able to share whatever it was that still weighed heavily on his mind.

For herself, she was happy to push that all aside and start to get back to being her. To let go of her fear that she'd made a mistake by sleeping with him. She usually made such bad decisions about men it was hard to believe this wasn't one of them.

She took off her thick sweater, and then her long-sleeved thermal underwear shirt and her bra, before she stood up and began to remove her pants.

"Wait a minute," he said. "Remember when you bent over last night?"

She nodded.

"Would you do it again? I was too turned on and you had those tights on, so I couldn't fully enjoy the view."

"What are you going to do for me in return?" she asked brazenly.

"Whatever you ask me to," he promised. She stood up and pushed her jeans down her legs and off and then walked closer to him, still wearing the thin silk pants that protected her from the cold.

She walked toward the tub and then stopped at the step that lead up to her side. She turned carefully around and glanced at him over her shoulder.

"Like this?"

"Yes. Now lean forward slowly and draw those pants down," he said, his voice getting huskier as he spoke.

She leaned forward as he asked and slowly drew the pants down her legs, and lifted first one foot and then the other to remove them.

She straightened and then slowly drew her panties down the same way. The water sloshed in the tub as he shifted and she felt his wet hand on the curve of her butt as she finished removing all of her clothing. He stroked his finger along her curves and cupped one cheek and then the other. She turned around to face him and he let his finger run along the side of her hip and then the bottom edge of her stomach.

He hooked his hand behind her waist and drew her forward. Dropped a wet kiss on her belly and then reached between her legs to lightly stroke at her center. "Sit on the edge. Put your legs in the tub and sit right here."

Penny climbed into the tub and sat down on the edge as he moved forward between her spread thighs. He parted her with his fingers and she felt the brush of his breath against her intimate flesh before he tongued her lightly. The side of the tub was cold under her backside, but Will was warm and his mouth on her made her forget everything but him.

The way he felt with his broad shoulders between her legs, his mouth moving over her and his arms wrapped around her waist, pulling her closer to him—it was pure ecstasy. He flicked his tongue over her and she shivered. Felt her nipples tighten.

Penny pushed her hands into his hair as she arched her back and felt shivers spread throughout her entire body. She was shaking but she wanted and needed more. He pulled her down into the tub on top of his lap. His mouth moved over her torso and licked her nipple. He traced her areola with his tongue and then sucked it into his mouth. She felt the tip of his cock between her legs and reached for it. Stroked her hand up and down his length as he continued to suckle her nipple. The warm water lapped around them and the scent of the vanilla candles she'd lit filled the room.

The jazzy sounds of Wynton Marsalis played in the background but really all she thought about was Will. He was consuming her and making everything—every part of her being—focus on him and him alone. There was something overpowering about him. He pulled his mouth from her breast and scraped his teeth over her nipple before tangling his hand in her hair and bringing her mouth down to his.

His kiss was carnal and raw. She tasted herself on his lips as he shifted beneath her and drove his cock up inside of her. He drove in deep and hard and she moaned against him as she felt the first wave of an orgasm wash over her.

It was powerful and shook her to the core of her being. He pulled out of her and tore his mouth from hers. He was still hard. He hadn't come and she wondered what he was doing.

But he turned her around so that she sat on his lap, facing away from him. Drew her back until he surrounded her with his arms. His cock slid between her legs and he found her opening, thrust up inside of her and then settled down.

"This is nice."

"Nice?" she said, her voice sounded wispy and lost even to her own ears. Her nipples were hard and her entire body felt like it was on the edge again. He moved slowly between her legs, in time with the lapping water but not rushing.

She tightened her core around his cock and he breathed in hard, then bit lightly at the back of her neck. "Not yet. I want this to last."

"I don't," she gasped. "I like the way you make me feel when you move inside of me."

"I like it, too," he said, pulling her farther back against his chest, gently moving around until her head rested on his shoulder. She turned to look at him and noticed that he was looking at her body.

At this angle her breasts were thrust back so that her nipples were exposed to the cooler air and the water surrounded the rest of her. He had one hand stroking up and down the middle of her body. Drawing his finger around and around her breasts and then lower to her belly button. He spread his fingers out and pressed her firmly back against him and the action drove his cock deeper inside of her.

She shivered and shook, so close to another orgasm. She wanted it. She needed it—needed *him*— but this anticipation was making her sensations that much stronger. She didn't want to think about Will, about how much he was rewriting everything she thought she knew about herself. But the truth was, no man had made her feel like this before. She reached her arm back, running her fingers through his hair, and pulled his head toward hers.

She shifted so she could kiss him. Suckle his lower lip and bite it gently. Their tongues tangled together and she felt everything in her body slow. She turned in his arms, straddled him again and took him deep into her. She kept her mouth on his as she rode him hard.

The water splashed around them and he held her waist in his hands, ripping his mouth from hers to call her name as he thrust up inside her and then came in a violent rush. She rocked against him at the same moment, finding her climax seconds after his.

She wrapped her arms around his shoulders and held his head in her hands as she looked into his eyes. They were half-closed but then he opened them and their gazes met and held. She saw in his eyes that he had been moved by this. It was more than sex to him.

Just like it was to her. It was something that neither of them had been searching for. She opened her mouth to ask him about it, but he put his finger over her lips.

"Not right now," he rasped.

"Okay." She settled next to him in the tub, rested her head on his shoulder, and tried to pretend that her Christmas wish hadn't changed from spending the two weeks with Will to keeping him in her heart forever. But she also wasn't going to lie to herself. She knew better than anyone how destructive that could be. She deserved better and so did Will.

He reached for the loofah sponge that was on the edge of the tub, and her scented soap, and then slowly washed her. She let him do it and pretended this would be enough.

PENNY WAS A challenge and every second they spent together made him question things he'd always known about himself. He'd made love to women countless times in the past, but with her it felt new.

Felt like he'd just discovered sex for the first time. He'd just come inside her and he knew that he was ready for her again. Something that didn't happen to him all that often. Granted, he hadn't had sex in almost six months, but he knew it was Penny affecting him and not abstinence.

"Want me to wash your hair?" he asked tenderly.

She looked over at him. "Really?"

"Yes," he said. "I love to play with your hair. It's so soft and pretty. Just like all the princesses from the books my mom read to me as a boy."

"I'm not a princess," she told him. "But I'd love to have you wash my hair."

"Okay. Let me get this set up right," he said, moving to the built-in bench at the back of the tub. "Come sit between my legs."

"Are you sure hair washing is all you have in mind?" she asked with an impish grin.

"For now," he said. He wanted to keep things light and it seemed each time he made love to her, the bond between them grew stronger. He wanted to figure out how to manage his response to her before he took her again.

He cupped his hands and let the water slowly spill out of them down her hair. She closed her eyes and tipped her head back toward his body. He kept pouring water over her until her hair was wet and then he ran his fingers through it. He reached for the shampoo and dispensed some into his palms.

"Lift your head," he said, working the rich lather

through her hair. He liked the way she felt sitting there between his legs, and despite his best intentions, washing her hair was turning him on. But he kept working.

Careful to keep her from brushing his erection as he rinsed her hair, slowly he filled his palms. "Close your eyes."

She nodded and her soapy hair rubbed against the inside of his thigh and his cock, the strands teasing him as they touched him. He poured the water over her hair again and again until all the lather was gone. Then she leaned back and smiled up at him. Her lips were full and pink, her nipples hard and irresistible. He flicked his fingers over them before he kissed her.

"I need conditioner, too," she said, her voice sultry. "Or my hair will tangle."

Will figured she was getting turned on, as well. He liked that. Liked the thought of bringing her pleasure. He wanted to surround her with it so that she'd never forget this or forget him.

He reached for the bottle of conditioner, but she took it from him. Poured it into her own hands and smoothed it through the length of her hair. "You can rinse for me."

After rinsing her hair, he pulled her to her feet, draining the water from the tub. Then he drew her into his arms and kissed her hard and deep. Stepping from the tub and lifting her out behind him, he wrapped a towel around her and carried her to the bedroom.

He put her in the center of the bed, her towel falling open as he came down over top of her. Passion roiling through him, he kissed her deeply as he thrust into her, and he felt her wind her arms and legs around him as he plunged deeper and deeper inside of her.

This time he didn't feel the urgency he'd felt earlier.

This time he made it last, building her to orgasm slowly and enjoying the feel of being entangled in her limbs. When she came, he came with her and then rolled to his side, reached for the edge of the comforter and wrapped them both up in it.

He held her close to him. Too close, because he knew she wasn't his forever and that was something that he was coming to understand that he truly wanted. He never wanted to let her go, but that was what he was going to have to do. He was beginning to fear he wouldn't be able to spend Christmas with her because memories weren't the only thing she was calling to life inside of him. She was also stirring his emotions.

Making him want things he was afraid he couldn't have. Long for things that fate had shown him were just out of his reach. But none of that seemed to matter in this moment. It almost seemed like he was holding everything he'd ever need right here in his arms.

11

PENNY AND WILL had fallen into a routine and on December 21—the winter solstice—he suggested they spend the longest night of the year together. First dining at Gastrophile West, the Lodge's five-star restaurant, then dancing in the nightclub, and then going to the second-floor patio bar and watching the night sky.

She had to admit she liked the idea. She'd gotten dressed in a cream-colored velvet gown—she loved wearing velvet at this time of the year—that was discreet in the front with a boat neckline, but in the back it dipped low to the bottom of her spine and the cut-out was lined with two strands of faux pearls.

She started to put on her ridiculously high-heeled shoes but then decided maybe she should wait until she got to the lobby to put them on. The snow was thick on the ground and the skiers had been having a great season on the hills, thanks to all the cold weather. And Penny understood from Lindsey, whom she'd had lunch with the other day, that the snow was just right for perfect conditions on the slopes.

The two women had been working together to plan

Elizabeth's wedding. Since they were both going to be her attendants—Penny as maid of honor and Lindsey as a bridesmaid—Lindsey's cousin was sending dresses for them to try on when she shipped out some wedding dresses for Elizabeth.

Penny put on the pearl earrings her mother had given her as a college graduation present and checked herself in the mirror before reaching for her heavy winter coat. She was having a good time with Will, and the work she'd been doing to plan Elizabeth's holiday wedding had kept her busy enough not to dwell on her secret fears. The ones that only crept up in the middle of the night when she was reminded that she'd only be in Will's arms for ten more days.

Live in the moment. She'd been repeating that mantra to herself day after day, and so far she was pretty successful in enjoying her holiday. There were moments when her control slipped, like when she'd been decorating her Christmas tree and Will had brought her a gift ornament of "Fifi." The dog was exactly as she'd described it to him and it had touched her.

It made her realize that he had the potential to be the kind of man she'd want to spend more than two weeks with. The kind of man that, if they'd met under different circumstances, she might have had a chance of convincing that he could be hers forever.

Another part of her thought that maybe he felt so right because it was only temporary. That she was better off cherishing every moment with him instead of analyzing it and trying to change him.

She was reminded of something her mother used to say when she'd been younger: don't worry about tomorrow or today will suffer. Until this Christmas season, she hadn't really understood that.

Penny looked back at her Christmas tree with its beautiful twinkling lights illuminating the darkness of the living room as she flicked off the lamp and prepared to leave her chalet. It was hard to believe, but this little chalet was starting to feel like home. She closed the door and walked up the lighted path toward the Lodge.

She and Will had been careful to balance their time together and apart. The temptation on her end was to spend every second with him, but she knew that wasn't healthy.

Elizabeth was near the concierge desk when Penny entered the lobby. The Lodge was having a special winter-solstice sleigh-ride program, and from the lines Penny noticed in the lobby it seemed to be very popular. She waved at her friend as she headed to the coat check, changed her boots for her high heels and handed in her coat. She kept her clutch with her as she checked her watch.

She had ten minutes until she was supposed to meet Will. She walked through the lobby toward the three-story river-stone fireplace. It was breathtaking as she stood in front of the roaring fire and looked up at the garland decorating it.

She knew every Christmas after this would have a hard time living up to the atmosphere here at the Lodge. It was like she'd stepped into one of those Currier and Ives cards that she'd recalled when she'd gone on her sleigh ride with Will. Everything so picture-perfect.

Even her man, she thought.

Not a detail had been overlooked and she wanted to believe it was real. Wished it could be, but life wasn't picture-perfect, was it? She'd learned that early on when she'd spent all her time with just her mom. Not having that ideal family unit that so many of her other classmates had was hard sometimes, but she didn't begrudge it. Her upbringing had been the best one for her.

And she acknowledged some of those "perfect" families had their failings, as well.

"Penny for your thoughts," Will murmured, slipping an arm around her waist.

"That's my line," she said with a smile, but it was forced. As much as she knew perfection was a kind of lie, she still wanted to find perfect. Wanted Will to be— No. He was her lover for today and she would enjoy it.

"I bet it is," he said. "So what were you thinking?"

"This Christmas is almost perfect. Like an old-fashioned picture with the Lodge and you and me. Just reminding myself not to buy into it."

He nodded. "Are you still okay with everything between us?"

What was she going to say? She wanted the rest of her time with Will, and as much as she was dreading the ending, she wasn't about to do anything that would cut it short any sooner than she had to.

"Yes," she said. Now if only she could convince herself.

THE NIGHTCLUB WAS jam-packed on the fifth floor. The electronic pulse of the music made conversation difficult, but Will pulled Penny closer to him in the banquette. She told him an amusing story about a flopped cake and no dessert at an office Christmas party.

"Sounds like it was fun," he mused. "Do you like hosting parties?"

It seemed like a Penny sort of thing. She was very social. He'd noticed that when they weren't together, he was sequestered in his chalet doing work and she was out and about socializing.

"I do like it a lot. I think part of it is that I grew up with my mom always throwing parties. As a lobbyist, she spends a lot of time schmoozing," Penny said.

"I bet she does," Will added. "My parents liked to socialize, as well. We'd have a big party every year for the Fourth at our estate. They'd invite everyone who worked for the family company out there. It was huge."

And fun. He remembered how hot it would get in Chicago in July. Not Texas hot. He had gone to school in the Dallas area. He wondered if he should tell Penny, find out where she lived now. But to what end? There was absolutely no need for him to know where she lived.

"Sounds like fun. We always did the Fourth in DC. It's so much fun. Makes me feel very patriotic."

The deejay switched from club music to a set of Christmas tunes. They played "Joy to the World," and when Penny closed her eyes and hummed along to the tune, he wondered what memories the song held for her.

He almost asked but then remembered his own caveat. Temporary lovers didn't need to know why. But he wanted to. It made him happy to know all the little details of what made Penny tick.

"You like this song?" he asked when the song finished playing.

"I do. I had a solo one year in choir and got to sing the second verse," she said. "My mom was very proud."

She blushed a little then rolled her eyes. "You know how parents are. Or do you? Did your folks ever get to see you perform in a holiday pageant?"

He rubbed the back of his neck. Maybe the loud music could start up again so he didn't have to answer. But it didn't. He had tried to forget about all those times when he'd been in a show at school and had no one except his butler to watch him. His parents had seen one or two performances, but after they died, that had all ended.

"They saw one," Will said quietly. "We didn't really put on that many shows at my school for parents."

"What was it like to be at a boarding school? Did you miss your home?" she asked. "I'd have been miserable without my own room. But my mom has always said I'm spoiled."

He laughed. "I can see that."

"Hey. A gentleman would have said she was wrong," Penny protested with a big smile.

"I thought we said no lies," he said, winking at her.

"Fair enough. Tell me about boarding school."

He had no idea what she wanted to hear. He'd kept to himself, not because he was ostracized but because his personality had always been more loner than anything else. "I played on the basketball team and tried rowing for one season. We were in double rooms and my roommate was okay. We both just did our own thing and left the other alone."

She took a sip of her seltzer water. He noticed she'd stopped ordering wine after he'd told her about his addiction. "I would have hated that. I probably would have been trying to pester you every time we were alone with questions."

"If you'd been my roommate, I think it's safe to say that I would have been chattier."

"You would have?" she asked flirtatiously. "Do you like talking to me?"

He smiled. "Yes, but as I was a teenage boy, I would have wanted more than conversation."

She nodded. "I remember those days. I'm afraid you would have found me…um…sort of high-maintenance."

"What were you like back then?"

"My mom and I were on our own and she had big dreams for me. I didn't want to take a chance on letting a boy put me off my path." She sighed. "Mom had warned me that love isn't always like it's portrayed in the movies. Sometimes it's difficult and leaves you both a mess."

He leaned back in his chair and studied her for a long minute. In a way he was surprised that was how she felt about love. "Is that why you fall for morons?"

"How did you know that?" she asked. "About the morons?"

"You warned me you were a moron magnet," he said.

"True. Sort of. I think maybe I just got so used to trying not to fall in love that I've never found a man that I could fall for," she said.

He tried not to take that comment personally. After all, he didn't want her to fall in love with him. Except maybe he did. To what end? He had no idea, but he didn't like being painted with the same brush as all the other men who'd been in her life. Deep down he wanted to be the one who finally made her dreams come true.

AFTER LEAVING THE NIGHTCLUB they strolled around the lobby, looking at the display of a model train and Christmas village that was along the south corridor. Penny kept her hand in the crook of Will's arm as they walked. She'd seen that expression on his face when she'd talked of love and she wondered what he'd been thinking.

They both knew that love wasn't an option between

them. Had he changed his mind about ending things between them? Doubtful, since he'd asked her if she was
still okay with their arrangement. She dropped her hand
from his arm and walked a bit ahead of him as she studied the model train track. She paused to look at the scale
replica of the Lodge and leaned forward to pretend she
was checking the windows.

But the truth was, she thought she'd caught a glimpse
of the man Will might have been if his parents had lived.
Because there was great potential in him for love. She
saw it—why couldn't he?

She understood that losing his parents had shaped
him. She suspected that more than anything was responsible for his attitude toward the holidays and toward longer love affairs. But she didn't know how to change him.

Could she even if she tried? She didn't think so. Will
had a strong desire to keep his life on the footing that
he'd found for himself.

"I had a train like this when I was a kid," he said.
"Come see."

He stretched his hand toward her and she walked back
to his side, slid her fingers through his and stood there as
the train chugged its way around the track and through
the Wasatch Mountains that were depicted around the
village. "Look at the steam. It's a replica of one of the
old-time trains that first came west. My dad had a huge
collection of these up in our attic. It was his hobby room."

Penny listened to him talking and wondered if he even
realized that he'd started talking more easily about his
parents and his past. She loved each memory he shared
with her, understood that he was becoming more and
more comfortable with her as he shared these things.

"Did he let you help him with it?" she asked, studying his handsome profile.

"Yes. We were building—"

He abruptly pulled his hand from hers and took a step back from the village. She turned toward him. "What?"

"We had been working on a model of our estate when he died. Dad promised me that we'd finish it when he got home but they never made it back."

His face was expressionless and she knew that he was retreating from her. Pushing his thoughts of his family and the trains down so he didn't have to feel the pain.

"I know that you don't want to remember how he never came home, but what about all the joy you two had working on it? Surely that counts for something," she said softly, walking over to him. She took his hand and led him to the rough-hewn bench that was situated in an alcove near the display.

She sat down and drew him down beside her. Turning to face him, she held his hand loosely in hers and looked into those blue eyes of his. Eyes that she'd seen happy and lusty and determined, but now were walled off.

"There are so many times when I want to pretend that all the bad things that have happened to me, didn't. That they were mistakes that I should shove so far out of my mind that I can never recall them, but I don't do that." She reached up with her free hand and gently stroked his jaw. "Because without all those things—the loser men I dated, the events I planned that didn't go perfectly, the jobs I interviewed for that I didn't get—I wouldn't be here today."

He didn't look away and she thought she might be getting through to him. Saw a softening around his mouth. She wanted him to understand she truly got it. "I still have my mom, so I'm not going to pretend that in any way we are the same, but I think if you remember all the good things, you will see that it makes your life richer."

He nodded. "Thank you. I forget sometimes how blessed my life was. How much they gave me. You're right that I wouldn't be who I am today if that accident hadn't happened." He swallowed hard. "It's just difficult to take the good and the bad, you know?"

She did know. It was so much easier to wish the bad things hadn't happened. But they were the things that truly gave her strength. "Without the bad the good would just be normal and everyday."

"Very true. Thank you," he said, lifting her hand to his mouth and brushing a kiss along her knuckles.

"You're welcome. Do you want to tell me more about the train you and your dad worked on?" she asked.

He shook his head and pulled her to her feet. "No. I think I've had enough of strolling down memory lane for this evening. What do you say we go and make some new memories on this longest night of the year?"

"I'd love to. So far I have to say it's been pretty good. How are you proposing to top it?"

"By taking you back to my place and making love to you. I want to spend the rest of the night wrapped around you and in the present," he said.

She wanted that, too. She kissed him softly and gently because she knew that a part of him was running away again, but he wasn't hers to fix. How many times was she going to have to remind herself of that until the message sank in?

12

WILL SPENT THE NEXT morning in Park City, pretending he wasn't hiding from Penny, but the truth was that last night he'd felt raw and exposed. It was one thing to make love to her, quite another to have her see the things that really mattered to him. He didn't know why she was dredging up all the old memories he'd drowned out long ago.

But he couldn't stop thinking of her and of a sort of future for them. Except he knew from his past that there was no way he could make anything like that work. He wasn't good at the day-to-day stuff—he'd had that one brief marriage as evidence—and had no plans to ruin what he had with Penny by making that mistake again.

The streets of Park City were busy and Will almost regretted coming to town today, but he knew that he had to get away. Maybe stay away for more than just the day. In all honesty, he was tempted to drive to Salt Lake City and…leave.

So there it was. The cold, hard truth. Maybe it was time to get out of here if he couldn't really deal with how Penny made him feel.

Will entered a local coffee shop and sat down at a table in the far back corner. He'd brought his laptop with him, and the plan was to distract himself with work and try to get her out of his head. But instead he found himself putting her name into Google search and then reading articles about her.

Yeah, this was helping, he thought sarcastically. But the truth was, he couldn't—or rather wouldn't—ask her about herself, because no matter how screwed up he felt right now, he didn't want to deceive Penny into thinking this could last. But more importantly, he didn't want to hurt her by making her think that he cared more deeply for her than he knew he was capable of.

He rubbed the back of his neck as he scrolled through the articles. There weren't that many but the ones that were there raved about her skills as an event planner. She was at the top of her game. He wondered why the fashion house she'd applied to hadn't already offered her a job.

He sensed sometimes that not having a job for after Christmas was worrying for her. As it would be for anyone. It was hard not to have something to go back to. Was there anything he could do to help her?

He didn't know anyone in fashion. He was about as far from trendy as a man could be, but he did know powerful men who owned big companies that put on a lot of corporate events.

He opened his email and sent a message to the five CEOs that popped into his head first. He mentioned Penny, attached the links detailing her shows and the rave reviews they'd gotten, and then asked them to contact him if they were interested in her.

It wasn't as if this was going to make parting any easier, but it was a gift he could give her, one that she wasn't expecting, and it made him feel good. He hoped it would work out. He knew from the past that coming back from a vacation like this one could be hard. It took time to adjust back to the real world.

"Will…right?" a woman asked, walking toward him.

He recognized the pretty blonde from the resort and thought she was Penny's friend. "Yes, and you are?"

"Elizabeth Anders," she said, holding her hand out to him.

He shook it, wondering where this was going to go.

"Do you mind if I sit here? There aren't any other chairs. I'm waiting for my fiancé so I won't be here long."

"Not at all," he said, pulling a vacant chair out for her at his table. "In fact, I was hoping to meet you, as Penny invited me to be her plus-one at your wedding."

"She did? I'm glad. Penny is doing us such a favor by planning the wedding. I'm not good at being spontaneous."

Will laughed at the way she said it. "Not everyone is. I think weddings planned on the fly can be the best because you don't have time to worry over every detail."

"Are you married?"

He lifted a brow. "Would I be seeing your friend if I was?"

"You never know."

"Well, I'm not. But I was a long time ago. And my bride was the biggest, most badass bridezilla to walk down the aisle."

Elizabeth laughed. "I'm not like that. *I hope*. I did have a short list of things that I wanted to make sure Penny included, but I left the rest to her. Did she tell you we were roommates in college?"

He realized he had a chance to learn more about

Penny, more than he'd find out on the internet, from Elizabeth. He had a twinge of conscience about it, but then shrugged it away. His intent wasn't to use the information for nefarious purposes. He just wanted to know more about the woman he cared for.

"No, she didn't mention that," he said. "What kind of roommate was she? She said she likes to *chat*." Elizabeth laughed and nodded at him. "She does. But she's the best at cheering me up when I'm down. I have a real desire to be the best at everything—it's a big flaw, I know—but when I'd get a bad grade or not be in the top one percent in our class, Penny would bake me cookies and sit on my bed and talk to me until I didn't feel bad anymore."

That sounded like Penny. She had a sunshiny personality and he wondered why she hadn't found a better man to love. He knew she'd said that she had wanted to wait to find a good man, but surely it was time for that.

And as much as he hated the thought of her with anyone other than him, he wanted her to be happy.

THE DRESSES THAT Bella sent for Elizabeth had been sent to her home, but she'd included three bridesmaids' dresses each for herself and Lindsey to try on. Penny opened the package and realized they were all gorgeous. She took them out of the box slowly and held them up to herself.

Not for the first time, she had to admit she was both happy for Elizabeth and a little envious of her, as well. She'd met a great guy, overcome her problems, and now she was getting married. As opposed to Penny, who had met a great guy and agreed to have a two-week affair with him.

She turned away from her mirror and tossed a dress

on the bed. She was a mess. She did a good job of pretending that she was dealing well with everything that was going on in her life, but she didn't have a job, her boyfriend was leaving her on December 31, and unless she got her act together, she wasn't going to be able to keep fooling her friends that she was okay.

She went downstairs to the refrigerator and opened the freezer section, taking out a pint of Ben & Jerry's ice cream, and then got a big spoon. She needed the kind of comfort that only Ben and Jerry could provide. Christmas music was playing, except right now it was a sappy ballad about New Year's Eve. She walked over to her smartphone and skipped the song. What she needed was something loud and cloying, something like "Rudolph the Red-Nosed Reindeer," not something romancey. Nothing about love or plans for New Year's Eve.

The last night she'd have with Will.

She sat down on the couch, tossed the lid to the ice cream on the table and went in for a big spoonful. But it was frozen. Like, really frozen. So damned hard she couldn't get the spoon into it.

Just her luck, she thought, fighting back tears.

She put the container on the table as the songs changed again, and "I'll Be Home For Christmas" came on. She just went ahead and flicked off the music. Silence would be better than songs that stirred too many emotions inside of her.

She knew she could do this. Her own mother was in the Caribbean having the Christmas of her life with her new husband. She was glad Will hadn't asked why she wasn't spending the holidays at home, because the truth was, she didn't have one right now. Once her mom and Peter had settled into being married maybe she'd go home for holidays, but not this year.

Instead, she was standing in front of a Christmas tree decorated by her and the first man she'd really cared for in a long time.

She knew she was close to falling in love with him. It was hard not to. He did all the right things. Said all the right things. Let her be herself and just got her.

She hugged the throw pillow from the couch to her stomach. She was losing it. She'd been doing so well but planning a wedding for her friend was stupid when she was with Will. It made her think of things she normally ignored. Like if she were planning her own nuptials she'd make sure they were married outdoors in the summer in a park. Because she knew he liked to be outside and she liked the idea of it.

She had been scanning wedding magazines for ideas so she didn't forget anything for Elizabeth, but she'd earmarked pages with things she'd want for herself. It was ridiculous—she knew it. But all the same, she couldn't really help herself.

She looked at her pint of ice cream and noticed that it looked softer. She picked up the container and took a big scoop before heading over to her laptop to look for a Christmas present for Will. She had to get something for him. She thought about it for just a minute, and knew her idea could be something that he'd either love or would really be upset by. But she wanted him to have the train that reminded him of his childhood.

On top of that, she wanted to give him something that would resonate with him long after he'd forgotten her. Which he would. Just like she knew that eventually she'd forget him. Or would she? She hoped she would. It would be easier to keep on pretending she loved being single and free if she didn't remember this time with him.

Penny placed her order and asked for overnight shipping and then got up from the computer. She was going to do something for herself now—not Elizabeth or Will. Like maybe baking a big batch of cookies and taking them to the homeless shelter that Elizabeth and Bradley volunteered at.

She liked that idea. It would serve her well to remember how good she had it. That her life was filled with sweet blessings and she was standing in the spot that she'd carried herself to. And even though she didn't want to say goodbye to Will, she had to remind herself often that this was what she'd originally wanted. A no-strings, red-hot Christmas affair so that she could go back home in January and start with a clean slate.

She just hadn't realized back then that she'd have such a drastic change of heart. That was sobering, but as she mixed up a double batch of her hazelnut chocolate-chip cookies and baked off ten dozen of them, she started to find peace inside herself again.

WILL THOUGHT HE saw Penny in town at the homeless shelter and followed her inside. "Wait up."

She turned toward him with a large box in her hands that had the Lodge's bakery's logo on it.

"What are you doing here?" she asked.

"I've been in town all day, trying to get some work done," he said. When he was at the chalet he saw Penny everywhere and it made him horny—not really the right mind-set for work.

Not that he'd been able to be very productive today, anyway. It had been enlightening talking to Elizabeth and he realized as she'd shared stories about Penny how much he cared for her already.

"Did you get a lot accomplished?" she asked.

"Not really. But on one project I learned a lot more." He gestured toward the box. "What have you got there?"

"Cookies. I was making myself a little crazy with wedding planning, so I decided to bake and now have ten dozen cookies."

He laughed. Weddings were a woman thing that he would probably never understand. But he got that they were important to some of them. "Are there more cookies in your car?"

"Yes. It's the SUV we rented the day we went snowshoeing," she said, handing him the keys. "Would you mind helping me?"

"Not at all," he said, taking the keys and leaving her to talk to the man who ran the shelter. He grabbed the remaining two boxes from the backseat and carried them carefully across the icy parking lot. He had spent the entire day trying to get some distance from Penny, but it seemed the harder he tried to keep her at arm's length, the closer she got to him.

He knew that she wasn't trying to do anything to bind her to him but it was happening all the same. Maybe it was because she was being so careful to not ask too many questions about his past. She seemed content to let him share the memories that he wanted to. But perhaps that was part of her plan.

Except he found it hard to believe that the woman who'd baked ten dozen cookies for the homeless of Park City had an evil plan to make him fall for her. In fact, logic said that the opposite was true. That he was falling for her because she *didn't* have a plan. Some of the women he'd dated in the past had played at being happy with a temporary affair, but with Penny, he knew that she'd really just wanted that in the beginning.

He wouldn't blame her if, like him, she'd found her feelings changing. It was hard to spend as much time together as they had and not start caring.

Releasing a ragged breath, Will wondered if he'd finally found the one thing that would make it hard to live up to his own promises to himself.

"Where should I put these?" he asked her.

"Follow me," Penny said. She was wearing a pair of tan-colored leggings that hugged her shapely legs and a pair of riding boots that ended just above her knees. She had a light blue sweater on that ended midthigh with a big cowl collar. Her blond hair was braided to one side.

She looked cute. Tempting. It was hard to keep his mind where it needed to be when she looked like that and stood close to him smelling of vanilla and yummy cookies.

He was only a man after all.

He put the cookies on the counter where she gestured for them to go and then he turned toward her. She smiled sweetly. "I sort of missed you today."

"You did?"

"Yes, but don't let it go to your head." She looked up at him. "I had already talked to Mr. Peabody about helping out tonight. Would you like to stay as well? He said the closer it gets to Christmas, the busier everyone is."

He nodded. "I'd enjoy helping. Do you do this often?"

"At home I try to go down to the shelter there at least once a month, but today I was feeling sorry for myself and needed a reminder of how good my life is."

He smiled at her. He doubted that she moaned too

much about her life—that would be anti-Penny. As the thought entered his mind, he knew he had to end this. He was getting in way over his head. His life had worked for him because he hadn't let anyone become too important to him, but already he could tell that she was. That Penny was the one woman he didn't want to have to leave.

He stood next to her, helping serve food to the homeless who came through. Talking to them as they came up with their trays, he realized that some of these people could really use his help. So instead of listening to Penny's chat with the family who were the last ones in line, Will went out to the dining room and sat down at a table with six guys and started a real conversation with them.

He found out a little about each of the men, the kind of work they'd done and how they'd ended up here. Then he talked about his own struggles with alcohol, partly because he knew from the AA meetings he'd attended in the past how helpful it was to learn that someone else was walking in your shoes.

"I had to start completely over with my career after I got out of rehab the last time. And I couldn't have done it without the help of a mentor. Here's my card in case any of you need any help getting back into the workforce."

He sat there nursing a cup of coffee until Penny was done, but when he looked up to find her, he noticed she was leaning against the wall near the door watching him. Slowly, the place cleared out and he walked over to her.

"Why are you looking at me like that?"

"Every time I think I know you, you surprise me."

13

THE SOUND OF sirens jerked her from a solid sleep, and she glanced around her bedroom. She was alone. God… was Will all right? She heard the loud, shrill wails growing closer, so she hopped out of bed, grabbed her robe and ran downstairs. Everything was okay in her unit. She shoved her feet into her UGGs and opened the door, sticking her head out.

The sirens were much louder with the door open, and she looked up toward the Lodge, where she saw a fire truck. She glanced at Will's chalet and saw him hurrying toward her in his robe and boots.

"Are you okay?" he croaked.

"Yes. You?"

"I'm fine," he said, reaching out and wrapping her in his arms. "Thank God you're all right. I was so worried. I should have stayed at your place tonight in case you needed me."

She hugged him close. "No more sleeping apart."

"Agreed," he said. "We only have a little over a week left together."

"I know," she murmured as she tilted her face up to

gaze into his eyes. He didn't have to remind her of how much time they had left—she'd been keeping close track of it in her mind. Although she'd been trying to keep herself from caring more deeply for him, to make their eventual parting less painful, it was virtually impossible to let her mind control her heart.

So why waste precious time fighting a losing battle?

"Will, I don't want to worry about you when we are apart," she said.

He kissed her long and hard, and in that kiss she heard and felt all the things that she believed he couldn't say. That he'd been scared for her and didn't want to be alone again.

He swept her up into his arms and strode toward her chalet. She'd left the door open and he carried her over the threshold and closed the door with his foot. She leaned down to lock it.

"I'm staying tonight."

"I know," she whispered.

"Just wanted to make sure there were no doubts," he said. "I don't think I can sleep without you in my arms."

He walked to the couch and sat down, cradling her on his lap. Her Christmas tree lights were the only illumination in the room. They heard the sirens stop. Penny hoped everyone was okay at the Lodge and wondered if she should contact Elizabeth. But she knew there was nothing she could do right now.

"Want some hot cocoa?"

"Yes," he said. "I'll make a fire."

She got off his lap and went into the kitchen area, then warmed some milk before melting chocolate in it and pouring it into two mugs. She heard her phone beep upstairs and Will looked over at her.

"Want me to go get your phone?" he asked.

"Yes, please. I'm worried about Elizabeth."

He ran up the stairs and was down a moment later. "It is from Elizabeth. Sorry, I didn't mean to read it, but it was on the screen. I met her in town yesterday. She's nice."

"She's the best. Is she okay?"

"Yes. Why don't you read her text?" he said, handing her the iPhone, "and I'll bring the mugs over. Too bad you don't have any more cookies."

"Well, we can bake some tomorrow. We'll need some to leave out for Santa," she said.

"What's that?"

"My mom always had me put out cookies for Santa, and now it's become a habit I can't quite break."

He smiled over at her as he poured milk and found the bag of marshmallows she'd left on the counter. She'd bought them when she'd been in town because Will had mentioned that he liked them in his cocoa.

"Where is your mom this Christmas?" he asked curiously.

"In the Caribbean with her new husband. She got married last July," Penny said.

"You don't spend the holiday with her?" Will asked.

"No, not usually. But that's because a lot of years she's working or I'm working. Last year, I had planned a big party that was for the families of our biggest sales winners. I didn't work on Christmas day, but the party was on December 24 so it made sense to just stay home instead of traveling. Mom and I go on vacation each February."

Penny skimmed the message from Elizabeth, which simply said that the resort fire alarm had been pulled and that they'd taken care of the problem, and she hoped that Penny was okay. Penny texted back that she was fine and sat down on the couch as Will brought the mugs over and settled down next to her.

"Why do you go on vacation in February?"

"It's silly but mom and I are usually single, so we get out of Dodge for Valentine's Day. Most of the time we go someplace we haven't been before. Last year it was Venice."

"It doesn't sound silly at all. I do the same thing, except it is more of a staycation in my house. I don't leave it for days." He grimaced. "It's impossible to go to a store, even the gas station, without being bombarded with all those hearts and flowers."

She took a sip of her cocoa and leaned her head back against the sofa. She had a feeling this year her mom might not want to go away. And she was thinking about her clean slate and her future and it didn't look as great to be starting over in January as she'd thought it might.

She was going to miss Will, true. That he was there for her in the middle of the night and whenever she needed him.

"What am I going to do with you, Penny?" he asked.

Love me, she thought. But she knew that wasn't the answer he was looking for. She surprised herself by thinking it. "Enjoy Christmas with me."

ENJOYING HIS TIME with her was becoming harder and harder. She stirred too much inside of him. Things he never wanted to feel or think about again. And he knew that no matter how much he tried to keep things from going any deeper, it was almost too late.

If he were a different sort of man…then maybe this

could work, but he wasn't and she couldn't change him. He drank the cocoa she'd made and remembered that he'd been sleeping at his place to preserve the distance he needed between them.

But waking up to an alarm, fearing something could have happened to her, had brought home to him that no matter what the future held, at this moment he needed her close to him. Needed to ensure her safety and well-being.

She seemed pensive and not her usual sunny self tonight. He toyed with a strand of her hair as she leaned back against the couch and sipped at her drink.

"Thanks for getting marshmallows," he said.

She shrugged. "It was no big deal." But he knew it was. She'd gotten them for him. It was the kind of small gesture that let him know she thought about him when they were apart.

"Actually, I'm lying," she confessed. "I've been thinking about you a lot and I like doing things that make you happy. But my intel on you is kind of limited, and I'm struggling not to ask too many questions or try to get to know you better."

"Why?" Will asked in a low voice. But he wasn't ready for this conversation. He'd thought they'd have at least until the day after Christmas before she started realizing how close they were to leaving each other.

"Because then it will be harder to say goodbye. I'm not going to try to change our agreement, but I can't tell if it's because we know when it will end that I find you so attractive…or if it's the real thing."

Will felt the same but there was no way he was going to let her know. He needed to keep her in the dark about his feelings so that he could continue to lie to himself. "Hell."

He stood up and walked over to the window that overlooked the Wasatch Range. It was dark and he saw only a shadow of his own reflection in the glass. He looked like a man who'd spent too long running.

But he couldn't stop. Wouldn't stop. Already Penny was making him confront things he'd thought he'd left in the dust.

"I'm not going to say I'm sorry," she said. "That would be a lie. But I will say I didn't mean to feel this way."

He turned to face her. She had her arms crossed around her waist and watched him with that level stare of hers that made him feel like he'd let her down. Hell, he knew he had. He'd let himself down, as well.

"Penny, I can't. There are too many things in my past that I just can't share with you. You have helped me recall some happy memories of my childhood that would have been lost forever, but there are other things that I don't want to relive. I can't do it. I'm sorry."

He didn't want to end things now. He wanted it to be like the Christmas song. "We are close to having a merry little Christmas," he said. "Penny, put your troubles away and let this continue the way it has been."

"I'm trying, Will. Really, I am. But it's hard. I want to know all about your past. I want to share things about mine. When you asked about my mom, it occurred to me that she'd like you. And I think you'd like her." She sighed. "But that's not what we are about, is it?" Will watched her carefully. He knew she needed more from him, and he had this moment. This one chance to buckle and give her what she needed, but he was afraid he'd just be fooling himself if he did that. Every relationship he'd had ended. First the one with his parents—he knew that was an accident but they were gone. Then his brief marriage had sort of cemented the fact that he didn't know how to make something last. He wanted to believe things would be different with Penny, but he wasn't sure that they really could be.

Because no matter how much it might seem as if the two of them could build a meaningful life together—away from the Lodge—he feared that was just a fantasy. Before long, the real world would intrude, and he'd end up breaking both their hearts.

Frustrated, he raked a hand through his hair. "Do you want me to leave?"

"No," she said. "I want you to care."

"Dammit, I do care, Penny. Don't think that I don't."

"Then why is this enough for you?" she asked, waving her arms around. "Just two weeks? That's not healthy."

"It is healthy. And it's all I have to give you. It's okay if you've changed your mind," Will said, but in his heart he knew it wasn't. He wasn't ready to say goodbye to her yet—he wanted all the days she'd promised. Those hours belonged to them.

"I haven't changed my mind," she informed him. "Maybe I've changed my heart. I thought I would be safe by knowing we were going to say goodbye on December 31, but I'm not. I care about you, Will. Each and every hour we spend together makes me want to hoard them in a memory chest."

She turned away and walked to the kitchen, putting her mug in the sink before she faced him again. She braced her hands on the counter and leaned over to stare at him. He thought he saw a sheen of tears in her eyes and he knew a better man would leave, end it now be-

fore this went any further, but he was also a little selfish
and he wanted her. Needed her.

"Should I go?" he asked again.

Penny said nothing. Just kept watching him. Then
she shook her head. "No, I don't want that. I want—"
She broke off and shook her head. "Never mind…I'm
fine. I think the fire alarm just scared me because I was
afraid for your safety."

"I understand that," he said, coming over to her, rubbing his hand over the back of her head to see if she'd
let him touch her.

She turned to face him and then sighed and curled
her arms around him. He held her loosely but inside the
vise around his heart loosened as they embraced. He
was afraid he'd lost her.

PENNY HAD PUSHED and hoped for better results, but at
the end of the day—or in this case in the middle of
the night—she didn't want to say goodbye to him. He
smelled so good and she felt safe in his arms. He
threaded his fingers through her hair, tugging gently
until she tipped her head back.

He brought his mouth down to hers. Kissed her long
and hard, their tongues tangling as he thrust his deep
into her mouth. He lifted her off her feet and set her on
the countertop. She cradled his face in her hands and
leaned down to keep kissing him.

His hands slipped inside of her robe and caressed her
body through the thin layer of her nightgown, and she
wrapped her legs around his middle.

He tore his mouth from hers and looked up at her.

"Is this enough?" he bit out. "Please let this be enough
for tonight."

She swallowed. She wasn't about to say no. Not to-night. "Yes."

He lifted her in his arms again and carried her up the stairs to the bedroom. The music continued to play downstairs and the lights from her tree were the only illumination. He let his robe fall to the floor and he was naked underneath, and obviously turned on. She reached for him. Touched his smooth chest with that thin smattering of hair that went down his abs.

She let her fingers explore him and he stood there with his breath catching in his throat as she brought her hand closer and closer to his erection. He was such a fine male. She felt lucky to have found him.

She wrapped her hand around his cock and walked backward to her bed, tugging gently, but he was right in step with her. She stroked him up and down, reaching between his legs to cup his balls.

She wanted this night to force him to realize how much she meant to him. To make this night one they'd never forget. She wished there was something she could say that would make him start thinking about staying with her for longer than the end of the year.

But for right now, she needed to have him inside her. To feel him possessing her…body and soul. She needed to reaffirm that her grasp on him, however tenuous, was still there.

He kissed her again and she saw in his passion-glazed eyes that he wanted to say something, but she felt like she was on the edge of losing it and just couldn't talk anymore.

Penny slid her robe off her shoulders and sat on the edge of her bed, scooted back until she was in the middle, then pulled her nightshirt up and over her head and threw it on the floor.

"Make love to me," she said. To her ears, her voice sounded raw and strained, but she didn't care. Hiding the fact that she wanted him was beyond her. Tonight she'd laid her cards on the table and she'd lost.

Lost.

God, she felt adrift, and the only thing that she was sure of was that she wanted him to make love to her until she could stop thinking. Otherwise she'd never be able to sleep and she'd have to do the one thing that she really didn't want to.

Say goodbye to Will.

But she wasn't going to let this be the end. She was going to prove to Will in any way she could that there was still more between them.

He walked forward and put one knee down on the bed and then crawled toward her.

"Penny—"

"Don't say anything. I just want sex," she said.

His eyes said he knew she was lying, but he stopped talking and came up over her. Used his chest to caress her from the apex of her thighs to her breasts, and then his mouth was on hers as he propped himself up on an elbow and stroked her from neck to waist and back again.

She was swept up in the passion, kept kissing and caressing him. Needing to memorize his entire body with the touch of her hands. She wouldn't stop. She needed him. Needed him *now*.

She reached between his legs and grasped his cock again.

He moaned her name and the sound sent shivers down her spine. The way he made love to her always made her believe that he must care deeply for her, but then she remembered that he was good at compartmentalizing things. Including women. Especially her.

"Are you ready for me?" he rasped.

"Yes," she said.

He shifted his hips and she felt him at the entrance of her body. He pushed forward slowly, just an inch entering her.

"Take me hard," she commanded.

He groaned and thrust all the way into her. Penny moaned his name, and as he continued to pound into her, she threw her head back. She wanted to keep him there. Keep him in her bed and in her body since he wouldn't allow her to keep him in her heart.

She stroked her hand down his back and cupped his butt, urging him to ride her harder and harder until her orgasm took her by surprise. She came hard, stars dancing behind her eyes and her breath rushing out of her in quick gasps.

He came a second later and collapsed on top of her, his body covered with sweat and his hot exhalations brushing over her breast. He pulled her close for a cuddle and she thought about turning away. Making him leave. But she knew that would be spiteful and she wasn't going to sleep without him by her side just to prove to herself that she could. Come January 1 she'd be sleeping alone every night.

That would be soon enough.

14

WILL DIDN'T SLEEP WELL. His dreams were plagued by fires and Penny. He was the one trapped inside and he couldn't get to her no matter how hard he tried.

He sat up, scrubbed a hand over his face and looked at the empty bed. Where was she?

He listened carefully but there were no noises from downstairs or the bathroom. Getting up, he pulled on his robe and went downstairs to find a note telling him that she had gone to meet her friends for breakfast and that he could let himself out.

She'd signed her name and added a little smiley face after it, but in his gut he knew that nothing was the same this morning.

He had let her down last night. Or maybe she'd let herself down, he couldn't say for sure. But something had changed between them.

He found his boots and put them on and then left her chalet for his. His Chrismas tree was arriving today and he'd asked her to dinner, but he wondered if she'd still show up. It was December 23. Only two more days until Christmas and a part of him wanted…to slow time.

But the other part, the realist inside him, wanted it to go more quickly. Needed to find a way to get her out of his life before she found her way deep into his soul. God, what a mess.

He entered his chalet, showered and changed, and then sat down at his computer. Work, which had long been his shelter from loneliness and his messed-up life, wasn't working. Instead, as he read the financial pages of various international newspapers, he was struck by the fact that none of the CEOs he'd written had gotten back to him about a job for Penny.

Dammit. She mattered to him. Really mattered to him.

What was he going to do? Maybe start pulling back. Make up excuses—lie? It was the one thing he'd promised her he wouldn't do. The one thing that he knew was the unbreakable promise between them. He was aware of how her last lover had deceived her. Understood why lying wasn't something she'd tolerate. And normally he'd agree, but in this instance, it might work in his favor. Give him the clean break he needed.

Because she had become too important to him.

If he thought there was a chance in hell that they could continue on, he might be tempted to take it. But he didn't believe in forever. Had tried it once to disastrous results. He knew that he wasn't like other folks. Or maybe that he was like the 50 percent of people who never could commit to someone else.

He'd felt superior to the men that had been in Penny's life before. Had told himself that he was better than they were, but now he felt like a total fraud. That by offering her this temporary affair he'd proved he was just the same as the others.

He wanted to be better. Wanted to give her everything but was too aware of the failings inside of himself. Things that made it impossible for that to happen.

Will left his chalet, but instead of heading toward the Lodge, he started down the path that lead to the hiking trails. He needed to clear his head. The air was cool and as he walked away from the Lodge and civilization and the signs of Christmas that were everywhere, he felt his pulse start to calm and that inner peace he worked so hard to keep returned.

This wasn't a "make it or break it" moment in his life. She was just a girl.

No, she wasn't. She was Penny. She had that thing that made him want to be better and to stay in the sunshine that she projected with her smile.

He stopped walking and sat down on one of the benches the Lodge provided. His legendary cool had deserted him and he had a sinking feeling that he wasn't going to get it back by running away from her.

But staying?

He hadn't lived with anyone since he'd tried marriage. Kara had lasted for exactly six weeks before she'd ghosted out of his life. Rightly so. He'd been…obsessed and controlling.

He knew how he got when a relationship was serious. It didn't matter that he'd been twenty-one then and in desperate need of someone to call his own.

At thirty-five he still wanted that and didn't like it. He didn't have that thing that other men did that made them normal in a relationship. He knew how he could be, and by adding the word *temporary*, he'd found a way to keep things from getting out of hand. To have companionship for a short time without losing himself.

Or scaring off the women. In this case, Penny.

He got up and started hiking again, but no matter how fast he walked, he couldn't outrun his past. Couldn't get the image out of his head of making an offer to keep her in his life only to have it ruin them both.

He needed to remember that Penny was different and special, but she wasn't meant to be his forever. He couldn't forget that.

Will heard the silence of the trees around him and the sound of the snow falling from the branches. It reminded him of the snowshoeing he'd done with Penny. He really wasn't sure how he was ever going to be able to be free of her.

Already he wanted her more than anyone else. And the feelings he'd had for Kara at twenty-one seemed like mere puppy love compared to the depth of need he now had for Penny.

He started running instead of walking. Felt the burn of each inhalation of cold air down his throat and into his lungs. He ran faster and found a pace that was punishing, and since the path was icy and uneven in places, he had to pay attention. Will did it for as long as he could and then slowed to a walk to cool down.

He put his hands in the pockets of his jacket and found a piece of paper he hadn't realized was in there. He pulled it out. The note from Penny that morning. He traced his finger over her signature and her smiley face, and knew he wanted to be the one who kept her smiling.

BREAKFAST WITH THE girls had never been so welcome. Elizabeth had picked both her and Lindsey up at the Lodge and driven them to her house. She and Lindsey brought the bridesmaids' dresses that Bella had sent them. The plan was to try everything on and pick a dress that morning.

Penny sat in the backseat, staring at the landscape as they drove to Elizabeth's house. The last thing she wanted to do this morning was talk. Last night she'd realized she couldn't keep lying to herself and pretending that temporary with Will was okay. She'd vacillated back and forth over the course of the days they were together, but she knew now she couldn't keep doing it.

She really cared for him—borderline loved him. She didn't want to admit that or let herself care that deeply, but she faced the fact that it might be too late.

"You okay?" Lindsey asked when they were in Elizabeth's house and her friend had gone into the bedroom to try on the first wedding dress.

"I'm fine…just tired," she said. "There was a fire alarm in the middle of the night at the Lodge."

"I heard about that from the staff at the recreation area. I'm glad no one was hurt."

"Me, too."

"I need help doing the back of the dress," Elizabeth announced, walking into the living room. The dress was in the art-deco style, which Elizabeth loved. It was made of white satin and skimmed close to her body at the top, gently flowing outward through the skirt. The neckline had very stylized platinum embroidery. She stood there in front of them with her hair flowing around her shoulders, and Penny thought she was absolutely stunning.

She hurried to help her friend do up the gown. The simple design showed off Elizabeth's own effortless beauty. Made her the one everyone wouldn't be able to take their eyes off of. It was a little big in the bust but otherwise fit like a dream. The bride's mom was com-

ing into town tomorrow and would handle the altera-
tions. They were trying the dresses on in Elizabeth's
living room because she had a panel of mirrors on the
wall. Her friend turned to look at herself and Penny
knew from that sparkle in her blue-green eyes that she
liked what she saw.

"I love it," Elizabeth said. "There's a veil to go with
it. Will one of you go get it? It's sort of a cap with a
long veil."

"I'll do it," Lindsey offered.

Penny hugged her friend and felt the stirring of tears
at the backs of her eyes. "You look so gorgeous. Bradley
isn't going to be able to take his eyes off you."

"It's perfect. I couldn't have picked something more
me."

"Here ya go," Lindsey said as she rejoined them. The
Nordic blonde helped Elizabeth get the veil on her head
and adjusted the long train of her dress and then just
stood next to the bride-to-be.

"Okay, that's my dress," Elizabeth said. "Now what
about you two?"

"Um, I liked the red and green colors. So I had a
thought…" Penny began.

"I like the green one best," Lindsey interjected.

Elizabeth looked at her best friend. "What's your
thought, Penn?"

"What if I teamed the dresses with some gray snow
boots for the outdoorsy photos?"

"I love it," Elizabeth said.

"Me, too," Lindsey added.

"Go try the dresses on," Elizabeth urged, and they
both went to separate bathrooms to get dressed and then
came back.

Lindsey looked so tall and graceful that Penny felt like a little kid standing next to her. But at least the dress she'd been sent fit her pretty good since they'd sent their measurements to Bella and she'd gotten even the skirt length right.

"You two look beautiful," Elizabeth said, wrapping her arms around each of their shoulders and drawing them close to her.

Staring at the three of them in the mirror, Penny smiled. They did look good. "I like it."

"I do, too. That was easy," Lindsey said. "My sister took four weeks of dress shopping before she ended up picking the very first dress she tried on."

"That's crazy…and since I only have a week until the wedding, I can't be too picky. Plus this is lovely. Bella really paid attention to the details I sent her. I love it," Elizabeth reiterated. "Thank you, Lindsey."

"No problem."

"I think we have everything sorted for your ceremony at the Lodge," Penny said. "I've booked you the gazebo near the pool and park area. It has a large circle drive and I was thinking you could arrive on the horse-drawn sleigh. What do you think?"

"Sounds heavenly," Elizabeth said. "Thank you so much for doing this for me. When you get married, I will plan yours."

Penny nodded but doubted she'd be getting married anytime soon. "That's not exactly in the cards for me."

"Why not? Will seems like a nice guy and he's not married already," Elizabeth said with a wink. "I asked."

"I did, too," Penny admitted. She quickly caught Lindsey up on her romantic track record with less-than-great guys.

"I've always been too busy to date and the only guys

I used to meet were competitors like me, and they all seemed too arrogant," Lindsey admitted. "But I do hope to get married someday."

Penny always had, too. But she had fallen for Will and he was not interested in marriage. By his own words, commitment wasn't for him.

"So what's the problem with Will?" Elizabeth asked after they changed back into their regular clothes and were having breakfast in her kitchen.

"He's not the marrying kind. He only does two-week relationships," Penny said.

"Uh, that's not what he told me," Elizabeth said offhandedly.

"What?"

"He's been married before," her friend explained. "We talked about brides and weddings when I ran into him in town."

A spark of anger started deep inside of her. All the excuses she'd been making for him…all the leeway she'd given him…now seemed like a big fat lie. Because the man who claimed he couldn't do anything longer than two weeks *could* do it. Just not with her.

WILL SAT IN the Lodge lobby listening to the Christmas music and watching the fire. He had a book in his hands. He preferred to read paperbacks over ebooks, though he did have the Kindle app on his iPad. But there was something about the tactile feel of the book in his hands that he liked.

He hadn't figured out what to do next with Penny, but he knew he could no longer deny that he wanted more with her. Now he just had to figure out how to bring it up. He had the thought that she might be amenable to meeting throughout the year for two weeks at a time until they figured out if this was a Christmas thing or something real.

Will rested his head against the back of the chair and closed his eyes. He thought he smelled Penny's vanilla-scented body lotion and turned to find her perched on the edge of the chair closest to him.

"Can we talk?" she asked.

He grinned. She looked so pretty she took his breath away. With her long silky hair, big blue eyes and those sensuous lips that always made him want to kiss her. He remembered the way she'd made love with him last night and knew he'd found something special with her. She was his equal on every level when it came to sex and her drive matched his. In fact, she complemented the things he was good at and evened out the things he'd never tried.

"Yes, of course. I wasn't sure when you'd be back from breakfast with your friends so I've been sort of hanging out and waiting for you. I wanted to speak to you, as well."

"That's good," she said, giving him a tight smile. "What did you want to discuss?"

"It's probably a conversation that would be better-suited to some privacy instead of here in the lobby," Will said. He hoped that when he suggested they continue their vacation affair, she'd be happy. But either way, discussing their private lives in the lobby didn't feel right to him.

"Sounds good. Want to go for a walk?" she asked. "There's a path that leads to a park. It's a location I need to check out again for Elizabeth's wedding."

"I'd like that. Let me get my coat from the coat check," he said. "I'll meet you back here in a few minutes."

She nodded. She still wore her coat and had the scarf he'd given her tied around her neck, but it felt like something was off. That he was missing something important. He claimed his coat and tucked the book into the pocket as he walked back to Penny.

He realized she hadn't touched him since she'd approached him. She always either hugged or kissed him whenever she saw him. He tried to pretend it wasn't important, but it felt as if it was.

Something had changed between last night and this morning. Perhaps he had been kidding himself when he thought that he could just keep things the way they'd always been. It had been wishful thinking to believe that he'd have what he wanted and still get her to agree to it.

He knew in business that risks had to be taken—but he was going to ask her to meet him again after Christmas. Wasn't that a big enough risk?

Perhaps she just didn't know where she stood with him. Maybe if he could convince her to give him more time…that would work.

He wasn't one to give in or give up lightly.

But as he headed back toward her, he stopped to observe her where she stood in the middle of the lobby by the fireplace. She looked small and lost, he thought with a pang. Unlike how he'd ever seen her before. He felt responsible.

He'd only wanted to give her a Christmas she wouldn't forget. Take the same thing for himself. But he seemed to have done something to hurt her. He wouldn't know what it was until they talked.

Will walked up to her, wrapping one arm around her,

and she gave him that stiff smile again as she pulled away. "Ready to go?"

"Not yet," he said gruffly. "What gives? Have I done something?"

She bit her lower lip. "I'd rather talk about that when we're alone."

"Fine. But I thought we left things in a pretty decent place when we went to sleep last night. I'm sorry I didn't hear you wake up this morning."

She shook her head. "It's not that. I was quiet so I wouldn't disturb you."

"Then what is it?" he asked, holding the door for her and she walked through, turning toward the path that led to the recreation area. He followed her. She was moving quickly. Her steps short and almost angry.

"Penny. We're alone here. Tell me," he insisted.

She stopped and shoved her hands into the pockets of her coat. Looked up at him with eyes that were sparking with outrage. "Tell me again how you always have two-week affairs because you can't commit to anyone longer than that."

"What?" he asked. "You know that's the truth. What's this about?"

"I had a very interesting conversation about weddings this morning with Elizabeth and was surprised to learn that you knew a little something on the subject of brides. That you'd been married."

Oh, crap. Kara was so long ago he didn't consider her anymore, but he understood how it might look to Penny.

"It's not what you think," he said.

"Really? Did you marry her?"

He felt cold deep inside his soul. This was not going to end well. "Yes."

"Then it's exactly what I thought," she said. "You're another liar."

15

PENNY SAW ON his face that he was scrambling to find an answer. Something to say that would placate her and make everything okay, but it was futile. She turned and stormed away from him and the Lodge. Walked farther down the snow-covered path and tried to force herself to remember he was only her two-week lover.

Forget that she'd started to believe he could be more. Forget that she had started to care about him and had hoped he cared about her, as well. Because Will had been playing her all along. Pretending to be one thing just so he could have his no-strings-attached affair.

The worst part was she would have been fine with it if he hadn't said he could *never* marry. She wouldn't have thought of marriage—she wasn't looking for forever. But knowing what he'd said, and the kind of closeness they'd shared since then, she felt betrayed.

She wanted it to just be anger. That would make it so much easier.

But it was hurt, too.

She'd been honest with him. Confided things that she usually kept carefully tucked away from the world to protect herself, but he'd made it seem as if it might be okay, and now she knew it wasn't.

He'd been playing a game. A different game than Butch had, but at the same time, it felt pretty damned similar.

"Penny!"

"Unless you have something new to say, something that will make up for the last week of you pretending that marriage was something you'd never consider, than forget it," she said.

He caught her arm and tugged her to a stop. "No."

"No?"

"That's what I said. I'm not going to let you throw out a comment like that and walk away." He spoke through gritted teeth, his eyes dark with pain. "The truth is, I was married when I was twenty-one. It lasted for less than a month and then it ended. I was horrible at being married and I learned from that and moved on. I never think of Kara as my wife, I think of her as a…mistake. I wished I'd been more mature so I wouldn't have made it."

She didn't want him to make sense. Didn't want to listen to him and let go of her anger. Part of her knew it was because if she were mad then she'd be able to just leave. Break things off with him now instead of letting her vulnerable heart become more attached to him.

Another part of her acknowledged it was too late.

"I'm listening."

"There's nothing more to tell."

"I think there is," she said. "Why didn't it work out?"

He sighed. "It's not a very flattering picture of me."

"That's okay. Your image isn't that great in my mind right now anyway."

He moved a few steps away from her and looked out at

the snowy landscape. "I had been alone for so long. First at boarding school and then at various summer camps and college. I dated Kara in college and we decided to marry. I never thought what it would be like when I had someone else to share my life."

She got it—he'd been alone. But she wasn't making the connections that would make this all seem sensible. He'd said he didn't do commitment, yet he had. That meant he'd lied. And she wasn't going to just let him off the hook. "What happened?"

He looked at her for a long moment. "I guess I panicked in a way. I got really possessive and didn't want her to leave my side. I had nightmares and woke up in a cold sweat. I scared her." He exhaled sharply. "She was willing to give me time to get over it, but I saw things in myself that I couldn't handle."

She felt a little sad when she thought of Will at that age. Finally finding someone to share his life and then being completely overwhelmed by it. "You were young."

"I was. I started drinking after she left and when I got sober, I realized that for me letting someone that close was like reopening the pain I felt when my parents left. I couldn't feel safe with Kara because I worried she'd die unexpectedly." There was a long pause. "So I stopped getting emotionally involved. I limited myself to two-week flings where there wasn't time to let anything serious develop." His jaw flexed as he stared into her eyes. "And that worked...until now."

Now? She didn't want to believe that she was different to him. But she could tell already she was. She had to believe that the love that had started growing in her heart would be mirrored in his.

"In what way?" she asked him.

"I can't just leave you on December 31," he said bluntly. "But I'm afraid to take a leap, as well. I wanted to ask you something, but first do you understand why I didn't mention my marriage?"

"Not really. I mean when you talked about how you were afraid of losing her, I get that. I think we all feel that way when we find someone to care about. I know I do."

"True enough, but it is so far back in my mind. That was fourteen years ago, Penny. I'm thirty-five and life looks a lot different now. I'm not the man I was at twenty-one, but those same demons still reside inside of me."

She looked at him with his thick head of light brown hair and intense blue eyes. That face that had become so dear to her over the last week…and she wanted to harden her heart. Find some way to keep herself safe from him. But she couldn't. "Is there anything else you haven't told me?"

"No."

"Think about it, Will. Be very sure before you answer. Because if I find out you've lied about anything else, I won't be able to forgive you," she said.

He closed the gap between them in two long strides, drew her into his arms and kissed her fiercely. "I promise you there is nothing else."

PENNY WALKED AROUND the gazebo and Will followed her. He really hadn't meant to talk about Kara with Penny's friend, but the truth was that Penny made him feel like his past wasn't a dark quagmire, and he was thinking about things that he hadn't really dwelled on in years. He trusted Elizabeth because Penny did…he had started to become involved with a community of people. She scraped some snow off the railing of the gazebo and turned to look at him.

"What do you think? I'm going to drape lighted garland around the pillars and the top. Pretty enough for a winter wedding?" she asked.

He shrugged. "You're asking me? Wedding planning isn't really my forte, but yeah, I guess it will be pretty enough. Is that what you want for your own wedding?"

"Wouldn't you like to know!" She curled the snow in her hand into a ball and he noticed it a second before she lifted her arm and lobbed the ball at him. He tried to duck but it caught him on the shoulder, splattering snow on his face.

"Oops," she said while laughing. "Sorry that hit you."

Yeah, right. "No problem."

Will noticed she was scraping more snow from the railings and he had a feeling he was about to become her target again. He reached down and grabbed a handful of snow, standing up just as another snowball hit him in the chest.

She giggled but when he looked up he couldn't see her. Then he noticed her pink knit cap behind one of the pillars of the gazebo.

He packed his snow into a round ball and strode toward her.

"Another misfire?" he goaded.

"Maybe," she said, popping out from behind the pillar to fire another snowball at him.

But he was ready this time and knocked hers away while throwing one of his own, which hit her on the shoulder. It shattered and got in her hair and on her hat.

She laughed and ran toward the open field behind the gazebo, and bent to scoop up another handful of snow.

He followed at a safe distance and made another snowball for himself. But as he bent to pick up more snow, he got hit on the back.

"Are there any rules to this game?" he asked in a mocking tone.

"Nope. I'm aiming to hit you when I can."

He fired one toward her and it hit her leg as she turned and ran toward the line of trees in the distance. He followed after her with his last snowball and tossed it as she turned to see where he was and it hit her square in the chest. She threw her arms out to the side and fell backward.

"You got me."

"I did," he said, walking over to her. She moved her arms and legs, making a snow angel, and he fell down a short distance from her and did the same.

"I'm sorry I didn't mention my marriage," he said as he moved his arms and legs. He'd never been with anyone he cared for as deeply as Penny, not even Kara. It scared him. Way more than he wanted to admit.

He looked over at her and noticed she was staring at him. "I just wanted to be special. Like the one woman who made you feel something more. And I thought I got you, but then when I learned about your marriage, I realized that I didn't. There are still things we haven't shared."

He sat up and turned toward her, messing up his snow angel. "I know. But you *are* special, Penny. Before you asked me about Kara, I wanted to talk to you about something that is important to me."

She nodded. "I'd get up but I don't want to ruin my angel."

He laughed and got to his feet. "Give me your hands."

She did and he lifted her straight up and caught her around the waist, setting her down next to her snow angel.

"Closest I'll get to wings," she said, wiggling her brows. Then she dusted the snow from her back and looked up at him. "What were you saying…?"

"Would you consider meeting me for vacations through the year? Giving the two of us a chance to see if there is more between us than just Christmas?"

Penny tipped her head to the side as she studied him. She licked her lips and then slowly nodded. "It will depend on my job situation. I'm going to be living off my savings until I get another position, but I would like that. I'm not ready to say goodbye to you yet, either."

He wrapped his hand around her gloved one, but she held him at her side, reaching up with her free hand to flick at the snow caught in his bangs. Then she kissed his jaw. "I'm not sure what to do with you, Will."

"I don't know how you mean?"

"It's hard because I've never gone into something like this knowing it will be just for fun."

"I know. You are making this all new to me. It feels like I've been waiting for you for my entire life and that scares me. Makes me want to retreat and yet, at the same time, I don't want to lose you." His Adam's apple bobbed up and down. "When I saw how angry you were earlier, I was afraid I wouldn't have any more time with you. I didn't want that."

"Why not?" she asked gently.

He couldn't confess to his emotions. Not now. Maybe not ever. He intended to do this until he had a chance to figure out how to keep Penny with him and not lose his mind in the process.

"It's not Christmas and I have some fun plans for us on that day."

She looked disappointed.

"I can't change overnight, Penny. I want more but I can't make any promises right now. I need to know that you're okay with taking this one step at a time."

PENNY FELT LIKE she'd been through the ringer today but there was something nice about standing in the snow with Will. Over his shoulder she saw their snow angels. Hers so perfect, thanks to him, and his just a little messier.

Sort of like the two of them. They were figuring things out together and his offer to see her again after the New Year was good. But already she knew it wouldn't be enough. She had to figure out what to do next. But not now.

She wanted to enjoy these next few days, and Christmas, and then she could try to deal with what would happen between them. She stepped back. "Want to go and bake some cookies with me?"

"No."

"Why? You have something else in mind?"

"Yes, in fact, I do. I want to go and make love to you," he said. "I want to make sure that everything is okay between us."

"Sex isn't an answer," she told him. "It didn't help last night, did it?"

"I thought it did," he said huskily.

"It left me feeling like I was grasping at you, trying to hold a man who was already gone."

He shook his head, then pulled her close, but she didn't want that. She realized that this was all like frosting on a cookie that had been broken. It might look nice on the surface but underneath the problems were still there.

And meeting for vacations was the same as what they had right now. In order for her to ever truly be happy with Will, she knew she was going to need more. Something that she feared he wouldn't be able to give her.

Learning about his marriage had revealed the truth that had been dancing just out of reach since they met. The solid reason why a handsome, successful man like Will was still a bachelor at thirty-five. And even though Penny was tempted to try to fix him—or change him— that wasn't going to happen.

Hadn't she learned anything from her mom and dad? It was like her mom said, love wasn't always hearts and flowers. Sometimes it hurt.

"What are you thinking?" he asked anxiously. "If it means that much, I'll make cookies with you."

She shook her head. There was no way she could explain this to him. She wanted to be the light, carefree girl she'd been when they'd met under the mistletoe, but she wasn't that same person anymore.

She would never be that girl again.

Falling for Will had changed something inside of her, and the way she'd fluttered through life, finding these meaningless little relationships that let her down, was no longer acceptable. She wanted it all.

"I can't do this," Penny said.

"Do what?"

"Pretend that I'm happy with a promise of more sexy vacations together. I think I want more from you," she admitted. "I'll understand if you don't. I get it. From what you said, that's not what you're looking for."

He dropped her hand. "It's not."

Blinking back tears, she nodded. It was the confirmation of what she'd already figured out for herself. "Okay. Then let's stick with our original arrangement."

"Are you sure? Seems like that isn't going to be enough for either of us," he said.

"What choice do we have? Spend the rest of our vacations in cabins next to each other, pretending we don't exist?" she asked. "That sounds ridiculous, doesn't it?"

"I don't want to do any of that. Why can't you agree to my suggestion?" He placed his hands on her shoulders and stared down at her intently. "It's a step forward."

"Because it's not really a solution. It's just postponing the inevitable. Unless you really do think you can change. Can you?" she asked softly. From everything he said and her own rotten luck when it came to men— Actually, that wasn't true. She didn't have rotten luck. She'd just spent so much time trying to keep from falling in love that it had snuck up on her when she wasn't looking.

And she wanted to believe that maybe that emotion was in his heart, as well. But the truth was, just because she had fallen for Will didn't mean he'd fallen for her. That wasn't the way the world worked.

There were no scales of fairness or balance that ensured couples loved each other equally. She knew that. So although she desperately wanted to cling to the hope that maybe things would be different, she knew she had to prepare herself for the worst.

Which meant steeling her heart and mentally readying herself to have this one and only Christmas with Will.

"So just our original agreement, then?" he asked.

"Yes. And sex is okay but no more spending the night together. That makes it feel like a relationship."

He hardened his jaw and shoved his hands in his pockets. Looking as if he wanted to argue but then thought better of it.

She sighed. The day that had started out so full of hope and promise was turning gray and stormy. Not just in her heart but also all around them. The snow clouds were heavy and the flurries started falling as they walked back toward the Lodge. A messenger from the concierge met them as they entered the lobby and told her that she had two packages waiting.

Will excused himself and told her he'd meet her later, and she watched him walk away. It hurt a little seeing him go, even though she knew she'd see him that evening. She told herself it was a view she should get used to, because before long he'd be walking away for good.

16

WILL WAS TEMPTED to go to the small grocery and sundries store in the Lodge and get a bottle of Glenlivet to take back to his room with him. He actually stopped in the store before he realized what he was doing. He couldn't let himself go backward, and yet at the same time he needed something to dull the pain he felt right now.

He hadn't wanted to hurt Penny or leave them both in this position, where there was no step forward and no way to go back.

He stood there in front of the whiskey display, trying to make himself leave, but he didn't want to. Sweet oblivion beckoned and all he had to do was reach out and pick up the bottle. He lifted his hand.

"Will?"

He glanced over his shoulder and saw Elizabeth standing at the end of the aisle. She gave him a tentative smile. He dropped his arm and walked over to where she was. Pretending he was okay. Faking it the best he could until he was alone. That was too damned close.

"Hi, Elizabeth."

"I think I might have spoken out of turn to Penny earlier," she began uncomfortably. "I didn't realize she wasn't aware of your marriage. I'm sorry."

He shook his head. "It's no problem. Besides, if you had known the circumstances beforehand, would you have really kept it from her?"

Elizabeth started to nod but then shook her head. "I couldn't. She's my best friend. I'd want to protect her if I could."

"I want to do the same. To be honest, it wasn't something I thought would matter," Will admitted. But he knew that Penny wouldn't like it if he discussed their relationship with her friend. "Thanks for being upfront with me."

"I felt I at least owed you a warning that I mentioned your marriage." Still looking uneasy, she cleared her throat. "So, how are you finding your stay at the Lodge?"

"Very nice."

Elizabeth nodded. "If there is anything I can do to make your stay more pleasant, please let me know."

"You've already gone above and beyond," he said. "I can see how the Lodge earned each of its five stars."

She flushed. "It's not really down to me. I've only been the GM for six weeks."

"Did you come in from another resort?" he asked, leading her away from the groceries and back out into the hallway. Now that he was talking, he started feeling normal again, like he didn't need the Glenlivet anymore.

"No, I have worked here for the last ten years. It's like a family. I doubt Lars would let an outsider have a position of power here or at his resort in the Caribbean."

"There aren't many resorts that can still have that kind of control over themselves," Will said.

"We're lucky that Lars has a great board who respect him. Most of them are friends he's made over the years. People who believe in his leadership and share his philosophy on running his luxury resorts," Elizabeth said. "I'd be happy to give you more information if you need it for your portfolio."

"Thank you," he said, but he had all the business information he needed from her. "I think I'm good for now."

"Okay, I will see you later." She flashed a smile. "Take care."

She walked away and Will made himself leave the store, as well. He headed toward his chalet but somehow ended up at Penny's instead. Taking a deep breath, he knocked on her door, and when she opened it, he stepped over the threshold.

"I'm sorry I can't be more."

"Don't be," she said. "We're going to have fun and pretend that each day is enough."

He wished it were that easy, but he was willing to give it a try because the alternative was that he headed back to the sundries store and bought that bottle of whiskey. She had two packages under her tree but not wrapped presents. They were big shipping boxes.

"What's in there?"

"Presents for you," she said with a half smile. "Are you someone who likes to peek?"

Will shook his head. Truth was, he hadn't received a present in years. He didn't have close friends and if he wanted something he'd get it for himself.

"I'm afraid I *am* the type that peeks," she confessed. "That's why my mom doesn't send my presents until the last minute. I wish I had your willpower."

"It's not willpower, I just don't get presents," he said.

"What? Why not?" she asked incredulously. She leaned back against the counter at the kitchen area, folding her arms across her voluptuous chest, studying him.

"I don't have friends or relationships that last more than two weeks. That makes it hard to have people who send you gifts," he said. It wasn't a topic he wanted to discuss, but he was curious as to what she might have gotten him. Two boxes, and they looked big. He'd already finished his shopping for her and thought she'd like the things he'd gotten her, but maybe he should get her a few more things...

"What about an assistant?" she asked. "My officemates and I all exchange gifts with each other."

"I work alone at my home and do all my research myself. I do send a box of cigars to my attorney and all my clients get a gift from me, and they gift back, but it's corporate giving—chocolate or donations to charities."

He'd never thought about gifts before this. Well, at one point he had, but he'd stopped thinking about them long ago. To be frank, getting a present from someone who he didn't care about wasn't something he wanted or needed. But a present from Penny was something altogether different. *That* he wanted.

"I'm glad you have me this Christmas," she said tenderly. "That's what I decided when I was walking back here. We need each other."

"Yes, we do," he agreed. "And I'm very glad I have you to spend this holiday with."

WILL PUT SOME Christmas music on the television and then joined her in the kitchen. She had all the prepared ingredients—softened butter, eggs, sugar and flour—

ready to go into the bowl. Over the years she'd baked cookies with lots of people, but never with Will.

She thought of this as another gift she was giving him. Something he didn't know he was missing but years from now he'd remember fondly. "Do you want to do wet or dry?"

"Um…what?"

She smiled, guessing that his mind was elsewhere. "Ingredients. You have to combine them separately and then put them all together."

"Wet?" he asked.

"Okay, here you go—eggs, softened butter, vanilla and sugar," she said, handing him the measured items.

"Sugar is not wet," he said, frowning slightly.

"I know but you always have to cream the butter and sugar together first."

He read the recipe and was very serious about adding all the ingredients together while she sifted the flour and other dry ingredients together. "Feliz Navidad" started playing and she danced around the kitchen as the mixer was working at getting all the wet ingredients combined.

"When I was little I thought the words to this song were 'At least my name's Da.'"

He started laughing. "You're kidding."

"Nope. And I loved it—it was my favorite song so I used to sing it really loud whenever it came on the radio. One night my mom had some people from her work over for dinner and I was dancing around singing it and one of them said, 'What is she singing?'"

"Oh, no."

"Yes, and my mom replied, 'She just makes up the words,'" Penny said. "And I was like, 'No, those are the words, Mom.'"

She laughed at the memory and how funny it was to everyone. "After that my mom told me the correct lyrics but sometimes, just to tease her, I'll text her 'at least my name's Da.'"

Will put his arms around her and swayed with her to the music, singing softly in her ear, and she was surprised that he had such a nice voice. It was another little memory that she put in her heart to remember him by when he was gone. But she wasn't thinking about that, not today.

She looked into the bowl where he had been mixing away. "I think that's creamed enough."

"Okay. What now?"

She talked him through adding in the rest of his items and then slowly added hers in. "Now we have to roll it out. Where are your cookie cutters? The ones you bought the other day."

"In my chalet," he said. "I came straight here from the Lodge."

"I thought you had more time. We planned to bake the cookies tonight," she reminded him. "Didn't we?"

"I stopped at the sundries store and ran into Elizabeth," he said. "She wanted to warn me that she'd told you about my previous marriage. I guess she could tell by your reaction that I hadn't mentioned it. I told her it was not a big deal." He smiled at her. "She's a good friend to you."

"Really? How do you know?" Penny asked, but she already knew Elizabeth was a good friend. She just wanted to know why he thought so.

"She got a little protective toward you. I'm glad you have people like her in your life."

"Me, too," Penny said. "We've known each other a

long time. It helps when you share all the ups and downs, you know?"

He started to say something but she laughed before he could. "No, you don't."

"Maybe I will soon," he said gruffly.

"Really?"

"Yes, with you," he said, turning to grab his coat. "I'll go and get my cookie cutters."

"Okay, hurry," she said.

He lifted a brow. "Why? What's the rush?"

"It's just…I'll miss you while you are gone," she said. That was more than the truth. She had decided to enjoy the rest of her time with him, and after their conversation in the snow earlier, she didn't have any misconceptions that maybe it could be more. She knew this was it.

Will pulled her into his arms, tangled his hands in the back of her hair and kissed her. She loved the way his lips felt against hers. She breathed in his masculine scent and held him to her. A sentimental Christmas song was playing on the radio and she felt tears burning in her eyes as she thought about how this wasn't something that could last.

She wanted to tell him that she'd compromise and give up on her own pride just to keep him by her side. But she knew that would poison what she felt for him. And she didn't want to let that happen.

Will lifted his mouth from hers, stared into her eyes with that intense blue gaze of his and pulled her close. He rocked them back and forth to the music for several long, tantalizing moments before he spun out of her arms and strode to the door.

"I'll be right back," he said.

She swallowed hard and turned away, forcing herself

to stay busy mixing icing and coloring while he was gone. She pulled out the cookie cutters she'd bought when they were together but also the model train one she'd special ordered for him.

She set them on the counter and then washed the work surface, drying it before putting some flour down on it and getting out the rolling pin she'd purchased. She was going to have more baking supplies in her suitcase than she did at home, she thought ruefully.

She cut the dough in half and started rolling it out, getting it ready for Will when he got back. The smell of the cookie dough reminded her of all the batches of cookies she'd made over the years. All the memories she had of cookies baked and frosted and eaten in the kitchen. She wanted that with Will. Wanted him to have those special memories, as well.

WILL STOOD OUTSIDE in the cold, letting the weather cool him off. There were things he wanted that he never knew he'd longed for until he'd met Penny. And all of them were in that chalet. All of them centered around that one woman. He knew if he reached out and asked her to give him a chance, she'd do it.

But he also knew that in this moment he felt fear in his heart alongside all the deep emotion she stirred to life inside of him. It would be easy to pretend that he could handle it, but for the first time in almost ten years, he'd been tempted to drink.

Not just have a sip of something but to drink until he was numb and the world disappeared.

That was dangerous.

And when he held Penny in his arms, he wanted something so much more from her, wanted to never let her go. And he meant never. Not today or tomorrow or any of the days for the rest of their lives.

Not healthy.

He wondered if he should try to talk to someone. But who? His therapist had retired almost four years ago and he'd been doing so well. True, maybe it had been ego and cockiness that had made him believe that he could handle himself now that he was an adult. But he suddenly realized that he'd been fooling himself.

He hadn't understood it before because he'd been meeting women on his vacations that'd been happy to have something superficial and just for fun. Fun wasn't overrated. He worked hard and needed to blow off steam at these two-week holidays he scheduled. But this year he wasn't so much blowing off steam as turning into someone different.

The same thing that Penny had said she wanted, but *she* was different, too.

She had been from the first moment he'd kissed her under the mistletoe and he doubted that would ever change.

No distance or time was going to make him be able to handle this without coming up with a plan forward. He stood there for a few more moments. The snow that had been threatening earlier started to fall in earnest fat flakes. He ran to the porch of his chalet, let himself in and looked for the bag from the kitchen store.

There was so much that he was doing for the first time with Penny. Maybe that was why she felt so different than the other women he'd been involved with. Because she opened up his world and introduced him to new things.

He was baking and talking about childhood memories and having more sex than he had had in the last few years. She was a mix of sweet memories and sexy nights and he had no idea where to go from here.

He felt as trapped now as he had been as a lad of ten when his parents died. When he'd realized he had to figure out a way to keep going forward. He'd thought he'd figured it out long ago. But he hadn't been moving—he'd been standing still and hiding from life.

Penny made him want to be more. To be a better man. He knew he was a good man but he wanted to be one for her. Not just an investor with integrity. He wanted things that had nothing to do with business.

And as tempted as he was to experience more, to reach out and grab it with both hands, he was afraid, as well. The loss he'd suffered, he knew that he should have gotten over it by now and thought he had.

But it still haunted him.

He picked up the kitchen-store bag and left his little chalet. He was overthinking this. They'd already come to an arrangement and he needed to just keep to it, and when he got back to his home and his routine, everything would be fine.

Maybe if he said it often enough it would become the truth.

He knocked on her door and then opened it and walked in. She was standing there in the hallway with her coat on.

"What's up?" he asked, seeing she had her scarf in hand and her boots on, as well.

She chewed the corner of her lip and then took her coat off. "You were gone a long time and I was worried about you."

"I'm a mess, Penny," he blurted. "I don't know what

I'm going to do about you. I'm pretending that all I have to do is get through Christmas and then everything will be normal for me again, but I no longer believe that is true."

She looked stricken and he didn't want to be a burden to her or anyone.

"It's not you," he said, scrubbing a hand across his face. "It's just that my life had been a nice comfortable shade of brown before I met you, and now I've got all these colors all around me and I'm not sure what to do. I'm not sure if it's something I need to worry about or if it will all go away when I get home."

"I know exactly what you mean," she confessed. "I had those same doubts and worries when I learned you had been married but now I know that it's not anything I can control. I want to spend this time with you for the selfish reason that I want this memory to keep," she said.

"I'd like that, too," he said gruffly.

17

Penny took Will's hand and led him to the kitchen. She took out his cookie cutters and handed them to him. Inside she was dying a little, but on the outside she smiled and just carried on.

That was what she'd done when Butch's wife had surprised him in the office, very pregnant and very in love with her cheating husband. It was what she'd done when her father had shown up at her elementary school drunk and rambling. It was what she'd do now. She'd get through this and find some kind of Christmas joy—if it could be found.

"We aren't going to think about this anymore," she said. "I see you have some interesting cutters here."

She held up the robot.

Will didn't say anything and Penny turned away. He was shutting down again, for reasons she couldn't fathom, and she couldn't do this on her own. Not really. For her it came down to the fact that if he wouldn't at least try to be happy, she was going to have to…what? She didn't want to say goodbye. No matter how many times she tried to tell herself she was fine with it, she knew she wasn't.

And she wondered if there was really any sense in prolonging this for another day or even hour. She wanted the memories, but the pain she could live without.

"Good thing I have this big Santa-hat cutter," she continued in a voice that sounded way too chipper. "I'm making some cookies for the concierges, and thought I'd write their names on these in icing."

She took her cookie cutter and started cutting out the large Santa hats, and in a moment, Will came over next to her and took his robot and started using it. She'd set a parchment-lined tray on each side of the dough and one of the cookie spatula's she'd purchased.

Nat King Cole's "The Christmas Song" came on the radio and Penny couldn't help the tears that burned in the backs of her eyes. She missed her mom. She wished she were with the people who loved her and made her feel safe.

Having a sexy Christmas might have sounded good in theory, but the truth was that Will had changed that dynamic—or maybe she had by falling for him. She put her cookie cutter down and turned away from Will and the dough, braced her hands on the counter and tried to get her emotions under control.

"I'm sorry," Will said softly, coming up behind her and wrapping his arms around her.

She nodded. She didn't want him to see she was losing it. Just totally losing it while making cookies. That wasn't cool.

"Penny?"

"Mmm-hmm?"

"I really am sorry. I wanted to give you a great holiday but instead it seems like I have brought you down."

She turned to face him. "What has got me 'down' is the fact that you refuse to admit you aren't the same man you were at twenty-one. I'm not like your young bride. We could make a go of this."

"How do you figure?" he asked with a resigned sigh. "I know myself better than you do."

"You don't know yourself," she said. "You keep hiding in your safe world doing things the exact same way you always have. I think if you were honest, you'd have to admit that I'm different and that you picked me for this two-week affair because you were bored with your routine."

Will shoved his hands in his hair, watching her with those beautiful blue eyes of his, but right now his face was hard and almost angry. She got it. She hated having anyone point out her faults, but the truth was that he wasn't doing either of them any favors by acting like he knew for sure what he could or couldn't do. It had been fourteen years since he'd tried anything other than affairs.

And not that she was looking for marriage— All right, she wouldn't *mind* marriage to him. Because when he wasn't trapped in his past he was a great guy. He made her believe in the kind of happiness she'd always thought was just out of her grasp.

"I'm not bored," he said, through clenched teeth. "I'm just sure of myself and what I want. You are the one who seems to keep changing her mind."

"Really? Because I wasn't the one who took fifteen minutes to walk between our two places. I'm not the one who made it seem like cutting out a robot cookie was going to take all my willpower," she said, not holding back anything. She was tired of always falling for the wrong men. Giving them the goodness of her heart and all of her soul and finding them not worthy.

The worst part was, Will *was* totally worthy. She had seen the potential in him, and in them as a couple, over the intense days—and nights—they'd spent together. But instead of reaching out and taking what she had to offer, he was shoving her away.

Again she was being left alone. She was so tired of doing this.

"We're not all bubbly little Penny who can just smile and keep on going when things get tough." He crossed his arms over his chest. "Sorry if I'm not smiley enough for you."

She shook her head, feeling like he wasn't getting the point. Wasn't hearing what she was saying. Because she didn't need him to be smiling and happy. She just needed him to at least try.

"Will, smiles aren't what I'm asking for. And I know I use that happiness as a defense mechanism sometimes… but it's my way of not breaking down and totally losing it," she said. "All I want from you is to try. To meet me halfway."

"I thought I had by saying we could plan to meet up again in the spring or summer," he muttered in frustration. "That's more than I've offered anyone else before."

She looked at him. "Seriously? That's the exact same thing we have now. How is going on vacation again together going to be moving forward? We'd still be two people who haven't done anything but get together in a stress-free environment and have great sex."

"So?"

This wasn't working. No matter what he said to the contrary, he didn't want to change. Didn't want to take a risk on…what? Did he love her? Did he care about her? Or was this about something else entirely? "Will, what is it that you are so afraid of?"

WHAT *WAS* HE AFRAID OF? Before all this, he'd have said nothing. He lived his life on his own terms. But this last week with Penny had proven that he did still have a few spots in his dark soul that were driven by fear. She had exposed them, shed light on them, and now she wanted him to talk about them.

Not happening.

He'd wanted sex and fun for Christmas. Had that been too much to ask? Why couldn't she just keep smiling… except she had been, and he'd seen straight through her pretend smiles to the aching hurt underneath.

Hurt he knew he'd caused.

He was mad. At himself. At his parents for dying and leaving him a big mess, which he'd thought he'd gotten over, but part of what she'd said was right. He'd ignored it, buried it deep inside of himself, and then hunkered down in his routine to move on.

And most of all, he was mad at her. For reminding him of all the things he had missed. But he couldn't tell her that. Instead, he clenched his hands into fists, standing with his legs braced apart, as he looked her square in the eye.

"I'm not afraid," he said. He'd given her too much already and that was part of the problem.

She'd made him feel from the first moment they'd met that he could let his guard down, and that had been a huge mistake. One he wasn't going to repeat.

"Liar. I thought we said no lies, and now every time we talk, I'm hearing more and more untruths from you," she told him. "But you know what? That's not the worst part. You know you're lying to yourself, as well. That's where the real destruction will be. I think you probably buy into your own lies."

"What about you? Smiling when you know that you're not happy inside is a lie. But you think that's okay. There's a big double standard here, Penny. One that works in your mind and operates in your favor alone." He flattened his lips, growing angrier by the moment. "I offered you something more. Something that I've never even considered with anyone else, but that's not good enough for you, is it?" This wasn't entirely his fault. She was stuck in her routine as much as he was his. "You're so used to being treated poorly by every man that you automatically go into that mode if things aren't perfect. I haven't treated you badly. I'm not some loser who wants to hide you from the world."

"That's not fair," she said.

"It's not, but it is true. That truth you are supposedly so fond of. It hurts, doesn't it? To find out that you're not the one who's right all the time. That maybe you don't know it all."

"I never said I knew it all. I'm just saying—"

He scowled at her. "That you want everything your way. All the cards stacked in your favor. You want me to be the one to take all the risks. I'm not going to do it," he said at last.

"I guess that's all I need to know. I thought we had something special," she choked out.

"I'm not saying we didn't. But if it's so special to you, why can't you try doing things my way?" he asked.

He wanted to hang on to his anger, but the truth was, as she stood there looking so small and vulnerable, he wanted to say the hell with it and do whatever he had to in order to make this right. But then he remembered the bottle of Glenlivet and how close he'd come to buying it. He knew that in order to keep himself under the tight control he'd always had, he wasn't going to be able to do this any way but his.

"I can't," she whispered. "I know you think I'm just being petulant, but the fact of the matter is, I have waited a long time to find a man like you, Will. Someone who checks all the boxes in my head and in my heart. Some of those boxes I didn't even know were there, so pretending that it doesn't matter is not something I can do."

She walked over to him and put her hand on his arm, squeezed his bicep and then let her hand drop. "I want it all with you because I know if we tried, if both of us stopped living in fear, we could make it work."

But deep down, Will thought, she didn't know that. After all, how could she? Penny had no more experience with making a relationship work than he did. "How can you be so certain? Neither of us has ever been in this situation before."

"I realize that," she said, taking a step back. "But at least I'm willing to try."

"Don't say I'm a coward again, Penny. You have no idea of the battles that I have to fight every day."

She bit her lower lip and stared at him through a sheen of tears. "You're right—I don't. I'm sorry for your struggles and I don't want to make them worse. But I can't just stand here and let you push me away time and again and keep making excuses for you."

"I'm not asking you to. Why is meeting again later

next year not good enough for you?" he asked. "That's a big thing. Like I mentioned before, we'd have a chance to see each other again and we'd know if what we feel now is real."

She shrugged. "But we wouldn't. Real is give me your phone number at home and tell me where you live so we can figure out how to see each other as soon as we get back. But you don't want to know where I live. You don't want to see my real life."

She had a point. Real life was harder than vacations, harder than making this two weeks work. And he knew he wasn't sure he could do it.

"I can't."

PENNY WASN'T SURPRISED. She'd seen it in the way he'd been acting since they'd met up in the Lodge this afternoon. Also, despite what she'd told him, a part of her really didn't believe in her own feelings. She'd spent most of her life running from love, and having found it now, she wondered if she'd ever be able to enjoy it.

"I guess you can leave, then," she said tightly. No sense in prolonging the inevitable now that he'd made up his mind. Plus, he'd said some mean things to her.

"Fine. But before I do, I want to make sure you know that I didn't want to walk out on you. I didn't start this with the intent to deceive you—"

"I know that, Will. God, we both had the best intentions, but the truth of the matter is that we weren't in the right place to meet. Maybe a few years from now, when I've gotten used to my new life, I'll be better. But right now I think I was searching for some kind of happy ending in my life. If not with my job, then at least with you."

"Just a happy ending?" he asked. "Then I don't matter? Any guy would have done?"

"Not at all," she said vehemently. "*You're* the reason I want more. The reason why I started to believe that love could be more than the lousy examples I've seen. You're not a cheater or a drunk."

She looked at him and this time she didn't feel as angry as she had before. She felt sad for herself, and for him, because in her mind she thought if they could have both bent a little in their beliefs they might have been able to figure out a way to make this last.

"I almost wish I wasn't so stubborn," he ground out. "But I am. And I know what can happen if I don't keep myself under control. I'd hate myself if I hurt you, Penny."

She nodded. She'd already figured that out. If she were different, if her romantic past had just once had something positive in it, maybe she would keep dating him from vacation to vacation…but she knew better. She knew that half measures were the biggest lie she could tell herself.

And with Will she needed more.

"Nah, if you weren't stubborn, I wouldn't have grown to care so deeply for you," she said. Penny couldn't bring herself to call it love. Not right now when she felt raw and ached inside. She wanted to keep a part of her pride and not let him see how hard this was.

"I guess that's something," he said. The anger had cooled in him, as well.

Penny walked past him, but he caught her wrist, wrapped his arms around her and pulled her close for a hug. She turned her head to the side as the scent of his aftershave surrounded her, and she tried to remember that this was going nowhere, but when he tightened his arms, she wanted to say to hell with it.

She wanted to just pretend that she didn't care if she ended up brokenhearted and alone. But then she knew that was a lie. No more lies, she reminded herself.

She rose on tiptoe and kissed the beard stubble on his jaw then stepped back away from him.

He drew her back into his arms and brought his mouth down on hers. It was tender but she could feel the tension in him, the residue of anger beneath the surface. She met his passion with her own, and they held each other until the fire burning between them was extinguished.

"Thank you for a really enjoyable time," she said. "I hope that you find what you are looking for two weeks at a time."

He stared down at her, his blue eyes smoldering with emotion once again. "Why is meeting again later this year such a bad idea to you?"

She finally realized that until he knew the truth of how she felt, he was going to think she was simply trying to manipulate him. She tucked a strand of her hair behind her ear and tipped her head to the side.

Taking a deep breath, she said, "Because I love you, Will. I've never let myself love another man before and I'm not asking for anything back from you. I know that love isn't something that can be weighed and measured and sometimes one person falls and the other one doesn't."

He started to speak, but she held her hand up.

"If I met you for a vacation, I'd spend every minute we were apart making you into the kind of man who would love me. The kind of man who had missed me so much that when we met up again, I'd be anticipating that you felt the same way as I did. But that's not going to happen." She sighed. "And then, when I came to terms with that, I'd convince myself that I could do two weeks because two weeks is better than nothing, but in the end I'd be dying inside."

He didn't say anything, just shook his head. "I don't know what to say. I care so deeply for you, Penny. You've shaken me to my moorings. But that leap to where you are standing, that place where you look and see a happy future, I'm not sure I can do it."

She knew that. She'd sensed it from the moment he'd returned with his cookie cutter and stood next to her as if he were afraid of what might happen next. Will's life hadn't been the blend of happy days mixed with sad ones that hers had.

"I know. That's why I think this is goodbye," she said brokenly.

She wished he'd left when they'd been arguing because then she'd have the hope that it had been anger driving him away. This quietness as he walked to the door was a million times worse. Because this was really goodbye.

He was leaving for good and all she could do was watch him go.

18

CHRISTMAS EVE DAWNED crisp and cold. Penny rolled over and hugged the pillow that Will had slept on when he'd spent the night with her. Last night had been long, with lots of Ben & Jerry's and tons of tears, but she'd made it. Each day would be easier.

She didn't have to worry about texts from Will. She knew that the break with him was clean and forever. He wasn't going to send her messages, begging her to change her mind, which made her sad because for him she thought she might change. But she knew that was just loneliness talking. She respected herself too much to settle for half measures. Penny forced herself to get out of bed even though a part of her wanted to turn on the television and mope around all day. Surely she could give herself permission to do that for one day, but she suspected that would make tomorrow even harder for her.

Her mom wasn't here, her friends would be spending Christmas with their loved ones and she, who had said she wanted to be alone this year, was going to get exactly what she'd claimed she wanted.

A big lonely day.

She went and had a hot shower, trying to ignore the bathtub and the memories she had of Will washing her hair and pretty much making her fall for him. He'd done things for her that no other man had before. Things she hadn't even thought would be sexy or romantic, but they had been.

She got dressed and then checked her phone. As if he'd send a message…and what was she hoping for? He wasn't going to suddenly realize he loved her and run back to her. But it would be so perfect if he did.

Shaking her head, she gathered the box of cookies she'd made for the front desk and concierge staff and left her chalet, defiantly not looking toward Will's place. The snow from last night sparkled in the morning sun, and Penny stopped thinking about heartbreak and loneliness and tipped her head back. God, it was a pretty day.

The kind of day that made her happy to be alive. She felt tears burning her eyes but that was just because she'd realized that she would be able to put one foot in front of the other. Once more, she'd be moving forward on her own and somehow, some way, she had to make that okay.

She entered the Lodge and the bellman greeted her by name and smiled as she walked by. There were worse places to recover from a broken heart, she thought. And to be honest, if falling for Will had shown her one thing, it was how superficial her feelings for Butch had been.

She hadn't realized what love felt like until Will had taken her on that sleigh ride and she'd seen her first glimpse behind the facade of that sexy smile and charming wit.

"Good morning, Ms. Devlin," Paul, the concierge manager, said as she walked up to his desk.

"Morning, Paul. I baked these for your staff to say

thank you for all the help you've provided with Elizabeth's wedding arrangements."

"It was our pleasure," he said. "Do you need anything else to prepare for Christmas?"

She needed something that he couldn't procure for her. Even though the concierges here at the Lars Usten Lodge were incredible, there were some miracles they couldn't perform. She smiled at him and shook her head, then walked down the hall toward the model village. Suddenly, tears blurred her eyes again as she remembered how Will had looked when he'd seen the train.

That special smile on his face, the one she'd seen on only one other occasion. After they'd made love the first time. He'd been truly happy when he'd recalled his childhood memories. Why was he resisting being happy with her forever? Why didn't he have the guts to risk his heart?

She did.

But while she was used to having relationships, Will had confessed that he wasn't. That he liked to keep himself all tucked safely away so that he wouldn't be tempted down the dark path of addiction. But was that the truth?

Or was it really just the fact that she wasn't the kind of woman he wanted to have in his life for more than a few weeks? Of course she didn't want to believe that. It would be too painful, and much too personal. Instead, she wanted to make some sort of blanket excuse that would seem like it was his failing, and not hers, that had driven them apart.

But like love, it wasn't all one-sided. She knew she was just as much at fault for needing and wanting more. She hadn't wanted to change him and didn't want to admit he had already changed her. But at the end of the day, she was looking for more from Will than she'd ever allowed herself to dream was possible before.

She sat on the bench and watched the train chug around the little village, and thought of the gift she'd bought for him. The one that was in a box in her chalet. She knew that no matter what, she still wanted him to have it.

Even if he couldn't be her man and didn't love her, he deserved to have a Christmas memory that he could cherish. Something to hold on to for the rest of his life.

Penny got up and walked slowly back toward the lobby, and when she heard the Christmas music playing, she couldn't imagine the thought of spending Christmas Eve alone instead of with Will in her arms. Despite the problems they still faced, she knew that the one thing she really wanted this Christmas was to see him standing outside her door. A part of her was disappointed when she walked back to her chalet and he was nowhere to be seen.

Nevertheless, she wrapped the presents she'd bought for Will and arranged for the concierge to have them delivered to him tonight while she was at the community nativity play. She wanted to make sure he didn't think she'd sent them so he'd come and find her. On the contrary, she simply wanted to do this one last gesture for him. The man who'd shown her what it was like to be in love.

PARK CITY WAS decked out in lights, and Penny tried not to feel that tug of nostalgia as she walked into the church for their children's mass and evening nativity service. But she did. She remembered all the masses she'd attended with her mom as a child. How, as she'd gotten older, they'd exclaimed over the cute kiddos in their costumes, and how her mom had said someday Penny would be a mom.

She knew it was foolish to let herself get too depressed about that. Because deep down she knew she'd find a man and have kids, if that was what she wanted, but tonight she couldn't help thinking about the kids she'd never have. A little boy with Will's dark hair and her smile, and maybe a sweet girl with Will's bright blue eyes and her hair.

"Is this seat taken?"

She glanced up to see Lindsey standing there. "No, it's not. I thought you had plans."

"I did, but they fell through. My friends are still on the competitive team so they couldn't take the day off as they'd hoped."

"I'm sorry."

"It's okay," Lindsey said. "I've actually been enjoying scouting out Park City. I've been living here since the summer but haven't really spent that much time in town."

"Why not?"

Lindsey shrugged. "I think I was still in training mode. I pretty much stay at the Lodge and just ski and teach skiing and then go back to my condo." She gave a little laugh. "Boring, huh?"

Penny smiled at the other woman. "It's hard to change your routine."

In a way, Lindsey was like Will. Stuck in her life, and even though her circumstances had changed, she still hadn't moved forward. Penny hoped that Lindsey wasn't stuck in that routine forever. "Park City is nice. Do you see yourself staying here for a while?"

"I don't know. I'm hoping to give competing another

try once this knee is completely healed. My doctor wants me to give it another couple months but I feel so much stronger now, and it's been almost a year since the accident and my surgery."

Penny understood what it was like to be in limbo and ready to get back on track. That was sort of how she felt about her career and the fashion house that had promised her they'd get back to her in January. "I hope you can."

"Me, too," Lindsey said. "But if not, I'll find something else to do. I have had a few offers from a television station to do their winter sports commentary. I might give that a shot."

"Maybe you'll get famous and I can say I knew you way back when," Penny said with a laugh.

"Who knows?" Lindsey replied. "In any event, I was glad to see a familiar face tonight. I love nativity plays."

"Same here. I used to think I was the star every year when my mom would drive me to church dressed in my peasant costume. Though one year I did get to be the angel."

"With your long blond hair, my preacher would have made you an angel every year."

"You're blonde, too," Penny pointed out. "Were you an angel?"

"Nah, I started training when I was eight so I didn't have time for plays and all that. But my little sister did."

"You sound envious."

"I guess I sort of was. Sounds surprising, right? I mean, I really loved skiing and everyone put me first. My parents had to sell one of their cars and my dad worked two jobs so my mom could drive me to my private lessons, so I get how much they sacrificed for me.

But there were times when I wanted to be a normal girl, you know?"

Penny understood that. She'd loved her mom and had had a wonderful upbringing, but there had been times when she'd wanted to be like everyone else. Have a family with a mom and a dad, maybe a sibling or two. But the older she got, the more she realized that no one had an ideal childhood. Hers was so much better than a lot of others, especially Will's.

The play started with the kids walking up the aisle like the procession to Bethlehem. Penny sat back on the hardwood bench and got swept away, forgetting all the troubles that had been plaguing her since Will had walked out last night.

When it was over, Lindsey saw some fellow ski instructors and went to join them. She'd invited Penny along but she didn't want to go and have to act like she was happy tonight. Instead, she strolled down the main street of Park City, looking at the Christmas displays in the windows, and then, when she was sure her presents would have been delivered to Will and enough time had passed that he wouldn't come looking for her, she caught the shuttle van back to the Lodge.

There was a darling family on the same shuttle. The kids were talking excitedly about Santa and they kept gazing out the window at the stars and the night sky, searching for his sleigh being pulled by Rudolph and his red nose.

She remembered her night ride with Will and knew that was the moment she'd started to fall in love with him. Under the stars, talking about following Fido and those dreams from her childhood that had turned into different desires as an adult. She missed him.

She admitted that to herself as she walked into the Lodge and grabbed herself a bottle of wine and another pint of Ben & Jerry's ice cream from the sundries shop. She wished there was a way to take his past and hers away from both of them so they could be the perfect partners for each other. But she knew that wouldn't happen.

It had started snowing as she walked back to her little chalet and she looked up at the night sky, searching for something but knowing it couldn't be found.

WILL'S DAY HAD been spent on the phone trying to secure a job for Penny. He didn't want to just leave her without giving her that. One of his friends who owned a winery in Napa Valley was in desperate need of an event planner and was willing to talk to her. He made a note of it and neatly printed out all of the information for her, and had it sent to her room.

Then he decided he'd had enough of relaxing and he was ready to go home. He tried to change his flight but December 24 was a busy travel day, something he normally would have been aware of, but because he'd been so consumed with thoughts of Penny, he hadn't paid close enough attention. He was able to change his flight to December 27, but that was still three long days away.

He wasn't sure he was strong enough to stay away from her. But for the sake of his sobriety, he knew that he had to. After he'd left her chalet yesterday, he'd gone to the sundries store, bought the Glenlivet, and now that bottle sat on the counter in his kitchen. It was unopened so far, but every second that he wasn't working on his computer, he glanced over at it.

It promised the kind of relief from the pressure inside of him that nothing else could offer.

Finally after lunch, when he'd almost cracked the seal on the bottle, he left the chalet and went for a walk. Being outside helped because it was bitterly cold and left no time to think about what could be. Instead, he just concentrated on putting one foot in front of the other, following each breath as it puffed out in front of him.

He wanted Penny to give in and say that she'd be his vacation lover for the rest of his stay here, but he knew that wasn't going to happen. She wasn't going to just give up on what she wanted.

The thing was, he almost believed if she'd just say yes this one time, that he'd change. That wasn't realistic but she made him want to. Penny was unique and no matter how much he'd tried to make her like every other woman, that had never happened.

She'd thrown her phone out her door and almost cracked him in the head. God, she was wonderful. She was exactly what he'd needed for too long but he was afraid for himself. That was it. The truth he'd been running from for too long.

She made him want to be the man she needed because he sensed she could be the one person that he'd been searching for since he was ten years old and all alone. Penny got him, even the dark parts, and she made him better.

But at the same time…if he hurt her, if she got hurt, he wasn't sure he could deal with it.

He ran, trying to distance himself from the frenzied images in his head, left the path and found himself under the trees and sheltered from the view of anyone who might be walking by. He fell to his knees and, putting his head in his hands, let the quiet of the day fall around him.

He finally admitted to himself that he couldn't live

without Penny. He had known that for a while, and even though being with her might be a challenge, anything would be better than this aching loneliness.

It had only been one day and already he wanted to share things with her. He wanted to have her next to him as he'd planned for the New Year. And not for only two weeks. For much, much longer. But he couldn't go back to her.

He missed the feel of her in his arms, her sweet, feminine scent surrounding him.

Not now. He had to figure himself out first. What did the future look like?

She'd said she loved him and he'd walked away because that was easier than admitting that he felt more for Penny than he had for any other being in his life. He loved his parents, he knew that, but the feeling had been gone for so long—*they'd* been gone for so long—that he had forgotten what that had felt like.

And his marriage had been a mess of two needy people trying to make something real out of nothing. But he and Penny had found that, for them, nothing had turned into something very real.

He got up, realizing the snow had soaked through the knees of his jeans, but the cold numbness didn't bother him. It was stinging as he walked back to his chalet. Reminded him he was alive and that life wasn't ever meant to be easy or perfect.

Finally, he felt like he understood why he had been so unsure of what to do with Penny. Why he'd been unable to resist her for so long. She had found her way into his heart without him even being aware of it. He'd been charmed by her. Enchanted by her. And he'd been afraid to admit that he loved her.

That he needed her in his life for the rest of it.

He knew he'd be a mess if she was ever taken from him, but he would learn to handle that. Each day she made him stronger.

He entered his chalet and the first thing he did was throw the bottle of Glenlivet in the trashcan. Then he changed his clothes and got down to the business of figuring out how to win back the only woman he'd ever loved.

19

WILL TOOK A shower and got dressed in the Santa suit that the concierge had special ordered for him. It had taken them the better part of the day to get it for him, but he didn't mind. He had what he needed now to make this the best Christmas ever.

There was a knock on his door and he went to open it. One of the hotel staff had a trolley with wrapped presents on it.

"Hello, Mr. Spalding."

"Merry Christmas," Will said.

"To you, too, sir. These are for you. Where would you like them?"

Will stepped back into the hallway. "Under the tree, please."

It had been years since he'd had any presents and he knew these had come from Penny. That despite what had been said between them yesterday during that heated argument, she'd still sent him the presents she'd bought for him. It made him feel humble but also more in love with her than ever. If he needed the confirmation that she was his other half, the part that would make him a better man, well, then this was it.

He tipped the bellboy as he left and then went to sit under the tree and look at the packages. One of them was bigger than the others but he truly had no idea what was in any of them. She wasn't planning to see him open the gifts...that much was clear.

Had he waited too long to go to her? He didn't care. He seldom lost when he put his mind to something, and he definitely had put his mind to Penny.

He sat on the floor in front of the presents and reached for the big one. He felt like he had when he'd been a boy and saw the presents under the tree that he and his parents had decorated. That anticipation laced with joy in the pit of his stomach. Not all that different from how he felt when he thought about Penny.

Will pulled the package toward him, slowly removed the wrapping and then felt shock reverberate through him as he realized she'd gotten him a model train. The same one that he'd admired in the lobby of the Lodge. The one he'd said he and his father had been working on together.

He sat the box on his lap and just looked at it. Realized that his hands were shaking. Penny had given him something he wouldn't have bought for himself because he wouldn't have wanted to admit how much he wanted it.

He opened the box and set the train up in the living room, taking his time with the track, and it felt almost like his father was there with him, watching him. For the first time that he could remember, he was thinking of his parents and it wasn't about the loss of them. It was about what they had both given him.

He set the train on the track and then sat back on his

heels and flicked the button so that it fired up and started chugging around the living room.

He left the train on as he opened the other presents she'd given him. There was a wool sweater with his initials monogramed on it. And then a pair of socks that had the three wise men on camels following the Star of Bethlehem. But it was the smallish flat package that he opened last. The one that held the picture of the two of them that he'd taken when they'd been kissing that really got to him.

He'd thought nothing could top the train but this did. She was the gift that he hadn't known he wanted. The one thing that he truly needed. He remembered every detail of that day. How her lips felt under his. The way she'd felt tucked up against his side, and how in that moment he'd realized how much he was starting to care for her.

He'd been a little scared but still so sure that he'd be able to manage that fear. And he felt that way again. He'd been running for a long time but it was only when he turned his back on Penny that he knew he had to stop.

There was no peace or happiness down the path of his life if he was by himself. Nothing was worth it without her by his side.

He thought of the gifts he'd gotten her, superficial things that he'd sent to lovers over the years, and he realized that he needed to do something for Penny that would show her how much she meant to him. Jewelry was nice but he wanted something that would be about the two of them.

He wanted to do more.

He glanced at his watch. It was six-thirty on Christmas Eve and he wanted to go and find a present. Talk about awful timing. But that wasn't about to stop him.

He changed out of the Santa suit and into a pair of jeans and the sweater that Penny had gotten him and left the chalet. He walked quickly through the snow-covered path toward the Lodge, and when he got there, he waited until the concierge manager, Paul, was free.

Then he cornered him and asked for a very special favor.

Paul wasn't too certain he could pull it off, but then he'd been working at the Lodge for a long time so he had the contacts that Will needed. He rented an SUV while Paul got him the information and then he left with a name, a number and directions that led him out of Park City to a rural farmhouse.

And after two cups of coffee—and promises that he was a decent man who would give it a good home—he left the farmhouse with a rescue corgi named Fifi. He knew that Penny wouldn't be expecting it. And to be honest, as Fifi whined in her crate as he drove back to the Lodge, he knew he hadn't been expecting her, either.

PENNY LIT A fire in the chalet, texted her mother Merry Christmas so she'd be the first one to message her on Christmas morning, and then changed into her pajamas and wrapped the scarf that Will had given her around her neck. Sighing wistfully, she sat down on the couch next to the tree, looking at the presents underneath it from Lindsey and Elizabeth and Bradley. It was nice that she was close to her friends. They'd invited her to join them for dinner tomorrow.

She had not taken them up on it and if she hadn't agreed to plan out Elizabeth and Bradley's wedding, she'd be tempted to leave Park City altogether. But she had and her best friend needed her.

She'd gotten the small note card from Will with the information for a job interview from a winery in California. Even though it hadn't been what she'd really wanted from him, she was grateful all the same. It was another avenue for her to pursue, and she'd never lived on the West Coast. Still, deep down, she didn't know if she could really relocate there.

She was too used to being close to DC and all that. She wondered if Will was from California. Then laughed. Why did she care? It was pretty obvious that he'd broken all ties with her. That the job interview was his way of making amends for hurting her feelings and letting her move on.

She wished it were that easy. She took a sip of the hot chocolate she'd made for herself and listened to the logs in the fire and the clock ticking on the wall. She was staying out of her bed, not because she thought that Santa might appear but because she just couldn't spend another night on the bed she'd shared with Will.

Memories of him were everywhere in the chalet. She thought she'd ask to move to one of the rooms up in the Lodge but then changed her mind. She liked being surrounded by him for as long as she could.

She was pitiful, she told herself. But then again, she was in love. Though, at this moment, it was hard to see the difference.

She heard a knock on her door around 11:00 p.m. and padded over to it and looked out the peephole. There stood a bellman with a pile of presents. Unless she was wrong, they were from her mom.

She opened the door and pasted a bright smile on her face. "Merry Christmas!"

"Merry Christmas," the young man replied. "I had

orders to wait until midnight to deliver these, but my girlfriend got off early and…"

"It's okay, your secret is safe with me. Can you put them under the tree?"

"I did the same thing for your neighbor about five hours ago."

He must have delivered her gifts to Will. "Did he seem to like them?" she asked.

"He seemed surprised to me," the bellman said as he finished arranging the wrapped presents under the tree.

Penny got some cash for a tip for him from her wallet and then handed it to him as he walked out the door. "Thank you. Have fun with your girlfriend."

"I hope to. I'm planning to ask her to marry me. Got to plan it the right way, though," he said.

"I bet. Good luck…I hope she says yes."

"Thank you, ma'am."

Penny closed the door as the bellman walked away. She thought of the nervousness mingled with the joy on his handsome young face. She hoped he got his Christmas wish.

With a heavy heart, she walked over to the tree and looked at the presents there. She sat down next to them and admitted to herself that she'd trade all the presents for one more day with Will. Maybe she should just take him up on his offer of a string of vacation affairs.

Was that offer still on the table? She wasn't too sure. That note with the job offer seemed like his final communication with her. Maybe it was time for her to…pour herself a glass of wine and start opening presents. Penny went into her kitchen and uncorked the bottle of white wine and then went back to the tree. She knew she should wait until midnight to open her mom's gifts. But it was technically only five more minutes until Christmas, so maybe if she opened the presents from her friends first, she'd be able to make it till then.

So she sat cross-legged on the floor and set her wineglass on the coffee table. Feeling an unexpected wave of childlike excitement, she pulled Lindsey's beautifully wrapped present toward her and carefully opened the package. It was a long narrow box, and when she opened it up, she found a pair of cashmere-lined leather gloves in a deep pink color that she loved. She slipped them on and then, because she was by herself, took a picture of the gloves and popped it on Instagram, tagging Lindsey in it.

She took the gloves off and placed them back in the box with the lid off. It was something her mom always did. So that for the rest of Christmas Day when they looked under the tree they could see all the presents lined up and on display.

Next she opened the present from Bradley and Elizabeth. It was a heavy, large square box. Inside she found a new pair of snow boots in her size and a matching pair of leggings and a sweater. All from Fresh Sno, which was the chain of outdoor retail shops that Bradley owned.

She arranged them in the box and tried for an arty photo for Instagram. Then, disgusted with herself, she tossed her phone aside. Making believe she was having a great Christmas by posting stuff on social media was totally lame.

She didn't want to spend the holiday alone. Decision made, she stood up and put on her new snow boots and her gloves. She was going to find Will. No more pretending she was okay with being apart from him.

She'd convince him that they should be together this Christmas morning and every other morning that was yet

to come. The doorbell rang and she opened the door…
hoping for Will…but found a dog on her step with a big
red bow around its neck. A note tied to it read "My name
is Fifi and I am so glad I finally found you."

She bent down to pet Fifi—a cute little tri-colored
corgi—and the pooch licked her hand. She glanced up
and down the path but couldn't find anyone. She brought
the dog inside wondering if this gift was from her mom.
She got a bowl in the kitchen and put some water in it.
The little dog wagged her tail and lapped at the water.

There was a loud knock on the door that startled her.
Fifi started barking and ran to the door.

"Ho! Ho! Ho!"

The deep voice sounded like Santa, and when she
looked through the peephole, she saw Will in a Santa
suit standing on her doorstep.

She opened the door.

"Merry Christmas, Santa," she said.

Fifi leaped forward and wagged her tail as she tangled
herself around his legs.

"Merry Christmas, Penny. I see Fifi finally found her
way to you," Will said in a deeper-than-normal voice.

"Yes, she did. Thank you."

"You're welcome. Um…can I come in?" he asked in
his normal voice. "I have this all planned out."

"Why do you want to come in?" she asked. Even
though she wanted to throw her arms around him, she
suddenly felt a bit gun shy. Unsure of his true intentions.

"Penny, you said you loved me and I was a fool to not
tell you in that moment how I felt about you."

She swallowed and took a step back, gesturing for him
to come inside. He did and closed the door behind him.

"First things first," he said, reaching into the big red

sack he carried. He took out two dog bowls and handed them to her along with a can of dog food. "She couldn't carry her own food. So I figured I'd bring it for her."

"Thank you," she said. "Why don't you go into the living room while I feed Fifi?"

"I will."

"Thank you for getting me this dog. I love her already," Penny said. And she did. She wouldn't be alone anymore. She should have thought of getting a pet a long time ago.

"You're welcome," he said gruffly. "I wanted to get you something that was as special as the train you gave me. I can't thank you enough for that."

"It was nothing. I knew it was the one thing you'd never buy for yourself."

She got the dog settled with her bowls of food and water and then took off her snow boots and the gloves and set them on the counter.

"So, Santa, before this goes any further, why are you here? Is it just for tonight?" she asked.

"No. I'm here because I love you, Penny. From the moment I walked away from you, every instinct I had was telling me to turn around and go back to you. But I was too afraid to do that. I wasn't sure I could figure out how to live with my fears about you."

She stayed where she was, afraid to rush to the wrong conclusion. "And now you are?"

He stood up and walked over to her, still carrying his Santa bag. "Yes, Penny, I am. All day today I kept seeing you in my chalet and then I went outside and you were there, too. I don't think running back home is going to change the fact that you are in my heart now, Penny. I don't want to live without you."

She watched him, trying not to get too excited, but she couldn't help it. "So what do you want to do about this?"

"What you suggested," he said. "Let's figure out how to bring our lives together. Date each other and figure out if this love is something that will last. That is, if you even still love me."

She shook her head. "Of course I still love you! I was mad at you for walking out, but it takes a long time to fall out of love. That is why I've always been afraid to let myself care about a man. A man like you who has everything I wanted but never knew I was looking for." Suddenly, she gave him an apprehensive look. "But before we go any further, Will, I need to know one thing."

"What?" he asked.

"Are you sure about this?"

He took a step closer to her, smiled broadly and framed her face in his large hands. "More sure than I've been of anything in my life."

Then he reached into his bag and took out a sprig of mistletoe and held it over her head.

"Really?"

"Wasn't sure you'd let me kiss you without it," he said.

She took a deep breath. Then threw herself at him, knocking his Santa's hat off his head, and his bag fell to the ground as he caught her. Their mouths met and they kissed. The embrace was long and fierce and they both whispered each other's names and promises they meant to keep.

He carried her to the sofa and made love to her in the reflection of the light from the fireplace and the brilliantly lit Christmas tree. She held him as close to her as she could.

He cradled her to his chest and stroked his hand up

and down her back. "I was so afraid that I'd done too good of a job convincing you that I didn't need you in my life, when the opposite was true. I've never been good at admitting I needed anyone. But I don't think I can live without you, Penny."

She leaned up on her elbow, resting it against his chest, and looked down into his face so dear to her, with those beautiful blue eyes. "I need you, too. You were right—I was afraid that I'd fallen for a guy who wouldn't love me again. I think I was projecting my fears on you—"

"While I was doing the same to you. But we're together now and we will be for good."

"Yes, for good." She gave him an inquisitive look. "Um…where do you live?"

"California."

"I wondered after you got me that job interview out there. I guess you were trying to make sure you'd see me again."

"I guess I was," he admitted ruefully. "I can't imagine my life without you."

He pulled her into his arms, bringing his mouth down on hers, and she felt as if she'd had the best Christmas ever. Will was the present she'd always wanted but never dreamed of having.

* * * * *

Ignited

KIMBERLY VAN METER

Kimberly Van Meter wrote her first book at sixteen and finally achieved publication in December 2006. She writes for the Mills & Boon® Blaze® and Romantic Suspense lines. She and her husband of seventeen years have three children, three cats and always a houseful of friends, family and fun.

1

ALEXIS MATHESON WAS dreaming of Christmas cookies and homemade candies and stressing over how her candy thermometer was not working properly—when the scenario changed abruptly.

Suddenly, she was wrapped in a shadow lover's arms, enjoying a sizzling kiss that was hotter than baking peanut brittle and she hazily wondered who her dream lover was and why she was torturing herself with a sex dream when she'd sternly declared a moratorium on sex until she got her head on straight.

Ugh. Plainly her brain thought that might take forever.

Ah, dream lover was pretty good with his tongue and hands! Now, why had she determined sex was a bad idea for the time being?

She moaned, wrapping her arms around her lover, sighing with pleasure as his mouth blazed a trail down the column of her neck, nipping and nibbling and sending goose bumps tripping down her skin.

Everything felt so real and yet dreamy at the same

time. Hell, if dream lovers were this entertaining, maybe she could give up wide-awake sex for good.

Ha! Very funny.

She groaned again as a strong hand found her breast and squeezed and suddenly her eyes fluttered open at the realization that something didn't feel right—no, it felt fabulous, but that's not what she meant—she no longer knew if what was happening was only in her mind.

Before her sleep-fuzzed brain could fully react, she was being kissed again and, damn, it was good.

But wait a minute…she'd gone to bed alone!

An instant shot of adrenaline chased away her sleepy enjoyment of Mr. Talented Stranger and replaced it with a holy-shit-I'm-about-to-become-a-statistic jolt of awareness and she shoved at the big body covering her, landing a strategic hit to his groin area as she kicked.

He grunted in pain and rolled to his side, doubled over.

Every serial-killer book and movie she'd ever happened to read or see jumped to mind as she used her feet to shove the stranger's massive body right off the edge of her bed and onto the floor.

"This bed is already *occupado*!"

Once she heard the thump of his body landing on her carpet, she sprang from the bed and flicked on the light, snatching the first thing she could grab, and hurled it at the stranger when he stumbled to his feet. *Oh, good Lord, he was naked.*

He dodged the shoe, yelling, "What are you doing? Stop throwing shit! You've already mashed my nuts, lady!" as he shielded his frank and beans and blinked against the light like a mole squinting at the sun. "Watch it!"

"No, *you* watch it, this is my room and, more important, my bed. You have ten seconds to tell me who you are before you get a Martha Stewart smackdown." She hefted the book in her hands with the smiling domestic goddess gracing the hardcover to show she meant business, but the sturdy, dark-haired guy looked strong enough to take a hit without breaking a sweat. Even under the circumstances, Alexis would've had to have been blind to miss the fact that her intruder had a body that was worth taking a second look at. Go figure. A sexy intruder. Why did she have the worst luck with men?

"Calm down," he grumbled. "Put the damn book down, you crazy lunatic."

"Wrong answer," Alexis retorted and heaved the book straight at his head.

He tried to evade the projectile, but it caught him on the shoulder. "Holy hell! That hurt!" he yelled and then snatched up his jeans and jerked them on even as he stumbled/ran from her room, but not before she caught a quick glimpse of a near-perfect ass. *What a tragedy*, she thought before leaping after him, determined to find out who'd had the gall to climb into her bed, but her foot caught on her suitcase and she went hard to the floor, twisting her ankle in the process.

She'd once been accused of having an obsessive type of laser focus when it suited her, which was why instead of babying her foot, she continued to run after the stranger with the hot ass as he skidded into her brother, Erik's, room.

"Your sister's crazy, man," the guy said, glowering in Alexis's direction just as Alexis realized that Erik was home and she'd offered her best friend, Emma, her brother's bed. *Oh crud.* Stopping short, Alexis registered confusion all around, which under different circumstances might've been funny as hell, but there was nothing funny about the way her ankle was beginning to throb.

"What the hell, Erik? Who *is* this?" she asked, wincing as her abused ankle started to really protest. What the hell had she done to her foot?

Alexis shot a brief, apologetic look to Emma who was watching the situation unfold with wide eyes, the blankets tucked tightly beneath her arms as if trying to superglue the cloth to her body. *Egad. Poor Emma.* Alexis was going to have to bake an extra batch of lemon bars for this little snafu.

Erik, ever the peacemaker, stepped between Alexis and the man scowling hard enough to freeze his face that way, trying to be the voice of reason in this awkward situation. "Hey, hey," he said when Alexis didn't immediately back down.

"Jesus, woman," the man beside Erik said to Alexis, still miffed that she'd tried to neuter him with a donkey kick to the jewels. "I didn't know you were in there. Give me a freakin' break."

"What are you still doing here?" Erik said, gently pushing Alexis back to protect his friend.

Alexis stepped back and winced as a jolt of fresh pain took her breath away. "Ow," she gasped, immediately lifting her foot to relieve the pressure. "I think I hurt my ankle," she admitted with an irritated glower when Erik frowned with concern. "And we're here because my memory sucks. I drove to pick up Em, but we decided to take her SUV from her place. Then just as we headed down I-25, I realized I left my laptop charger and we swung back because there wasn't going to be time to get a new one once we got to Emma's parents' place. By the time we could leave again, they had closed parts of the interstate. We figured we'd wait until midmorning to leave. Roads should be clear then."

"So that's why your car wasn't in the driveway," Erik surmised.

"Yeah. I thought you were working," Alexis huffed, moving past Erik to sit on the bed next to Emma so she could get a better look at her ankle.

It was then that Emma whispered, "Lex, you don't have any pants on."

Oh yeah, there was that. She hadn't exactly been planning to entertain and most times she slept naked, so the fact that she had a shirt and underwear on was a bonus. She shrugged, more interested in the state of her ankle than anything else at the moment. "How different is this from my bathing suit? Crap, my ankle is really swelling," she muttered, momentarily forgetting about the guy, her brother and the whole shebang because *holy hell, that smarts!*

But apparently someone else was still holding a grudge because Stranger with the Sexy Ass piped in with, "She punched me and then threw a shoe at me."

"You scared the crap out of me," Alexis said with

a glare. As if he had any room to bitch—if he hadn't been in her bed, she wouldn't have had to defend herself. And she wasn't even going to mention how Grabby McGrabbyhands had been all over her—she wasn't in the mood to clean up a massacre. As even-headed as Erik was, he might take exception to the fact that his friend had been touchy-feely in his supposed sleep.

"Okay, okay." Erik held his hands up, obviously bone tired and not in the mood to deal with this nonsense all night. "Let's all just calm down. This was a big misunderstanding. No harm, no foul."

But Alexis was feeling more petulant by the moment as her ankle ramped up in pain. "Speak for yourself," Alexis muttered, rubbing her ankle. "I tripped over my suitcase when I was chasing that pervert out of my room."

"Pervert?" the guy said. "I'm not a—"

Erik looked aggrieved and shook his head. "He's not a pervert. Well, not usually. This is Layton Davis," Erik said by way of introduction. "He drove me home after we worked a blaze. I told him to take the spare room. I thought you were gone. You were supposed to be gone."

Oh sure, blame it on Alexis's inability to keep details straight. She shot a withering look Layton's way. Was she being irrational? Possibly. Sure, they could chalk it all up to a weird, unfortunate coincidence that would make really funny sitcom fodder, but pain made Alexis ill-tempered and she'd never been much of a good sport when it came to being on the losing end of an argument.

"Well, we weren't gone," Alexis said, unable to keep the grumpiness from her tone. "And who doesn't check where he's going to sleep before plopping down on top of someone?"

"Someone who's tired as shit and unaware someone's friend's sister is occupying the bed he was given," Layton said, clearly just as annoyed and as ready to put the argument to bed as she was.

Erik shrugged, rubbing his eyes. "Like I knew. Let's shelve the accusations and take a page from Emma's book and not freak out."

Everyone looked at Emma. *Oops.* Alexis had forgotten about Emma again. Emma managed an awkward smile and Alexis wanted to say, *I feel ya, sister—this bites,* but didn't because she didn't want to embarrass Emma any more than she already had. And Alexis held no illusions that Emma wasn't mortified to her dainty toes over this mishap. Of the two, Emma was the more reserved, more conservative and least likely to be voted Most Outrageous in a peer poll.

Awkward silence followed as they each came to the conclusion that no further beating could be done on this particular horse and it was time to lay it to rest.

"Okay, good. Now, since it's cold as frick outside and the roads are too dangerous, let's bunk up and get through the night," Erik said.

"Your sister probably needs an ice pack or something," Layton said with a reluctant sigh as if he hated to be helpful in this regard because he was still holding a grudge, and gestured to Alexis's swollen ankle. "How about I grab some ice while you figure out the sleeping arrangements."

It was on the tip of her tongue to tell him not to worry about it, that she could tend to her own injuries, but Layton had already split. Maybe he needed ice for his nuts, too.

It was then that she realized her brother was swaddled in a blanket like a Scottish laird.

"Why are you wearing a quilt?" Alexis asked.

"'Cause I'm naked under here," he said, tugging the quilt up higher.

Ah. *Yeah, good idea.* Therapy for getting an eyeful of her brother's junk was not in her budget. But wait a minute…if he was naked under there…her gaze swung to her friend.

"Wait, did you climb into bed with Emma while you were naked?" Alexis asked, grossed out for Emma. Not that Erik wasn't good-looking, but, *eww*, Erik was like a big brother to Emma, too. He used to torment Emma just as enthusiastically as he'd tormented Alexis. He'd been an equal-opportunity torturer.

"Yeah," Erik admitted, and color climbed Emma's cheeks. Was Emma embarrassed because she'd seen Erik in his birthday suit or, worse, because she'd liked what she'd seen? *Ugh.* The very idea… Alexis couldn't handle it.

"Well, how come you didn't scream?"

"I rarely scream," Emma said, as if that made perfect sense.

"Well, if a big bozo sat on you, you would," Alexis countered, not quite buying Emma's explanation.

But there wasn't time to push the argument because Layton reappeared with a bag of frozen broccoli wrapped in a dish towel. "Here. I'm happy to take the couch," he said.

"And I'll give you your bed back and sleep with Alexis," Emma said to Erik. "I feel so bad about being here when you—"

"I told you to,' Alexis interrupted, still thinking about Emma's reaction. "He was at work."

A beat of awkward silence made ten times weirder because of the questions popping around in Alexis's head followed, until finally, Emma said, "I'm not exactly dressed. And neither is Erik. So…"

"Right," Alexis said, grabbing the frozen-broccoli bag and sliding from the bed, only to gasp at the sudden and unforgiving pain. Erik started as if he wanted to help her but couldn't without dropping the quilt and risking a full-frontal show.

"Well, hell," Layton said with a low grumble before sweeping Alexis into his arms.

"Hey! Put me down," Alexis said, mortified that a) he'd picked her up as if she weighed nothing and b) there was no mistaking the delightfully solid muscle lifting up her backside.

"I will. In your room." Layton strode to the door, ignoring her protests. Alexis shot Emma a pleading glance— as if her friend was going to jump to her rescue when all Layton was doing was being mildly chivalrous—and suffered the knowledge that she was just going to have to suck it up and deal with the fact that this situation couldn't get any more uncomfortable.

But then Alexis knew full well that tempting fate with a thought like that never ended well.

2

LAYTON WAS TIRED, grumpy and his balls ached, but he had to admit that in spite of the fact that Alexis was a firecracker with a short fuse, she felt pretty good in his arms.

And that thought right there was why it was apparent that he wasn't right in the head.

"For what it's worth, I'm sorry about…uh, you know."

Eloquent. He nearly bit his tongue in half with embarrassment at his bumbling apology, but was there a more suave way to apologize for sleep-sexin' someone up?

"All I'm saying is that I'm not that kind of guy," he added gruffly.

Alexis seemed to accept that he was being truthful and nodded, though her cheeks brightened a bit. "Sure. Honest mistake, I guess."

"Yeah."

Layton set her gently on the bed and started to leave, but Alexis stopped him, saying, "Um, so, yeah, sorry about your balls. Self-defense 101, take out the jewels."

"Effective. It'll be a miracle if I can have kids."

She bit her lip around a smile when she realized he was kidding.

Layton exited the bedroom just as Emma was entering. Emma shot Layton a quick look and then joined Alexis on the bed.

"Well, that was eventful," Alexis said with an embarrassed laugh to break the ice. "I bet that was hecka awkward with Erik. Sorry about that. Are you traumatized for life?"

"It's okay," Emma murmured, but there was a subtle flush to her cheeks that made Alexis wonder if Emma had enjoyed the view. Okay, so if Alexis were being objective, her brother was pretty decent to look at, so she supposed it wouldn't be far-fetched to imagine Emma liking what she saw. But Alexis couldn't go there. Emma was her best friend since grade school. Erik had pulled Emma's pigtails and made fun of her braces. Alexis shuddered. "Let's chalk this night up to one unfortunate incident and try to forget about it. Tomorrow, we'll hit the road as soon as the roads are clear. Sound good?"

"Mmm-hmm." Emma climbed into the bed and was already snuggling up to the pillow, all too ready to return to dreamland.

But it wasn't that easy for Alexis. Her adrenaline was still pumping and, worse, the memory of those heated dream kisses that turned out to be real, after all, was making her restless.

She should've known that something was off when

she'd been so incredibly aroused in her dream. No dream was that good.

Not even if chocolate was involved.

She liked to think of herself as relatively smart—she was, after all, in the master's program for her business degree—but if one looked at her track record with relationships, she might not appear to be so intelligent.

Which was why she'd made a vow to herself that until she finished school she was not going to even *think* about guys. Boys, as her dad used to warn her, were bad news.

Except her brother, of course; Erik was a doll.

But all other boys…were persona non grata.

A small sigh escaped her lips. Goodbye fun times, hello celibacy.

It wasn't for forever—just until she got her act together and on track.

So why did it feel like a death sentence?

LAYTON RUBBED THE sore spot on his dome and tried to ignore the dull, throbbing ache from where the book had connected with his shoulder, not to mention the residual sore spot from where Alexis had abused his groin.

Erik had mentioned his younger sister was living with him for the time being while she finished her master's degree, but he hadn't mentioned anything about the woman being a live wire.

Erik also hadn't mentioned anything about how gorgeous his sister was.

That part shouldn't matter, he reminded his randy self as he closed his eyes against the pain. Sexy and crazy were a bad combination—like pickles and eggs on a peanut butter sandwich or Tabasco sauce on chocolate. All sorts of bad and bound to give you indigestion.

But even as he knew it was better to just go to sleep and forget all about Alexis Matheson…how was he supposed to forget the memory of that hot woman writhing in his arms, her mouth on his? Guilt nudged at him. If Erik knew where Layton's mouth had been, Layton would have more than an aching dome to contend with. But damn, if she'd been that hot asleep, what was she like when she was awake?

Those kinds of thoughts were not helpful, he told himself.

Neither was the fact that when she'd leaped from the bed wearing next to nothing, he'd gotten an eyeful of rounded, feminine hips and a rack that wouldn't quit. A nice, generous handful for sure. And that thin silky chemise hadn't given much coverage. He was pretty sure he'd caught a tantalizing view of her breasts—and what his eyes had only caught a glimpse of, his hands had touched, albeit without his conscious knowledge, and he couldn't stop replaying the memory.

Aaaannnnd cue the boner.

Goddamn.

Erik would set him on fire if he knew what kind of thoughts he was having about his little sister.

Hey, it's not as if she's a kid, a voice protested in his head. Likely the same part of his brain in charge of his downstairs region. Layton pushed at his growing erection with irritation and an increasing sense of frustration. He wasn't going to jerk off on his buddy's couch. *Just go to sleep.* Tomorrow would come soon enough and he could bail. Right about now he wished he'd just ignored Erik's offer to stay and taken his chances on the road.

Erik was his buddy, a good man and a better fire-fighter. They shared the same shift and looked out for one another and that meant he couldn't start looking cross-eyed at the guy's sister.

Layton tossed back the blankets and climbed from the couch, needing aspirin for his head. Padding quietly into the kitchen, he began opening cabinets in search of a painkiller when a voice at his back made him turn.

"Okay, I'm willing to overlook the fact that you climbed into my bed without asking, but now you're rummaging through my cabinets? Should I be worried? If I find you going through my underwear drawer next, we're not going to be friends."

Alexis stood there, wrapped in a filmy robe that wasn't much more coverage than the shirt and panties she'd been sporting earlier, and he wondered what he'd done in a past life to deserve such a test. He also noticed she was still favoring her right foot.

"Just looking for aspirin. Someone hit me in the head with a shoe," he responded, trying to keep his eyes from straying. "You really did a number on that ankle. You ought to have it checked out."

"It's nothing. I twisted it a little when I was chasing after you. It'll be fine by morning."

"Are you sure? Sprains can do some damage."

"I'll take that under consideration." Alexis limped in his direction and went to the last cabinet to retrieve some aspirin. She tossed the bottle his way and he caught it with a small smile.

"Thanks," he said.

"Sure." She waited as he shook out two. "So...sorry about the shoe. It was the first thing I could grab and I thought you might be a murderer."

"How many murderers stop to take a snooze before they do their murdering?" he asked, tossing back the aspirin with a swig of water straight from the tap. He wiped his mouth. "I mean, if you really think about it, highly unlikely that I was a murderer."

"Logic and reason don't play when you're jolted out of a dead sleep."

"Okay, I'll give you that," he conceded, wondering if she was going to mention the other thing that happened. What was the protocol on something like this? Should they pretend they hadn't been wrapped in each other's arms, about to do the deed if they hadn't woken up? Sobering thought, even if she was sexy as hell. "So why are you up?"

"Funny thing about getting an adrenaline shot laced with pure survival instinct...hard to sleep after that."

"Sorry," he said. "I should feel guilty, right?"

"A little."

"I do feel bad," he admitted. "I mean... I didn't know you were in the bed. I'm not that kind of guy."

She nodded, accepting his apology, and they both knew he wasn't only talking about the mishap with her ankle.

"Don't worry about it. I've done worse and been just fine. Thanks for caring." A small smile played on those luscious, pouty lips and he had to remind himself that she was off limits. But he couldn't seem to stop himself from thinking about things that were better kicked to the curb. Alexis limped to the fridge. "However, when I can't sleep, I drink warm milk. Want some?"

Yuck. "Not since I was a toddler," he quipped. "But by all means, help yourself. Don't let me get in the way."

"I won't." Alexis grinned more broadly. Yeah, firecracker was right. This gal was all sass and vinegar wrapped in a sizzling package of hips and luscious breasts. Thank God he was leaving in the morning or he might be sorely tempted to see if she tasted just as good when he was awake as when he was dreaming. Alexis poured a mugful and stuck it in the microwave. "So, how long have you and Erik been friends?"

"Awhile. Same shift. Makes for tight friendships under the right circumstances. He's a cool dude."

"He is a very cool dude, but then I'm biased."

The microwave dinged and she retrieved her mug of milk. "You're really going to drink that?" he asked, grimacing.

"Every drop."

"All right then." He watched her leave and damn if his eyes didn't go straight to her ass. Yeah…it was definitely a good thing he was leaving as soon as the roads were clear. He was only human and he really didn't want to lose Erik as a friend.

But Alexis Matheson was going to haunt his dreams.

3

ALEXIS WOKE EARLY in spite of the night's events, but mostly because Emma was already up and showered, anxious to hit the road.

"Aren't you a bowl of sunshine?" Alexis said, yawning. "Did you sleep okay? I mean, after everything?"

"Slept fine. But I'm sad to report that you still steal the covers. If I hadn't wrapped myself up like a burrito, you'd have left me with nothing."

Alexis laughed softly. "Bad habits are hard to break. Sorry."

"It's okay, I still love you, but I feel bad for whoever you marry. It's always going to be a battle for the bedding."

"True story." Alexis climbed from the bed, stiff, and still not quite awake. She needed coffee and quick. She swung her legs over the edge of the bed, but as soon as she put pressure on her right foot, she nearly yelped from the shock of pain. *Well, if that isn't a fine way to wake up.* She lifted her ankle and grimaced at the black-and-blue bruising and swelling. *Crap, this doesn't bode well.* Alexis tried to put some pressure on her ankle, but it was a no go. She bit her lip. "Em? We have a problem."

Emma plainly hadn't heard Alexis. "Can you be ready to hit the road in about an hour? I think the roads should be open by then," Emma called out from the bathroom where she was doing her hair.

"Em? Come here a minute," Alexis said, sinking back down on the bed. When Emma appeared with a concerned frown, Alexis said flatly, "Houston, we have a problem."

"What's wrong?" But just as the question left her mouth, her gaze fastened on the nasty bruising on Alexis's ankle and she gasped. "Oh my God! Oh no! That looks terrible, Lex. We need to take you to the doctor. It definitely looks worse."

Alexis had to agree, but she wasn't about to ruin Emma's weekend by spending it in the ER. "It's the weekend, which means an ER visit, and I cannot afford a bill like that right now. I just paid for all my books for the semester. I'm practically living on ramen noodles at this point. I'll just have to wait until my regular doctor's office opens. Besides, what can they do for my foot that I can't?"

"What if it's broken?" Emma fretted.

"It's not broken," Alexis insisted, feeling fairly confident that she was right, but there was a shadow of a doubt that was dogging her. It hurt pretty bad. And the swelling wasn't helping, either. "I probably just need to ice it."

"And elevate it," Emma added with a fatalistic shake

of her head. "There's no way you can sit in the car for the next two hours."

"No. This is not going to ruin our girls' weekend. I've been looking forward to this party for weeks. You know Arnold is going to be crushed if I don't share a cookie with him. I've already promised."

Emma's parents ran a school in Colorado Springs for mentally challenged adults, and Alexis and Emma were planning on surprising Emma's parents at the annual Christmas bash. They were going to serve dinner on Saturday with a full-fledged girls' weekend thrown in the mix.

Alexis enjoyed volunteering at the school. The residents never pretended to be something they weren't—unlike the guys she seemed to attract like bees to pollen.

"Arnold will have to take a rain check," Emma said, then decided, "If you're not going to go to the hospital, then I'm canceling my trip, too. I can't leave you alone like this."

That was exactly what Alexis didn't want Emma to do. "No," Alexis said emphatically. "You are not canceling your trip over this. It's no big deal. It's not as if my foot is going to fall off or something. I just need to baby it a little."

Emma pointed. "Your foot looks like it was beaten with a bat. If it's not broken, I'm willing to guess it's badly sprained."

There was no denying her foot looked terrible. So much for her idea of getting a pedicure. "Please don't cancel on my behalf."

"I can't leave you like this," Emma said, appalled that Alexis would even suggest it.

"Seriously, I'll just putter around the house and watch a movie marathon all day. There's no need for you to cancel your plans because of this, and I would feel ten times worse if you did."

But Emma knew her too well and called her out. "No you won't. You'll try to hang lights and bake and decorate the Christmas tree because you can't stand to sit still. You have the attention span of a gnat and an inability to sit still for any length of time. I'd have to tie you to a chair if I wanted you to stay off that foot."

"That's a little extreme." Alexis pretended to appear offended. "For your information, I recently took up crocheting and that takes a lot of patience."

"You tried it once and then got frustrated and haven't touched it since."

"Okay, fine. Crocheting isn't my thing. But neither is yoga and you're the one who told me to find something to help me relax."

"Yes, and you're still looking because you have a hard time being still. So, forgive me if I don't believe you when you say that you'll take it easy."

Alexis knew Emma was right, but it killed her to think that Emma would cancel over something so dumb. Miserable for ruining her friend's weekend, she rose on unsteady legs with the intent of hobbling her pathetic self to the kitchen for some coffee, but Emma was already slipping her arm beneath her to help. "I'm sorry," Alexis said, feeling like doggie poo. "I didn't mean to ruin our weekend."

"It's okay."

But it wasn't okay. Alexis could hear the sharp disappointment in Emma's voice even as she tried to hide it with a cheerful smile. That was Emma in a nutshell, always thinking of others before herself and it broke Alexis's heart that she was the cause of Emma's disappointment.

Erik and Layton were in the kitchen getting coffee when Emma and Alexis made their way in.

Erik frowned. "Lex? Is that ankle still bothering you?" he asked.

"It hasn't gotten any better," she answered glumly as her butt found a dining room chair. Her mood was rapidly plummeting as quickly as the temperature outside. Another storm was coming. "It actually seems to have gotten worse during the night."

Layton came forward. "Let me take a look."

"It's fine."

But Erik chimed in, saying, "Let Layton take a look, Lex. He's got paramedic training."

Hard to argue with that, seeing as she didn't want to rush to the hospital. "Fine," she grumbled, allowing Layton to gently examine her foot. He slowly manipulated her ankle, carefully gauging her reaction. She winced a few times and then yelped when he pressed her foot. Layton nodded and released her foot with care. "Well, I don't think it's broken, but you've probably got one helluva sprain. If you go to the ER they'll order an X-ray, which won't show soft-tissue damage, but it'll definitively show whether or not you have a fracture."

"But you don't think it's broken, right?" Alexis said.

"I don't, but that doesn't mean you couldn't have a hairline fracture. Best to check it out."

"See?" Emma said, lightly tapping Alexis's head for being difficult. "I'll drive you to the hospital."

"No, I'm not going to the hospital," she said stubbornly. "And you're not missing out on your parents' bash. Erik, please tell Emma that I'm a big girl and I can handle myself, even slightly injured."

"Lex, it's fine, really. I don't really want to drive alone anyway, so we'll just do that movie marathon you mentioned. It'll be fun."

"Erik can go with you," Alexis volunteered, shocking Emma. She didn't know why she'd offered her brother's services, but it seemed to make sense. Erik was a total gentleman.

"Oh! That's not necessary. I'm sure he has plans," Emma said, darting a look at Erik. "It's fine, really. I don't mind canceling. Lex really shouldn't be alone with her foot the way it is."

Alexis sent an imploring look Erik's way, *C'mon, bro, don't let me down!*

But it was Layton who spoke up first. "I can't believe I'm going to say this, but… I could stay behind and help you out so your friend doesn't feel like you're being left behind all alone. It's kind of my fault you're all banged up anyway."

All eyes turned to Layton. Did Layton just volunteer to babysit her?

Erik said, "That's okay, man. You don't have to do that. It's not your fault. It was a misunderstanding all the way around."

"I know, but hell, I've got nothing to do today that

didn't include drinking a few beers and being a slug. Besides, I've got the training. If her ankle gets worse, I'll bundle her up and force her to go to the ER."

"He has a point," Erik slowly agreed, nodding. Then he looked to Emma. "How do you feel about that?"

Alexis hesitated then looked to Erik and Emma, saying, "Well, if Erik agreed to go with Emma... I guess that would solve both problems. Are you okay with that, Em?" As soon as the words left her mouth, Emma started shaking her head, but Alexis wasn't going to budge on this one. "Em, it's dangerous on the roads. You know it's stupid to drive alone and I refuse to let you cancel your plans. Erik will be the perfect gentleman, I can promise. He's one of the good guys."

Emma's cheeks flared as her gaze darted. "I know Erik is a good guy. I just don't want him to have to do something he doesn't want to do."

Erik chimed in. "I don't mind," he said. "And I agree with Lex. You shouldn't drive alone in these conditions."

"The storm doesn't seem to be letting up as I'd hoped," Emma said, biting her lip with indecision. "Are you sure you don't mind the drive?"

"Not at all. We can catch up. Tell me what's new in your life since you were just my bratty little sister's friend."

"Bratty?" Alexis repeated with indignation. "Like you were the epitome of well behaved. Just because Mom and Dad were blind to your antics doesn't mean everyone was. For your information, I told them that it was you who broke Mom's ceramic elephant from Africa during that party you held your senior year."

"You little snitch. You promised you wouldn't tell. I paid good hush money for that," Erik said, grinning. "I should've threatened some kind of punishment for reneging on the deal."

"Good times," Alexis said, laughing. "Okay, so is it settled? Erik will go with Emma, and Layton will stay with me?"

They all shared looks and then nodded, agreeing. Emma heaved a breath and then said, "All right, if that's the case, we need to get moving. If that storm is determined to dump another load of snow, I want to put some miles on the road before it happens."

"I can be ready to roll in fifteen minutes. That work for you?"

Emma nodded and they both split off to finish getting ready.

"And just like that, it was you and me," Layton said.

"Yeah…you know you don't actually need to stay," she said in a conspiratorial whisper. "I appreciate what you did. Emma wouldn't have agreed without Erik and you volunteering. As soon as they take off, wait about a half hour and then you can take off, too."

He shook his head, grinning. "Sorry, no can do. My offer was legit. What kind of guy would I be if I left you to fend for yourself when you're plainly injured?"

That surprised her. He really wanted to stay? To be truthful, she'd thought he was just giving her backup. "Seriously?"

"Yeah, I mean, I know it's not actually my fault, but I do feel a bit responsible for your laid-up foot. The least I can do to assuage my guilt is to help you out."

Alexis didn't know what to say to that. She paused

for the tiniest of moments only because a hot guy was her personal weakness, and the last person she needed to mess around with was her brother's best friend, but what were the odds that anything would happen between them over a weekend? She could be around a hot guy and keep her hands to herself. She smiled with determination—mostly to prove something to herself—and said, "Okay, but don't say I didn't warn you. I wasn't lying when I said I had a movie marathon in mind."

"I like movies."

"Chick flicks."

"Movies with hot chicks? Sounds good to me."

She laughed at his devilish charm. Yeah, he was just the sort of guy who'd turn her head. But not this time.

Nope.

Layton Davis...it ain't gonna happen.

TRUE TO HIS WORD, Erik was ready to go within twenty minutes. With Emma in her SUV waiting, Erik paused to give the obligatory big-brother speech, which Layton didn't fault him for, but he was tempted to remind Erik that Alexis wasn't a kid.

"I know you're a good guy or else I wouldn't even think of leaving Alexis with you, but I feel I have to warn you about my sister. She's...spirited."

Layton's brow rose. "Spirited? Erik...*horses* are spirited. Be more specific."

"Hell, this is the most awkward conversation ever. Look, she has a thing for falling for the wrong guy and I don't want to see her hurt. She's been through enough. Her last boyfriend... Let's just say I wasn't a fan. So, yeah, what I'm trying to say is…don't mess with her and for God's sake, don't let her mess with you. Keep things friendly, but not too friendly."

"C'mon, man, like you would have to ask. I'm not here to hook up with your sister. I'm just helping out."

The look of relief pinged Layton's conscience. The fact was, Alexis was hot. She was a grade-A hot piece of ass if he were being honest, but he meant what he'd said. He wasn't here to mess around with the woman.

Erik clapped him on the shoulder and climbed into the car. "Help yourself to whatever's in the fridge. I'll call you when we get there."

"Drive safe," Layton said, waving.

The snow started to drift lazily from the sky, dissolving into tiny wet spots on his face almost instantly. He glanced at the sky. Hopefully, they made good time before the storm really started up again. Layton turned on his heel and returned to the house, where Alexis was already up and hopping around the kitchen.

"What are you doing?"

"Nothing. What are you doing?"

"Preventing you from overdoing it. What happened to the movie marathon?"

"There's plenty of time for that. I want to make some kettle corn. Want some?"

Kettle corn. How did she know it was his weakness? "You know how to make it?"

"I sure hope so, otherwise I'm about to make a huge mess for nothing."

He chuckled. "Okay, wiseass, as much as I would love to scarf down some kettle corn, you are getting off that foot. I told you I didn't think it was broken, but it's certainly sprained and you need to elevate it with some ice."

Alexis scowled, but he didn't give her a chance to argue and simply scooped her into his arms, shocking her into stunned silence as he carried her to the living room. He deposited her on the sofa and then put a pillow under her foot. "You sit here while I get the ice."

"Is now the appropriate time to admit that Emma was right and that I don't sit still well?"

"I already had that figured out."

"Story of my life. I've never been able to just sit around. Once I had the chicken pox and I drove my mother crazy because I couldn't stop itching and squirming, which then made it worse. My mom says it was the longest two weeks of her life."

Alexis's story was telling. He held no illusions that Alexis would be an easy patient, but there was something about her that drew him, in spite of all the reasons he ought to keep his distance. Maybe it was the memory of those dream kisses or maybe it was the memory of that near-perfect ass. Ha! Neither memory was safe enough to entertain for longer than a heartbeat.

He returned with an icepack wrapped in a towel and gently draped it on Alexis's ankle. "That ought to help, but you really have to keep off your foot if you want it to heal."

"Yeah, yeah," she grumbled. "Are you sure you want to hang around? There's nothing exciting about watching paint dry."

"Depends on the company."

Alexis met his gaze and cocked her head to the side

with a sweet, beguiling grin that he didn't trust in the least but found extremely compelling. "Is that so? And are you saying that you would enjoy my company? The woman who nearly turned you from a rooster to a hen with one kick?"

"In spite of that...yeah."

Were they flirting? It felt like flirting. And he liked it.

Hell, he'd always been a sucker for the girl who was just out of reach; she didn't need to make it ten times more difficult by being sexy, too.

Erik's advice rang in his head like a gong and he pulled back even though there was something captivating about Alexis—and he wasn't just talking about the sweet rack she was sporting.

"You're going to get me into trouble," he said with a chuckle as he rose from his haunches. "You know your brother has it in his head that you're this fragile thing who might break if handled too roughly." He waited a heartbeat, then asked with a sly grin, "What do you think about that?"

She met his grin with a saucy one of her own. "I think I'm a big girl and I don't need my brother to run interference for me."

"That may be true, but I'm not the kind of guy who would go behind a buddy's back to get at his sister. You know what I mean?"

"That's admirable," she admitted with grudging respect.

"And why does it feel the opposite when you say it like that?"

She laughed and the sound tickled his bones like

fingertips dancing down his vertebrae. "I told you, you don't have to stay. I'll be fine."

"I gave your brother my word. I'm not going anywhere."

There was the slightest, most minute, almost indiscernible hitch in her breath, and that sexy little sound almost caused an immediate erection to tent his jeans. Ah hell, this was going to be the hardest test of his life. For crying out loud, they'd only just met, but there was electricity bouncing between them that was hard to ignore, and if she didn't stop looking at him as if he were the choicest cut of beef, he was going to have a helluva time keeping to his word.

"Tell me about this guy who did you wrong," he said, moving to sit beside her on the sofa. Act like a friend. Not a hungry wolf ready to pounce. "According to Erik, he was a douche."

"He said that?"

"Well, not in so many words, but I got the impression he hadn't thought much of him."

She shrugged as if it was no big deal, but beneath that negligent shrug was the faint show of heartache that surprised him. Alexis gave off the vibe that if anyone was doing the heartbreaking, it was her and not the other way around.

"What can I say? I'm a terrible judge of character," she said.

"I don't believe that."

"No? Well, I can't deny that I've been drawn to the worst sort of guy. My track record isn't the best."

"We all have unfortunate hookups in our past," he said. "It's called live and learn."

Alexis laughed and adjusted the ice pack. "Yeah, well, until I get through with my master's degree there will only be one kind of learning going on."

"Sounds like a solid plan."

And it was. So why did he want to make her break it?

4

CIRCUMSTANCE WAS A funny thing. Alexis stared at her ankle, amazed at how much could change in the blink of an eye. Last night she was lobbing objects at Layton's head and today, she was noticing how nicely his cropped, dark hair set off the masculine cut of his jaw. Maybe she wouldn't mind if Layton played nursemaid after all. Even if she had the very best intentions to keep her hands to herself, she could certainly enjoy the view.

And the view was quite spectacular. Muscled chest and arms, solid abs narrowing to a trim waist and hips… Yes, indeed, Layton had the goods.

"Okay, so tell me the real reason you volunteered to stay behind," Alexis said, putting Layton on the spot, trying to make things interesting.

"What makes you think I wasn't being completely altruistic in my offer?"

"Were you?"

Layton paused, then that little glint in his wondrously dark eyes gave him away. "Okay, full disclosure…you're a beautiful woman and I happen to have a weakness for women like you, but even with that said… I promised your brother that I wouldn't do or say anything inappropriate."

"Such a gentleman," she murmured as her heart rate did a little jump at his admission. Was it terrible that she was already imagining him naked beneath her? Good grief, her hormones were out of control.

"I wouldn't go that far," he said ruefully. "I'd be a liar if I didn't admit that keeping my thoughts on the straight and narrow has already proven to be a challenge."

She smiled, enjoying that she wasn't the only one thinking about inappropriate things. "Seems we have more than my brother in common," she returned.

"Careful, those kinds of comments are dangerous."

"To whom? Because I'm an adult and don't need a chaperone."

He laughed. "I promised your brother."

"That was your mistake."

"Hot damn, Erik warned me about you and it seems he was right on the money."

"Did he? And what exactly did he warn you about?"

"Just that you have a taste for trouble and that I ought to steer clear."

She pouted. "That's not flattering at all. Makes me sound like a kid."

"You are definitely no kid," he said, his gaze feasting on her ample breasts. If there was one asset she knew she owned, it was her impressive cup size. He cleared his throat as if he realized that he was staring and actually made a concentrated effort to look elsewhere. "But I've gotta hold on to a shred of integrity, you know?"

"So noble."

He smirked. "Well, I respect the hell out of your brother. He's a good man. I'm not about to start looking at his sister like a piece of meat."

"Is that one of the lesser-known 'Bro Code' rules?" she teased.

"Call it what you want, it's just how I operate."

"You're playing into that firefighter-hero stereotype pretty hard," she said with a mischievous smile, enjoying their banter. "I wonder if there's a bad boy lurking underneath that polished exterior."

He chuckled, the sound tickling her senses. "You have no idea."

Was she completely wicked that she suddenly had a desperate hunger to find out just how bad Layton could be? Probably. Particularly when she'd made a pact with herself to keep on the straight and narrow until she had her master's. It was a good plan at the time. Now? Seemed stupid as hell.

"What would you say if I told you I was attracted to you?"

He held his easy smile, but something in his gaze changed and her body tingled with awareness. "Then I'd say that you'd better keep that on lockdown because things could get awkward."

She could call his bluff. Alexis knew when a guy was into her. Layton was throwing off signals that a person would have to be blind not to see, but she felt a bit like a predator chasing after a poor doomed gazelle. He was plainly telling her it wasn't going to happen and she respected that—to a point—but his gaze was also throwing sparks that were bound to catch fire at some point.

Alexis sighed dramatically, leaning casually against the sofa, idly gazing at her injured foot. "Well, the truth of the matter is the fact that I want to give you a tongue bath must mean that somewhere, deep down, you're defective."

He startled with a laugh. "I think you just insulted me, but for the life of me all I can think of is that tongue bath."

"See? It's hopeless. Let's be honest, we're both adults and we're both attracted to one another. We also both know that we shouldn't act upon the dirty thoughts in our heads. So…it's probably best that you go home before something terribly unfortunate happens between us."

"Unfortunate?"

"Yeah, like all our clothes flying off and landing on the floor."

He swallowed and she privately delighted in the way the thought made him stutter a little. "Are you always this blunt?"

"Pretty much. My mom says I've always suffered from a lack of tact, but my dad says I don't seem to suffer from it at all."

Layton laughed with a slight twinkle in his eye that she found highly alluring. "Okay, well, not leaving. I made a promise to Erik that I'd stick around and make sure you stayed off that foot, so you're just going to have to deal with my company."

Alexis held his gaze for a moment then shrugged.

"Okay, but I can't be held responsible for what may happen between us."

"Nothing is going to happen," he said with amused laughter. "You don't quit, do you? You're like a dog with a bone."

Alexis shrugged. "We'll see."

"How about this? You pick the movie and I'll scramble up some eggs and bacon for breakfast."

She perked up. The only thing capable of jarring her one-track mind was the introduction of her second favorite distraction: food. "You can cook?"

"A necessary skill when you live with a bunch of other guys several days out of the week. Yes, I can cook. Any requests?"

Oh, how could she not take him up on that offer? She hated to cook but she loved to eat. "A Denver omelet would be fab," she admitted. "I think we have everything you need in the fridge."

"Denver omelet coming up," Layton said, going to the kitchen. "And while I'm making breakfast you can throw out movie ideas."

On the surface, that sounded well and good, but Alexis didn't want to sit around the house all day. She spent so much of her time studying that she needed a physical outlet. Her gaze drifted to the window where soft snowflakes fell lazily from the sky. The storm hadn't hit yet. There was probably just enough time to get the lights up before the snow really started coming down.

Maybe she could convince Layton to help her string the lights? But how to do it was the question.

She wasn't above using her charm to get what she

wanted and she had a feeling Layton wouldn't mind fresh air...once he realized that spending too much time cuddled up on the sofa wasn't a good idea, particularly if he was determined to keep things Disney-rated.

Before too long, Layton returned with two plates of omelets and toast, and Alexis's opinion of her brother's friend went up a notch.

"Did you pick out a movie?"

"No, I did something better," she said around a bite of omelet. "Oh, that's good. You're a handy guy to have around. Cute, built like a Roman god and can cook? Okay, just level with me, what's your hidden defect?"

"I have a weakness for pretty, sass-mouthed women," he admitted wryly as he shoveled in his food.

"How much of a weakness?" she asked, curious.

Layton leveled a wry look her way. "Enough of one. Eat your breakfast."

"So bossy."

"Has anyone ever successfully told you what to do?"

She affected a serious expression. "My dad." But she couldn't keep a straight face for long, laughing as she said, "But you're not my dad so don't even try to boss me around."

"Duly noted." He gestured to her plate. "Good?"

"Fan-freaking-tastic," Alexis openly admitted with glee. "You're quite a catch. So tell me, Layton, do you chase the ladies or do the ladies chase you?"

Layton gave her a sideways grin that showcased a nice row of white, even teeth. The man could audition for a toothpaste commercial without an ounce of reservation. "I've chased my share, but I've been chased, too."

"It's all about the chase though, isn't it? Once you've gotten what you want…where's the mystery? Where's the thrill?" She couldn't help a twist of hidden bitterness to shape her words. Maybe she was still smarting from her last boyfriend. He'd been all about the chase, too.

But Layton frowned, shaking his head. "Some guys are like that. I'm not."

Alexis barked a laugh, not believing him for a second. "You don't have to put on an act for me. I know guys are all about getting laid."

"When I'm with a girl, I only have eyes for her," he said with such seriousness that she paused for a moment, thrown off track. How could a man who looked like Layton be a one-woman kind of guy? She didn't buy it. "Seriously?"

He shrugged as if he didn't care if she believed him or not. "The chase is fun, don't get me wrong, but the real good stuff? That happens after you get to know each other. Never underestimate the value of being able to be yourself with your partner."

"Whoa there, Dr. Phil," Alexis joked, a little uncomfortable with how quickly things had gotten serious. "I was just kidding."

But she wasn't entirely. Riker had screwed up her internal sensor so badly she wasn't sure it worked any longer and she didn't trust her own judgment. Sure, Layton seemed like a good guy, but didn't they all in the beginning? It was better to keep things superficial than risk getting hurt later. She'd happily step over the line and break her own rule for the opportunity for some hot blow-your-mind sex, but that's where it stopped.

"For what it's worth, you don't have to try to convince me that you're not a player. I don't really care one way or the other."

"Why is it so hard to believe that I'm a good guy?"

"Because I've known too many guys like you to know better," she quipped.

But Layton set her straight with a quiet "Something tells me you've never met a guy like me."

He said it with such confidence that for a split second Alexis stopped to wonder if he was telling the truth. But wasn't that the problem? She always thought they were being truthful until that terrible moment when she discovered otherwise. She was done with being played. "You can drop the act, buddy. I'm not interested in the game. I mean, I'm down for a little fun, but I don't need the white lies to smooth the way."

Layton frowned, shaking his head with faint irritation. "Boy, Erik wasn't wrong. You must've been screwed over big-time to be so jaded at such a young age. So, for the sake of every other man that happens to cross your path, why don't you tell me what happened with this other dude so I can assure you that not every guy is like that."

He wanted to listen? Alexis covered her surprise with an airy laugh. His comment hit too close to home for comfort. Riker's betrayal still stung. But she didn't feel like opening up her chest and revealing her broken heart to a complete stranger. Sex was one thing— being vulnerable was another.

"Okay, Mr. Wonderful…why don't you have a girl-friend?"

Layton leaned forward to put his plate on the coffee table. "Guess I'm taking a break from it all."

"What do you mean?"

"The dating thing. I'm over it."

She handed him her plate and he set it on top of his. "Explain."

Layton shook his head with a small smile and then went to gently lift the ice pack from her foot. "I'm tired of the game. First dates, the obligatory small talk, the uncertainty of the outcome…it's all one colossal drag on my time. I'd rather spend it hiking or riding my bike than sitting across the table from someone I just met to try to make some kind of connection. I don't know…just not into it right now."

Alexis laughed. "Okay, so it seems I'm not the only one who's been burned in the past."

"Touché."

"What was her name?"

"What was his?"

"Riker."

Layton did a double take. "Riker?" he repeated with a fair amount of incredulity. "Well, there's your problem right there. Anyone name Riker is bound to be trouble."

She couldn't argue that point. "He was hot."

"So was she."

Alexis laughed, strangely enjoying the way they both flirted around the edges of something personally painful without poking too hard for the other's comfort. If she were being truthful, she was terribly curious about the woman who'd been stupid enough to break this man's heart.

If she were smart, she'd keep everything surface level.

But then if she were smart, she wouldn't be in this position anyway, so why start now?

5

THAT SASS WAS ADDICTIVE.

Alexis was a ball of contradictions. Hot and spirited and yet, beneath all that burning sex appeal was a girl who'd obviously been hurt enough to withdraw from anything or anyone who might be able to hurt her again.

He could understand Erik wanting to punch the last boyfriend's lights out, because he was feeling a little punchy himself and he had no reason to.

But turnabout was fair play so he let loose with a little intel. "All right…you shared, so I'll give you something in return. Her name was Julianne. Jules for short."

Alexis snapped her fingers with a definitive shake of her head. "Yep. Gotta steer clear of anyone named Jules—immediate problem."

"Is that so?"

"Absolutely. You should also avoid anyone named Tiffany or Brittany and if they spell their names with an *i* run like hell."

"Good advice." He nodded, adding for her benefit, "Conversely, any guy named after a *Star Trek Next Gen* character you should avoid like the plague. Born players. They're all concerned with going 'where no man has gone before.'"

Alexis broke into peals of laughter, prompting a grin of his own. She had a way about her that was unabashed and free, definitely different from most girls he met, and it was getting harder to remember why he was supposed to keep his distance.

"Any other advice you might want to impart from the other side of the curtain?" she asked playfully.

He made a show of thinking, but all he was really thinking was that he wanted to kiss her. Strands of dark hair escaped her low ponytail to curl around her jaw, but she made no move to fix it and he was glad. There was something about her devil-may-care attitude about her hair that he found refreshing. Jules had always been picture-perfect, or at least worked hard to appear so and it got old. *Don't touch my hair* or *don't smudge my lipstick* were familiar admonishments before the end had come crashing down around them. "How's your ankle feeling?" he asked, redirecting his own thoughts to safer ground.

Alexis's gaze dropped to her ankle and she nodded. "Better. The ice helped."

"You should still stay off it," he said, trying to stay focused. "Now…are we going to watch movies or what?"

"Is there a third option?"

"Such as?"

"Such as…hanging lights."

"Come again?"

"Here's the deal, I can't sit here for hours on end and just zone out. I need to be doing something, and since I'm stuck home when I thought I'd be elsewhere, and since you've already shared that you don't think it's a good idea if we knock boots, that leads me to suggest that you help me hang lights…seeing as I'm laid up and all." She paused for effect then added, "Or, I suppose we *could* stay indoors, cuddled up on the sofa… just you and me and no one else in the house…with total privacy to do *whatever* we wanted and *no one* would ever know…"

"You don't play fair," he groaned, his groin immediately jumping into the conversation, happy to join the fun, which was a terrible, bad thing in the way of trying to keep his hands where they belonged—off Alexis!

"I never said I played fair," she said with a beguiling smile. "I play to win."

Damn straight, she did. He had to respect that. His choices were: ignore his better judgment and allow Alexis to hop around outside hanging lights or keep her indoors and try to be a good guy and keep his hands to himself. Yeah, not much of a choice. He wasn't a damn saint. He gave in with a sigh. "All right, you win this round. I suppose being outside doing something is better than staring temptation straight in the face with you cuddled up beside me. But on one condition…"

"Which is?" she asked warily.

"You sit your ass in a chair and let me do the work. The last thing I need is your brother asking why I let you hop around on an injured foot and you end up hurting yourself worse."

She made a face. "You make me sound like an invalid. I'm fine. However, I concede to your demands. I will direct the labor and you will do the heavy lifting."

He chuckled and grabbed the dishes. "So when is this decorating frenzy scheduled to begin?"

"Well, in the interest of not being outside when that storm hits, I'd say about five minutes after you put away the dishes and we get dressed. Sound good?"

Layton agreed, and she was actually ready to go a minute earlier than he was. He gave her a once-over ostensibly to gauge whether or not she was dressed warmly enough, but actually, his gaze was far from simply friendly. Hot damn. That girl could melt snow. White fuzzy boots, white fur-lined jacket and white snow pants, she looked like a snow bunny from an upscale ski resort who didn't plan to actually do any skiing but would look plenty cute just sitting in the lodge sipping hot chocolate. "Trying to blend in with the snow?" he teased, needing desperately to treat her like a little sister so he stopped seeing her as a full-fledged woman with hips and curves. "I'm not sure you have enough white."

She fake scowled. "Pardon me if I don't take fashion tips from a man who thinks pajama pants are acceptable for going out in public."

"Correction—*lounge* pants. Not pajamas," he said, adding with a wink because he couldn't help himself. "As you've already discovered, I sleep in the nude. No need for pajamas."

Her cheeks flared adorably and he had to admit it

did nice things to his ego. *Knock it off, Romeo. Erik's little sister, remember?* Layton reined in his giddy libido with effort. "Okay, show me where the lights are and let's get this started." If Alexis sensed the fact that he was struggling with the need to be the good guy, she didn't let on and he was thankful. He was quickly becoming a powder keg and she was the match. Just how would Erik react if he found out that the guy he'd left his injured little sister with had ended up boning her like some jerk-off who couldn't keep his dick in his pants for one damn day. Yeah, Layton knew exactly how he'd react—badly.

And with good reason.

Layton hefted the box of lights from the garage and followed Alexis's instructions, bringing three big boxes from their storage spot to the front porch.

"I'll test the strands, you hang," she said cheerfully, her breath pluming in front of her as her eyes sparkled. "I'm so glad I'm getting a chance to hang these a bit earlier than expected. Typically, I like the lights to go up right after Thanksgiving, but with midterms and a brutal professor who seems to hate me, I've been knee-deep in school stuff."

"So master's degree…that's pretty impressive."

She grinned broadly. "My dad calls me the perpetual student. He swears my decision to get my master's was to get out of finding a real job."

"Was it?"

Alexis gasped with mock outrage. "Of course not. I just want to land at the top of the food chain, and the only way to do that is with a master's degree."

"You want to be the boss?"

She looked wistful and aggressive at the same time as she nodded. "Hell yes. I don't know if you could tell, but I'm not the type of person who takes orders very well. I'm much better at giving than following them."

Why did he just think of her giving orders in bed? And why the hell did he find that idea hot as hell? *Get your head in the game and focus, Layton! Thoughts like that are gonna land your ass in a pan of boiling water.*

"The world takes all sorts," he said with a forced grin, watching as she tested the first strand. Satisfied when all the lights twinkled and blinked, she handed the strand off to him and moved onto the next. He took the light hooks and began lining them along the porch rafters so he could hook the strand into each one. "Okay, so don't take this the wrong way but you don't seem the Suzy Homemaker type. What's with the driving need to decorate for Christmas?"

"Christmas is my favorite holiday and always has been," she answered with a small shrug. "There's just something about the holiday that recharges my battery and restores my faith in humanity."

"Christmas does that for you?" he asked incredulously. "That's funny, all I see are a bunch of people trying to screw each other over for material stuff."

"Sure, that happens, but what about the stories of people who go out of their way to help a stranger?"

"Yeah, I suppose that's nice."

"You suppose?"

"No, that didn't come out right…it is nice. I guess I just don't see enough of that. Christmas always seemed the greediest time of year. Really turned me off the holiday."

"That's a tragedy."

He shrugged. "Nah, it's just life. I like St. Patrick's Day, if it means anything."

"And why is that?" she asked.

"Because it's a day sanctioned for drinking beer." She rolled her eyes and he grinned, adding, "Can't imagine a better holiday than that." Layton held the strand, inspecting it for loose wires of any sort as a force of habit. "Actually, I'd be lying if I said that I don't enjoy Christmas a little bit. I like the lights and the displays but I've seen too many house fires caused by Christmas trees that it's hard to forget what's left behind."

Alexis sobered, pausing in her strand detail. "That must suck."

"It does. I don't want to be a Debbie Downer, but Christmastime…can be kind of scary for public service. Do you realize that suicides and domestic violence go up during the holidays?"

"You're a bowl of sunshine," she said, handing him the strand. "You should really think of going into inspirational speaking."

"Sorry. Occupational hazard, I guess."

"You're forgiven, but I don't care what you say, nothing can dim my holiday spirit. I love the holiday and I'm determined to enjoy every last moment."

Layton had to respect her determination to get her Christmas on, no matter the obstacles.

"One question though."

"Yeah?"

"Why are you decorating your brother's place? Is he as nutty about the holidays as you are?"

"Gracious no. Erik is about as observant as a lawn gnome. He's not much into the whole decorating thing, which is why he lets me do what I want. Someday I'll have my own place and I'll be able to stop commandeering my brother's place."

"Heaven help the man you settle down with. I can only imagine what your house is going to look like."

"It's going to be fabulous and whoever I end up with will be the luckiest guy in the world because I make the world's most insanely delicious gingerbread-men cookies and I give a pretty hot blow job."

Layton stumbled back, missing the step and going down hard on his ass in the snow.

"Are you all right?" she asked, barely holding back her laughter.

"I'm fine," he grumbled, climbing to his feet and wiping the loose snow from his pants. "You shouldn't say things like that to a man you barely know."

Alexis smiled with the innocence of an angel, but that impish twist at the corners of her lips ruined it in the most tantalizing way.

"Just stating facts." She held out the next strand as if she hadn't just rung his bell hard. "Better hurry, that storm is moving quick."

"Are you the devil?" he muttered, mostly to himself, but she heard him loud and clear.

"Not the devil but quite possibly a fallen angel."

A fallen angel with an agenda.

And he was running out of willpower to stay the course.

Heaven help him, what had he gotten himself into?

6

ALEXIS KNEW THE minute the words came out of her mouth that she shouldn't have said them. What was wrong with her? It was as if she were bound and determined to make the worst mistake of her life in record time.

"I'm sorry," she said, quickly making amends. "I shouldn't have said that. It was totally inappropriate. I don't know what's wrong with me. My brain is certainly not acting responsibly—not that that's a big surprise given my track record, but I really am trying to change bad habits."

His chuckle seemed forced, but what could she expect after she'd just let her potty mouth get the best of her. "Hey, it's okay," he reassured her. "Don't beat yourself up over it. We've all made mistakes that we're not proud of. Besides, there's nothing wrong with being proud of a skill."

She couldn't help herself. "When you say things like that it makes me not sorry at all."

A beat of charged silence flowed between them,

filling the crisp air with heat. Layton shook his head. "We're a pair to draw to, aren't we?"

"As in, we both have the same problem recognizing what boundaries to pay attention to?"

"Exactly," he agreed ruefully. "I know it's wrong to look at my buddy's little sister the way I'm looking at you now, but it's getting harder and harder to remember why I was supposed to keep my distance."

A delighted flush tickled her cheeks. "And if I wasn't your buddy's little sister?" she prompted.

He didn't hesitate. "Then we sure as hell wouldn't be hanging lights right now."

What he didn't say was plainly in his gaze. Her breath caught. "Maybe we could pretend that I'm not your buddy's little sister. Just for today."

"I'm not sure that would work. Eventually Erik would find out and I really don't want to lose a friend because, you know, I couldn't keep my hands to myself."

It was solid reasoning, and that he was holding back to protect the feelings of a friend meant something, but it really didn't change the fact that she wanted him and she wasn't sure she wanted to deny herself. "I understand and I think it's awesome that you're the kind of guy who cares, but there's something about you that I can't quite get out of my head and maybe it's because I'm in a reckless frame of mind or maybe it's because you're the hottest guy I've seen in a along time, but right about now, I'd much rather spend my weekend making all sorts of mistakes with you than anything else. So what are we going to do about that?"

"You're making it real hard to be good."

"I guess what I'm saying is I'm not interested in you being good this weekend."

"Yeah, but you're not the only one who's been hammered by bad decisions. I'm trying to change, too."

Was it wrong that she couldn't care less about his past or how he was trying to make amends? Okay, so the fact was, her heart was a little broken. Maybe she didn't like to admit it out loud, but she could feel the jagged pieces scraping and poking and sometimes it was just hard to ignore. "Have you ever just wanted to do the exact thing you know is wrong for so many reasons and yet it felt so right?"

"Story of my damn life."

"At least we have that in common. Erik has always been the responsible one, the one who could be counted on, whereas I was the one people always thought of as the flake. I don't want to be that person anymore, but habits are hard to change."

"But not impossible," he told her. "If you want to be a different person, you have to take steps to be that different person. And that means not doing the things that you want to do the most. At least, that's the advice I've been given."

"So why do you want to change so bad?"

"There just comes a time when you realize that you can't keep doing what you've been doing and hope to have a good life at the end of your days. I mean, I don't want to get all sappy, but I want a family at some point. And that's not going to happen if I don't stop chasing after the wrong tail."

"You have a point," she said, trying not to let his admission hit a soft spot, but she wasn't accustomed to hearing men talk about the idea of settling down. "And I don't think that's sappy at all. I think that's really sweet—and shocking—coming from a guy like you."

"Shocking? How so?"

Alexis shrugged. "I don't know, I guess I'm playing into the stereotype, but guys who look like you and are built like you are usually more interested in sowing their oats rather than putting down roots."

He laughed. "Well, a year ago I was definitely the stereotype. For lack of a better word I was a little… *free* with my affections. But I realized the hard way that people were getting hurt. And that's not the person I want to be."

He had no way of knowing, but his statement had just tingled her ovaries as effectively as if he'd clanged a bell. "If I were more of a cynic, I'd say that was the most effective line I've ever heard."

"Not a line, it's the truth. There's only so many times you can do the walk of shame without it affecting you."

"Men do the walk of shame? I thought it was always the woman."

He chuckled. "I don't know, I've done some shameful things."

She laughed. "Am I a bad person that I want to hear details?"

"Not a bad person, but you're not going to get them, either. Those stories are going to go to my grave."

"Okay, now I'm intrigued. I have to make it my goal to crack open that safe."

Layton scooped up the empty boxes and carried them up the porch where Alexis was sitting in a chair.

"And on that note…what else are we going to do out here? I'm about to freeze my balls off."

"No fair. You can't mention body parts if I can't mention skills. But you're off the hook, the lights were all I wanted to do today."

"Good." He carried the boxes into the house, but just as Alexis started to hobble after him he returned and scooped her up as if she weighed nothing.

She gasped, her cheeks warming. "I'm not crippled. I can walk."

"Maybe I just want to feel you or maybe I'm just being a gentleman. Either way, I come out on the winning side when I have a fine woman in my arms."

Couldn't argue that logic. The man had a way with words, and that smile was quickly becoming her weakness. She laughed and enjoyed the feeling of Layton holding her as if she was precious cargo. He returned her to the sofa and elevated her foot. "You know, if this firefighter gig doesn't work out, I think you could have a real future in home health care."

Layton smirked. "I'll keep that in mind. But only if all of my patients look as cute as you."

"Can't make any promises there. I am pretty cute."

"And modest. Dangerous combination."

Layton went to pull away and she snagged his shirt by the lapels and dragged him straight to her lips. "Since we've already agreed we both suck at making good decisions, we might as well just go with it. I'm tired of fighting what I desperately want to do."

And then she sealed her lips to his in a searing kiss so hot that any good sense between the two of them went up in smoke.

Danger! Abort!

Red sirens and flashing neon lights blazed in his conscience, but if there was an angel and devil sitting on either shoulder, the angel had just been duct-taped and hog-tied, because he sure as hell wasn't in charge.

Alexis's skin was like soft silk beneath his fingertips as his tongue danced with hers, the urge to taste every inch of her body burning through his brain like a fever. This was the sweetest, most tantalizing lunacy, but he couldn't stop. Heaven help him, he couldn't stop if he tried.

Her hands, as eager as his own, pushed at his shirt and within seconds he'd ripped off the offending piece of clothing, his skin burning at her insistent touch. He slowed only long enough to help her remove her top and he nearly swallowed his tongue when she revealed the most achingly perfect breasts God had ever created. Sweetly upturned pink nipples pearled and pouted, demanding a hot mouth to suck and tease them and he wasn't about to disappoint.

Wasting no time, he sucked a tightly budded nipple into his mouth and teased the tip with his tongue. Alexis groaned and her belly trembled as his hands kneaded the soft, pliant flesh of her glorious breasts and he knew there was no going back. They were in too deep now. And he wasn't going to think about Erik—hell no, talk about a buzzkill—all he wanted to think about was how to make Alexis squirm in his arms. He wanted to hear her breathy moans in his ear, taste her sweet juices as she came and feel her shudder beneath him.

How did they get here? One minute they were hanging lights—totally platonic, right?—and now, he was ready to flip the switch and go down on her. "Alexis, tell me if you want me to stop," he said, hating the words but needing to say them anyway. They were playing with fire, but he'd pull back if she said to.

"Don't you dare stop," she growled, pushing at his head as she shimmied out of her pants, wincing briefly as she cleared her injured ankle. Following her lead, he grinned and helped her out of her panties, grabbing the tiny scrap of lace and inhaling the unique scent.

"Mmm, perfect," he said, unabashedly enjoying Alexis's unique scent. "God, you smell incredible."

Alexis blushed but seemed to revel in his enjoyment. He grinned and tossed the panties, ready to dive into the real thing. Everything about Alexis excited him. At this point he figured he deserved a medal for holding out as long as he had. He positioned himself between her legs, careful not to jostle her injured ankle, and then feasted on the honeyed sweetness between her legs. He teased the tiny button nestled between her damp folds, licked and laved the bare flesh, tickling the tiny strip of pubic hair seaming her cleft.

A breathy shudder escaped her lips as she tensed, her body shaking almost immediately. Manly pride surged through him as he sucked and licked her pleasure spot until she stiffened and broke apart with tiny, mewling gasps that would have sent him over the edge if he hadn't already been sporting granite in his pants, full and thick, ready for action.

He was more than ready to sink into that slick heat, but he wanted to make sure she got hers first, because as he'd admitted to Alexis, he was a gentleman at heart even if he had the mind of a lecherous pervert.

Layton gave her clitoris one final tease and she jerked, her belly spasming involuntarily. "You're a bad boy," she said with a satisfied grin. "And I like it. Do you always let ladies come first?"

"Seems a good rule to live by," he said, rising to seal his lips to hers, loving that she gripped him hard and didn't shy away from the fact that she could taste herself on his lips. He pulled away and Alexis helped him out of his underwear, revealing his thick and eager erection. He grinned and palmed himself. Now he didn't mind that he was naked. "Like what you see?"

"Not bad," she said coyly. "But let's reserve judgment until after it's over. You know what they say about guys with talented tongues…"

"They're lucky bastards?"

She laughed. "They say they're good with their mouths because that's all they got."

Layton laughed and pulled her gently off the sofa, lifting her into his arms. "Honey, I guess I'm the exception. We'll see if you can handle this action."

She smelled like sex and he liked it. "I like the feel of your wet pussy against my arm. Reminds me of where I've been."

"You have a dirty mind," she said with sly approval. "I like the way you think."

"I think we have a lot in common." He placed her on the bed and gazed at the perfection wrapped up in one saucy package. "How is it that I've never met you until this point? Your brother was smart to hide you away."

She snorted. "You make me sound like a virginal princess in the medieval days."

"I'm just saying…if you were my sister I wouldn't want the guys at the station house seeing you, either. You have no idea what a bunch of guys cooped up together start to talk about. It's raunchy."

"Do tell."

"How about I show you?"

She shivered with open delight. "Do your worst."

"Well, sometimes when there are no calls and the station is otherwise dead, we try and one-up each other with tales of sexual adventures."

"Okay, now I'm intrigued. What's the kinkiest place you've had sex?" she asked, scooting onto the pillow and leaning back, giving him the best view of everything she had to offer.

"Easy. Bathroom of the Lotus. She had to cover her mouth to muffle the screams as I banged her hard up against the bathroom wall."

"The Lotus…are you saying you had sex in the swankiest restaurant in town…the same place that takes weeks to get a reservation unless you're a celebrity?"

"As it happened…I was with a certain up-and-coming starlet who I'd met on the slopes in Vail. We hit it off and saw each other a few times until her schedule got too hectic and we lost touch."

"Who was it?"

"I don't kiss and tell."

"You're lying," she said, calling his bluff.

"No, I swear to you. True story. She was a hot lay,"

he admitted as he climbed onto the bed. "But enough about her... I'm all about you right now."

"Good answer," she said, pulling him to her for another kiss, their tongues sparring with one another in a sensual assault. She was good with her mouth. He could only imagine what she'd do with that mouth on his cock, but he couldn't wait for more foreplay. He was willing to forgo a little head if it meant he could sink into that sweet pussy.

But first... "Condoms?"

"First drawer, full box."

"I love a woman who's prepared," he said, jerking open the drawer. He ripped open a foil packet and sheathed himself, his hands shaking. Damn, he was never this eager, but there was something about Alexis that turned him on his ear. So much for the suave act he usually had down to an art form.

Pulling her injured leg up over his shoulder, he slid himself into her damp heat and nearly lost his mind from the instant pleasure cocooning him from all sides. She gripped him with her internal muscles, squeezing him from the inside, and he nearly came like a prepubescent boy in a circle jerk.

"Oh my God," he breathed, unable to stop from uttering a guttural moan. Sweat popped along his hairline. He wanted to pump into her like a piston, to ram his cock into her with the force of a machine, to put his stamp on her insides, and the ferocity of his need shocked and embarrassed him a little. "You feel so good," he admitted with a tight groan.

He drove into Alexis, burying himself to the hilt, losing all sense of cool as he thrust against her. Remembering some semblance of himself, he slowed his thrusts to focus on her, loving the way her cheeks flushed with each moan as her generous breasts bounced with the motion of his hips, everything about her was sexy.

Within moments, she was tensing and her thighs shaking and he knew she was close, which was a blessed relief because he didn't think he could last much longer. He liked to pride himself on being able to go the distance, but something about Alexis stripped him bare and made him vulnerable at the same time.

All he wanted was to lose himself in her, to watch as she came and to taste her on his tongue. He wanted to bury his face in her pussy and lap at her folds until she cried out his name. He'd never been one to wax poetic about a woman's lady parts, but he thought he could write a sonnet about the sweetness that was Alexis.

"L-Layton!" she cried out, gripping the pillow beneath her head, thrusting her breasts up as she came hard. She shuddered and a long exhale escaped her lips as she completely lost herself to the moment. It was beautiful to watch and almost interrupted his own orgasm, but within seconds of that undoing, he followed, coming with a loud groan.

He rolled off and pulled the condom free, tossing it carefully into the trash before collapsing to the bed, spent. It took him several minutes before he could form words, but Alexis didn't seem to mind the silence. If anything, the satisfied smile on her face said more than words could, and that made him want to crow.

"I needed that," she said with a happy sigh. "Thank you."

He paused and then nodded. "You're welcome."

A happy gurgle of satisfaction escaped her sweet lips and he wanted her all over again. Could this become his newest bad habit?

7

LAYTON ROLLED ONTO his side. "If you're this good in bed laid up, I can only imagine what it's like being with you when you're fully recovered."

She leveled a playful look his way. "I like to switch positions. A lot."

"Sex is great cardio. Best way to work up a sweat in my book. Should I stock up on Gatorade?"

She laughed. "Getting ahead of yourself, don't you think?"

"Not really. I think we both had a good time. Am I wrong?"

"Oh no, you were good, no doubt about that. I rarely come that easily, so I either chalk that up to the fact that you're pretty talented or I was pretty horny. Either way, I count that as a win."

"I think it's because I'm pretty talented," Layton said with cocky swagger. "I don't mean to brag, but... I'm pretty good."

Alexis made a show of thinking then decided. "Sorry, buddy, I think I was just really horny and needed an itch scratched. Thanks for that, by the way," she repeated.

He laughed, reaching for her. "All right, not sure who's winning this argument because I feel as if I'm coming out the winner either way, so let's call it a draw and proceed with funky times."

Alexis pealed with laughter. "Funky times? That sounds like something that needs an antibiotic."

He kissed her and she enjoyed the feel of his lips against hers, but after a long moment of wrangling tongues, she gently pulled away, leaving him perplexed.

"What's wrong?"

"I just want to be clear about what we're doing."

He grinned. "Isn't it obvious?"

She pushed at him, needing him to be serious for a minute. "No, I mean, I want to make sure that we're both okay with the agreement that this is just for today."

The sweet warmth in Layton's dark eyes faded and she suffered a twinge of guilt, but they both knew they couldn't mess around once Erik returned. For one, Alexis would never come between Erik and his good friend and, two, Alexis didn't think she was ready to start seriously dating again. She still had...*issues* she was working through about her breakup with Riker and it wasn't fair to Layton to drag him down that dark road.

"Kind of a downer conversation after such a great start," he said.

"Agreed, but one that needs to be had, right?"

He sighed. "Yeah," he said, but he looked as if having this conversation wasn't high on his priority list. "Still a bummer."

"Can we be friends after this?" she asked.

"We're not friends," he reminded her. "We just met."

"And what better way to build a great friendship than letting our naked parts rub up against one another. I had an anthropology instructor once tell me that everyone should use sex to defuse conflict, like the bonobo monkeys. Any time they are confused or conflicted, they bang it out and, voilà, everyone is happy again."

"If only things were so easily resolved," he said wryly, plainly not impressed or on board with her suggestion to keep things platonic going forward.

"You seem irritated," she said. "Are you mad?"

"No, not mad. I get where you're coming from. Just feels weird to be on the other side of that argument."

"Aw, how cute," she crooned with a laugh, and he broke a small grin. "But I'm really serious about not getting involved with anyone until I have my degree in my hot little hand. You have no idea how it feels to be the one that everyone writes off. I'm not saying it wasn't my fault and that I didn't make things worse with my choices, but it still sucks."

"Your brother adores you," Layton said with a mild frown. "And he's proud of you. He's told me so."

"Really?"

"Yeah, really. The only thing he's ever said that was remotely negative had everything to do with that douche you were dating. Erik didn't like him."

No, Erik hadn't thought much of Riker. Neither had

her dad, now that she thought about it, but she'd been too head over heels in love to see the warning signs. "I wish I'd listened to them in the first place and dumped him," she admitted.

"Hey, don't be so hard on yourself. You know that saying, you have to kiss a lot of frogs before you find Prince Charming? Well, I think that's applicable here."

A warm smile found Alexis's lips. "So full of wisdom, aren't you?"

"Only because I've made my share of dumb moves and I have the scars to prove it."

She tucked her robe around her. "I would've thought that this would've been a convenient out for you. Not many guys would find a weekend fling outside of their wheelhouse."

"I didn't say it was outside of my wheelhouse. I've done it before," he corrected with a shrug. "I just didn't think you'd be okay with a one-and-done."

"I'm not…but a day of sex with you sounds just about perfect."

"You sure about that?" he asked, his dark eyes threatening to drown her in their beautiful depths. And those eyelashes! Criminal!

She hadn't lied when she'd said she'd come faster with Layton than anyone else and it'd been a pretty fantastic orgasm—not like some weak little tingle that barely registered but one of those earth-shattering oh-my-God-was-that-real kind of things and that was hard to give up, but she was determined to stay the course. "Yep," she said with more force. "Now, I'm going to bake cookies. You can help if you want."

"Cookies? Why now?"

"Because it's part of my holiday tradition, just like hanging the lights, and keeping to my schedule is one way to stay on track with my goals."

The fact that I'm already thinking of you in ways I shouldn't is enough of a warning sign. Yep, so go bake cookies, Alexis!

And then she left him in her bedroom.

HUMMING UNDER HER BREATH, Alexis hobbled to the kitchen, determined to bake some gingerbread cookies before Erik returned. Erik was a sucker for her cookies and Alexis was not above using his love for cookies to get what she wanted, such as premium cable when Erik had been adamant that it was a useless expense. Erik was far more frugal than her—hence the belief by their parents that he was the more responsible one.

Well, that and the fact that he seemed to have his life on track whereas she had made more than a few stops and starts.

Such as when she agreed to let an internet start-up company slap their logo all over her car with the promise of paying her rent for six months when, in fact, the company had gone belly up within a month and she'd been left with a hideous logo blazoned across her bumper, which had to be professionally removed at her own cost.

In hindsight, she should've known that any company named Jiggity, with the tagline *The jig is up!* wasn't going to last.

And then there was, of course, her experience with Riker that certainly rose to the top of the pile.

And now that she'd shagged Erik's best friend, Alexis thought it might be prudent to have some tasty yumminess around the house to soften the blow, if he were to somehow find out, which she was going to do her best to ensure that he didn't. But a girl should always have a Plan B, right?

Too bad she hadn't had a Plan B with Riker.

Ugh. What had she been thinking? She had to stop being swayed by a hot body and a bad-boy attitude. Bad boys didn't hold down solid jobs, and they spent your money and slept with your former sorority sisters.

She set the cookie tin down with more force than necessary just as Layton joined her in the kitchen. Alexis hit him with a blinding smile and began chattering as if they hadn't just spent time in each other's arms because, frankly, she needed to put her mind on a different track.

"So, tell me about yourself," she started, grabbing the ingredients for the cookies and the mixing bowls. "What's it like to play the hero all day?"

"I wish it were that simple. Being a firefighter isn't saving kittens and rescuing damsels from fiery buildings all day. Sometimes, on slow days, it's scrubbing a station toilet that's been used by twelve other guys."

She wrinkled her nose. "That sounds like punishment."

"Let's just say, some of my station brethren aren't as diligent about hitting the pot."

"I would murder someone," Alexis said, biting back a laugh. "I mean, that's really gross."

"Yes, it is."

"Tell me more about this unglamorous side of being

a firefighter," she said as she worked the dough, loving the smell of fresh cookie dough. In a past life, she was a French baker, she was sure of it.

"You really want to know?"

"Sure. We've got time to kill."

"I can think of other ways to kill time," he suggested, walking over to her. Her hands were stuck in dough, trapped in the sticky glob, and he took delightful advantage. His lips brushed across hers and she melted a little. "Are you sure you want to talk about station life?" he murmured against her lips.

"No fair," she said with a breathy little sigh. "You are one of the best kissers I've ever had the privilege of kissing."

He grinned and kissed her again. He swallowed her moan and she accidentally put too much pressure on her sore ankle, causing her to yelp and pull back. "Ouch. Sorry," she said, lifting her foot. "Still tender."

"You shouldn't be on it," he reminded her. "It won't heal if you don't let the swelling go down."

He surprised her by lifting her up on the counter, spreading her legs to stand between them. She automatically looped her arms around his neck. "See? Isn't that better?" he asked.

"Of course it is," she agreed with a laugh. "But you're messing with my plans."

"Make new ones," he murmured right before sealing his mouth to hers, stealing her breath and for a moment, her will to be a good girl. But this—*this exact thing!*—was the reason she kept making the wrong decisions in her life.

Alexis reluctantly pulled away. "I really need to get these cookies done."

"Please tell me that's a unique euphemism for getting it on in the kitchen."

She laughed and pushed him away so she could slide from the counter. "Sorry, bud. Not this time. You'll just have to shelve your dirty mind for a minute."

He groaned as if that were impossible and she wanted to say, *I feel your pain*, but she didn't want to make things harder—ha! No pun intended—than they already were in the *hands-off* department.

She cast a playful scowl his way. "Don't get in the way of my baking. You don't want to see me when someone has blocked my cookie habit."

He raised his hands in mock surrender. "Far be it from me to prevent the lady from whipping up something delicious and sweet."

Alexis grinned and returned to her dough, which was just about ready. She grabbed the rolling pin and began rolling out the dough. "Do you like gingerbread cookies?" she asked.

"Not really."

She did a double take. "What?"

"Sorry. I don't care for the taste of molasses."

"Well, you've plainly never experienced a good gingerbread cookie, which you will once you eat mine."

"I'm willing to be wowed, but you ought to temper your expectations, just in case."

"Never."

He laughed. "Okay," he conceded and then added, "You asked about unglamorous station life? Well, it's like this… When things are slow, we're out mowing the grass, washing the trucks, doing outreach at the schools and renewing our certifications. Like I said, totally unglamorous."

"Well, it beats being a perpetual student," Alexis admitted. "I'm ready to be done."

"You're smart going all the way. Being at the top of the food chain is a good thing."

Alexis appreciated his vote, even if they were going to keep things casual. "I wish you weren't my brother's buddy," she said, mostly under her breath, but it was a titch louder than she'd meant it to be. She risked a glance at Layton and he seemed to understand her comment.

"You're the one making the rules," he said by way of saying, *Hey, things can be different if you want them to be*, but she knew better than to give in to that flimsy hope. Layton read her mind and added, "I think Erik would be cool."

She chuckled. "No, he most definitely wouldn't be cool about you and me. He's very protective, especially of late. It feels good that he cares, but it does get a little tiresome when he treats me like a kid."

"Older-brother gig. Occupational hazard."

"Yeah, I guess so. Anyway—" she cast a wry look at Layton "—he won't be chill about his best buddy shacking up with his little sister, and I would never want to come between you and Erik."

"I can handle Erik," Layton returned stubbornly, and in that moment she believed him, but she didn't want Erik and Layton going to blows just because she'd practically seduced Layton and now they both wanted more. "Besides, you're an adult. He has to come to grips with the fact that you're capable of making your own decisions, good *and* bad."

"True, but it's probably not a good idea to shove it in his face."

Layton leaned in. Her breath caught and, for the life of her, she couldn't speak. His big, rough hands gripped her ass and pulled her to him. Their parts fit together so perfectly it was almost a sin not to allow them to interlock. His tab was aligned exquisitely with her slot and she almost giggled at the ridiculous bent of her thoughts only because laughter was her defense mechanism when she was nervous.

"Here's the way I see it," he said in a seductively low voice, "for whatever reasons, we mesh pretty good. Unless I was mistaken and you're the world's best actress, you were having a pretty good time, too. The cat is out of the bag, babe. Can't stuff that genie back in the bottle now."

"I get the idea," she said, lifting her chin and meeting his gaze. "Doesn't mean I'm willing to put a wedge between you and my brother just because epically good sex is on the line."

He gently backed her against the counter. "Are you sure about that?"

"Positive," she said with a breathy tone that even to her own ears sounded like a come-on. But before she could try again and set him straight, he turned her around and she was bent over the counter and his hand was up her robe, squeezing her bare ass. "What are you doing?" she asked, biting her lip to keep from smiling. She knew she ought to stop him but she'd always been a sucker for a good time and a bad idea. "The cookies!"

"Screw the cookies," he said with a growl as the sound of foil tearing made her turn and she gasped when she saw him sheathing himself in a fresh condom. He'd brought it with him out of the bedroom. Kudos for thinking ahead, but she really ought to give him hell for being presumptuous. Except she was lifting her ass, closing her eyes against the inevitable sensation of his cock pressing past her folds, going in deep, and she couldn't wait.

"Do it then," she said, eager to feel him again, even though she'd just made a big show of saying they should forget it ever happened. Okay, maybe just one more time and then she'd really put her foot down.

And then, as if he'd read her mind, he didn't waste time sliding inside her, pushing hard and hitting that sweet spot with unerring accuracy when most guys had to have a little direction. She groaned like a cat in heat, losing herself in the pleasure of being bent over, taken and used mercilessly. It worked for her, and the fact that Layton seemed to appreciate that hidden part of her was an even bigger turn-on.

Riker had always made her feel bad for expressing her needs, but then he'd cheated on her with every woman who happened to twitch her hips at him, which had only served to do a number on her self-esteem.

But right now, Riker was the last person she wanted to think about. Layton was doing her right and that was all that mattered.

Maybe those monkeys were onto something. Sex was certainly working to alleviate her stress!

This time wasn't as quick, but that served them both well. Layton took his time to really give it to her good, alternating slow and hard thrusts with fast piston action. She couldn't catch her breath, but it was so good all she could do was hang on for dear life as he pounded her with the single-minded attention of a man on a mission.

God, she loved a man with purpose. Just when she thought she might scream from the building pressure, she burst and wondrous explosions of pleasure blasted her nerve endings, squeezing her muscles and sending her into orbit. She didn't notice the pain in her ankle or the granite counter grinding against her hips, only sweet, sweet oblivion.

"God, yes, Alexis," he gasped, gripping her hips as he pushed into her, coming hard as he pumped erratically, all semblance of finesse out the window. She loved that he lost control with her, that he couldn't seem to get a handle on his game. She didn't want to be the only one losing all sense of reason and cool.

He shuddered and his grip fell away from her hips, even as he remained firmly inside her. She pulsed with residual spasms as her orgasm slowly receded. She didn't remember the sex being this good with Riker. Surely that was just the mind playing tricks with the memory because she'd discovered Riker was a dick? It couldn't be that she and Layton, of all people, had some serious sexual connection that they were both slave to?

He withdrew and removed the condom, tossing it in the trash and then, without a word, scooped her up and carried her to the sofa.

"What are you doing?" she asked, amused that he always felt compelled to carry her. It was sexy and made her feel distinctly feminine, even if it embarrassed her a little because she could still walk.

"Movie time," he said, leaving and returning with Erik's robe and slipping it on.

Alexis gasped and then laughed. "Erik will kill you if he finds out you're wearing his favorite robe."

"Wearing his robe is the least of my offenses today."

"That's true," she acknowledged, admiring how sexy he looked in nothing but a robe. They were like a couple, spending the weekend together—except they weren't a couple and never would be. The jarring thought dampened her enthusiasm for a minute but if all they had was this weekend, she supposed they might as well do it right. "You really want to watch a movie? Why can't we just spend all weekend screwing each other's brains out?"

"As much as I'm down with that, a man needs a little recovery time. We also need to fit in a shower at some point because we might start to smell."

She laughed, loving how easy it was to hang out with Layton but soon enough the jab of reality was too much to ignore. "You know we can't just pretend that whatever this is will work out in the end because it won't."

Layton regarded her with a slight smile. "Are you an all-or-nothing kind of girl?"

Alexis stopped to think. "Maybe. I don't know. I don't know what kind of girl I am right now. Riker messed with my head in a big way. I thought I was in love with him. Finding out that the man you imagined building a life with is a douche kinda throws you into a tailspin."

"I hear ya," he agreed easily. "I thought Julianne was the one until I found out she was screwing her boss. I'd say that threw me for a loop."

"How'd you find out?" she asked, intrigued. It was somehow soothing to commiserate with someone else who'd been equally screwed over by their ex. "Was it like something out of a movie?"

"Nothing so dramatic, actually. I didn't bust in on them during one of their trysts. I found a text message."

"That must've been a pretty incriminating text message."

"No, not terribly, but I sensed there was something off about it and I just asked her point-blank if she was screwing the guy. She caved pretty quickly and admitted it. Told me she'd been trying to break it off with me for months but I was such a good guy she didn't want to hurt me. And you know what, when she said that, I was feeling pretty much the opposite of a good guy because of the things I wanted to say to her, but I didn't say shit. I just packed my things and told her to have a nice life."

"You let her off easy," Alexis said, remembering her own showdown with Riker. She was embarrassed to admit she'd gone a little loco. "I keyed Riker's truck. Actually, I carved *cheater* into the hood. It's going to cost him a bundle to fix that."

Layton whistled low. "Damn, girl, you went after the man's truck? That's cold."

"No, what was cold was catching him jerking off in

the middle of the night on his webcam to my former sorority sister. He thought I was asleep and I caught him with his pants down. Literally. Actually, it turned my stomach. I couldn't believe he would do something so low. But after that, I discovered that wasn't the first, and probably wouldn't be the last, time he cheated on me, so I bailed."

"After leaving him a lovely parting gift," he supplied helpfully, and Alexis nodded. "Sounds appropriate."

"I thought it was."

He chuckled and they shared a quiet moment together. It was weird to share something so incredibly painful with a virtual stranger and yet feel relieved to let it go. Not even Erik knew the full details. At the time, Alexis had been too embarrassed to share the nitty-gritty, choosing instead to say Riker had cheated and leave it at that.

"So, after Julianne, you jumped into the dating pool?"

"Yeah, probably too soon. A buddy told me the best way to get over a woman was to find another one right away. I wasn't sure that was the best advice, but I was hurting and desperate to feel better, so I went on a dating spree that mostly turned into a blur of sexual mishaps, one-night stands and unfortunate mistakes that I knew I had to stop or else I'd never stand a chance of respecting myself again."

Compassion softened her voice as she said, "You know, I get it…the need to feel good after hurting so bad. I went the slutty route for a little while, but when I realized that it wasn't making me feel better I invested in a good vibrator and stopped chasing dicks."

"What kind of vibrator?"

She pushed at his shoulder with mock indignation. "You never ask a lady about her toys. That's private."

"Is it bad that I would give my right nut to watch you pleasure yourself?"

Now she gasped for real and the blush heating her cheeks could warm a small country, but the fact that he wanted to watch her turned her on in a big way. "Are you a voyeur?" she ventured, curious.

"With you, I think I'd be anything you wanted me to be."

"Stop it," she said, his openness tickling her. "You're making me blush and you're playing me like a fiddle."

"I don't know what it is about you, but everything I've said is true. You're different, Alexis. I don't know why and, trust me, I wish I could figure it out so I could put the kibosh on it. I get it, we are complicating everything, but I can't seem to stop and I don't want to. You turn my crank in the hottest way, and that's saying a lot."

What could she say in the face of such brutal honesty? It was a breath of fresh air after everything she'd been through with Riker. He was a born liar. The words that'd popped from his mouth were always peppered with half truths, a fact she'd only discovered after she'd been thoroughly humiliated. "Julianne was an idiot," she murmured, shooting him a quick look. "If she didn't see what a good guy you are… She was blind."

"Same goes for Riker. I can't imagine letting someone like you go."

"What is happening between us? This can't be natural, right?"

"We have insane sexual chemistry," he agreed, equally mystified. "I wonder what would've happened if we'd met before we both were burned."

"I wouldn't have been attracted to you."

He did a double take. "Come again?"

She soothed his ego. "It's not you. It's me. Honestly, what attracted me to Riker was his bad-boy attitude and the fact that he drove a motorcycle. I wouldn't have been attracted to you because you have a good job and you're a decent guy."

Layton relaxed and laughed. "Yeah, well, I know I would've looked twice your way. You have the kind of breasts I dream about."

Alexis giggled, loving how free he was with compliments. "Did Julianne have big boobs, too?"

"Yeah, but I gotta say, and I'm not just saying this because we hooked up, but your breasts...damn... they're so awesome."

He grinned then added, "However, hindsight being what it is, I've since realized that I couldn't marry a woman that didn't stimulate me intellectually."

"I know what you mean. Riker was smart but in an arrogant way. He enjoyed one-upping people. It was embarrassing at times."

"He sounds like a peach."

"A rotten one."

"There is that." He shifted and as he did, the robe gaped, and she got an unobstructed view of his cock, lying semi-erect against his thigh. He tracked her gaze and grinned, allowing the robe to open farther. "See something you like?"

"I can't believe you're getting hard again. You have the stamina of a horse."

"Not always. I'm telling you…it's you."

He'd been so giving thus far, going down on her, making sure she came first. Riker had been an inordinately selfish lover, almost never seeing to her needs first. God, why had she stayed with him as long as she had? Sliding her robe down, she bared her breasts for Layton's gaze. Interest flared in his eyes and his cock sprang to life as if given a shot of Viagra. She couldn't help but laugh. "That's a cool party trick in some circles."

Layton grinned and she was struck by how damn adorable he was. Sure, he was sexy, that was a given, but how had she missed just how sweet and cute he was? And he deserved a little selfish loving. She leaned over and slipped his cock in her mouth, delighting in the way his hand automatically went to her hair and stroked her head lightly as she sucked him. His cock held the faint taste of latex but she didn't mind. Soon enough his touch became more urgent as she worked his cock, using her hands and tongue to tease him to his breaking point without pushing him over. She took him to the edge several times until he was practically begging her for release and then, because her jaw was getting tired, she allowed him to come.

Layton groaned as he spurted his load down her throat and she gulped greedily, wanting to know his taste just as he'd eagerly acquainted himself with hers.

He gripped the sofa cushion as he lost control, shouting her name as he came—and that was hotter than hot.

She wasn't sure how she was going to quit Layton Davis.

In record time, he'd just become her most wicked secret vice.

8

THE STORM ARRIVED by midafternoon but by that time Alexis and Layton were quite comfortable to ride it out snuggled with each other. They'd even managed to bake a batch of cookies in between some serious fooling around—several orgasms—and a shower later.

"You know, I expected to hear from Emma and Erik by now," Alexis said, feeling slightly guilty for not even thinking about her brother and best friend until that moment. She grabbed her cell and quickly called. It rang twice and then went to voice mail. She frowned. "That's odd. Em never turns off her phone. She's addicted to it."

"They're probably in a bad service area," Layton said. "I wouldn't worry. Erik will take good care of Emma."

"I know he will." She settled on the sofa with the popcorn she'd just popped. "Want to know a secret?"

"Sure," he answered, grabbing a handful.

"Emma has always had a raging crush on Erik since

we were kids. She thinks I never noticed but it was plainly obvious."

"How'd you know?"

"Well, for one, girls always know when a girl likes a guy. Second, it was easy to catch her mooning over him, staring at him like a starving puppy whenever he was around. It was really annoying, actually."

"So, has Erik ever shown an interest in Emma?"

"God no. And I'm glad for that! How weird would that be to have my best friend shacking up with my brother? I can't handle the imagery."

"It's no weirder than what we're doing," he reminded her.

"No, it's totally different."

"How so?"

"Because it is." She left it at that. There was no way he could convince her that the situations were similar because she didn't want them to be similar. "Besides, Emma and Erik are complete opposites. They'd never suit."

"Your brother is a good guy. Why wouldn't you want your best friend to find a man worth her time?"

"Oh, come on, don't throw sensible arguments my way. I think we've already established logic and reason have no bearing on my decision-making process. They aren't good together—end of story."

He laughed and tossed back some kernels. "You're a hypocrite."

"Am not."

"You are. But you're still cute so I forgive you."

"I am not a hypocrite. I just…ugh. I can't stomach

the idea of my brother getting jiggy with my best friend since grammar school. Is that so wrong?"

"It's a little selfish," he said with a shrug.

Alexis gasped. "You don't know me well enough to pass judgment."

"Maybe not, but it seems to me that you'd want your best friend to end up with a good guy. I'm surprised you haven't tried to hook them up."

Alexis frowned. Emma and Erik? It made her feel squicky. "Erik looks at Emma like a kid sister."

"Not the way I saw him looking at her."

"What do you mean?" Alexis stared hard at Layton, wondering what the heck he was talking about. "Erik thinks of Emma like a sister," she repeated, stubbornly refusing to believe that her brother was thinking of Emma in any other way besides brotherly.

"Look, it's not a big deal, but I think Erik was seeing that Emma was all grown up. I mean, she's hot. I can't blame him for looking."

Alexis glared, feeling a tad bit jealous, and she had no right to. "I know what my friend looks like."

Layton leaned forward and surprised her with a kiss. "Calm down, tigress. Emma's not my type."

"And I wouldn't care if she was," she quipped a little too quickly. Her heart rate had kicked up a notch and she realized she was being ridiculous. "Okay, I'm a little reluctant to admit that you may have a point. But there's no sense in worrying over something that hasn't happened, right?"

"Right," he agreed. "But I know what I saw."

"You *think* you know what you saw," she returned

stubbornly. "But in the meantime, I just want Emma to call so I know they're all right."

Layton nodded with understanding. "So, where are your parents this holiday?"

"Scotland," she answered with a sigh. "Something about checking off items on their bucket list before they die. I think my mom just didn't want to host Christmas dinner and this was a convenient way to get out of it."

"Scotland is pretty far to travel to get out of dinner."

"You don't know my mom," she said dryly. "She's not your average-mom type."

"How's your foot?"

She slowly rotated it. "Not bad. It feels much better. Just a small twinge."

"That's good. You should still baby it though."

"Yes, Doctor."

His gaze turned playful. "I'll play doctor if you'll be the naughty nurse."

Alexis tossed a popcorn kernel at him with a grin. "And that is not happening, so lose that idea. If anything, I'll be the doctor and you can be the naughty nurse."

"Intriguing. I'm secure enough in my manhood to try a little power exchange. Are we talking spankings and bondage? Be gentle, I'm a beginner." She barked a shocked laugh and he tackled her to the sofa cushion to kiss her hard and fast. "You're just full of surprises, Alexis Matheson," he said, pulling away.

"That was not an invitation to go buy whips and chains," she joked. "I'm mostly vanilla with a dash of chocolate on top."

"My favorite flavor is vanilla," he said, smiling. "So that's fine with me."

She sobered. "What are we doing?"

"Whatever we want," he answered.

"Will it be weird to see each other socially like nothing happened?"

"Yes."

She frowned then groaned. "I wish you would lie to me a little."

"No you don't."

"You're right. I hate liars."

He brushed a soft kiss across her lips. "I don't know what's in store, all I know is that right now you are the center of my universe, the storm is going to knock out the power at some point and all I care about is spending whatever available moment with you. I'm not even thinking beyond this weekend."

"Me neither," she admitted, looping her arms around his neck. "Is it bad that I don't want to think about tomorrow?"

"If it's bad, I'm right there with you."

"It's strange, don't you think, that we have this connection? I've never felt so comfortable with another person I just met, especially a guy."

"I can't explain it, either. Maybe it's fate."

"Do you believe in fate?"

He hedged with a guilty smile. "Not exactly, but I am a closet romantic and I like the idea that fate exists."

"Me, too."

Too bad it wasn't as black-and-white as *I like you, you like me.* Erik had always been her champion, always seeing the best in her. How would he react to knowing that she'd gleefully seduced his best friend? She couldn't stand the idea of suffering Erik's disappointment in her behavior. She should've kept her hands to herself and just white-knuckled her attraction to Layton.

But even as she knew they'd both jumped feet first into the pool without caring if there was water beneath them, a part of her wasn't sorry and maybe that was a problem.

Maybe the worst part was knowing she'd do it again.

LAYTON KNEW HE was playing with fire, but the more time he spent with Alexis the more he wanted. He had an insatiable need to know her more deeply, to touch and feel, and he was a little disconcerted by how easy they slipped into an effortless familiarity with one another. Would they be able to pull off a nonchalance among other people? Erik would know right away. Hell, maybe he ought to just spill his guts and hope for mercy.

He sat up and pulled Alexis with him. "How's this for an idea…let's just tell Erik that we hooked up and let the chips fall where they may."

"That would go over like a lead balloon. I don't recommend it."

Clearly, Alexis didn't find as much merit in the idea as he did. "Don't you think Erik would respect our decision to come to him instead of letting him find out by accident?"

"No. A big fat no. My brother is very protective of

me, and ever since I broke up with Riker, he's been superprotective."

"I'm not like Riker," he pointed out, trying not to suffer a ruffled ego at any accidental comparisons. "And your brother knows I'm not a bad guy."

"Of course not but just because he thinks you're a swell guy to go fishing with doesn't mean he wants you hooking up with his little sister. Besides, what's the point of sharing? We're not planning to be a couple anytime soon, so why rock the boat unnecessarily."

Ah, there was the heart of the matter, right? Maybe he wanted to explore the possibility of a relationship with Alexis. But did she want that? He decided to test the waters. "And what if that changed?"

"What if what changed?" she asked, confused.

"What if…we wanted to try out a relationship?"

For a split second he caught a sliver of yearning in her gaze, as if she might like to try a relationship on for size, but she shut it down quickly. "You know that's not going to work between us. Let me just tell you… I'm a mess right now. I'm smashed against deadlines, midterms, impossible classloads and I'm moody as hell, to boot. I am not girlfriend material."

"Usually people list the pro points instead of just jumping straight to the con list."

"Yeah, well, maybe if more people were starkly honest there'd be a whole helluva lot less heartache. I think people should just put it all out on the table and let people decide if it's something they can handle. I mean, I wish Riker had admitted to me on our first date that he was a serial cheater without a loyal or faithful bone in his body because then I could've decided right then and there that I didn't want to take that on. But instead, I had to find out the hard—and painful—way." She drew a deep breath before asking, "Don't you think you would've liked to know that Julianne was a cheater before you took a chance on her?"

"Sure. But love is a risk. Even if I had known up front she had a wandering eye, I'm not sure I would've done anything differently."

"Yeah, well, I'm telling you right now… I'm a bad investment."

Layton heard the pain in her voice, hidden beneath the false bravado, and it struck him that she was scared of being hurt again. That's what it was all about for them both, right? Maybe that was the connection drawing them, which meant eventually such a flimsy connection would fade. Rebound relationships were transient for a reason.

"Okay," he accepted her reasoning with a small nod. "I guess you make a good point. We'll keep our weekend to ourselves and I'll do my best to pretend that I don't know what you sound like when you come." She sucked in a wild breath and he grinned. "Sorry?"

"You're not sorry. You did that on purpose."

"Guilty."

She allowed a small smile and he wanted to kiss away whatever was making her secretly sad. She regarded him with those beautiful, soulful eyes that snapped with mischief most times but right now were filled with wells of yearning that seemed so deep he might drown. He ran a knuckle down her soft cheek.

"Circumstances change us but they don't have to

ruin us," he reminded her gently. "Don't let one ass-hole destroy the part of you that's precious."

"Easier said than done," Alexis said with a forlorn sigh. "Most times I just feel so incredibly stupid for letting him into my heart when he clearly didn't belong there."

"It's all just a rehearsal until the curtain goes up on opening night, babe. That dick was just a bit player in your show."

She smiled wider. "Got some theater in your background?"

"Father was a drama teacher at my local high school," he admitted with a short grin. "Can't seem to help myself. They're the only metaphors I seem to remember."

"I like it," Alexis said, slowly losing the sadness. "It's kinda profound. Made me think of things in a different way."

"My dad will be happy to know that his words live on."

Alexis grabbed his hand and pulled him from the sofa, leading him to the bedroom.

"I seem to remember someone wanting to watch…"

Layton nearly swallowed his tongue.

And just like that, Alexis managed to turn on a dime from broken butterfly, struggling to fly, to sexy temptress ready to eat him alive, and the contradiction was a wild turn-on.

Hell, everything she did turned him on!

How was he going to get Alexis out of his system when the weekend was done?

Something told him Alexis was in his blood—and there was nothing he could do about it.

Funny thing…he was okay with that.

9

THE FOLLOWING MORNING Alexis woke up to the stillness of fresh snow outside the window and Layton curled around her as if it was his natural place to be and for an instant she just savored the moment.

It couldn't last, but that didn't mean she couldn't enjoy every second until it was over.

But even as she was snuggled against his solid warmth, she was troubled by the fact that neither Erik nor Emma had called to check in yet.

Erik was a stickler for calling when he reached his destination. As a first responder, he'd seen too many tragic accidents to not call. The fact that she knew that about her brother only served to make her more nervous.

Layton stirred and his hand found her breast, causing her to smile briefly. Man, he wasn't joking about being a boob man.

"Morning," he murmured, his breath tickling her neck. "You talk in your sleep."

"I know. Did I say anything interesting?"

"Nothing that I could make out. It was mostly gibberish."

"Did I keep you awake?"

"Nope. As soon as I realized you were out like a light and just talking in your sleep, I went right back to sleep."

She smiled, happy to be in bed with him, but soon enough she remembered her concern about Emma and Erik and voiced them. "You know, I'm really stressed that Erik and Emma haven't checked in. It's not like Erik to go radio silence."

"They probably got in late and didn't want to wake you."

She shook her head. "No, Erik always calls. It's sort of an OCD thing. He wouldn't have been able to sleep without letting me know that they were okay."

Layton rose on his elbow and she rolled to her back to gaze at him. He frowned. "I'm sure there's a logical explanation, but I understand your concern. Erik is pretty consistent in his habits."

"And Emma would call, too. She's a worrywart by nature and she'd never forget to call because she wouldn't want me to worry."

"Well, we can call the road patrol and see if there were any accidents," he suggested and she shivered at the thought. "It might, if nothing else, ease your mind."

"Or it could send me into a panic if it turns out they're not okay."

"Let's not jump to the worst-case scenario," he said, kissing her softly and instantly soothing her nerves. "Breakfast first and then we'll figure out what's going on with your brother and Emma."

"You're such a good guy," she gushed, wrapping

her arms around his neck. "Tell me again why I don't want to keep you forever?"

"Because according to you, you're a bad girlfriend," he supplied, tongue in cheek. "But I think it's because you don't want to be tied down with someone like me who's serially monogamous."

She made a face to hide the sudden racing of her heart rate. Was he right? Was she afraid of trusting again? *Possibly.* "That was the most passive-aggressive statement I've ever heard so early in the morning," she said with a small roll of her eyes. The best defense was a good offense.

But Layton wasn't giving up. "Fair enough. How's this? Because you're afraid I'm going to be clumsy with your heart like that last douche even though we're nothing alike."

Oh, he hit the nail on the head. "No one ever starts out acting badly," she told him quietly, hating that she was still affected by what Riker had done. It was hard to think of yourself as a strong, independent woman when you were still licking the wounds from the past. "That comes later."

"Only if you're hardwired that way from the start." He kissed her—perhaps to stop her from thinking too much—and it worked. Within moments, they were touching, feeling, tasting and loving each other as if the world were about to end.

By the time they emerged from the bedroom, they were starving and raided the kitchen to make French toast and bacon.

"Easiest way to my heart," she admitted around a generous bite of French toast. "I swear I'll be four hundred pounds by the time I'm middle-aged. I love food.

I cringe at the thought of cutting out carbs or going paleo or doing any of those crazy restrictive food plans. I need variety. I need sugar and carbs and grains! I rue the day someone tries to put me on some kind of diet."

"Hey, more meat on your bones means one thing. Bigger boobs, so eat up all you want."

She laughed. "You're impossible. There's more to life than boobs."

"Debatable."

She finished her breakfast and then she grabbed her phone only to find it dead. She'd forgotten to charge it last night and now it was completely dead and it would take about fifteen minutes to even get a tiny signal.

"Can you call Erik and see if he answers? My phone is deader than a doornail."

Layton fished his phone out of his pocket and quickly dialed Erik.

To her relief, Erik picked up.

"Hey, man, there you are," Layton said, gesturing to the phone with a thumbs-up to indicate everything was A-okay. "Your sister was freaking out because you didn't call."

But then Layton sobered and frowned with concern and she knew something was wrong. "What is it?" she asked, tugging at Layton's sleeve. "Is everything okay? What happened?"

He held up his hand to quiet her as he was listening and then said, "All right, that sucks but glad to hear you're okay. That could've ended a lot worse. So you're going to stay there until the car is repaired?"

Car? Her eyes widened. "What happened to the car?"

Layton covered the microphone and whispered, "They were in a minor car accident. The SUV slid off the road and landed in a ditch but they're okay." He returned to Erik. "Alexis's foot is fine. The swelling went down and we didn't need to take her to the hospital. I've been taking real good care of her."

At that, Alexis pinched his nipple and he tried not to yelp. "Don't worry about Alexis… I got everything under control." Then his expression changed and he frowned. Something told her Erik was giving him an earful about something he didn't like. "We'll talk more when you get home. Drive safe."

Once he clicked off, Alexis pounced. "What happened?" she demanded to know. "Is everyone okay?"

"They're both fine but it was a little scary. They slid off the road into a ditch and because of the snow no one saw them right away. No injuries, just a little shaken up."

"I knew something was wrong. Erik and Emma are both OCD in that they would've called." She worried her bottom lip. "Poor Em! She just wanted to spend the weekend with her parents and all these terrible mishaps happened. It's almost as if the universe didn't want her to be there. I wonder what that's about."

"Well," Layton said with a small shrug, "if I'm right about Erik seeing Emma as more than just your friend…maybe spending some alone time worked out for them."

She scowled. "There you go again talking about things that make me want to vomit. If you knew Emma, you'd never suggest that she'd have sex in a vehicle. She's very shy."

"The right man, the right circumstances can bring out hidden qualities."

"Hush your mouth. I don't want to hear that. You don't know Emma like I do."

"Is she a virgin?"

Alexis scowled a little harder. She shouldn't answer, but she was curious as to where Layton was going with his question. "No, of course not. She's not a nun."

"Then you have no idea who she is behind closed doors. Sometimes the most prudish people are wild things when no one is looking."

"Gahhh," she gargled, putting her fingers in her ears. "I don't want to speculate on my best friend's potentially freaky sex life—particularly when you're suggesting that she ought to hook up with my brother! *Ew.*"

Layton laughed, enjoying her discomfort. "You're adorably contradictory. One thing is for sure, one has to stay on their toes with you."

Alexis pursed her lips, unsure of whether she wanted to continue the argument or let it go, but Layton had already moved on.

"Well, there's nothing we could've done. Emma's phone died, which is why she wasn't answering, but they're okay and that's what matters."

"That explains it."

"Yeah…so they'll be back tomorrow after the car is repaired."

"What was he saying that made you look annoyed?"

He hesitated then answered, "Uh, he was telling me to keep my hands to myself."

"Too late."

"Yeah, that ship has sailed and it's not even circling the port."

She chuckled, but it brought up a bigger issue. "How'd he even know?"

"I don't know, big-brother sixth sense?"

"Maybe. Must've been in the tone of your voice or the inflection?"

"Who knows. But who cares? You're a big girl. You don't need your brother's approval for anything, much less who you date."

"I know, but like I said, the last thing I want to do is to come between you and Erik."

"It won't come to that."

Alexis nodded but her thoughts were wandering. The snow was still coming down in fat, lazy flakes, but the lights looked cheery and festive. Erik wouldn't admit it, but he liked when she decorated for the holidays. For Alexis, decorating for the holidays made them feel more real. She looked to Layton. "Want to help me drag the Christmas tree from the garage and start decorating?"

"Is there a second option?"

"Remember that thing I did right after the shower…"

He blushed a shade of red that didn't look natural on his skin tone, but she found his reaction cute. "Yeah," he choked out. "I remember."

"Well, I'll do it again if you help me get the tree ready."

He started walking briskly toward the garage. "Show me where the tree is stored. Let's get it started."

Alexis laughed and followed him out.

Two hours later, the tree was up and decorated and Alexis was beaming with excitement as the house started to look Christmassy. "Have I mentioned how much I adore Christmas?"

"You might've mentioned it."

"I do. I love it." She drew a deep breath and smiled. "'Tis the season to be jolly, you know."

But Layton only had eyes for her and even though she was delighted with the way the decorations had turned out, she couldn't ignore the pleasant tingle in her belly knowing that Layton was looking at her the way a wolf eyed a lamb.

The primal pulse of desire between them was almost palpable. So when Layton grabbed her and pulled her to him, she went with giddy anticipation.

He sank onto the sofa and she quickly straddled him. "This is going to be a hard habit to break," she told him between kisses. She reached down to fondle the bulge in his boxers. "How are we going to stop?"

Instead of answering, he pulled his erection free and she reached over to grab a condom from the box they'd left carelessly on the end table after their last session. Within seconds she had him sheathed and even faster than that, he was inside her. She shuddered as she came down on his cock, loving the way he stretched and filled her perfectly. She braced herself against the sofa cushions behind his head and slowly rode him, taking her time to savor each sensation as they built up the tempo and the rhythm. "Layton," she breathed, ending with a load moan. "Oh God, Layton…right there…"

He gripped her hips and helped guide her as he met her grind with slow thrusts and within moments, they were both nearing their edge. Layton reached down and pinched her throbbing clitoris, sending her hurtling into an epic orgasm that stole her breath and killed any semblance of lucid thought.

Layton tensed and shouted her name as he came,

thrusting hard into her sheath until he'd spent his load. She fell forward against his chest and for a long moment just focused on catching her breath.

Was it normal to be so consumed with another human being? Not even with Riker, who she'd been certain she was in love with, had she been so perfectly in sync. It was a little frightening, to be honest, that she was already questioning everything she thought she knew about herself. Was it possible to fall so hard, so fast for someone?

"Penny for your thoughts?" he asked in a husky tone that sent shivers down her spine.

She drew up, smiling as she traced her finger down his fine, muscled chest. "I was just thinking that I don't know what to do about you."

"What do you want to do?"

"Well, there is what I should do and what I want…"

"And?"

"And what I want is in direct opposition with what I should do."

"You're talking in circles."

"Yeah, welcome to my process."

Layton tightened his hold on her, anchoring his hands on her bare hips. "There are no guarantees in life, babe. We take our chances with what we've been given and you either have to have the balls to just go for it or live in the shadows of your life, always wondering what might've been. You don't seem to be the type of person who wants to live a half life. So grab life by the balls and squeeze."

"So you're saying I should just take a chance that you won't hurt me like Riker did and just let Erik know that we're testing the waters and then what?"

Layton caressed her cheek in a sweet gesture that plucked at her heart strings. "I'm not interested in a fling with you, Alexis. I'm not down with 'testing the waters.' I want the real deal."

She bit her lip. "What if I'm difficult and you discover that I'm truly a bad girlfriend? I get grumpy. And moody. And Erik says that I'm a slob. Can you deal with that?"

"Only one way to find out."

Was there nothing that she could say that would scare Layton away? "You're asking me to trust you."

"I am."

"I'm not really all that strong in that department right now." Her voice a tremulous betrayal of the anxiety twisting her nerves and making everything seem so dangerous to her heart.

He brushed a kiss across her lips. "Then let me help restore your faith."

And there it was. She had to take a leap to find out if there was firm footing when she landed. Riker had been a painful life lesson, one she was determined not to repeat, but as far as she could tell, Layton and Riker were nothing alike. So what was holding her back?

"I'm scared."

He gazed at her so tenderly that her heart nearly broke from the sweetness. Of course Layton was nothing like Riker. How could she even think that he was?

"We don't have to make big decisions right this second. Just give yourself permission to enjoy whatever this is…at whatever pace we deem appropriate but just know that I'm ready for the real deal with you."

"But what about Erik?" she asked, a little fearful of her brother's reaction. And what would her parents say? Ugh. She could already see her mother rolling her eyes at another one of her impetuous decisions.

"Erik isn't your warden," he said firmly. "Whatever is happening between us…it's private. No need for anyone else to weigh in with their opinions."

She liked Layton's no-wavering stance. He didn't back down at the hint of pressure. A man like that was handy to have around. A man like that was husband material— *Whoa, don't get ahead of yourself. There's no picking out the linens just yet.*

Layton tapped her behind and she lifted off him so he could discard the condom. She giggled at the most inappropriate thought. "We can never let Erik know that we've had sex all over his house. He will freak out. He's a bit of a germophobe."

"And he lets his messy sister live with him?"

Alexis shrugged a shoulder. "He loves me."

"Yes, he does. He's a good man, which is why I'm not worried. He might be pissed at first but he'll come around."

Alexis nodded, realizing that Layton was right. Erik wasn't an ogre and, generally speaking, he was pretty levelheaded. Not to mention, Erik had never truly been able to control anything Alexis did. Whatever Alexis put in her head she usually went after, no matter the consequences.

"I'm going to be unavailable a lot of times because of my school schedule," she warned, but she was already smiling because, oddly, it felt right. "I might be too tired for all this hanky-panky we've been doing all weekend. It won't always be like this."

"Thank God for that," he said. "I'm not sure I could live up to the hype," he teased and she laughed.

"You're a freaking stallion, who are you trying to fool?"

She snuggled up to him, loving how perfectly they fit together, whether they were banging the pictures off the walls or just watching movies. That felt like a sign—that the universe was trying to tell her something and she was trying like hell to listen this time around.

"I live at the station four days out of the week and I'm often on call, which means I could leave at a moment's notice, right in the middle of anything."

"I know. I'm used to it with Erik. Actually, I think that works out just right because I can't stand spending too much time with one person for an extended period. So, right about the time I'm starting to get sick of you will be the time you have to leave for your shift."

He laughed. "Sounds about right."

Wow. Were they really thinking of being together? She thought of Riker and how he'd burned her so badly, and now, everything she'd gone through with him seemed like a faint memory. There was one thing she had to say, though, before they embarked on anything resembling sharing a toothbrush holder.

Alexis rose up to meet Layton's gaze with all seriousness. "Do not abuse my trust. Whatever you do… just stay true. Can you do that?"

"I can do that," he agreed solemnly, sealing the promise with a kiss. "Now I just have one thing to ask, too."

She nodded. It was only fair. "Go ahead."

"I want to see you in a naughty-nurse costume at least once."

Alexis squealed and slapped him playfully. "Damn you, Layton, I was being serious."

"So was I," he quipped with a devilish grin, and she fell just a little harder for the man she never saw coming.

"Are you going to be a bad patient?" she asked coyly and he nodded vigorously. "Will I have to punish you?"

"Yes and yes."

She liked the idea of a power exchange. She'd never tried it, but damn if it didn't make her skin tingle at the fantasy.

"Are you game?" he asked, and she realized he was asking about more than just a kinky sex game—he was asking about it all.

Sobering, Alexis slowly nodded, her heartbeat fluttering at the implications of what felt like a momentous change in her life with that single affirmative nod.

Layton's arms tightened around her and she felt as if she'd come home after a long journey.

"Me, too," he said, sealing the deal.

And then just as he was about to kiss her, the lights dimmed and went out. She laughed. "Well, there goes the power. Now what?"

"Can't watch movies, can't bake…that leaves one thing," Layton said with mock resignation as he helped her from the sofa.

"Which is?" she asked playfully.

"This."

And then he shocked her by throwing her over his shoulder as if he was saving her from a burning building, and she squealed with laughter as he carried her straight to the bedroom.

He kicked the door shut with his foot and then gently tossed her to the bed and started to strip.

"Nothing to do but each other?" she supplied, enjoying the show as Layton got gloriously naked. Man, that body! She could swoon every time.

"You read my mind, babe." He grinned as he came toward her.

And then she was in Layton's arms, which, as it turned out, was the best place she'd ever been—or ever wanted to be.

The last thought zinging through her mind before she lost all sense of reasonable thought was...*Riker who?*

And that was the best feeling of all.

Layton was the best unexpected holiday gift of all time.

Merry Christmas to me! Fa-la-la-la-la, la-la-la-la!

Now, where to find a naughty-nurse costume... someone was going to get a spanking!

* * * * *

Where There's Smoke

LIZ TALLEY

After finalling in RWA's prestigious Golden Heart in Regency romance, **Liz Talley** found a home writing sassy contemporary romance. Her first book starred a spinster librarian—V*egas Two Step*—and debuted in June 2010. Since that time, Liz has published fourteen more novels. Her stories are set in the South, where the tea is sweet, the summers are hot and the men are hotter. Liz lives in North Louisiana with her childhood sweetheart, two handsome children, three dogs and a mean kitty. You can visit Liz at www.liztalleybooks.com to learn more about her forthcoming books.

1

ERIK MATHESON HAD fought a lot of fires, but he'd never been so damn tired before. Of course, a three-alarm blaze in an apartment complex was a rarity in the small town an hour north of Denver. And he was usually better rested before hitting his shift. Multiple late nights moving his sister back to Pine Ridge paired with accidental smoke inhalation had taken a toll. After knocking out the blaze, he could hardly stand on his own two feet.

"You okay, man?" Layton Davis asked, glancing over at him as they turned into the subdivision where Erik had bought a house a few months before. Layton shared a shift with him at the fire department.

"Yeah, I'm still kicking. But damn if I'm not beat."

"That's 'cause you're getting old," Layton said, ever the smart-ass.

"I've got five years on you. Not twenty." Erik rubbed his eyes. They still stung from the intense heat.

"Dude, I've never been to your place. Which way?" Layton asked, slowing the truck, his voice weary.

They'd been about to end their shift when the call came in. Being on their feet actively engaged in fighting the fully involved fire for over six hours had been brutal. Erik figured he'd sweated away the extra calories he'd packed on from all the Christmas cookies Alexis had been baking. His sister was a traditionalist when it came to the holidays, even forcing him to buy a Christmas tree and silly stockings to hang on his mantel. Since it was the first house he'd actually owned and his parents were currently in Scotland, he hadn't made too much of a fuss about his sister's attempt at an old-fashioned family Christmas.

"Take a left, then a right on Timber Ridge Drive."

Layton followed his directives. His younger friend was a solid guy, a little too pretty—a request from the Colorado firefighters' calendar project manager for Layton to model in the 2016 charity calendar had arrived last week. Poor dude had endured plenty of ribbing from the guys at the station. Good thing Alexis and her friend Emma were on their way to Colorado Springs and not still at his place. Alexis could never resist a pretty face, and she didn't need heartbreak on her menu.

"Right here," Erik said, pointing to the house with stacked stone columns and a wide front porch. His new place had plenty of room, which was a good thing, because the roads had already started icing up. No doubt his friend would have to stay the night.

"Nice place," Layton said, nosing the truck up the slippery driveway. The tires spun a bit, before catching and shooting them forward. "Damn, it's slick out."

"Which is why you're staying," Erik said, his words

sounding oddly slurred. Hell, he was more tired than he thought.

"Naw. I can make it back to my place. I'll swing by and get you tomorrow once the roads are clear and take you back to the station to get your truck."

"Dude, it's past one o'clock in the morning and the roads are shit. I have an extra bedroom."

"Thought your sister was staying with you for a while."

"She's in Colorado Springs spending the weekend with her best friend from high school." Her very grown and very hot best friend. Emma had stopped by yesterday as he was leaving for his shift. He hadn't seen her since she'd been in high school and he'd damn near choked on his hello. She was stunning, no longer leggy and awkward with braces. Emma Brent had grown into a full-fledged woman.

"I'll take you up on it. I could audition for the *Walking Dead*." Layton turned off the engine, glancing at Erik. "You need help?"

"It was a little smoke exhaustion. I'm fine." Erik opened the door and slid out, wincing at the sharp cold and the ache in his lungs. Toward the end of the fire, he'd slipped in the gook covering the ground floor when he entered a cleared room to set up the pressure fan. He'd knocked off his mask and couldn't get it back in place before inhaling too much smoke. He'd been cleared by the medics but had begrudgingly accepted Layton's offer to drive him home. Being light-headed and exhausted wasn't an appropriate mix for making it up the steep grade to his subdivision perched off Jackson Ridge.

By the time the men got to the porch, dodging the stinging sleet, Erik remembered he'd left his keys locked in the glove box of his truck. "Shit."

"What?" Layton asked.

"My keys."

Layton blinked in the glow of the porch light shaped like a lantern. "You're kiddin'."

"I have an extra. Wait here." Erik jogged around to the garage and lifted the speckled planter bearing the Christmas tree–looking bush his sister had brought him for a housewarming gift. The bottom bore a special compartment for a spare key.

Turning, he ducked his head down and ran back to the porch. "Got it."

A second later they pushed into the warmth of the house. Alexis had thoughtfully left on the light over the oven, casting a soft glow over the new furniture he'd picked out only weeks ago. The place still had new-car smell. Or rather, new-house smell.

"Let me grab you some stuff to change into. You'll probably want to take a shower." He glanced over at Layton, hoping his friend took the hint. Just about everything in the house was new, including the coverlet and sheets in the spare room his sister had been using.

"Thanks. Yeah, I do have to shower before I sleep."

"Me, too," Erik said, nodding toward the open door at the end of the hall. "Guest bath is through there. My sister's not exactly neat, but it should be clean."

"Don't care if it's not. I need a shower and ten hours of shut-eye. Just set the clothes outside the door. Night."

"Night," Erik echoed, trudging toward his bedroom with the en suite bathroom holding a steam shower. His room was dark and he didn't bother switching on the light. His eyes ached and his head throbbed. Smoke inhalation could make a person feel crappy.

Five minutes later he padded into his room, towel over his head. One more scrub at his damp hair and he tossed it in the direction of the chair that sat by his chest of drawers. He pulled back his covers and climbed into bed bare-assed naked, hungry for sleep and the warmth of his down comforter.

The first thing he noticed was how warm the bed was.

The second thing he noticed was the body curled up in the center of the bed.

The third thing he noticed was the scent of freshly laundered sheets.

And though his brain felt sluggish, he concluded pretty quickly that the person softly snoring in the center of his pillow-top mattress was his sister's oldest friend.

Emma Rose Brent.

His eyes adjusted to the moonlight streaming in between the curtains and he saw the outline of her body, the one he failed to see when he first entered his room. The light fell across her neck, highlighting her jawline and the loveliest pair of plump lips. For an upper-crust literature professor, Miss Emma Rose had lips that belonged in a porno.

And though his head pounded, his throat ached and his thoughts felt as jumbled as the storage room full of Alexis's junk, he couldn't help himself from drinking her in.

Emma had always been thin and awkward, stingy

with her shy grin. She rarely spoke, seemingly content to observe those around her, a shadow outside the spotlight. When he'd been around, she'd been especially quiet, so he'd been surprised at the confident woman who'd greeted him yesterday.

"Mmm," she murmured, turning over, pulling the covers with her.

This was so incredibly wrong, but he couldn't stop watching her. The wrinkle impression on her cheek, the tangle of her sandy hair, the small sigh of contentment escaping as she sank back into slumber.

And then his sister's scream shattered the silence.

EMMA HAD BEEN dreaming she was back in high school. Mrs. Vonnegut—not related to Kurt—had been fussing at her for screwing up the spring recital. She'd given Emma a piece she'd never seen before and instructed the orchestra to play along. Emma had struggled to keep up and Ertha Vonnegut had screamed at her to stop at once.

Then she woke up to someone actually screaming.

And noticed the man sitting next to her.

A naked man.

"Emma, Emma," the man whispered softly. "It's okay. It's me."

It took her a moment to register that the "me" was Alexis's older brother, Erik. "Wh-what are you doing?" she whispered as she scrambled away from him, clutching the covers in her fists, trying to figure out what was happening.

Erik was in bed with her. And he was naked. And Alexis was screaming.

"I'm sorry. I didn't know you were here," he said, grabbing the quilt at the foot of the bed and pulling it around himself.

"Alexis?" she whispered, still confused.

"Look, I'm sorry about all this, but I got to go save Layton. She's probably thrown something at him." Erik switched on the lamp, causing her to blink. The alarm clock on the nightstand showed her a steadfast 1:42 a.m.

Alexis had stopped screaming, but then a masculine yelp and curse followed.

"Too late," Erik said, rising, the patched quilt clutched around his waist. His broad back narrowed to a trim waist above the intriguing curve of his butt. She rubbed her eyes and zeroed in on his ass. Which she knew from past viewings was really nice.

There was a crash and then a wail.

"What the hell is going on?" she murmured as Erik opened his bedroom door. He'd taken only one step when another man, this one clad in jeans, came bounding by.

"Your sister's crazy, man," the guy said, raising his arms as if to fend off attack.

Alexis appeared, clad in a camisole and a pair of postage-stamp panties. "What the hell, Erik? Who *is* this?"

"Hey, hey." Erik caught his sister. Alexis looked ready to fight someone.

"Jesus, woman," the man beside Erik said. "I didn't know you were in there. Give me a freakin' break."

Emma remained rooted to the bed, covers tucked beneath her arms. She'd worn a T-shirt to bed, but her bra hung from the bedroom door and she'd shucked her pajama pants before climbing into Erik's bed. She tugged the covers up.

"What are you still doing here?" Erik said, gently pushing his sister back.

"Ow." Alexis winced as she stepped backward. She immediately lifted her foot and frowned down at the dangling appendage. "I think I hurt my ankle. And we're here because my memory sucks. I drove to pick up Em, but we decided to take her SUV from her place. Then just as we headed down I-25, I realized I left my laptop charger and we swung back because there wasn't going to be time to get a new one once we got to Emma's parents' place. By the time we could leave again, they had closed parts of the interstate. We figured we'd wait until midmorning to leave. Roads should be clear then."

"So that's why your car wasn't in the driveway," Erik said.

"Yeah. I thought you were working." Alexis hobbled into Erik's room and sat on the bed. Erik and the dude behind him watched as she tenderly prodded her ankle.

"Lex, you don't have any pants on," Emma whispered.

Her friend glanced up. "How different is this from my bathing suit? Crap, my ankle is really swelling."

Alexis was the person Emma wished she could be. Bold and confident, her best friend since third grade was a ball of energy, sass and smack talk. Being seen in her underwear didn't faze her.

"She punched me and then threw a shoe at me," the guy behind Erik said, sounding incredulous.

"You scared the crap out of me," Alexis retorted, her dark eyes blazing.

"Okay, okay." Erik held his hands up, pressing them against air. "Let's all just calm down. This was a big misunderstanding. No harm, no foul."

"Speak for yourself," Alexis muttered, her face twisted in pain. "I tripped over my suitcase when I was chasing that pervert out of my room."

"Pervert?" the guy said. "I'm not a—"

"He's not a pervert. Well, not usually. This is Layton Davis," Erik said, tilting his handsome face heavenward in what looked to be a prayer for patience. "He drove me home after we worked a blaze. I told him to take the spare room. I thought you were gone. You were supposed to be gone."

Guilt nudged Emma. Their being stranded was all her fault. She'd tried to run too many errands on her list that morning and it had pushed them back on getting everything done for the Christmas dinner and dance being held at the school her parents ran for mentally challenged adults. The party was scheduled for Saturday night and Alexis had volunteered to go with Emma to surprise her parents, who were receiving a community-service award at the annual function. Since Emma had recently moved to Greeley, which was just east of Pine Ridge, to teach at North Colorado State, she'd been thrilled when her bestie had suggested they make a girlfriends' weekend of it.

"Well, we weren't gone. And who doesn't check where he's going to sleep before plopping down on top of someone?" Alexis asked.

"Someone who's tired as shit and unaware someone's friend's sister is occupying the bed he was given," Layton said, flashing an annoyed glance toward Erik.

Erik shrugged. "Like I knew. Let's shelve the accusations and take a page from Emma's book and not freak out."

Everyone looked at Emma. She managed an awkward smile.

For a few seconds the room fell silent, the animosity dissipating.

"Okay, good. Now, since it's cold as frick outside and the roads are too dangerous, let's bunk up and get through the night," Erik said.

"Your sister probably needs an ice pack or something," Layton said, gesturing to Alexis, whose ankle looked swollen. "How about I grab some ice while you figure out the sleeping arrangements."

Layton disappeared and a light came on, lending a glow to the hallway.

"Why are you wearing a quilt?" Alexis asked.

"'Cause I'm naked under here," he said, tugging the quilt up higher. Emma had noted it slipped a bit during the whole Alexis-trying-to-kill-Layton incident, revealing washboard abs and the hint of the delicious narrowing to… No, she wasn't going to think about the crush she'd always had on him.

This was Alexis's brother.

And, yeah, he was hot as butter on a biscuit, but he was practically *family*. Erik was the guy who had given her noogies, who had pulled her pigtails. Okay, not literally, but pretty much the same thing. She wasn't supposed to notice the quilt dipping low to reveal the curve of his ass or how nice his naked torso looked or the fact he had a tattoo of an eagle on one side of his chest, which looked so…tough and male and—

"Wait, did you climb into bed with Emma while you were naked?" Alexis asked, still cradling her swelling ankle.

"Yeah," Erik admitted, looking unabashed.

Alexis glanced at Emma, eyebrows arched above amused eyes. "Well, how come you didn't scream?"

"I never scream." Emma sniffed.

"Well, if a big bozo sat on you, you would," Alexis grumbled.

The big bozo appeared with a bag of frozen broccoli wrapped in a dish towel. He frowned at Alexis but shouldered his way inside, handing the bag to her friend. "Here. I'm happy to take the couch."

"And I'll give you your bed back and sleep with Alexis," Emma said to Erik. "I feel so bad about being here when you—"

"I told you to," Alexis interrupted. "He was at work."

Erik looked as though he wanted to say something more, but he bit his tongue.

They all stood around. Finally, Emma said, "I'm not exactly dressed. And neither is Erik. So…"

"Right," Alexis said, sliding off the bed and hobbling toward the door. Erik frowned as if he wanted to help her, but he still clasped the quilt around his waist.

"Well, hell," Layton said, sweeping Alexis into his arms.

"Hey! Put me down," Alexis said, her nearly naked bottom staring Emma in the face.

"I will. In your room." Layton strode to the door, ignoring her friend's struggles. The man looked like a model, with hair flapping over one eye and sleek, knotted muscles bulging at Alexis's weight. Emma dropped her eyes down to Layton's tight butt and that's when she noticed Erik watching her.

She jerked her gaze away, begging the pink not to creep into her cheeks.

Which was a fail.

"Uh, I'm gonna grab some pants and then let you get dressed," Erik said, lifting her lacy pink bra off the doorknob. He eyed the sexy lingerie and then smiled as he handed it to her.

Desire punched her in the stomach.

Damn. Erik Matheson was an absolute fox. Layton may look like an Abercrombie model, but this man was like sex on a plate…just waiting for someone to take a satisfying bite.

Emma licked her lips before plucking the bra from his fingers. "Thank you."

"Need any help?" he asked, sounding serious, as his gaze dropped to her breasts covered by his blankets.

"Uh, no," she managed to say, her cheeks still likely bright red. Why couldn't she be like Alexis? Have the flippant, flirty comebacks? Be cool?

"I'm just kidding, Em," Erik said, grabbing his jeans off the chair in the corner and following Layton and his still-struggling sister from the room. Just as he was about to close the door, he popped his head back in. "Not that I wouldn't like to."

Then he shut the door, leaving Emma red-faced… but slightly turned on.

2

ERIK EYED THE ROADWAY, looking for patches of ice, and then glanced over at his sister's best friend. "The road looks okay. They're clear around Denver, but my buddy at highway patrol said traffic was still a nightmare. This shortcut will get you there faster."

"Good," Emma said, her hands folded primly in her lap. She wore a thick sweater with a scarf, a pair of black leggings and suede boots that stretched up her long legs to the bottom of her thighs. She looked amazing, especially with her blond waves falling over her shoulders and those pretty green eyes flocked by thick sooty lashes.

How in the hell would all those frat boys stay focused on Chaucer instead of their English lit professor's nice ass?

Probably with her cool demeanor. There was something so untouchable about Emma.

He'd insisted on driving her after fighting with a hobbling sister who had finally admitted she was in no shape to travel with her friend. Luckily, he'd showed no effects from the temporary smoke exhaustion. Apparently, eight uninterrupted hours of sleep worked wonders.

"Thank you again for driving me. I really wanted to be there to see my parents receive their award." Emma twisted her fingers and glanced over at him with those guileless green eyes.

"I wasn't letting you go alone in this weather, and, hey, at least I don't have to listen to Alexis bitch all weekend about her ankle."

"Poor Lex. Her ankle was so swollen. I feel bad for leaving her."

"It's a sprain. Layton said he'd drive her to get an X-ray, but it's not serious." Erik narrowed his eyes, looking for the turnoff. Normally, he'd never take a back road when the interstate and other well-traveled highways would be salted and much safer, but the dinner and dance honoring Emma's parents started in less than two hours. If Emma wanted to make it, then he had to make up for lost time. The ice storm had been bad and the interstate had opened a mere hour ago. Finding the correct turn, he slowed and carefully steered Emma's Lexus SUV onto the narrow two-lane highway.

Emma made a face. "I've never been this way before."

"I came this way all the time when I was in college. Don't worry. I've driven it in weather worse than this."

"I forgot you went to the Air Force Academy."

"For a year." He gave a shrug, slightly embarrassed he'd abandoned academia for something so mundane as being a firefighter. Deal was, he loved his job and knew it was where he belonged. Every hour he'd spent in a classroom had been excruciating. College hadn't been his cup of tea.

A few miles down the road that no longer felt familiar, he noted more frequent patches of ice. The road had been plowed at some point, but the salting had either been overlooked or the county hadn't bothered spending the money on a seldom-used byway. He needed to be very careful, so he decreased his speed and vowed to stop eyeing Emma's firm thighs. However, he could do nothing about the sensuous perfume that took his thoughts to places they had no business going.

The tires on the car slipped a few times, making Emma clutch the dashboard. "I'm sorry I'm being a nervous Nellie," she said, laughing at herself.

"Well, it's a bit worse than I remembered," Erik admitted, though he didn't want to state he'd been wrong about taking the shortcut. He probably should have stuck to the cleared interstate, getting Emma to the community center late, rather than trying to play macho hero. He'd just seen that look of longing in her eyes and wanted to impress her for some odd reason.

A sharp curve lay ahead and Erik tapped the brakes to slow down. Just as he started the turn, he hit black ice. The car slid sideways, veering toward the guardrail and a steep embankment.

"Ah," Emma squeaked as the back of the SUV fishtailed. He felt her grab the handle above her head but kept his eyes focused on the road and hands on the wheel. He managed to get control of the vehicle and had just breathed a sigh of relief when the back fender clipped the guardrail.

The Lexus did a 180-degree spin. The tires could find no traction as the SUV tilted backward over the embankment.

The seat belt jerked him against the seat and he heard Emma screaming.

Oh, shit.

He pressed the brake, locking up the tires, but he couldn't slow the momentum. They went down the steep embankment. Branches whooshed by and then the vehicle hit something that spun them another 180 degrees so that they were hurtling right toward a—

Huge tree.

The Lexus plowed into a bank of snow and then smacked the tree.

Hard.

His head snapped forward on impact and then something slammed into his body.

Air bag.

The entire time Emma had been screaming. Or maybe it was him? He didn't know. He couldn't see anything. He couldn't breathe.

Instinctively he fought the air bag, gasping for breath. The air bag immediately started deflating. "Emma?"

He didn't hear anything.

"Emma! Are you okay?" he shouted.

He heard the sound of spitting and then her hand connected with his leg. "I'm here. I think I'm okay."

Erik pressed down the expended air bag and looked over to find Emma covered in a powdery dust. Right when their gazes made contact, something slammed into the roof. She screeched, ducking down. He recoiled, too, before realizing the tremendous thump had been snow dislodging from the branches above them.

His heart beat in his ears and his body felt numb.

"Are you hurt?" he panted, adrenaline igniting, coursing through his body.

"I don't think so." She moved her legs, wincing a little. "My neck hurts a little, but I'm okay. You?"

"Yeah," he said, flexing his arms, wiggling his legs.

They'd been *very* lucky. The thick snow at the bottom of the hill had helped slow them before impact. If they hadn't had that bank of snow, they might have been gravely hurt. As a firefighter he'd seen plenty of head-on collisions.

The engine had died and he couldn't see anything through the spiderwebbed windshield. A fir-tree branch pressed against his driver's-side window, blocking his vision, so he looked past Emma, who still struggled with the air bag, to see they'd landed in brushy woods.

Erik breathed a sigh of relief when he pushed the unlock button and the doors made a telltale clicking sound. Then he unbuckled himself and dug his cell phone out of his pocket. He pressed the home-screen button and his apps appeared along with the signal display that read No Service. "Goddamn it."

He smacked the steering wheel, sending up a cloud of white powder that made him cough.

"What?" Emma said, stamping down on the fabric of the air bag.

"No frickin' service." He wagged his phone. "Try yours."

Emma unbuckled and felt around for her purse. Things must have fallen out, because she mumbled something that could have been a really naughty word before pulling out a pink phone with a bow on the top.

"Oh no," she breathed.

"What?"

"I forgot to charge it last night. Only one percent battery life."

"Who forgets to charge a phone?" he asked, feeling aggravation welling in him. It was like dealing with Alexis. No common sense. And now they had no way to phone for help.

Emma's eyes flashed fire. "Someone who was unfamiliar with the place she slept. Someone who had a naked man slide into bed with her. Someone who doesn't have to answer to you."

Touché.

Erik sighed and ran a hand over his face. "I'm sorry. Stress. Can't you charge it with the car battery?"

She ignored his apology. "Mine only charges when the engine is cranked. So who should I call?"

"That doesn't make any sense. It runs off the battery. Did you check your fuses?" Emma gave him a flat look, so he said, "Dial 911."

After getting the particulars about where he thought they were, Emma dialed the number. He watched, fear seeping into his gut. The temperatures weren't arctic, but they would drop when the sun went down. They needed to find help before that happened. He glanced at his watch: 4:33 p.m.

"Um, hi. Uh, my name is Emma Brent and my friend and I were traveling out here on—what's it called again?" She looked at him.

"Old Fox Farm Road," he said.

"You heard him? And we were cutting over to 105 when we hit some ice and ended up going over the shoulder, um, about ten miles past Mill Creek Run. Hello? Can you hear me? Hello?" Emma pulled the phone from her ear and looked at it. "No, no, no."

Then she lifted those pretty green eyes to him. "Sorry."

Erik wanted to slam his hand against the wheel again, but he didn't. "Okay. No big deal. I'm going to climb out and walk up the incline. I should have service once I'm on the road. You stay here. Put your coat on and stay warm."

Erik pulled his coat off the back floorboard and struggled into it. Tucking his scarf under the zipper, he opened the door, pushing hard against the bent metal, and climbed out into the bitter-cold day. Just as he slammed the door shut, sleet started falling, pinging on the smashed hood of the car. Not bothering to look over the wreckage, he began the climb up the steep embankment, praying that another vehicle might pass by, hoping beyond all hope he might get a signal.

Ten minutes later he turned and headed back down to the wrecked car. He'd not seen a single car pass by and his phone couldn't catch a signal no matter where he stood along the road. Which was ridiculous because every cellular commercial promised nationwide service. Such bullshit.

He pulled the door open to find Emma sitting bundled in her coat, teeth chattering. "Any luck?"

"No." He didn't want to admit how badly he'd fucked up by trying to take that shortcut. He'd gotten impatient about her phone not being charged, but the blame for this fiasco lay squarely on his shoulders. The only good news was that the sleet had stopped. But low mean clouds gathered in the distance. "Let's try to start the engine and charge your phone. Should have thought of that in the first place."

He pressed the button that should start the car. Nothing but a click. He pumped the gas pedal as if that would help. Nothing.

Emma pulled her hands from her pockets, holding her phone. "While you were gone, I managed to get my phone on again and sent a message to Alexis. I think it sent. Just said we'd wrecked off Old Fox and we were okay. That was the best I could do before it shut down again. I'm sorry I didn't charge it. We wouldn't be in this situation if I had."

Guilt sucker punched him. "No. This is my fault. I stubbornly insisted on taking this way."

"What are we going to do?"

"We're going to walk back to the highway and wait on someone to pass. It's a back road, but people live out here. Someone will come by."

No one came by.

It was like a movie. Two people stranded. Brutally cold weather. No one for miles. All they needed was an escaped serial killer.

"I can't believe this shit," Erik said, holding his phone up as they trudged back down the road in the direction from which they'd come. They'd waited for a car for a good thirty minutes before they decided to start walking. They'd only driven ten or twelve miles since they'd turned off the marked road. And the walking kept them somewhat warm. At least Emma's teeth had stopped chattering.

"Look," she said.

Erik had been moving his phone up and down, left and right, watching the left corner of his phone's screen. If he could just get one freaking bar. For the love of Pete, one bar.

Ripping his attention away, he followed her pointed finger to a small reflector buried in the grass.

Erik shoved his useless cell phone into his coat pocket and jogged over to the reflective glass. "I'll be damned. It's an old driveway."

3

EMMA WAS OFFICIALLY creeped out. The musty cabin hadn't likely hosted occupants in years. "This is so strange. Feels like a B movie and any minute a guy with a chain saw will pop out at us." She ran her gloved finger over the layer of dust on the small table.

"Already had that thought," Erik said, pushing the door he'd kicked in closed. The gray skies looked threatening and she could smell the snow in the air. Temps had already dropped since they'd hiked to the cabin.

The place was rustic…if run-down was considered rustic. But at one point it must have been a nice getaway. A small frozen pond sat just beyond, at the edge of the thick woods. The cabin was a one-roomer with a small kitchenette, a fridge and an unmade double bed. Faded gingham curtains hung in the two small windows and the decor was decidedly eighties with a focus on fish.

Emma pulled open the fridge and then immediately

closed it. It had been empty but smelled like death. "Ugh."

Erik rifled through a few cabinets. "Here's a flashlight that, uh, doesn't work. And a box of crackers dated 2001 and a tin of Spam. Matches." He shook the box.

Emma opened the only other door in the cabin and found a small bathroom with a toilet, sink and tiny shower. She twisted the faucet and water came out. "We have water," she shouted back to Erik.

"And the stove is gas. Though it's probably not hooked up any longer," Erik said.

"At least there's a fireplace." She pointed toward the empty grate. She walked over to the wood box. "Oh, and they left wood in the bin."

"I'll check the flue and then start the fire," he said, walking toward the fireplace.

"Does that mean we're staying here tonight?" she asked, knowing the answer but dreading his confirmation. A storm gathered outside and they were ill prepared…and very much alone.

"We'll have to. It's getting dark and looks like snow is on the way. We'll stay here and then tomorrow morning we'll head back to the road and try our luck finding help. Now, let me get that fire going. I'm frozen."

Emma plucked the matches from his hand. "You walk back to the car and get my luggage while I start the fire. I have some cookies and a wrapped tin of chocolates. It won't be much to eat, but it will be better than old Spam."

Erik looked as if he would argue, but instead

shrugged. "Okay. Check the flue and stack the wood. We'll light it when I get back."

"I can manage lighting a fire, Erik."

He pressed his lips into a line. "Look, I'm a firefighter and that's a fireplace that hasn't been used in years. Just let me have control of this one thing. Please."

She started to argue because he treated her like the kid she used to be. The awkward twelve-year-old who wandered into a beehive on the campout she'd gone on with his family, the newly licensed driver who had to call him to bring the gas can, the graduating senior who'd accidentally started a fire in the Matheson side yard on the Fourth of July. But Emma wasn't that gauche girl any longer. She could build a freaking fire without burning the place down.

But something in his expression stopped her.

Here was a commanding man accustomed to being in control of all things. At that moment he had none.

"Yes, Firefighter Matheson," she said, saluting and trying out a smile. If she was going to be holed up with a bossy firefighter in the middle of a potential snowstorm while missing her parents' award presentation, she needed to find her sense of humor.

And some self-control.

One bed, a roaring fire and the sexy guy she'd always had the hots for felt like an assload of temptation.

He looked hard at her and for a moment she wondered if he could see her thoughts. Did he know she wanted him…that she'd always wanted him?

No. She was the master of hiding feelings. Besides, Erik had never seen her as anyone other than his younger sister's nerdy friend.

"Okay. Stay here. Be safe."

A blast of cold air roared in when he opened the door. "Be careful," she called as he walked back into the world of white. If he was going to give orders, so was she.

Thirty minutes later, Erik pushed back in. While he'd been gone, she'd scoured the cabin looking for supplies. There wasn't much left behind in the place, but she'd found pillows, sheets and a few wool blankets in the bathroom closet. She'd aired them out, snapping them over the two tweed chairs centered in front of the fireplace. She'd also found some old rags under the sink along with a near-empty bottle of cleaner and had wiped down the counters and tabletop. The place still felt grimy, but at least now spiderwebs and dust weren't adding to the ambience.

"Jesus, it's cold outside," Erik said, rolling in her suitcase and dumping her emergency car kit on the floor. Inside, she had a first-aid kit and a few other things like bottled water, an extra blanket and a pack of tampons.

"And snowing hard," Emma said, watching as he unwound his plaid wool scarf from his head and shrugged out of his jacket. Snow coated his dark hair and he brushed it off. He wore a navy cable-knit sweater underneath, worn jeans and work boots. He'd been better prepared than she had. Her poor suede boots were ruined and the leggings she wore a flimsy barrier against the cold.

"You cleaned up a bit," he said, his gaze sweeping the place. When he looked at the bed, something hot slithered into her belly. "Brr, let's get that fire lit."

Emma dragged her damp suitcase toward the table and wiped away the excess moisture, glad she'd gotten a hard-shell case. Hoisting it, she pulled out the box of homemade chocolate-chip cookies along with the cylinder containing the expensive bottle of wine she'd gotten for her epicurean father. A flat box of handmade chocolates for her aunt Della also joined the stack. And as a plus, she found two protein bars she'd tucked into the pocket lining the case. Not the best dinner, but it would do until they could get back to civilization tomorrow.

The crackle of the lit fire drew her attention and instantly made the space cozy and—she licked her lips—intimate.

"Ah," Erik said, stripping off his gloves and warming his hands in front of the blaze. "Good thing this wood is aged and dry. Instant warmth. Come on over and warm up."

Emma hesitated for a moment, trying to regain a calm, less amorous demeanor. So they were alone in a cabin in the middle of nowhere with a bottle of wine, chocolate and a double bed? Big deal. She could handle it. After all, she'd never allowed her attraction for him to show through.

She walked over and crouched beside him, sighing at the warmth. Exploring the cabin had kept her moving, but her fingers and feet were numb.

"Here," he said, grabbing the nearest chair and dragging it close to the dancing flames. "Sit."

Seconds later they each sat in matching chairs, thawing out.

"I can't believe we're stuck here," she mused aloud,

the warmth making her drowsy. She suppressed a yawn. "This is like a movie I once saw."

"*Misery*?" he joked.

Emma laughed. "Are you planning on incapacitating me and making me write you a romance story?"

He wiggled his eyebrows. "That could be fun. But I could think of better things to do."

"Well, I saw some puzzles in the back of the storage closet. We can do one of those," Emma said, nervous about the direction the conversation headed. She wasn't a dumb-dumb; she knew that as a firefighter, Erik would never sleep with an unattended fire, which meant at some point he'd have to extinguish the fire. The room would get cold. Really cold. And there was that one bed sitting there like an elephant in the room… just not as noisy. Pair that with the fact she could easily be persuaded to find an upside to sharing body warmth and Emma could be in trouble.

"Are you suggesting rather than tying you up, I should do a puzzle with you?" he teased, hopping up to grab a blanket and place his scarf and coat nearby so they could dry.

"Or I can write that bad romance book."

"Or you can write a really good one. I'll volunteer for market research."

"Are you flirting with me, Erik Matheson?"

He grinned and crickets started hopping around her belly. Dang, but his smile could seduce a vestal virgin. He looked awfully yummy wrapped in a worn army blanket, hair ruffled from his trek through the woods wearing the scarf. Normally Erik was a buttoned-up sort of guy, which she totally dug. Nothing like a hard jaw, no-nonsense demeanor and a clean-cut style, but seeing him a bit smudged around the edges was a different turn-on.

How would he be in bed?

Commanding? Or content to let her take the lead?

She could probably find out.

"Of course not," he said, sobering a little. "You're like my sister."

He said it as though he was reminding himself, which lessened the dart of hurt. He was right. They had been like brother and sister. Still, they hadn't seen each other in years. Emma was a whole different person from the girl she'd been when she hung around the Matheson house, scarfing down ice cream and watching 'N Sync videos. She'd graduated with a BA from the University of Colorado, completed her MA in comparative literature and was presently enrolled in a doctoral program. Not to mention she'd lost her braces, flat chest and virginity along the way. She most definitely was *not* his sister.

"If that's the case, you're a shitty brother. I haven't seen you in…seven years?" she said, jerking her head toward the blankets piled on the table. "Hand me a blanket?"

He tossed it to her and she tucked it around herself, sighing at the warmth. "How about some wine? Think we can find a corkscrew around here?"

"You have wine?" Erik shifted his gaze over to her.

"My dad's Christmas gift, but it must be sacrificed. And I pulled out the cookies and handmade chocolate, too. We may not have much to eat, but what we do have is the good stuff. Give me a few more moments of warm up and I'll wipe off a plate from the cupboard and make us dinner." She chuckled at the thought.

"Nah, I'm thawed out enough to do the dirty deed," he said, struggling from the depth of the chair. Emma snuggled into the dusty tweed warmth, trying not to think about spiders and other creepy crawlies that might have done the same over the years. She heard drawers slamming and Erik shout "bingo," then she heard the clink of glass and the pop of the cork.

"Let it breathe," she said.

"You're much bossier than I remember. Is that what they taught you in college, Miss Fancy Pants?" Erik asked, his voice light. Similar to how he'd talked to her when she *was* sixteen. "Hope you don't mind drinking out of water glasses."

"Of course not. Do you need help?" she asked.

"Nope," he said, sliding by her, holding two tall glasses with sunflowers etched on the side. He handed her both glasses then turned and grabbed the cleaned plate he'd loaded with the chocolates and cookies. *"Bon appétit."*

"It's a travesty to drink this pinot noir in such ugly glasses," she said as she held up the offensive glasses to the firelight. The vintage was brilliant ruby in the glow. It smelled as advertised, with notes of cherry, anise and sandalwood.

"What do you mean? My maw maw has these glasses," Erik said, settling into his chair, tugging the blanket around his knees. He balanced the plate of cookies in his lap.

That made Emma laugh.

"You're so different now," he said. The teasing in his eyes had disappeared and he stared at her thoughtfully.

"How so?"

"I don't know. It's like you're Emma, but you're not. Just different."

"Did you expect me to stay the same? I was a teenager. You should know that when you feed and water them, they grow up to become adults," she joked, swiping a chocolate off the plate and biting into it. "Mmm, these are so good."

She felt him watching her and something zipped in the air. Like the crackling of static electricity. Or the prickling of hair at the nape of her neck. She chewed the decadent candy she'd bought at Belvedere's when she'd gone shopping in Denver.

Turning, she caught him watching her, hunger present in his eyes. He blinked, cleared his throat and said, "I'm going to grab one of those jigsaw puzzles."

ERIK WAS IN TROUBLE. Not because he was stranded in a cabin in the middle of nowhere with no electricity and no way to communicate with the outside world. No. The danger wore diamond earrings and fuzzy wool socks. And she smelled like exotic perfume and had hair soft as spun silk. Not that he even knew what spun silk was. But it was probably soft since everyone compared soft stuff to it. Everything about her was womanly. She had curves that begged to be traced, plump flesh ready to yield to the hardness of a man.

Yeah, little Emma Rose was big-time trouble.

"You really want to do a puzzle?" she asked, her

tongue darting out to take care of the small chocolate fleck in the corner of her luscious lips.

No, I really want to do you.

But he couldn't actually say that to *her*.

"Uh, sure. We can drag the table in front of the fire. It would be easier to set the glasses and cookies on the table, too."

Emma made a face. "Okay, if you really want to." She struggled from the grasp of the scratchy blanket and padded in her socked feet to the small bathroom. A few minutes later she emerged with a water-stained box.

Erik jumped up and set about hauling the kitchen table as close to the fire as was safe. Then he moved the wingback chairs, already warm from their bodies, over to the table. He'd found a couple of candles on the back of a shelf in the kitchen, which he set on the table and lit.

The overall effect was very cozy.

Maybe too cozy for two single warm-blooded people drinking wine by candlelight.

"This was the best puzzle in the bunch." She held up the box showing a large whale breaching an Alaskan bay. Or somewhere cold. As if they needed something else to remind them of being cold and wet. Why couldn't the former owners of the cabin have bought a tropical-landscape puzzle?

"That'll work," he said, settling in the chair, pouring another slug of wine. Normally he went for beer, but he couldn't deny how warm the wine made him. "Let's try to create the border first."

Emma started flipping puzzle pieces. "I wonder if

Alexis got my message. I started to text my parents, but they'd have been too worried. They would have canceled the dinner. Ugh, it was so stupid to forget to charge my phone."

"You were out of your element," he said, finding two pieces that fit and tapping them down.

"I've been out of my element for a while now. Ever since I finished my master's, I've lived with my parents. It was easy. I taught high school, worked on my thesis and my mom cooked every night. It's not like I'm spoiled, but this past month of moving and starting a new job has been difficult. But I know I'm settling in to where I'm supposed to be."

"In academia?"

She nodded. "Hey, I've always been a nerd."

"Nothing nerdy about you, Emma. You're a beautiful, accomplished woman. I know your folks are proud."

Emma glanced up at him. "You're being awfully kind to the girl who broke your Stratocaster."

Laughing, Erik passed her a few pieces that looked as if they would fit the border she worked on. "I forgot about that. You should have stuck to air guitar."

"You were always nice to me."

He wanted to be nice to her now. Really nice. The fire cast a glow onto her golden hair, and her cheeks were flushed from the wine and heat. She'd abandoned her wool coat and the long sweater she wore molded to her high breasts. "Why wouldn't I be?"

"Some of my other friends' brothers were so nasty to their sisters. You and Alexis always had such a good relationship."

He shrugged. "My parents gave us no leeway for anything else."

For a few minutes they fell silent, sipping wine and squinting at the somewhat warped puzzle pieces. Every so often she shifted a certain way and he got a whiff of her perfume. Something about her sexy subtleness revved his blood.

He'd been single for half a year. His last girlfriend had been unwilling to move past anything casual. Not that Erik was jonesing to move toward the altar. He'd just wanted something more than casual sex and half-hearted dating.

"Are you seeing someone?" he asked.

Emma jerked her head up at his question. "As in dating?"

"Just wondering if you had someone significant."

She shook her head and something inside him did a tap dance. "I haven't had time to meet anyone since I moved to Greeley. I had been seeing a guy in Colorado Springs, but it wasn't serious. We agreed to end it when I made the move north."

"Oh."

"Why?"

"Just wondering. Casual conversation. Uh, so what are your plans for Christmas?"

"I was planning on staying with my parents until after Christmas then heading back to Greeley. I'm staying in a friend's duplex but need to find another place. He's in Italy and will return in the spring."

"It's just me and Alexis this Christmas. Mom and Dad went to Scotland for the holiday. That was their big dream—to visit my father's family."

"Good for them," Emma said, capturing her tongue between her teeth. She scrutinized the 982 remaining pieces. "I'm going to be honest, this makes me glad I have Netflix."

Erik chuckled, trying like hell to keep her from seeing just how much he was attracted to her. After all, she'd never given him cause to think she was interested in him in any other way than being Alexis's brother. "Yeah, peace and quiet sounds nice until there's no TV or Wi-Fi."

For the next few minutes while they completed the outline of the puzzle, they chatted about their favorite movies, TV series and the upcoming NFL playoffs. It amazed him that smarty-pants Emma loved the Broncos so much. All the while, he kept sneaking peeks at the way the firelight danced on her hair, at the way her plump lips teased him, at the way her breasts rose and fell when she laughed.

After an hour, they had a fourth of the puzzle completed.

"I need a break," Emma said, stretching her arms overhead and yawning.

"It's only seven thirty," he said after looking at his watch. Because that was safer than staring at the swell of her breasts jutting out as she arched back.

Damn.

He needed a cold shower.

Instead, he rose and walked over to the window, pulling back the dusty curtains. "Man, it's really coming down out there."

And then she was behind him, looking over his

shoulder. "Thank goodness we found this place. It might not be the Ritz, but at least we won't die."

"There's that," he said, turning back toward the room. She didn't move and only a foot stood between them. The air grew heavy with something he'd denied up one side of the room and down the other...but wasn't going away.

Emma raised her beautiful green eyes, her gaze meeting his.

For a moment he merely watched her. At the way her breathing increased, at those sweet, sweet lips. They were made for kissing and other things he couldn't allow himself to dwell on. When she licked them, it was nearly his undoing.

Almost family be damned.

A faint pinking of her cheeks gave her away. She stepped back. "Want another cookie?"

Inhaling quickly, he stepped around her. "Sure. I always liked dessert before dinner. Um, except I guess we're not having dinner."

4

WANT ANOTHER COOKIE?

Jesus, who said something like that to keep a guy from kissing her?

Because, if Emma were a betting woman, she'd lay a cool hundred down that Erik had almost kissed her.

And she'd allowed her cold feet to ruin it.

Not her literal cold feet, which weren't too bad now that the fire had warmed the room. But the cold feet sticking out from behind the flimsy curtain of propriety she'd strung across to hide her desire for the man she'd always wanted to take a bite of.

And why not?

What was the issue with having a fun little one-night stand?

After all, they were adults. Healthy, somewhat-horny adults with desires, needs and nothing to do but put together an old warped puzzle of a sperm whale. Not to mention Alexis never had to find out that she and Erik had entertained themselves by giving the old iron bed some action.

What Alexis didn't know wouldn't hurt her.

"You want a cookie, too?" Erik asked, jarring her from her internal argument over should she seduce him or shouldn't she. He wagged a cookie at her.

"No, thanks."

He took a bite and chewed thoughtfully. "You know, with the snow coming down as hard as it is, we might be stranded for longer than one night."

The desire she'd been flirting with took a backseat at the thought of them being in danger. They didn't have anything more than half a bottle of wine, a dozen cookies and two protein bars. "And my parents won't be worried because they didn't know I was coming. If Alexis thinks I'm home safely and my parents don't know I'm missing, the only shot we have is someone will miss you."

"But not until tomorrow. Alexis will assume I stayed the night because of the storm."

"Well, we can hope that the storm will be over tomorrow and we can head back to the road to look for help. Someone will be along at some point."

"Right," he said, grabbing another log and placing it carefully onto the blaze. The fire had warmed the room nicely, but because the wood was so dry, it burned fast. "Last one for tonight. We can't go to sleep with the fire roaring."

Unwittingly, she darted a glance to the bed she'd put sheets on. How in the hell were they going to make it through the night without things getting awkward?

He followed her gaze. "Don't worry. I can sleep here in the chair."

"But you'll freeze," she said.

"Let's not worry about that now. Want to work some more on the puzzle?" he asked.

She shook her head. "My eyes hurt from staring at the pieces in the low light." She walked back to the table and picked up the wine bottle and poured herself another glass. Then she sank back into the chair, tucking the blanket around her. "Tell me about being a firefighter."

"What's there to say? It's a job."

Emma tilted her head. "Not to you."

Erik's lips twitched. "Yeah, I love what I do. Nothing's better than pitting yourself against nature and winning."

"Never thought about it like that. Must be a high."

"To an extent, but there are plenty of boring days when we sit around the firehouse with nothing to do. It's feast or famine for an adrenaline junkie like me." He popped up, eyeing the trunk serving as a bedside table for a useless lamp.

"What?"

"Did you check that trunk?"

Emma shook her head. "Guess I didn't think about it."

Erik rose and walked over, setting the old lamp on the floor. One good kick to the flimsy lock and he had it unlatched. He opened the lid.

"Score," he said, lifting up a bottle of golden amber. "Tequila."

Emma hopped up and padded over to the treasure trove Erik had unearthed.

"Here's a pack of playing cards and poker chips. And—" he lifted up a box "—some condoms."

Emma took them from his hand. "So tequila and condoms. What did the former owners use this place for anyway?"

Erik lifted out a stack of magazines. They were an assortment of *Penthouse*, *Juggs* and *Hustler*. "I'm thinking whoever they are, they had some teenage sons."

"Well, thank goodness," Emma said, taking the tequila and the pack of cards. "We have a drinking alternative."

"What? You don't want the 1999 July issue of *Juggs*, too?" Erik cracked, dumping the magazines back in the trunk. "There's also some chewing tobacco, a pack of smokes and a box of peanut butter crackers. They expired in 2006 but I'm seriously thinking about eating some."

"They'd go great with the wine," Emma joked, setting the half bottle of tequila on the table along with the playing cards. "Or tequila."

Erik joined her, eyeing the barely put-together puzzle. "You want to adios Moby Dick?"

"If we do, we can play cards."

"Strip poker?" Erik asked, his eyes glinting naughtily.

This was her chance to flirt back, to let him know she wasn't opposed to dropping her clothes and making the best of a bad situation.

But did she want to go there with him? Sure, she'd wanted him only forever and a day, but if they got nasty, there was no undoing it. They'd have that between them forever. And that might get rough since both Emma and Alexis had moved within thirty miles of each other. More than likely she'd not go another seven years without seeing Erik.

"Well, if I had known we were going to play that, I wouldn't have drunk so much wine. I need my wits about me or I'll end up as naked as the day I was born."

"More wine?" he asked.

"You're a naughty man, aren't you?" she teased.

"You say that like it's a bad thing." Erik opened the warped puzzle box and slid the pieces inside, clearing the table. Then he removed the cards from the box and started shuffling them expertly. "And I will give you this one warning. While you're talking about Milton and Chaucer, I'm playing Mexican Sweat with the fellows at the firehouse. So if we go the strip route, you will be naked."

His blue eyes sparkled and he looked even more insanely attractive than normal. He'd skipped shaving that morning and now his face looked gruff and sexy. "You know I can't resist a challenge."

"My gain then because I'm betting you look spectacular naked."

Emma smiled. "Maybe you'll get to find out." She opened the tequila, not because she needed liquid courage at the moment. Okay, maybe she did a little. She wasn't like his sister who bought men drinks when they were at bars and dressed in tight dresses that showed off her curves. Emma had always been the more cautious of the two friends, but one thing she knew, she could hang with any man in the bedroom. "Now, what are we playing?"

Erik rattled off some game she'd never played, going

over the rules. Then they played a practice hand that he easily won.

"Give me another practice round…and another shot. Then we play for real." Emma said, feeling the warmth of the Jose Cuervo all the way down to her toes. Her tongue felt a bit thicker, her thighs tingly.

"You sure you want to do this?" he asked.

Something told her this wasn't just about the game. He knew what tequila, strip poker and a box of condoms could get them. He was giving her a way out, as only a guy like Erik could do.

Emma shrugged. "It's nearly a blizzard out there and we have to stay warm someway."

"That's usually not by taking your clothes off."

"Who said I'm taking my clothes off anyway," Emma said, giving him her best card-shark grin. "Deal me in, fireman."

AN HOUR LATER, Erik was down to his Calvin Kleins.

Emma, however, had only lost her pants. Even the fluffy wool socks stayed on her feet. And damn if she didn't look sexy in that sweater and fluffy socks.

"How did this happen?" he asked, truly baffled. He was good at poker. Really good. "You must be the luckiest woman I've ever met."

"Or really good at five-card draw," she said as she shuffled the cards and eyed his naked chest. "And from where I'm sitting, the view is very nice."

"Oh, now the cardsharp gets flirty," he said, lifting the tequila and taking a swig.

"Hey, I sang a burlesque tune when you took off your pants," she said.

And she had. Her green eyes had sparkled like emeralds in the light of the fire as she *ba-ba-ba-da-dummed* him as he unbuttoned his Levi's and shimmied out of them.

"I want you to know my feet are freezing," he said.

"Just one more hand," she teased, wiggling her eyebrows.

He nodded, hoping like hell he could keep his boxers on. Already he'd had an embarrassing thickening of his cock when she tugged off her leggings and again when she'd licked her lips. He felt like one of the boys who'd no doubt flipped through those girlie magazines. Horny as hell for Miss Emma Rose.

He dealt the hand. Emma rearranged the cards in her hand several times, frowning and making a moue with her pretty lips. "Hmm, I'm going to give these two and get two more."

He slid two cards from the deck and handed them to Emma then discarded three from his hand and took three new cards for himself.

He looked at his hand and nearly shouted hallelujah. A flush. "You in or out?"

Emma took five poker chips from the stack in front of her. "In."

Was she bluffing? No way could she beat him this time. That sweater was coming off. Or the socks. Please let it be the sweater. Please.

"You?" she asked.

He picked up ten chips, one that had the eye of the whale. "I'm in."

"Show me what you got," Emma said.

Erik laid down his cards, spreading them with flourish. "Boo-yah!"

"Oh, wow, that's really good," she said, her eyes widening.

"Yeah, so don't cry when you take off that pretty little top of yours."

Emma spread her cards. "But I think I'll keep it on."

She had a fucking straight flush.

"No," he said, shaking his head. "No freaking way."

Emma grinned. "Hey, you dealt me those cards, and now I will take my prize. Off with the boxers."

Erik stood. "Are you cheating?"

"Absolutely not. I'm lucky, I suppose, so give me my prize, big boy," Emma said, clapping her hands like an empress.

He had to wonder if this was really Emma or Jose Cuervo talking because she was so, so, so different from the put-together, reserved woman he'd observed the day before. It wasn't that she came across as the shy-virgin type…just not a woman who would clap her hands and order him to remove his drawers.

"Are you sure?" he said, hooking his thumbs into the waistband of his boxers.

Emma only hesitated slightly before nodding. "Yeah, I want those cute little hearts to hit the floor."

Yeah, he had on the heart boxers his ex-girlfriend had given him a few years back. Not the most manly of underpants, but they were comfy.

"Okay," he said, jerking the waistband down.

Right at the moment he was about to clear his junk, the door to the cabin flew open.

Emma screeched as the door slammed into the wall,

making the cabin shudder. A gust of wind roared in extinguishing the candles and blowing the fire wildly, making embers and ash fly out of the grate.

"Shit," Erik yelled, not only because the wind was icy as shit, but also because embers from the fireplace scattered across the floor. "Get the door, Em!"

He lunged toward the fireplace, grabbing the puzzle box lid and slapping at the glowing embers that had scattered across the wooden floor.

"Holy crap," Emma said, pushing against the door, finally getting it closed. The busted lock had failed against the storm. Snow had spilled into the doorway. "I can't get it to stay."

Smacking the last of the burning embers, he stood and grabbed one of the kitchen chairs and wedged it underneath the doorknob, sealing the door and preventing it from blowing open again. "Thank goodness it opens inward. This should not only keep the storm from scaring the shit out of us again, but also slow down the chain-saw murderer who could show up while we're sleeping."

"Oh, thanks for making me feel safer," Emma joked, slumping against the door. "And now my poor wool socks are wet and I missed my reward for winning at poker. Did you plan that?"

Erik laughed. "Yeah, I have secret powers."

"Exactly what I was trying to find out with the removal of your undies." She sighed, a twinkle in her eyes.

"I can still shuck them," he said.

She shook her head, making her honey waves tumble seductively. Or maybe it just seemed seductive because neither one of them was wearing pants.

"Nothing like a windchill of five below and a pair of cold wet socks to sober a girl up. Keep your hearts on, big boy," she said, moving past him, snapping the band of his underwear.

And damn, if that wasn't the sexiest thing a woman had done to him in a long time.

So confident, so breezy…and it had nothing to do with the wind that had just blown through.

"You want to play some blackjack or something?" he asked, moving back to the table where Emma perched on the arm of the tweed chair, tugging off her socks. "Hey, if I knew that could get you out of your socks, I would have summoned the wind earlier."

She smiled and said, "So, do I get some burlesque music?"

"Only if you do it sexy," he joked as he tugged on his shirt and jeans. He found one of his socks on the back of the chair, the other near the fireplace.

"I'm not sure you can pull polka-dot fuzzy socks off in a sexy manner," she said.

"So blackjack?"

"Actually, I'm tired," she said, eyeing her suitcase. "I brought some flannel pajamas and extra socks. Just going to slip into the bathroom and put them on. And brush my teeth."

"Oh, sure." He didn't have anything to change into. Not even any deodorant to freshen up with or a toothbrush.

"Uh, I have an extra toothbrush you can use if you want. I always carry an extra in my toiletry bag. Unfortunately, I don't have anything for you to sleep in. Unless you like lacy lingerie."

"You have that with you?" he asked, his mind immediately flipping to the image of Emma in pink silk and lace. A most delicious fantasy.

"No. That was a joke, silly." Emma grabbed her suitcase and rolled it behind her to the tiny bathroom.

Erik dashed the kinky vision from his mind. He had to if he was going to survive the night with her without giving in to something that probably wasn't a good idea. After all, he couldn't seduce his sister's BFF, could he? Of course, after their game of strip poker, he wasn't so sure he'd be the one doing the seducing. Miss Emma Rose held her own. Still, where would they go from there? Emma wasn't the kind of girl a guy had a one-night stand with. Yet maybe it didn't have to be a one-night thing, maybe…

He looked up to find her staring at him with a quizzical expression. "Uh, you go ahead and get ready. I'll put another log on to give us some heat. That gust of wind made it too cold in here."

"Okay, thanks," she said, disappearing into the bathroom.

Closing his eyes, he sucked in a breath. He needed to get ahold of himself and remember they were in a dicey situation. Sure, things could be worse. They had found shelter from the storm and had some food…if cookies and chocolates counted. Not to mention a nice fire and a place to bed down. But still, if things deteriorated with the weather or if no one came to find them, they could be in trouble.

Before stoking the fire, he grabbed the large pot

he'd spied under the sink and wiped it out. Filling it with water, he took it to the hearth and set it as close as possible to the fire. It was too late to wash tonight, but some lukewarm water for a spit-shine bath might be good in the morning. By the time Emma emerged from the bathroom, he had the fire crackling once again.

"Feels much better in here," she said, lugging her suitcase behind her. She wore mint-green pajamas with puppy dogs frolicking on them. It was a firm reminder that this was the kid who'd hung out at his house wearing flannel shirts and ripped jeans, braces flashing when she gave a rare smile. Emma wasn't a sex kitten…even if she'd behaved like one.

"Nice puppies," he joked.

Her cheeks pinked. "Yeah, they're silly but warm."

"And new fluffy socks."

She lifted her foot and twisted it back and forth. "Only the latest in fuzzy haute couture."

She joked but she looked nervous. Like a patient awaiting the dentist. Something about it was endearing. "You know I'm not going to pounce on you."

Pressing a hand to her cheek, she said, "Oh, jeez. Give me some credit. I know you're not interested in me that way. I'm your sister's friend. You said yourself that I'm like family. It's just weird to think about sleeping with you."

"For one thing, we're *sleeping* together. Not having sex. Think of it as a survival thing and not a big deal." Much. He knew that it would be hard not to touch her when they climbed beneath the scratchy wool blankets, especially since they'd already been a little naughty by shooting tequila and playing strip poker. Who did that with someone he professed to be like his sister?

But she wasn't his sister, was she?

And she was no longer that little girl who stared at him with yearning eyes.

"But don't fool yourself into thinking that I don't think about how you'd have looked in your undies. You're a beautiful woman who is *not* my sister. I'm really pissed I dealt myself shitty cards."

The darkening of her pink cheeks had nothing to do with the warmer room. "Oh."

"So where's that extra toothbrush?" he asked.

5

Emma sank onto the bed while Erik took a turn in the bathroom.

Oh, come on, silly. It's no big deal. It's like sitting next to someone on the train. Except you're lying down. In your favorite dog pajamas.

Minutes before, she'd been warmed by tequila and wine, feeling a bit saucy and bold. That girl didn't care if Erik lay next to her. That girl wanted him next to her. So why was she having such misgivings?

Because a gust of wind cooled her ardor?

Or because she was truly afraid of herself?

That image of Erik standing before her, sliding his boxers down had imprinted in her mind. It was like a sexy GIF that kept repeating, revving her up. Making her want to see more. Do more with the guy she'd dreamed about her entire junior year of high school... all because of that one summer night.

She'd seen him in the Mathesons' pool with a girl.

Sleeping over at Alexis's was a weekly deal in the summer. Erik had dropped out of the Air Force Academy and was in the middle of firefighter training. He'd moved back to his parents' house to save money, but he was rarely around. But one weekend the Mathesons had gone to Vegas, leaving Alexis at home with Erik. He'd been sidelined. Rather than go out, he'd brought home the fun. In the form of one Whitney Kellogg. The beachy blonde had been the head cheerleader at Pine Ridge Academy and made wearing short shorts and knotted plaid shirts that showed her tight belly an art form. With more curves than a mountain road, the perky Whitney was the antithesis of Emma.

All weekend Whitney had perched on the arm of Erik's chair, swigging beer and laughing with the most annoying bray. She'd touched him all the time, too. But then Saturday night, Emma had padded into the kitchen to get some markers for the project she and Alexis were working on and she'd seen them in the pool.

The moon had been full that night, framing the two lovers in the water. Erik stood in the middle of the pool, kissing Whitney and untying a string bikini that looked like a rubber band trying to hold back toddlers at a playground. The fact it hadn't already snapped and rendered Erik unconscious was a miracle in itself. But now he was intentionally taking it off. And Emma couldn't look away.

It was like a car wreck—visceral, horrible and oddly fascinating.

His lips had traveled down Whitney's jaw to her neck, as his hand slid up to cup the gargantuan boob that had escaped the constraints of the bikini.

And pervy Emma had stood there, watching, wondering what it felt like…to have his hands touch her there, to have his mouth slide down and—

She had turned away, knowing she couldn't continue to watch them do it in the pool.

But at the same time, she'd been so turned on. Not by vapid Whitney of the Big Boobs but by the sensuality of Erik. He hadn't been like dorky Tyler McMurty who'd tried to feel her up in the church van with not so much as a how-do-you-do. No, Erik knew what he was doing. He was like a guy in a movie, gorgeous, sexy and knowledgeable.

And so she'd become obsessed with him that summer. Every time he was around, she couldn't keep her eyes off him. Alexis noticed, of course. Her friend noticed everything. She was a regular ol' Nancy Drew type. And she'd said things like "Stop looking at him like that. It's so gross."

But nothing about Erik was gross.

Actually, quite the opposite.

Erik Matheson became her ideal.

Now, the door opened and Erik emerged, still wearing a sweater and jeans. Disappointment at not getting another glimpse of the flesh she'd seen earlier that night filled her.

"Whew, that water was cold as hell," he said.

"I know. My teeth felt frozen."

"I set a pot of water by the fire. Figure tomorrow morning we'd light the fire again and it would get lukewarm enough to wash up with."

"Good thinking." She wondered if she should get up from the bed or fake being super sleepy and say goodnight. Those infernal crickets that always showed up when Erik was around started chirping and hopping in her belly.

"I'm going to sit here for a few minutes and let the fire get low. Want to make sure we're safe tonight."

"Okay, I guess I'll go ahead and go to bed," she said, rising and picking up the blanket she'd left on the chair. Another one lay folded on the kitchen counter and Erik had already tucked the third one around himself. With three blankets atop the faded sheets, they should be warm enough. She set about placing the blankets on the bed and fluffing her pillow while Erik sat staring thoughtfully at the fire. Her actions were a bit sloppy because she still felt the effects of the booze she'd consumed. She wasn't drunk, but maybe a little tipsy. The snap of cold wind earlier couldn't erase two glasses of wine and a shot of tequila. Or was it two shots of tequila?

With nothing else productive left to do, she slid into the double-size bed. The sheets were like ice and so she swished her fuzzy-socked feet back and forth to warm the bed, drawing his attention.

"Cold?" he queried.

"Freezing."

"Go ahead and warm my side, too."

"Fat chance," she said, cracking a smile.

"I always wondered what you and my sister did during all those sleepovers. Should I expect to get my hair highlighted and have a spontaneous pillow fight?"

Emma punched the pillow and sank onto it, ignoring the musty smell from no doubt being stored for too many years. "Guys have weird fantasies about that, but to tell the truth, most of the time we watched a movie or worked on class projects."

"Ah, I forgot what little nerds you were," he teased.

"Little nerds grow up to be successful women, thank you very much," Emma said, lifting her nose in the air and giving a sniff.

"Indeed you did," he said. "I'll try not to wake you when I slip into bed. I know it feels weird, but you're right. If I tried to sleep in this chair, I'd freeze once the fire died. We're big people. We can handle this, right?"

Maybe. When said out loud it made a good deal of sense. Body heat and all that, but the reality of the situation was they'd been flirting with each other all night. And though she had worn her bra under her jammies and he would no doubt still be dressed in some manner, they would be more intimate than they'd ever been.

And with the torch she'd always carried for him reignited, it wouldn't take much before she'd lose all rational thought. She was primed to go up in smoke for this firefighter.

"We can handle this. Good night, Erik."

He smiled. "Good night, Em. I had a lot of fun tonight. Maybe I should get stuck in snowstorms more often with you."

Emma lay back, pulling the covers to her chin, burrowing as best she could into the lumpy mattress. A broken coil prodded her, so she curled on her side, scooting to the right, leaving Erik the left side. At some point they'd brush against each other. There would be no way to prevent it. Erik was a decent-size guy and she wasn't exactly petite.

She wouldn't be able to sleep.

No way she'd be able to with her stomach doing loop-de-loops and feet cold as Popsicles.

Sighing, she flipped over onto her belly, a tried-and-proven way to relax herself. With the fire crackling and the bed finally growing warm with her body heat, she found herself sliding from thoughts of her evening with Erik to regret about her poor car and missing her parents' award presentation. Nothing that couldn't be fixed or remedied by a YouTube video that her brother had promised to post, but still a loss. And then there was the fact the roads might be too bad tomorrow. Alexis might not have received her text. But she'd be worried about Erik. She'd call both of them and not get an answer. Her friend wasn't the kind of girl to sit on her laurels. No, Alexis would send out the cavalry. And someone would find them tomorrow.

And then a fox appeared, sniffing the snow, making little paw prints.

And then she drifted off.

ERIK WATCHED THE fire until only a small flame remained and then he pulled the dusty fire screen in front of the hearth, assured that no small sparks would escape and ignite on the scraped wooden floors. The room was plenty toasty and he had to send a silent thank-you to the man who had built a one-room cabin rather than a much larger place. Easy to heat.

Emma breathed rhythmically letting him know she was asleep.

Which was good.

That's why he'd stayed awake. Oh, sure, the fire and all, but he knew he couldn't lie there with her awake, knowing that he wanted to do more than sleep. Knowing that she probably wanted the same thing.

Deal was, nothing about it was a good idea. Except the pleasure it would bring. He had no doubt they'd be good together. Beneath Emma's cool intellect burned a passionate, funny woman. But they were from two different worlds. She with her highbrow professor friends and he with his lowbrow good ol' boys at the station. The only opera they would consider watching would be *Days of Our Lives*. And that was only because Grant Teague claimed he had to be able to talk about it with his mother who was in assisted care and obsessed with the show. Erik suspected Grant was addicted to the show and needed a reason to watch.

And then there was his sister. Alexis loved Emma. Even when Alexis had moved away, she planned girls' trips with Emma and he knew they spoke daily. If things went south between him and Emma because they gave in to desire, there would be hell to pay. He didn't want Emma hurt. Hell, *he* didn't want to hurt. But he damn sure didn't want his sister up his ass about being a hound dog and messing with her friend.

So, yeah, he let Emma go to bed and waited for her to fall asleep. Might have been cowardly, but he knew it would be an added protection against anything happening between them.

Slowly he rose and walked to the bed. Emma lay on her side, waiting like a gift beneath his Christmas tree. Tawny strands of gold spilled off the pillow she'd punched into a ball. She looked angelic.

Yet he still wanted to gather her to him and slowly unbutton her puppy-dog jammies.

Tugging off his jeans, he lay them on the ransacked trunk filled with girlie magazines. Then he shucked off his sweater, leaving him clad only in his boxers, undershirt and socks. Not the sexiest of outfits, but he'd be way more comfortable.

Carefully he pulled the blankets back and eased ever so gently into the bed. Luckily his side was warm because of Emma's body heat. It took a minute for him to fully relax, mostly because the pillow was total crap and the sheets smelled like his aunt Marmie's house.

But then he caught the scent of the warm woman sleeping next to him. She wore some sultry perfume that smelled like a field of flowers and money all rolled up into one. And she snored softly. Nothing obnoxious, just little puffs of air.

He carefully rolled onto his side, turning his back to her and tucking up the covers. The bed was a bit hard and sprongy, but he'd slept on worse. Closing his eyes, he vowed to fall asleep.

But then she turned over and snuggled up to him, her hand inching across his waist. And that was all it took for his cock to twitch.

Jeez, what the hell. He reacted like some knock-kneed schoolboy who'd never gotten laid before. But obviously that part below his belt hadn't gotten the memo that nothing was going to happen.

"Mmm," she moaned, snuggling into him, tucking her legs up so they fit the back of his thighs, her warm breath penetrating the cotton of his undershirt.

"Emma?" he whispered.

"Mmm?"

"Nothing," he said, because if he asked her why

she'd cuddled up next to him, she'd withdraw. And if he had to sleep with a hard dick, he'd do it. Because the feeling of her pressed next to him was worth the blue balls he'd wake up with in the morning.

He let loose a sigh and stared at the rough-hewn wall. The low light from the fireplace tossed shadows against the grain.

Emma's hand flattened against his belly, moving ever so slightly, almost a caress.

Pure torture.

Her breathing changed and it was at that moment he knew she'd woken.

"Emma?" he whispered again.

"What?" she whispered back.

"You can't keep doing that."

"Doing what?" she whispered, her hand stilling.

He turned over.

She didn't move, her hand fell across his abdomen and her head dropped just beneath his shoulder. Sleepy green eyes met his gaze. "What are you doing?"

"Trying to stay warm," she whispered.

"Oh," he said, wrapping an arm around her and pulling her to him. She lifted her head onto his shoulder and even her knee crooked over his leg slightly. He set his hand on her shoulder, rubbing it to warm her. She felt plenty warm, but the fire had nearly died out and the insulation in the small cabin didn't look up to date.

Raising her hand, she set it on his chest.

"Your heart is beating fast."

No shit.

He was a hair's breadth away from rolling her onto her back and showing her just how much he wanted her. With every fiber of his being he wanted to sink inside her and lose himself in something so good. It took every ounce of strength he had to reach up and grab her hand. "Em, you're playing with fire. I have pretty good self-control, but just so you know, I'm on the edge, sweetheart."

"What if I want to go over the edge with you?" she asked, lifting her head slightly and studying him.

He couldn't see if she was being a tease or serious.

"Have you thought about what that would mean?"

"Yes, but no one will ever have to know, would they?" she asked, wriggling her hand from his grasp. She petted his T-shirt seductively. "I mean, we don't have to tell. It could be like a little secret. Like one of those things that happen at a party when you're drunk…and you never talk about it again. Pretend it away."

Briefly he closed his eyes because he really wanted to do as she suggested. Opening them, he said, "Can you handle that?"

"Sure I can," she said, but her words seemed hollow. As though maybe she wasn't the kind who could ever handle a true one-night stand, no matter how much she wanted to believe it. But was that his problem?

"I don't think—"

"Maybe you shouldn't think," she said, pressing a finger against his lips. "Thing is, Erik, I'm a big girl now, a big girl who knows what she wants. So you either want me or you don't. And honestly, you not wanting me might be ten times worse than you and I having crazy cabin-fever sex."

"Not want you?" he asked, finding it incredible she didn't already know how hot for her he was. "Here."

He grabbed the finger that had slid down to imprint the cleft of his chin and tugged her hand downward to the raging erection he'd had since she'd first draped her hand over his waist. Placing her hand on the length of himself, nearly coming at the contact of her fingers, he said, "Does that feel like I don't want you?"

"No, it doesn't," she said, fitting him to her palm.

"Oh, uh," he groaned, wrenching her hand away before he made a total mess of the sheets. Again, he wondered how she'd relegated him to a green boy, inexperienced to such a degree he ejaculated on first contact. "I think we better slow down, Miss Emma Rose."

"So are you going to warm me up, Matheson?"

He laughed and lifted himself on one elbow, pushing her back onto the creaky bed. "Oh, I'm about to see what lies beneath those puppies."

Emma laughed and brushed her hands across his forehead, capturing a loose lock and twisting it around her finger. "I knew these pajamas would drive you mad. That's why I left my fancy lingerie in the suitcase. I could see right away you were a dog man."

Erik looked at her face in the dying embers of the fire. Conviction sat in those emerald depths, in the set of her chin. He'd never known she was so stubborn. This Emma was no delicate flower waiting to be tended. This Emma was a woman who asked for what she wanted.

What she wanted was him.

And that was damned sexy.

6

EMMA COULDN'T BELIEVE she'd made the first move.

She'd slept for a good fifteen or twenty minutes while Erik waited on the fire. But when he'd sneaked into bed, she'd felt him…this time. A night ago, at his house, she'd been so unaware and so tired from moving, she hadn't felt him climb into bed. But tonight, she had a hyperaware thing going on. She'd thought about it for a few minutes, faking sleep.

Her mind kept flipping back to all those times she'd clammed up when he was around, tongue-tied and gauche. A girl who didn't think she was worthy of a stud like Erik. So many opportunities to talk to him, to flirt even, washed away because she was too afraid to be vulnerable. Even last night, when he'd climbed into his bed naked, she'd acted shy. But she wasn't that woman anymore, damn it.

She'd grown, gained her wings and thanks to Alexis, she had started asserting herself.

Okay, this was truly the bravest she'd ever been.

But when she'd thought about going back to the real

world, without taking the opportunity to be with Erik, she felt disappointed in herself. She knew he wanted her. And she wanted him. So what was the big deal? Fear that their virtually nonexistent relationship might be damaged? Fear that Alexis might get miffed?

No.

None of that was reason enough to pass up what she'd always dreamed about.

Being Erik Matheson's girl…for at least one night.

So now she lay beneath him, looking up at the sexiest man she'd ever seen—she lifted her hand and caressed his cheek.

"You're so damn beautiful, Emma," he said.

She couldn't see his eyes, but she felt him take her in. Her pulse sped up and her breathing amped. "Kiss me. Please."

Erik lowered his head and nipped her lower lip with his teeth. It was erotic, making her nipples harden and liquid heat pool inside her. Then ever so softly he traced her bottom lip with his tongue. "Mmm, you taste good, Em."

"I brushed," she whispered.

A flash of white teeth and then he lowered his head again. This time he pressed his lips against hers, light as an angel's kiss.

She moaned and lifted her head.

"Oh no, sweet girl. I want to take my time with you. I want to tease you, drive you crazy, until you beg. Will you beg me, Emma?"

Emma nearly lost her breath. She'd imagined Erik as her lover many times before, but she'd never guessed he'd be so…erotic. He wanted her to beg.

Well, she wanted him to make her beg.

Dropping her head back, she said, "Let's see what you can do."

He started unbuttoning the top of her flannel pajamas. "First I want to see you. Then I'll kiss you."

A slave to the desire unfurling inside her, she could only nod and watch him as he slowly unbuttoned, pausing at every button to deliver a kiss on her flesh as he peeled back each layer.

"Oh, you wanted to make it harder for me," he said, fingering her nipple through the lace of her bra. Emma inhaled audibly. "That's okay, sweetheart. I love a challenge."

Then he bent and sucked her nipple into the wet heat of his mouth.

"Ah," Emma said, arching toward him.

The devil laughed, nipping her with his teeth before releasing the rosy nipple.

Once the pajama top lay open, he reached for the drawstring of her pants. Tugging them, he gave but one command. "Lift."

Emma did as she was bid, raising her hips so that he could pull the flannel pants from her body. Languidly he tossed them toward the foot of the bed. Running a hand down one leg and back up the other, he boldly traced a finger through the damp lace at the juncture of her legs. "Oh, good girl. You're already so wet. Do you know what that does to me? Oh, I think you do, baby."

She reached for him, drunk with passion. She needed to touch him. Use her mouth on him. Something. Anything.

"No, no. There will be time for that later. Right

now, I have a mission. You remember what that was?" he asked.

Emma nodded.

"What?"

"You're going to make me beg," she whispered.

"Mmm-hmm," he said, lifting himself up and settling his body onto hers. His erection pressed against her thigh, a portent of what would come.

Then he started kissing her jaw, nibbling a little path down her neck, across her collarbone and back up to her lips.

Emma panted, no other way to put it. Liquid heat soaked her, and her lower pelvis ached to be filled. She could feel how wet she was, soaking her panties with slickness, permeating the air with the smell of arousal. She opened her mouth to say "please," but then remembered. She wanted the torture Erik seemed intent on providing.

Finally, he caressed her jaw, tugging it lower, opening her mouth to him. Then he pressed his lips to her, tenderness gone, as he plundered her mouth. She met him eagerly, kissing him back, tangling her tongue wildly with his. Her heart galloped and she felt nearly frenzied. She'd never felt this way. Never so out of control.

Instinctively she raised her hips, opening her legs. Erik took the hint and slid so he fit between them. Then he rocked his hips, allowing the rigid length to slide against her slick heat, driving her crazy.

One hand twined in her hair as he continued the onslaught on her mouth, his tongue parrying against hers, leaving her nearly sobbing for release. She'd never felt so out of control, so caught up in desire. Finally, he lifted his head and made his way down to her neck. His beard prickled her skin and it should have irritated, but instead it was another sensation vaulting her toward what she craved.

With one flick of his hand, he released the front clasp of her bra and cupped her breast.

"Ah, so, so pretty, Emma. Like small rosebuds," he said, capturing one peak with his teeth, biting softly before sucking her into the heat of his mouth.

"Oh, oh, yes, pl—" Emma groaned.

He lifted his head and quirked an eyebrow. She bit down on her tongue, making him laugh. "Close. Very, very close."

And then he bent his head again, giving equal attention to the other breast. Emma squirmed against him, enjoying the feel of his hardness sliding against her sensitive flesh. He did amazing things with his mouth. She'd never been so stimulated by her breasts.

His hand traveled down to her hip, stroking, squeezing, pleasuring her. And then his mouth was on hers again, and she knew by the way he kissed her that his control was on a short leash.

Their breaths mingled, soft pants of urgency.

Erik slid down the length of her body, bestowing a kiss on each tip of her breast before using his scruffy beard to tantalize her belly. He dropped little kisses down to her navel before slithering so he knelt between her legs.

Rising, he pulled his T-shirt off, revealing a chiseled torso. He had a fine sprinkling of hair across his chest that converged into a darker Y between his pecs.

The screeching-eagle tattoo swooped down from the left side of his chest, lending a roguishness to him. His waist was trim and stomach tight enough to show the hint of a six-pack. Emma had never been with a man so manly. He was like a lumberjack or a Viking…or just a superhot firefighter.

Lifting herself on one elbow, she reached out and traced a finger down his stomach, enjoying the way his flesh contracted. She hooked a finger in his boxers, which were tented from the large erection straining against the cotton. "My turn?"

"No." He smiled, capturing her hand and bending to bestow an almost courtly kiss on her wrist. "You haven't begged yet. So—" he pushed her back onto the subpar pillow "—I need to step up my game."

ERIK LOOKED AT Emma still tangled in her pajama top, lacy bra parted to reveal her perfect pink-tipped breasts, and felt something weird in his chest.

Yeah, he was hard as a baseball bat for her and had nothing more on his mind than making her scream his name, but still something struck him. As if the moment was somehow more than what it was.

So strange.

He pushed her back when she tried to rise again. "Later, okay. Right now, I need to taste you."

Lowering himself, he settled deeper under the covers. He slipped his hands beneath her perfect ass and pushed her up toward the creaking headboard. "Are you too cold?"

She shook her head, pretty emerald eyes wide and

riveted to him. He grabbed the abandoned pillow and handed it to her. "Use this."

Then he turned his attention back to that which drew him like steel to a magnet. He kissed a line across her belly, stopping every so often to nip at the lace. Then he nuzzled the plump flesh that covered her pubic bone, allowing the delicate silk to catch on his beard as he moved his face back and forth, inhaling her unique scent.

He clasped her knees and lifted them, pushing them back so she was more open to him. She still wore the fuzzy socks, which should have looked silly, but there was something erotic in half-dressed Emma spread before him. She squeaked, but her breathing increased and he knew she was turned on. "Hold your knees, baby. I'm going to be too busy to do it myself."

Emma did as she was told, holding her legs back, socked feet planted on the lumpy mattress. She looked like an offering to him.

Which, of course, she was.

Erik nuzzled her through the silk and lace, groaning when the slick damp fabric yielded the taste of her. Nothing turned a man on more than knowing how wet a woman was for him. Carefully, he used his finger to slide beneath the crotch, stroking the outside fold that was slick and oh-so perfect.

Emma moaned and her head hit the iron of the bed, but she didn't release her knees. And a second later, he felt her watching him as he licked her through her panties.

Another turn-on. He loved when a girl watched him go down on her.

Slowly he lifted the material, sliding it to one side, revealing what he'd been dying to get to. He'd wanted to make her beg, but he was near to begging himself at the sight and smell of her. He ground his cock against the bed, needing some sensation, some relief.

Then he traced a finger through her slick heat. Heaven.

"Oh, oh…" Emma sighed, her eyes never leaving his as he sucked his finger into his mouth.

It was an erotic move and it made her close her eyes. "Oh, Erik. I want more."

He watched her as he lowered his mouth toward the prize. Her mouth fell open as she panted and her eyes dilated. He paused right over the tight rosy bud he knew ached for him. And he blew on it.

"Oh, Erik. Oh, you have to…oh…"

He blew again, nearly losing it himself. "You know what you have to do."

Her eyes widened. "Please."

"As you wish," he said then closed his mouth over her clit and sucked.

"Ah," she said, thrusting her hips forward, rocking against him.

He let up on the pressure and used his tongue to stroke her. She tasted incredible, like turned-on woman, and it drove him mad. He increased the pressure and speed of his tongue and then he felt her tighten.

Her scream was the most satisfying sound he'd heard in forever. Her body shook, thighs closing around his head as she rode her climax out. He didn't stop the delicious torture. For one thing, he knew she needed more. For another, he was a selfish bastard who couldn't get enough of Miss Emma Rose's thighs locked around his ears, her honeyed treasure belonging only to him. To do with as he wished. He slid a finger inside her, nearly sighing at the sweet clenching heat of her. He crooked his finger, rubbing her G-spot as he returned his mouth to pleasuring her.

Again she tightened, and again she screamed as she came apart again, her body twisting, ass grinding into the sheets covered with faded forget-me-nots. He held her firm, preventing her from twisting away. Dampness had flooded her with her release and he relished the reward of his efforts. So he continued moving his finger inside her, sucking her clit lightly.

She came again.

Finally he felt a tug at his ears. "Stop, Erik. Please. I can't take any more."

He lifted his head, allowing the lace material to fall back into place. "Good?"

Emma fell back onto the pillows. "Oh, shit."

"I'm going to take that as a yes," he said, wiping her slickness from his mouth and sliding up to kiss her. She didn't shy away from the taste of herself, another mark in her favor. He loved a lusty woman, one who didn't pull back from adventure…from getting really down and dirty in bed.

"You wore me out," she said, brushing another kiss against his lips. "But it's time for *you* to beg, Mr. Matheson."

She pushed him back, rising to her knees, her pajama top still on but parted so her breasts teased him. The air was chilly, so her nipples were hard but her body felt warm enough. She kissed him, twining her arms around him, twisting her fingers in his hair. She kissed him in a way he would never have expected Emma to kiss him—hard, passionately and with wild abandon. Everything about her was so giving...so, so damned sexy.

Drawing back, she traced the ridge of his shoulder. "Are you cold?"

He shook his head. "Not after that. You are so gorgeous. Thank you."

She didn't look at him. Instead, she ran her fingers down his chest. "What for?"

"For not letting me talk myself out of this. I've never been so hot for someone before. You're driving me crazy, lady."

"Mmm," she said, leaning forward and flicking his nipple with her tongue before nipping him. He drew back with an inaudible hiss. But then he stilled himself as she dropped tiny kisses down his stomach, ringing his belly button, hooking her fingers in the waistband of his boxers.

Quickly she slid them down and his cock wagged out to greet her.

Wrapping a hand around his length, she looked up at him. "Very nice."

The pressure of her hand was such sweet torture, but her words of approval were an equal turn-on. She moved her hand slowly, teasing him. Then she cupped his balls, giving them a light squeeze. Erik nearly came right then and there.

"And since you had a taste, it's only fair, right?" she asked, but she didn't wait for permission. She bent, thrusting her ass deliciously into the air, and licked the tip of his cock.

"Ah," Erik breathed, reaching immediately for the golden hair that spilled against his thighs. He pulled it to one side so he could watch her mouth work him.

Grasping the shaft, she wrapped her hand around his rigid length and fastened her pretty mouth around the head of his cock. Slowly and confidently, she began to move.

"Oh, sweet mother of…" He couldn't finish his thought. His entire length was consumed by her and she knew what she was doing, giving pressure, lightening it, releasing her fingers to make a circle lubricated with her saliva, which gave a mind-numbing sensation.

Damned if Miss Emma Rose wasn't incredible at giving head.

He could feel his orgasm building, balls tightening.

It was as if she knew and she slowed her machinations, the pressure on his shaft lifting. She pulled her mouth from him and looked up. "Good?"

He nodded because he had no words and he didn't want to ejaculate yet. He wanted to sink inside her. Of course, as close as he was to coming, there wouldn't be much of an effort given.

Emma leaned forward and ran her tongue over the tip again. "You know what you have to say."

He almost laughed. But couldn't. "Please."

"Good boy," she said, taking him into her mouth again, wrapping her hand around his length, resuming the steady rhythm that had him thrusting his hips forward. The sensation built again, harder and stronger, and then he couldn't stop if he tried. He rode the lightning of his orgasm, pumping into her mouth, half horrified at himself, half out of his mind with pleasure.

Emma didn't stop working him, the torturous pleasure went on and on, making chill bumps ripple over his body. With one last grunt, he emptied himself fully.

She lifted her eyes and unwound her hand from his length. With light suction, she pulled her mouth from him and then scrambled off the bed. He collapsed backward onto the pillows, breathing hard, embarrassed that he couldn't control himself.

There was just something about Emma that made him lose all focus. All control. This wasn't supposed to happen, but there was no way he'd ever regret it.

Besides, they had some unfinished business that the box of condoms could help them with.

Emma came back wiping her mouth. He could smell the toothpaste. She paused at the side of the bed. "I don't swallow."

He started laughing. "Holy cow, woman. Get your sexy ass back in this bed."

Emma smiled and climbed into bed. She'd taken off her bra, but left the open pajama shirt on. Snuggling up, she pulled the blankets over them, straightening the tangle of the sheet as she did. Finally, she sank onto his chest. "That was incredible."

"Mmm-hmm," he said, twisting a length of her hair around his fingers. "Never could have imagined just how talented you were with that mouth."

"I'm a woman of many surprises."

He smiled. "Yes, you are."

She yawned.

"You're not planning on sleeping tonight, are you?"

She popped up. "Why? You have something better we can do?"

"Give me ten more minutes and I'll show you," he teased, dropping a kiss on her stubborn chin. Funny how he'd never noticed that before. Such a thrill to learn the reticent Emma was a freakin' wildcat in the sack.

She lifted herself and kissed him. "Only ten minutes?"

"What can I say? You make me feel like a teenager. Short recovery time."

"This is crazy, but I'm so glad it happened. I've wanted you only forever."

Erik's heart leaped. Which was weird. This wasn't about anything other than one night of crazy sex, right? Still, he kept getting these feelings about Emma. She was so familiar, yet a mystery to him. Gorgeous, smart and sexy, Emma was nearly the perfect woman. She didn't fill silence with noise and she was patient. Still, she didn't let anything stand in her way. He had such admiration for her and at the same time he wanted to consume her. "Have you?"

"Ever since I saw you making out with Whitney in the swimming pool."

"Whitney?"

"Kellogg. She was the head cheerleader. Sort of easy."

"Oh, yeah. Had a big set of jugs?"

"That would be the one."

"You saw me and her making out?"

Emma nodded. "Up until that point, I had always thought you were cute. You know, in that benign way teen girls do. But then I watched you in the pool. Oh, I'm not a pervert. I didn't stay long, but I saw enough to make me feel different about you. I wanted your mouth on me, your hands untying my bikini top. It was like a hunger awoke, and I guess it never really faded."

"Wow," he breathed, stroking her face, running a finger over her bottom lip. "I never knew."

"I'm not like Alexis. I don't usually reveal my feelings. I can't believe I'm being this honest with you now. I guess things just feel different."

"I'm so glad you are. This is so strange, but so wonderful. And we're not finished, sweet Emma. There's so much more I want to do to you. I feel spellbound, like I'm not even me. But then I am, and I want you with everything I am."

7

His words made her heart ache.

I want you with everything I am.

It was the sort of thing every girl wanted to hear from the guy she'd worshipped for years. Oh, sure, she'd had boyfriends and hoped for love with them. Erik seemed unattainable, totally off her radar. Until two days ago.

Then he was on it.

Very much on it.

"Should I fetch the box of Magnums?"

He smiled, pulling her down for another kiss. "I think I'm ready," he murmured against her lips.

"Let's see," she said, sliding her hand down to clasp his stirring cock. "Not quite, but I can do something about that."

"Oh no. You nearly killed me a few minutes ago." He curved an arm around her, pulling her to him, capturing her mouth in a sweet kiss that literally curled her toes that were still in the fluffy polka-dot socks.

He pulled her hand from his crotch. "Let's take this one slow, baby."

Erik rolled her over onto her back, tugging her hip so she slid beneath him. Propped on one elbow, he proceeded to kiss her thoroughly. By the time he'd finished and moved to the sensitive shell of her ear, her pulse galloped and a new achiness had awoken in her pelvis.

She stroked his shoulders, enjoying the feeling of his smooth, strong arms, as she allowed her nails to trail back and forth across the span of flesh. Goose bumps emerged and he moaned with pleasure. Against her leg, his erection grew harder, making sweet heat pool in her belly.

Moving down to her breasts, he lazily loved her, pausing to kiss, suckle and tease.

Finally he lifted himself, shifting over to drag the trunk toward the bed. Cool air rushed in between them, but seconds later, he was back, covering her, warming her. In his hand he held a condom package.

She took it from him and he kissed her once again, his hands stroking the length of her body, pausing to roll a nipple or tease her belly button. Pulling back from him, she used her teeth to rip the package, withdrawing the circular condom. "I can put this on with my mouth," she teased.

He closed his eyes and breathed deeply. "I think you better use your hand if you want this to last."

Giving him a mischievous smile, she placed the condom on the head of his cock and slowly rolled it down his length. He was the perfect size for her. Big and thick, but not porno monstrous. She loved the feel of him in her hand, even with the condom on.

Erik pushed her back and settled himself between her legs, sliding himself back and forth in the slickness of her body. His lips caught hers again and he whispered, "I could fall in love with a woman like you."

He lifted her thighs and tilted his hips before sliding inside her, burying himself to the hilt.

"Oh," she breathed as he filled her. It wasn't just the physical act of taking her, but the words. Again, his honeyed words wrapped round her, sweet nothings whispered in the act of passion. But somehow they seemed to be more. She wanted them to be. She needed them to fill the small box of hope inside her heart.

He began to move, eyes closed.

The sensation was so good, she closed hers, too. She lost herself in the moment, his hands clasping her hips, his breathing ragged in her ear as he dropped tiny kisses sporadically on the shoulder that had slipped out of the pajama top. Emma lifted her knees, hugging his lean hips, and rode with him toward that beautiful pinnacle.

"So…so…" he panted, kissing her jaw before capturing her lips again. "So good."

He increased the tempo and she lifted her bottom so he touched that spot. Inside, she felt the tension build, gathering deep in her pelvis. She surrendered to it, letting it rip through her, washing over her with tingling warmth.

Seconds later, Eric joined her, his guttural cry in her ear as he pumped into her.

Finally, he collapsed atop her, breathing hard, kissing her shoulder, whispering things about how good she was, how tight, how perfect, how sexy. Emma wrapped her arms around him, holding him close to her.

Their hearts beat together as time slowed and the chill around them permeated.

Erik lifted his head and studied her.

"What?" she asked after several seconds.

"I'm amazed by this. Sounds silly but I never planned on feeling so...so...right with you."

"Why not? Because of Alexis?"

Erik swallowed. "Maybe. I don't know. I guess I just never imagined that you were a possibility. I always liked you, but never allowed myself to see you as anything other than what you were to me—a cute friend of my sister's. But you're so much more and it's like stumbling over a winning lottery ticket. Where there once was not much, now there is such possibility."

Emma watched him, wondering what he meant.

She'd said this was supposed to be a one-night thing, a crazy act they'd never discuss again, but maybe he saw there could be something more. She wanted that. Oh, how she wanted that, but she didn't want to be that kind of girl. The kind that said one thing to get what she wanted but changed the game to suit herself later. She'd never press him for any kind of relationship if he saw this only as a hookup.

Erik withdrew from her, reaching down to deal with the spent condom. This time he was the one padding to the bathroom. Seconds later, he returned, handing her a length of the precious toilet paper so she could do cleanup. Afterward, Erik tugged on his socks and T-shirt, handed her the pajama bottoms and pulled her to him. Flipping the blankets back atop them, he sank into the lumpy mattress, settling her beside him.

After a few minutes of contemplating the darkness, Emma asked, "What did you mean by all that?"

"Hmm?"

"That there is 'possibility'?"

"Oh, well…" He hesitated as if he wasn't even sure what he'd meant. "I know we kinda agreed that this would be a one-time thing, but…"

"You want more?" She took the hope out of her voice. She didn't want to sway him, didn't want him to know how much she wanted him to say yes.

"I don't know, Em," he said, kissing her forehead. "I think right now we should enjoy what we have. We can talk about how this will shake out later."

In the light of day.

She knew how that worked. In the intimate darkness of the now-not-so-cozy cabin, what they had was one thing. Come morning, with the bright light creeping in between the gingham curtains and the nearly empty bottle of tequila staring them in the face, it would be quite another. Neither would have to take a walk of shame, but no doubt he'd regret doing his little sister's BFF.

"Go to sleep, baby," he said, kissing her softly.

His words had the intended effect and she closed her eyes and snuggled deeper into his side. Her thoughts were a tangle of possibility, hope, embarrassment, but no shame. She wouldn't change the amazing night she'd had with Erik. Even if the morning brought a painful resolution.

Softly, fatigue crept on her and with the warmth of the man next to her, she began to fall into sleep.

The last thought she had before she checked out was that she didn't think she'd ever come so many times in one night.

ERIK WOKE BEFORE Emma to weak light streaming through the crack of the curtains. The cabin still looked shrouded in darkness and part of him longed to burrow under the covers with Emma, shutting out the world.

But the cabin was ice cold.

Carefully he slipped from beneath her arm and slid out of bed, grabbing the jeans he'd discarded the night before. Quick as a cat, he used the john, brushed his teeth with the extra toothbrush and built a fire, wishing like hell they had some coffee. He puffed into his hands while he waited for the fire to catch and once it had, he hotfooted it back to the bed, shucked off his jeans and climbed in next to Emma.

"Oh," she said when he wrapped his arm around her. "You're so cold."

"Had to start a fire. It's freezing in here, but you're warm as toast, babe," he said, bundling her into his arms.

"Ah, you feel like ice," she squealed, pushing him away.

"Come on, I need your warmth," he said, hauling her against him.

This time she didn't struggle. Instead, she rubbed her hands up and down his arm, trying to warm him. Generous Emma. His heart beat harder in his chest as he thought about her last night.

She'd been spectacular.

He'd been with a lot of women. He wasn't a man whore, but he rarely turned down the company of a beautiful, willing lady. And he couldn't remember ever being so blown away. The sex had been hot as hell. But not only that, they'd had fun together, putting together a puzzle, shooting tequila and teasing one another. Thing was, he genuinely liked being with her, which surprised him. He thought he'd had her pegged as an uppity intellectual, but Emma had an earthy charm, a whimsical sense of humor and a giving nature. She was a dream package of a woman.

"Warmer now?" she asked.

He gathered her in tight to him, resting his chin atop her head. "Perfect."

"I wish I had a cup of coffee." She sighed against his chest.

He laughed. Great minds do think alike. "Can I interest you in half a glass of wine or tequila?"

"Ugh," she groaned.

"Oh, come on. You know what they say about tequila."

"It makes your panties drop?"

"Oh, is that what it is?" he joked, twisting a finger in her hair. "I thought it was something about not remembering things."

"Is that what you wish? Not to remember?" Her voice had grown serious and his remark from last night came back to peck at him. He hadn't meant to suggest they had to follow up their night of kick-ass sex with something more. Hadn't she been the one to suggest that it could be like one of those bizarre encounters both parties blame on the liquor and loneliness? He didn't want to change the rules when she'd been so careful to brand it as a onetime thing.

"No. I will always cherish getting stranded with you in this cabin. And so you know, we're still stranded, so how about—" he slid his hand up her thigh, relishing her flesh even through the soft flannel "—we not waste this fabulous lumpy bed with the broken springs?"

He lowered his head to kiss her.

But her hand stopped him. "I want to brush my teeth first."

"Don't worry. A little morning breath won't hinder me."

"Nope. You brushed yours. Besides, I can still taste the booze." She sat up and gave a little shiver. "Be right back."

Erik flopped back, smiling as he watched her run to the small bathroom off the main room, teeth chattering. He liked her pluck…and that she was thoughtful about hygiene. It took him back to last night and her hopping from the bed after giving him the most excruciatingly wonderful pleasure with her pretty mouth.

In less than a minute she ran back, jumping into bed, her body shaking. "Holy Moses, it's so cold."

"The fire will get us warm…but first let's make our own heat."

Emma giggled.

"What? Too cheesy?"

"Yeah, but I like cheesy sometimes. Come on, big boy. Come light my fire." She curved a hand around his neck and tugged him to her.

"Isn't that a song?" he murmured, dropping kisses on lips that tasted of toothpaste.

"Mmm-hmm," she moaned, opening her mouth to him. He started unbuttoning her pajama top, dying to see her breasts in the faint light of day. In the flickering light of the dying fire, they'd been so perfect, but he needed to see the pink-tipped breasts, taste them once again.

When he reached the last button, he broke the kiss, pulling the covers back so he could see her. It had grown lighter in the past half hour and now the darkness had been replaced by the grayness of dawn.

He had been right. Her breasts were perfect, gently sloped, fuller on bottom than top, the nipples a dusky pink. They were hard for him, begging him to taste them.

So he obliged, softly kissing the one closest to him, sucking her into his mouth.

Emma hissed, her head falling back on the pillow. "Oh, Erik. That's so nice."

"Is it, baby?" he said, turning his attention to the other breast, pressing her back onto the bed.

Emma nodded, her eyes closing as he worshipped the beauty before him. He traced a finger down her belly, which was flat and much smaller at the waist than he remembered. Slowly he slipped a hand into her pajama pants, burrowing beneath her panties to cup her sex. She was slick and ready for him.

He allowed his middle finger to slip inside to the sweet dampness and, finding her clit, he began to make tiny circles.

"Oh," she said, arching her back before thrusting her hips upward.

"Easy, babe," he said, allowing her nipple to slide from his mouth. "I want to watch you come. Will you come for me, Emma?"

"If you keep doing that," she said, opening her eyes to watch him.

At that moment, he knew he needed to see all of her. He slipped his hand from her and lifted himself slightly so he could slide her pajama pants down past her knees. Then he did the same with her panties.

"Oh, sweetheart, you're so pretty," he said, feathering through the trimmed hair covering her. He parted her folds with his fingers, catching a peek of the small bud. He started the circles again, shifting his gaze from her sweet womanhood to the pleasure on her face.

"Oh, heavenly days. Don't stop. Don't you dare stop," she groaned.

"Not even if a herd of buffalo stampeded," he said, quickening his movements, pausing only to move down, slipping his finger inside her before returning to her clit again. He loved the feel of her—so warm, wet and womanly. It was addictive.

Emma moved her hips, her eyes screwed closed as her breath came in short pants. Then suddenly her entire body tightened.

"Ah," she moaned, her hands slamming down to clutch the sheets as she rode her orgasm.

He didn't let up. Watching her come was also addictive and he wanted to see it again. And again. And again. Making love to Emma was one of the best things he'd done in forever. He wanted to savor the sight of her coming undone, the smell of their passion, the feel of her body clenching around him.

"Oh, oh, please," she panted, sliding her hands up to cup her own breasts. That sight refueled him and he slid his finger inside her, moving rhythmically, finding that sweet, sweet spot that would launch her anew.

And it did.

A new round of tightening, legs shaking as she found her release again.

"Don't stop," she yelled, thrusting her hips in time with him, feet planted, mouth open. "What are you doing to me?"

"No, what are you doing to me?" he asked, meaning it. This gorgeous woman was splendidly wrought, made to be played by his hands.

Suddenly she pushed his hand from her body. "I want you. Inside me." She reached for his waistband.

"You don't have to ask twice." He shucked off his boxers and reached for the box of condoms. She tried to take the package from him, but he brushed her hand away. Jabbing on the condom, he rolled it down his length and nudged her legs apart so he could settle into the sweetest place imaginable.

Slowly he inserted the head of his cock, sighing at the tight warmth. He bit his lip, trying to go slow, wanting to savor every inch of pleasure. Emma had other ideas. She clamped her thighs around his hips and lifted her ass, taking him all the way inside her.

"Yes…" She sighed.

He started moving again, so slow it almost hurt.

"No, no," she said, smacking his ass. "Harder, please."

Smiling, he tossed his intentions aside and gave her

what she wanted. Several minutes later he found his own release.

Their breaths and cries of pleasure twisted together in the oldest song known to man.

And it was so good.

8

THE LIGHT OF morning had not brought regrets. On the contrary, it had brought more of the fantasy Emma had wrapped herself in. She wasn't tugging it off until she had to.

She lay twined in Erik's arms, totally sated. "That was nice."

"Nice? Don't you mean spectacular?"

She gave him a little pinch. "You think highly of your abilities, don't you?"

He looked at her and crooked an eyebrow, making her laugh.

"Okay, okay, I can honestly say it was spectacular," she said, giving him a kiss.

Just as she was breaking the kiss, the front door slammed open, breaking the chair, sending it careening across the worn floor.

She screamed, clutching the covers to her. Erik jumped out of bed and grabbed the lamp he'd set beside the trunk, raising it like a weapon. At first she thought the wind had gusted hard enough to once again blow the door open. But then she saw the man…and the gun.

"Get your hands up," the intruder yelled, stepping into the cabin holding a shotgun.

She didn't want to put her hands up. If she did, her boobs would be out there for all to see. Tucking the covers under her arms, she pressed her upper arms to her sides and held up her hands. Erik dropped the lamp and the ceramic base shattered on the floor.

A large man wearing a brown cowboy hat and a fluffy khaki ski jacket with a star attached strolled in. Removing his mirrored glasses, he made a face. "Just what in the hell is going on here? You know you're trespassing, don't you?"

Erik kept his hands up. "We had an accident up on the highway yesterday and we couldn't find help."

"So you broke into my cabin?" an older man asked, stepping forward.

"Well, our car was dead and neither of our cell phones worked," Erik said, gingerly lowering his arms while eyeing the shotgun still pointed at them. "We stayed on the highway for a long time, but no one came. We saw the reflective marker on the highway and found this place."

"We'll pay for repairs to the door," Emma added, sliding her eyes to the shattered lamp. "And the lamp."

The deputy turned to the older man, who had a bristly mustache and wore hunting coveralls. "You gonna press charges, Walt?"

Walt looked at Erik and then looked at her. A knowing gleam appeared in his eyes. "Ah, hell. I can't press charges against people taking shelter from the storm.

Gave us nearly a foot last night. Besides it's Christmas and all."

"Thank you," Emma said, looking over to Erik, who looked like a man with his hand caught in a cookie jar. Yeah, her cookie jar.

"We would appreciate that, sir," he said finally.

"Ah, hell, this place ain't been used in years," Walt said, stepping in and closing the door. "No electricity or anything. If you'd have come a quarter mile more, you would have hit my spread. This here was my groundskeeper's place back when I needed someone. Sold most my land but kept this old cabin. My boys always liked to have friends over to play cards, drink hooch and blow up stuff. So don't worry about the lamp. No loss there."

The deputy looked around and then resettled his gaze on them. "Why don't we let these two get decent and then I'll run them up to your house so they can call a tow truck."

Walt nodded. "Yeah, come on up to the house and I'll get you some coffee and a proper breakfast. Maria made enough muffins for Cox's army. I'll wait outside."

The deputy followed Walt out, closing the broken door.

Her heart raced and she felt sweaty despite the new chill in the air.

"You okay?" Erik asked, reaching for his jeans and pulling them on. The tender teasing was gone, replaced by something she couldn't put her finger on. Probably that whole light-of-day thing. Or the sober realization they'd stepped over a line they couldn't backtrack over. Or maybe it was just having a shotgun trained on him.

"I'm fine," she said, suddenly feeling shy about her nudity. Minutes before, she'd been crying his name, shattering in his arms. But now it felt sordid. She'd seen the look in those men's eyes. They knew what had gone down in the cabin last night. And it damn sure wasn't completing a puzzle.

"At least we don't have to go up to the highway and look for help. It came to us."

"Yeah," she agreed, reaching for the pajama top she'd shed earlier. She didn't want to bare her breasts. Silly, of course, but she felt so vulnerable. In the blink of an eye, Erik had gone from tender lover to a man ready to stride back into his regular world. "Guess I better go get my things out of the bathroom."

"The water in the pot should be warm enough to wash up a bit. I'll put it in the bathroom," he said, tugging on the sweater he'd left by the fire before lifting the pot.

Emma couldn't help it. She blushed. If anyone needed cleaning up, it was her. They'd had sex three—or was it four?—times. She needed a good long soak, but lukewarm water dipped from a pot would have to do.

She scrambled from the bed and five minutes later emerged from the bathroom with her hair braided, face scrubbed clean and lip gloss firmly in place. She pulled on her ruined boots and shrugged into her wool coat. "I'm ready."

Erik had donned his coat and scarf and had moved everything back into its original order. He'd bundled the sheets into a ball, which he carried out with them. Walt and the deputy sat in a cruiser emblazoned with the Douglas County Sheriff's Office on the side. Erik held the back door for her and then set her suitcase between them, holding sheets that were the last reminder of their wild winter night.

"I brought the sheets. Figured they'd need to be washed," Erik said to Walt.

"Sure. My housekeeper, Maria, will wash them and I'll run them back later. Probably should clean that place up a little anyway. Maybe stick some rations in there in case another couple gets stranded again. Probably would have been nice to have some food."

"We survived on wine and chocolate-chip cookies," Erik said.

"Don't sound bad at all," the deputy said, backing around and turning toward the highway. "You folks were lucky to find shelter. A man died last year in the same situation. He stayed in his wrecked car and died of carbon monoxide poisoning. The snow clogged the tailpipe."

Fifteen minutes later, Emma was seated in the kitchen of Walt's enormous house, sipping a cup of coffee and trying not to wolf down the fluffy blueberry muffins Maria had set in front of her and Erik. Christmas music played in the kitchen and a pretty flocked tree glittered in the living area opened to the kitchen. Quite the opposite of the dusty cold cabin they'd abandoned moments ago.

Still, Emma longed for the cabin and the sweet love that had bloomed there if only for a night. Nothing seemed to remain of what they'd shared. Erik had withdrawn, passing over the sheets and blankets to Maria, erasing any evidence of their lovemaking. Or maybe she read too much into how easily he went back to normal. She didn't feel normal. More like confused and scared of all the feelings she'd unearthed for Erik.

He glanced at her. "You okay? You're awfully quiet."

"Sure." What else could she say? That she already mourned the loss of him. That her heart already felt wounded. Maybe actually broken. But that was crazy, right?

"I called a tow-truck company and they're supposed to get back to me on when they can make it down here. Deputy Shane said he'd write out a report. Here's his card for when you call your insurance company." He handed her the card.

"Thank you. I called my parents while you were on the phone. They flipped out but they're glad I'm safe."

"More muffins?" Maria interrupted with a gap-toothed smile. She filled Erik's mug and arched a brow.

"You bet," he said with a nod of thanks. "Good as my grandmother's and that's saying something."

Maria giggled and waddled back to the stove.

"I don't think Alexis ever got your text," Erik said, munching on the muffin Maria brought over. "I tried calling but her phone is off."

Walt toddled in. "Bad news. Roads aren't passable yet. Called the sheriff and he said he'd call the county to send the snowplows out. You're probably going to have to stay here tonight. Got plenty of room and we're stocked, right, Maria?"

"*Sí*, Señor Grider, and I'm preparing a wonderful dinner tonight for your guests," she said.

"We don't want to be a bother," Emma said, feeling

disappointed though she knew she should be grateful they were warm and safe.

"You no bother," Maria said, swatting a hand at them. "Señor Grider loves having company. And his boys are not coming till Tuesday, *sí*?"

Walt nodded.

Erik looked at her. "At least we'll have hot water."

"And something more than cookies and chocolate for dinner."

"Yeah, but I liked having dessert first," Erik said.

ERIK STEPPED FROM the shower, drying the rivulets streaming down his face. He glanced at himself in the mirror and noted his beard had gotten way too thick. He looked like a wild mountain man and, after the night he'd spent with Emma, he felt like one.

She'd asked for her own room and that told him all he needed to know.

Maybe she'd just needed some space.

But the way she'd looked at him, the way she'd shut down, worried him. He'd tried to tease her with the whole dessert-first thing. That's how he felt about them. As though maybe they'd had dessert first when they'd indulged in each other at the cabin, but he hoped they could use their lovemaking as a starting point for something more.

Wrapping the plush towel around himself, he walked into the bedroom. Folded neatly on the bed was a pair of jeans and Henley shirt. A new package of boxers and a neatly folded pair of socks sat on the end of the bed, convincing him Walt likely had sons the same size. In the bathroom, he found enough toiletries to make himself presentable. Glancing at his watch, he saw it was only ten o'clock in the morning, but he felt bone weary. Eyeing the bed, he wondered if he should nap…and then he wondered if he could talk Emma into napping with him.

His cell phone vibrated on the rough-hewn dresser.

"Hey, man, there you are," Layton said. "Your sister was freaking out because you didn't call."

"Well, I took a short cut that didn't work out so well. I hit a patch of ice, overcorrected and ended up plowing Emma's car into a tree. We didn't have cell service and had to take shelter in an abandoned cabin overnight. But we're good. All our toes and fingers are still intact." No need to mention exactly how they'd stayed warm.

"All right, that sucks but glad to hear you're okay. That could've ended a lot worse. So you're going to stay there until the car is repaired?"

"Yeah. Won't be able to get a tow truck until tomorrow, but both Emma and I are safe and warm. The owner of the cabin is putting us up for the night," Erik said, oddly glad he still had one night left with Emma…even if she was acting weird. He wasn't ready to go back to his version of reality. "How's my sister?"

His friend hesitated. "Alexis's foot is fine. The swelling went down and we didn't need to take her to the hospital. I've been taking real good care of her."

"Have you now?"

An uncomfortable silence sat for a few seconds.

"Dude, my sister doesn't need what you can give her," Erik said, knowing he overstepped but also know-

ing his sister and the reputation of his friend with the
ladies.

"Don't worry about Alexis… I've got everything
under control." Layton's voice lowered.

"You're a good guy, but she's had it tough these last
few months. She doesn't need any more heartache. She
needs stability and to get her life straight again before
jumping into something."

No doubt Layton and Alexis had some little flirta-
tion. His sister could use the ego boost after her last
boyfriend had gutted her self-confidence. Which was
hard to believe when it came to a woman like his sister.

"Hey, bud, I do appreciate your looking out for
Alexis while she is banged up. I wasn't trying to dis-
parage your character. You're a good guy. I'm just a
big brother concerned about his sister."

"We'll talk more when you get home," Layton said.
"Drive safe."

Erik hung up and sank onto the bed. The whole
Alexis-Layton thing bothered him. But to a degree,
his friend was right. There was only so much he could
do. His sister had to live her own life, and he had to
live his.

Thing was, he wanted to live his life seeing his sister's best friend.

Emma Rose had knocked him for a loop. Never
could he have imagined how incredible the woman
behind the image he'd painted in his mind could be.
He'd loved being with her, loved her teasing, the way
she launched herself into any task, the way she listened
to him, respected him…loved him.

Okay, he couldn't be so presumptuous, but damned if there wasn't something strong…and magical between them.

Weird to think of it as some fated thing, but that's what it felt like. It was as if everything that had happened was preordained, designed for him in the stars. He'd never been the kind of guy to need a relationship, but something about Emma made him want more. Maybe he was going bonkers. But he didn't think so. Because beneath his tough-guy exterior beat a heart longing for something more…and he was almost certain that Emma was part of it.

But she'd withdrawn from him both physically and mentally.

How could he reach her and show her he wanted more?

9

EMMA FINISHED DRYING her hair and slipped into the dress and tights she'd planned to wear to her parents' party last night. It was a bit fancy for dinner at Walt's house, but she didn't have anything beyond a long-sleeved T-shirt and jeans. The clothes she'd worn yesterday held too many memories for her to handle… along with the fact she'd torn a hole in the knee of her leggings.

After gulping down the coffee and muffins, she'd requested a room and had been so exhausted she'd conked out on the bed without even taking off her boots. She'd slept for four hours, waking stiff and sore from her adventure, both inside and outside the cabin. Groggy, she'd run a bath and lay in the bubbles for another half hour. After washing her hair and scrubbing her body with a lovely lavender herbal soap, she felt almost human again.

At least on the outside.

Inside, her mind kept tripping back to Erik's reaction

to their being discovered. He'd been so unaffected…
so normal.

Like nothing had happened.

And that hurt.

Last night she'd implied she could handle whatever
happened between them, but she couldn't. Wasn't as if
she'd lied—she wanted to be the girl who could sleep
with a guy without dreaming about their babies. She admired modern women who could love 'em and leave 'em,
but she wasn't wired that way. Never had been. And even
if she was, her problem was she'd already been half in
love with Erik before she'd slept with him.

So where did that leave her?

She'd sensed Erik's surprise when she requested
her own room, but she didn't feel comfortable sleeping with him at the moment. Not when they were back
in the real world. And Walt arching a questioning look
at them at her request only made her feel worse. He
didn't know they weren't a real-life couple. So why not
continue the facade for another night?

Didn't she want to spend more time wrapped in
Erik's arms?

Shaking her head, answers escaping her, she swiped
on her lip gloss and opened the door. Walt's house was
like none she'd ever seen. The rancher obviously took
great pride in his Colorado mansion, sprawling against
the evergreen landscape. A small creek ran through
the vaulted foyer built of solid stone. Everything was
wrought by a master craftsman and the effect was stunning. She found Erik and Walt in the vast great room.
A fire roared in the massive stone fireplace, a huge

Christmas tree glittered and the two men looked relaxed, sipping liquor out of highball glasses.

Walt stood. "Well, now, don't you look pretty as a tulip."

"Thank you," Emma said, ducking her head, before remembering she wasn't supposed to be the old Emma. Lifting her chin, she smiled. "How are you gentlemen this afternoon?"

"Well, thank you," Walt said, extending a hand toward the built-in bar. "Pick your poison, madam."

Erik rose and met her at the bar. "I'll fix you something."

"I can do it myself."

"Well, hell, since you're over there, Matheson, fix me another double. Maria will bring in some hors d'oeuvres in a few," said Walt, clearly oblivious to the tension.

Erik touched her hand, making her stomach tremble nervously. She wanted to let go of her fears, but the uncertainty between them kept her guarded.

"You okay?" he asked.

"You keep asking me that," she said, grabbing a glass and pouring a measure of what looked to be small-batch bourbon. She wasn't much of a bourbon drinker but she needed something to calm her. "I'm fine."

"We need to talk."

Emma nodded. "But later. Mr. Grider has been so kind to us, it would be rude to excuse ourselves now. After dinner."

He nodded and she took a sip, restraining herself

from crinkling her nose at the strength of the whiskey. "Tell us about yourself, Mr. Grider."

"Honey, call me Walt," the older man said, a twinkle in his eye. "I do love having a pretty woman to dine with me. I'm tempted to throw this one out in the snow and keep you for myself, but I'm thinkin' I'd have a fight on my hands."

Erik nodded. "That you would."

"I gather you're not originally from Colorado?" Emma asked, settling in a gorgeous chair straight out of *Architectural Digest*.

"Heard my Georgia accent, huh?" Walt teased, before launching into the tale of a Southern boy falling in love with the mountains.

Hours later after a dinner that Emma could only describe as one of the best of her life, they retired to the great room to enjoy after-dinner drinks. After another hour of chitchat, Erik looked at Emma. "Mr. Grider—Walt—I hope you won't mind if I steal Emma away for a moment?"

The older man stroked his mustache. "Can't say I haven't enjoyed the company, but I'm an old man who firmly embraces early to bed, early to rise. I'll say good-night now."

Emma and Erik both said their good-nights, reiterating their gratitude for his hospitality.

After Walt had left, Erik turned to her. "Have I done something wrong?"

She shook her head. "No. I suppose I'm a little freaked out by…everything."

"Do you regret what happened?"

Emma wanted to pace. She felt so unsettled, like

a caged leopard. She forced herself to sit. "I said I wouldn't and I mean that. I'm merely having some issues reintegrating myself in reality."

He came to her and brushed a hand across her jaw. "I don't want you to think I'll be any different than I was before."

Her heart leaped at his touch and then sank at his words. His declaration was a needle popping her balloon of possibility. She'd hoped he would want to see her again. That they might not be a one-night thing. But rather something more. "I know."

Her voice wobbled. Damn it.

"Hey," he said, lifting her chin. "I want you to be happy."

Unshed tears clogged her throat.

She pressed her fingernails into the palm of her hand and willed herself not to cry. This was why he'd had reservations about making love to her in the first place. He had asked if she could handle it. So no tears. No regrets.

"Me, too," she managed to say.

"Then why do you sound not okay? I'm worried that we ruined everything."

Emma looked up. "How is anything ruined? I know the score. I get it."

Erik studied her. "What do you get?"

"That it's over. I told you I could do this and I am. It's just—" she swallowed and averted her gaze from his brilliant blue eyes "—harder than I thought."

He tugged her to her feet. "Emma, what are you talking about?"

"I'm talking about me being an idiot. I knew the

way I felt about you would make this difficult. I should have been able to sleep with you and it not be a big deal, but—"

His kiss cut her off.

And it was a sweet, sweet kiss. One hand rose to cup her face, the other gripped her waist, bringing her fully against him. After a few seconds, he drew back and studied her. "I told you that I liked dessert first, remember?"

Emma squinted at him. "Dessert?"

"What we had back at the cabin was like having dessert first, you know? But I want the main course… and the appetizer—" he dropped his head and nuzzled her neck "—and the salad."

"You mean…you want to see me again?" she asked, hope gathering inside her.

Please say yes. Please.

He lifted his head. "Only if you want the same."

EMMA TILTED HER face up, her lips beckoning, her green eyes shimmering with emotion. "I want that more than anything."

He smiled and dropped another kiss on her lips.

Pulling back, she looked up at him. "But I didn't think you wanted anything more. You were so cold this morning."

Erik didn't know what she was talking about. "Cold? Uh, yeah. We both were."

"No, not physically," she said, regarding him with a puzzled look. "Just the way you acted."

"Like how?"

"Go wash up. Here's the sheets. Call your insurance

company." She crossed her arms over herself. "I felt like you were a different person."

"Well, I couldn't stay naked, whispering sweet words in your ear, babe. There was a man holding a gun on us and I was in my underwear. Makes a man feel a bit shaky."

"It wasn't me?"

"Hell no. I felt a bit out of sorts. Just a natural reaction to our situation. But you? You I haven't stopped wanting since we first got into the car yesterday."

"I feel so stupid. I assumed you were done with me, and I didn't want to press you. Didn't want to be that girl who changed the rules."

He pulled her into his arms. "It's okay. We're both new to this thing between us. I'm relieved you want more than last night with me."

She looked up at him, a tear managing to escape. In her eyes he could see more than possibility. In her eyes he saw a future.

Emma Rose Brent hadn't just grown up.

She'd grown up to be the perfect woman for him.

Erik kissed her and then slapped her behind. "Now, about our sleeping arrangements…are you up for, say, an appetizer?"

Emma nodded, a devilish twinkle in her eye. She opened her mouth, but he knew what she was going to say and pressed a finger against her lips.

"Don't even joke about main courses and bringing the beef." He laughed, wrapping her in his arms.

"How did you know?"

"Because dirty minds think alike," he said, sweeping her off the ground and into his arms. He headed toward the guest suites. "And that tells me all I need to know."

She wrapped her arms around him. "What?"

"That you're the perfect girl to spend Christmas with...you're the perfect girl to fall in love with."

* * * * *

MILLS & BOON®

The Rising Stars Collection!

1 BOOK FREE!

This fabulous four-book collection features 3-in-1 stories from some of our talented writers who are the stars of the future! Feel the temperature rise this summer with our ultra-sexy and powerful heroes. Don't miss this great offer—buy the collection today to get one book free!

**Order yours at
www.millsandboon.co.uk/risingstars**